Berlin Dancer

CINDY HURST

CELDIN PUBLISHING

While set in a particular era of history, this book is a work of fiction. References to real people, events, or organizations are intended only to provide a sense of authenticity, and are used fictitiously. The primary characters and incidents are drawn from the author's imagination and are not to be construed as real.

A book by Celdin Publishing
berlindancer.com
celdinpublishing.com

Cover designed by Brand Group Inc.
brandgroupinc.com

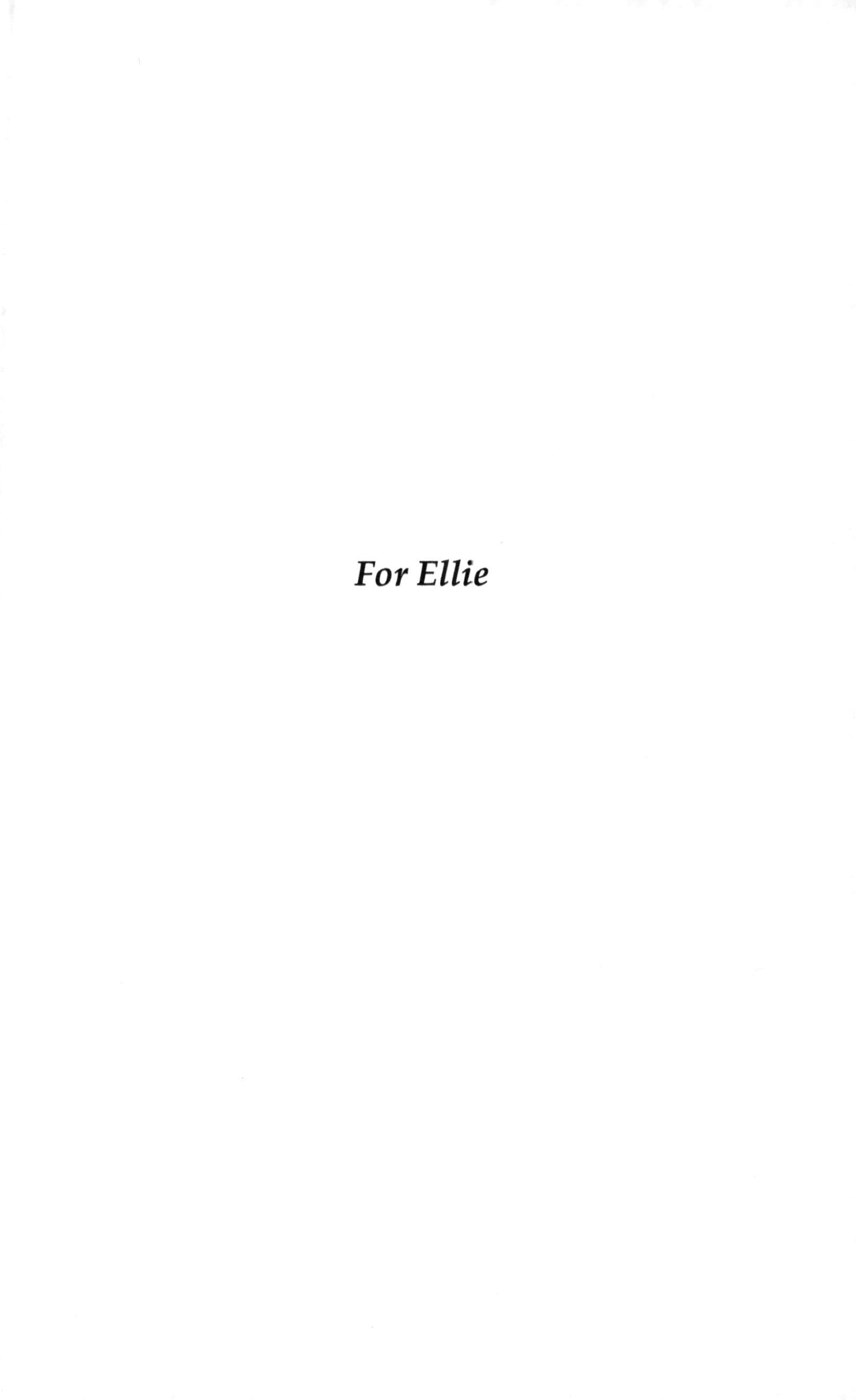

For Ellie

SPECIAL THANKS

I would like to thank the following individuals, without whom this novel probably would have never seen the light of day. My Aunt Benedicte Martin, who spent countless hours over the course of two months combing through the first draft of the manuscript, and offering valuable insight into the historical and human aspect of the story. My Uncle Louis Martin, who read through the next iteration and provided valuable commentary while also becoming my biggest cheerleader. Harold Orenstein, a gifted editor with an eye for content and grammar. All my amazing colleagues, past and present, at the Foreign Military Studies Office, in particular Dr. Les Grau, Dr. Jacob Kipp, Karl Prinslow, and Tim Thomas, all of whose mentorship throughout the years have given me the confidence I needed to succeed as a researcher, writer, and now novelist. A special thanks to Les for being my constant sounding board for the novel over the past few years and who taught me that real coffee was almost impossible to find in East Berlin! My friend Shonna Belian for taking time to review the manuscript and for her encouragement. Tom Britt and Bill Snowden, who helped me to conceptualize the legal and crime sequences that I needed to tie up the story. Julie York for providing connections to law enforcement in support of my research.

Steve Guerra for helping me to better understand the world of criminal forensics. Cynthia Benson, my former high school English teacher, whose initial edits sprouted the seed to my writing career. My godmother, Hannelore Gehman, for her German translations. Ed Hurst, my brother, for his constant encouragement and for Internet and other technical help. Beate Vollack, a choreographer and dancer who grew up in East Germany. Even though we have never met in person, she dedicated many hours reviewing a major section of the novel, and offered invaluable insight into what it was like growing up in the German Democratic Republic, as well as in the world of dance, which added a much greater depth and authenticity. Finally, and certainly not least, my good friend Patty Herb and her fabulously talented team at Brand Group Inc, who pushed my dream over the top by coming up with an amazing cover design and a complete plan on how to market my dream. Thank you! Thank you from the bottom of my heart!

NEW YORK CITY
DECEMBER 13, 1989

It was nearly two o'clock in the morning as the shadowy figure darted through the dimly lit alley. Thick clouds covered the moon. Confused and in pain, the man clutched his left shoulder tightly with his right hand. A burst of cold wind howled, sending a garbage can lid clattering to the ground only a few feet away. Startled, the man jumped away from the sound. His heart rate sped up, and then slowed back down when he realized that he was alone. Clad in black Levi's and a black leather jacket, he blended in with the night. In only a few more hours the sun would rise and the streets would fill with cars and people. There was no time to waste. He had to figure out what that woman wanted and confront her before anyone saw him. "How dare she threaten me," he muttered to himself.

His conversation with the woman replayed over and over in his head. Two days earlier, while the man brushed his teeth, the telephone rang. He shook his head and spat out a mouthful of toothpaste. After quickly rinsing his mouth, he wiped his hands dry on his white t-shirt. *Why is someone calling at night?* Nighttime was for relaxing. Most of the time it was a wrong phone number or, even worse, a faceless person hoping to sell insurance, vacuum cleaners, or some other dreck. By the time the man reached the phone, the answering machine had kicked on. He picked up the receiver.

"This better be important," he stated in his thick German accent. He could hear his own voice echo from the answering machine in the kitchen.

"*Wir mussen sprechen,*" a woman responded in perfect German. The voice was harsh and muffled.

"*Wer spricht da?*" he snapped, switching to German. "*Andrea, is that you?*"

"*Meet me at two o'clock in the morning, at the corner of Third and Jefferson, in two days.*"

"*Wait a minute. Two o'clock in the morning? Are you insane? This is a joke.*"

"*I know what you've done. I know everything about your bloody past. The rest of the world will soon find out unless you do as I say. Be there if you don't want me to call the police or the press.*"

The man stood in sickening silence. Was she bluffing? How could… Then he spoke again. "*You're completely insane! I don't know what you're talking about.*"

"*Be there… at two o'clock sharp.*"

He opened his mouth to protest, but the phone line went dead.

He spent the next two days obsessing over the telephone call. It sounded like Andrea, yet her voice was different… raspy. Maybe she had a cold, or maybe she had been disguising it. It had to be her. What was she up to?

Two days later, just before midnight, the man decided to telephone Andrea Brandt at home, now convinced that it was she who had made the menacing phone call. No matter how hard she tried, she could not disguise her voice enough. It was too distinct. Even disguised, her voice still had its rhythmic lilt. He would beat her to the punch. He dialed her telephone number. The line rang four times before her answering machine picked up.

"*Andrea*," he began with a menacing growl, "*you won't get away with your empty threats. You won't!*" He slammed down the receiver and ran out to his Mercedes. He had to confront her in person. He had to see her face to face. He started the car and slammed his foot down onto the gas pedal, peeling out angrily from his parking spot. A short time later he was weaving through the narrow streets of Soho. As he turned the corner, midway up Prince Street, he saw the familiar beige building with its cast-iron façade. Before it, spread over the window on the first story, he saw the large white letters, *Brandt Academy of Ballet*. There was no light on inside.

He parked his car across the street from the entrance, looking for any sign of life inside. He scanned the upper levels of the structure. The lights were also out on the second floor where Andrea lived. The man sat quietly in the darkness, watching vehicles and occasional pedestrians pass by. Nobody paid much attention to him. The air was freezing outside. Hot steam poured out of a nearby manhole. Suddenly, he saw a gray Buick Park Avenue driving toward him. He slumped down into his seat as the car passed without slowing down. *Good. She didn't see me sitting here. Hopefully she did not notice the Mercedes either.* He sat back up in time to catch a glimpse of her car as it disappeared around the next corner.

He stepped out of his car and walked across the street, turned the corner of the building and entered it through a nearby doorway. There was no one around. He walked a short distance through the bare passageway until he reached the old freight elevator. The location button showed that it had stopped on the second floor. He depressed the dimly lit button to summon the car. After about 15 seconds, the elevator groaned back into life and slowly made its way down to his level. He pushed open the cold steel door and stepped onto the checker-patterned floor. A single, 60-watt incandescent light bulb dangled in the elevator several feet above his head, emitting a soft yellow glow. He closed the doors behind him and pushed a lever to the right. The elevator slowly rose to the second floor, where he stepped out.

Still consumed with anger, he knocked on Andrea's door four times and waited. As the door began to open he thrust himself through into the loft, knocking her to the floor. A short while later the man, dazed and confused, stumbled out of the building. He had been shot by his own pistol through the left shoulder. He cringed and grasped his shoulder in pain. Warm blood oozed down his arm. He found his way back to his car. How would he explain this? *Hopefully she's dead!* He did not want to go to the hospital. That was too risky. He decided to head home where he could tend to his wound.

By the time he reached his apartment complex his head was spinning from the loss of blood. He pressed his body against the front door of his apartment building, struggling to hold himself up. He dug deeply into his pockets and pulled out his keys. They dropped to the floor. *"Scheiße!"* He leaned down and retrieved them.

Finally, opening the door, he made his way into the kitchen, where he poured himself a glass of brandy. He swallowed the entire drink in one gulp, then poured himself another before picking up the telephone. "I need to make a reservation for your first flight out in the morning to Paris, France."

He jotted down some notes then walked into the

bathroom. As he reached into the medicine cabinet for an ace bandage, the telephone rang. He winced in pain. Dropping the bandage, he returned to the living room to answer it.

"I will see you at two o'clock tonight, as planned," she said in German and through a strained voice. The line went dead.

The man's blood ran cold and his head began spinning out of control. He knew that Andrea was a fighter, but her nerve far surpassed his expectations this time. Despite his wound, the man pressed on. He had to finish the job. This insane woman had to be stopped and he knew what to do.

Now, standing in the shadows of a dark alley, he waited for her. A gust of wind parted his jacket, chilling his exposed neck. He grasped both sides of the leather and quickly zipped the jacket all the way up. The sky grew a little brighter as the clouds parted momentarily, allowing the moon to peek through. The man lightly brushed his right thumb against the old brick building beside him. He felt the grit and dirt that had built up on the wall from years of neglect and New York City traffic pollution. In disgust, he quickly shoved his hands into the pockets of his jacket and wiped his thumb on the soft, white lining inside. Beyond the lining he felt cold, hard steel at his fingertips. It was his 9mm-short Walther PP semi-automatic pistol. Its seven-round magazine was not full, but he only needed one round. He was not worried.

Nobody threatens me. Nobody ever threatens me and lives to tell about it. He cocked his head to the right and stretched his neck. *Andrea will pay. She will pay with her life!*

Then, like a spirit in the night, another figure appeared from around the corner. She moved carefully. The man opened his jacket, reached into the side pocket, and pulled out a pack of cigarettes, forcing himself to remain cool, carefully gathering his thoughts. Twenty… nineteen…

eighteen meters away. He calculated the distance between himself and the woman moving toward him. Seventeen… sixteen… fifteen. She did not see him standing in the shadows. He reached into his back pocket for his lighter, encased in a worn brown leather pouch. It used to be his father's. He watched the figure draw nearer and nearer. Did she see him yet? He could not be too certain. He pressed his lips together. Despite the cold, the palms of his hands were damp with sweat.

Holding both the lighter and the pack of cigarettes in his right hand, he slapped the pack twice against his left hand. He kept his eyes on the woman, who had stopped only ten meters away. Without taking his eyes off her, he removed a cigarette from the package and placed it between his lips. He then flicked the lighter open and, carefully shielding the cigarette with his right hand, managed to light it. Inhaling deeply, he felt temporary relief as the smoke filled his lungs.

His eyes narrowed as he watched her. She wore a black overcoat and a dark blue scarf. She carried a red shawl. The man continued to watch her from the shadows of the building. Another gust of wind came swooping down and blew back the woman's scarf slightly. She fumbled with the shawl then quickly brought her left hand up to readjust it.

"Care to join me for a smoke?" he finally asked in German. The woman took a few more steps toward him, but said nothing. *"Let me see your eyes…or are you too afraid now that you've pushed me away? You surprise me, Andrea. You have incredible endurance, but I am stronger."* He smiled confidently. *"Let me see your eyes, Andi."*

"Do you understand why you are here?" she said finally, ignoring his words. Her voice was hoarse, almost guttural. A street lamp shone directly behind her now, making it impossible to see her face. She took a few more steps toward him then stopped. She kept her hands beneath the shawl

and took a final step toward him. *"I think you know why we are here. You will never be prosecuted for your crimes. Therefore I have elected myself judge, jury, and executioner."*

A shot rang out. He heard the crack of the bullet as it grazed his right ear, causing him to let out a shriek. He ripped open his jacket and struggled to take out his pistol as a second shot hit him in the right arm. He staggered backwards. His arm was numb and his fingers were not responding. A third shot hit him in the right shoulder. He felt his knees buckle as he slid to the ground. The pain set in as the woman advanced. Quickly, in seconds, she stood over him. He was now staring straight down the sleek, dark barrel of a pistol. It looked cold and foreboding.

"Go ahead and shoot me!" he hissed. *"Finish the job, whore!"*

"I'm going to send you to hell for the pain that you have caused me all these years." And with that, he caught a glimpse of her cold eyes as the wind swished her scarf away from her face.

"I… I don't understand," he sputtered.

"The biggest mistake you could have ever made was to not finish the job when you had the chance. But now it's too late, isn't it? You should never have come into my life." The woman stepped around the man and into the light. *"Think about it."*

His lower jaw dropped instantly. *"Mein Gott!"* he gasped. *"No! No!"* He struggled to free his gun one last time as a final shot rang out. His body jerked, and then he grew still with the fatal shot piercing his heart.

The woman saw her own reflection in the lifeless eyes of the madman staring straight up at her. Even dead it was difficult to avoid feeling his empty gaze penetrate her soul.

"I think you do understand," she muttered one last time before turning and walking away. After all these years, she had finally gotten her revenge.

CHAPTER ONE

COUNTY JAIL - NEW YORK CITY
DECEMBER 17, 1989

Stanley Nolen was anxious to see his longtime friend, Andrea Brandt. Early that morning he received an emotional telephone call at home from her, begging him for help. After being released from the hospital, she was arrested and booked at the county jail for murder. The story had not yet been made public, but Stanley knew it was only a matter of time before word got out. Andrea was a world-renowned prima ballerina and a constant target for photographers and popular magazines. She was a graceful woman, forty-one years old, with blonde hair rippling softly past her shoulders. Her blue eyes were gentle, yet showed a hidden inner strength and intensity.

Stanley was familiar with the county jail. As a criminal attorney, he often visited inmates there. Andrea was the last person he would expect to find in such a place. He approached the front desk.

"Hey, Stan," the man in uniform greeted him, setting down a newspaper. "What brings you here on a Sunday?"

"Hi, Len," Stanley said, throwing him a smile. "I'm here to see Andrea Brandt."

The guard's face lit up. "Nice. You gonna dance

with her?"

Stanley glared at him. "Where is she housed?"

The guard cleared his throat and straightened up. "Block B," he responded, handing him a small device that served as a panic button. "You know the routine."

"Thanks." Stanley headed toward a large steel door. It slid open and he stepped inside. He stood there momentarily as the door slammed behind him with a loud clang. The second large steel door then slid open. He walked through it then waited for it to close behind him. Walking past inmates and prison guards, he made his way to Cell Block B, where he entered a small, stark room and waited. Inside, a heap of dirty laundry lay crumpled in a corner. Stanley made his way to a table and waited.

When Andrea walked in, Stanley was taken aback by her appearance. She looked sickly, gloomy, no longer the majestic figure he knew. Her eyes were void of all their expression, and her face was pale.

"How are you doing?" Stanley asked, trying to conceal his surprise. He pushed his tiny, black-rimmed spectacles up onto his nose. At times he seemed awkward, but he had successfully defended numerous clients, and he was the first person Andrea contacted when she had a chance.

She forced a smile. "It's not exactly the Ritz Carlton here," she said as she walked up to him. "They set my bond at one million dollars." Stanley wrapped his arms around her and she placed her head onto his shoulder. She wanted desperately to cry, but was too exhausted. They sat down across from one another at the table.

Stanley cleared his throat. "We don't have that much time to figure this out," he said. "I have a feeling they are going to push the case pretty quickly." Andrea watched him reach into his blazer pocket and pull out a blue notebook and a pen.

"You're taking notes?" she asked.

He pointed to his head and tapped it twice with his index finger. "Poor memory, as you know."

"Well you can start with this in your little blue book." Andrea leaned forward and hissed, her German accent becoming more prominent, "The devil got what he deserved!" She slumped back into her chair and looked away.

Stanley's eyes grew wide at his friend's sudden outburst. "Did he? That's a pretty big price to pay, wouldn't you say?"

"Not big enough," she retorted. "He came after me. He tried to kill me first. He was always a demon of a man. He was born a demon and he died a demon."

"So, you're admitting that you killed him?" Andrea did not answer. Finally Stanley broke the silence. "Here's the problem, Andi. The victim was a very well respected and affluent man and…."

"The truth is, Stan, that I don't remember that much. How could I have killed someone and not remember it?" Andrea interrupted him.

"You've got to remember *something*," he said, leaning toward her. "Andi, I'm here to try to help you. I can only do that if you cooperate and are completely honest with me."

"I *am* telling you the truth."

"So, what I'm hearing from you is that you could have killed him, but you're not sure?"

Andrea nodded her head slowly. "I suppose, but…" She stopped talking.

"We need to figure out what actually happened that night if you want to have any kind of chance of not finishing your life behind bars," Stanley urged. "Right now you're sitting in the hot seat. The investigation has already turned over some interesting evidence. They found a message on his answering machine from someone who sounds like you. The victim even identifies you on the phone and…"

"He attacked me. It was self-defense, but…"

"That would explain the bruises and your gunshot wound. It's obvious that there was a struggle that night."

"Something just doesn't make sense," Andrea said. She grew silent.

"So, why did you want him dead?" Stanley finally asked.

"*Mein Gott.*" Andrea rolled her eyes. "I don't even know where to start."

"Why don't you start from the beginning?"

"It's a very long story."

"You're my top priority today, Andi. You're my friend and you have my full attention," Stanley said gently.

"It's…" Andrea flinched slightly, but then pressed forward. "It all started with my mother… during World War II." Stanley sat motionless, waiting for her to continue. After carefully searching her memory, she began, "My mother was a dancer. She danced in a handful of productions. She even danced in *Swan Lake*, which had always been her most cherished part.

"During the War, when she was only in her mid-twenties, she left the ballet and went to live with her ailing father in Hamburg. In 1943, after most of the city had been destroyed by bombs, my mother fled to Berlin…"

"What about your grandfather?" asked Stanley. "What happened to him?"

Andrea shook her head. "He died. They lived in the center of the city, which was bombed. Even if he had made it to the basement, there was so much poisonous smoke that it sucked the air right out of the basements. He didn't have a chance. My mother wasn't with him that night, which saved her life. She had nothing, but managed to hop onto a truck headed to Berlin, where she knew a couple who owned a club, which held a nightly cabaret. They had always told her that she had a place to stay in Berlin if she ever needed one. In exchange for shelter and food, my mother agreed to dance in the cabaret. The club was not an extraordinary place, but the hospitality was good, and in the evenings the place was always packed with people hoping to escape the grueling realities of the war. It was in this very club that my mother met Johann Brandt..."

CHAPTER TWO

BERLIN
OCTOBER 1943

The loud music drummed in Johann's ears as he sat motionless, gazing with reverence upon the graceful dancer. Her name was Ingrid Stahl. She was a tall woman, not beautiful but indeed impressive. She wore tight fitting, translucent apparel with a sparkling array of colors. With her blonde hair set in a bun, she stood out among all the other dancers. Johann had first noticed her several weeks earlier when he stopped into the club for a drink. He was immediately captivated by her. Ingrid had become somewhat of a celebrity to the many patrons of the club. Dancing was her lifeblood and she adored being a part of that magical world. The cabaret was exhilarating, but at times Ingrid wished she could go back into time, before the war and before the air raids, and dance once again in one of the grand ballets that she had almost grown accustomed to. Unfortunately, the war had changed everything: her goals, her destiny, her life.

When she finally finished her dance solo, Ingrid gazed out into the audience and gave a refined curtsy. Catching her breath, she stood there for a moment as the audience, one man in particular, applauded warmly. Blinded by powerful stage lights, all she could make out was his silhouette as he stood by his chair yelling, *"Bravo! Bravo! Zu...ga...be! Zu... ga... be!"* A moment later, Ingrid left the stage. For her, the evening had once again come to an abrupt end.

Once in her dressing room, her body aching from fatigue, Ingrid sat quietly in a meditative state. The excitement of the stage, which had enveloped her in its mystical power, was slowly wearing off as she drifted back into reality. The show was an excellent means to relieve some of the tensions brought about by the war, which now threatened Berlin. Memories of not so long ago still haunted her. She felt the room closing in around her, and the walls became blurry as vivid recollections of bombs exploding, and screams, seemed to fill the air. They grew louder and louder and her entire body shuddered as she clasped her hands tightly over her head, trying to push it all out of her mind.

Suddenly, a knock at the door brought her back into the present. Ingrid quickly collected herself and opened it to find a stranger carrying a small bouquet of white, pink, and blue flowers. He flashed her a warm smile, causing her to blush slightly. Despite the stranger's charm, Ingrid remained cautious.

"May I help you?" she asked politely.

"I was hoping for an opportunity to meet you, Fräulein." He reached out and offered her the flowers.

"I'm sorry, but... well... you are not permitted back here," she stammered as she glanced up and down the hallway.

The stranger looked behind himself and apologized. "I'm sorry, Fräulein, but are you expecting someone?" Ingrid did not answer. "Ehhh...Please forgive me, Fräulein. I saw no signs posted." The stranger kept his eyes on her and continued smiling.

"How did you manage to slip past our security?" she finally asked.

"What security?" He gave her a boyish grin.

A moment later they were both startled by a menacing voice behind him. "Excuse me, but you are not permitted back around the dressing rooms. You have to leave."

The stranger turned. Behind him stood a large, burly man with a thick, black mustache and a belly that flowed immodestly in several layers over his belt. Suddenly, Ingrid snapped to and took the stranger by the arm. "It's all right, Rudolph. I know this man. He is...Well, he is an old friend of mine." She then jerked him by the hand into her dressing room and shut the door behind them.

"A frightening reception for a stranger," remarked the man melodramatically. "Thank you most graciously, Fräulein, for coming to my rescue." He reached out and took a hold of her hand, pulling it gently to his lips.

Ingrid blushed slightly. "That was Rudolph Kaisendorf, the owner of this club. I was not about to leave you out there for him to tear apart."

"Not only are you beautiful but you are also quite thoughtful," chanted the stranger melodramatically.

Ingrid blushed again. "He's extremely protective of me. He treats me like a daughter. He is really a wonderful and gentle man."

"Gentle? That's a bit hard to believe," he quipped.

Ingrid motioned the stranger to sit down on a nearby sofa. "Would you care for some tea?" she asked him.

"I would like that. Thank you."

Ingrid poured hot water into a cup. "You know..." She chuckled as she poured a second cup. "I don't even know your name."

"Oh! Please forgive me, Fräulein. It's Brandt... Johann Brandt."

"Pleased to meet you, Herr Brandt."

Johann smiled. "I really enjoy watching you dance. I've

seen you dance before. You are very talented. You move like a ballerina. You belong in a theater, dancing lead roles," he opined.

Ingrid lowered her head and smiled modestly. Now in the light of her dressing room, she was better able to see the stranger. He appeared older than she was, by at least ten years. His hair was graying on the sides. He was rugged in nature, a hard life evidenced by the lines clearly displayed around his eyes.

They both sat in awkward silence, watching each other and sipping their tea. Ingrid finally broke the silence by asking, "So tell me, Herr Brandt, what you do in your spare time?"

Johann shrugged and replied, "I do many different odd jobs. I enjoy building things, working with my hands." He held out his hands. They were rough and calloused. Ingrid noticed a ring on his finger.

"Are you married?" she asked

"Oh, this? No." He chuckled. "This was my father's. He gave it to me shortly before he passed away."

"It's nice. What does it say here?" she struggled to see the tiny inscription on the outside of the ring. Johann pulled the ring off his finger and handed it to her. She read aloud. *"Dem Alten Vaterland Die Treue zu beweisen Gab Ich in schwerer Zeit Ihm Gold fur dieses Eisen* (For the old fatherland, loyalty to show, gave I in difficult time, to him gold for this iron)." She looked back up at him. "What is this?"

"My father donated quite a bit of gold in 1914 to help Germany. He always joked that this was probably the most expensive piece of iron in the world." Johann smiled. "He treasured it, though. It symbolized his great deed to the fatherland."

Ingrid turned the ring in her fingers. Seeing a greenish notch on the front of it she smiled. "It's defective," she quipped.

"Oh, that? That little notch gives it a charming individuality. It makes it unique."

Ingrid ran her fingernail along the cross on the front, before handing it back to Johann. "I like it." More silence. "Are you from Berlin?"

"No, I come from Frankfurt."

"Why aren't you fighting in the war?"

"I injured my leg when I was much younger."

"What happened?"

"You ask a lot of questions," he teased with a smile.

"A strange man appears at my dressing room door unannounced. I think I am entitled to ask questions."

Johann chuckled and explained, "I fell off my father's roof." He shrugged. "I was hiding from my mother. I fell so hard that it snapped completely backward." The description made Ingrid cringe. A moment later a knock came at the door. "Did father bear return to check on his cub?" Johann mocked.

"Oh stop," Ingrid chuckled before opening the door. On the other side Frieda greeted them. "I am sorry to disturb you, Ingrid, but I have some news I want to share with you." Upon seeing Johann, she continued, "as soon as you have time." Frieda extended her arm and tapped Ingrid lightly on her wrist.

"Oh!" Johann stood up and prepared to leave. "Please don't let me interfere with anything. I merely wanted to say hello." He headed toward Frieda and then turned around to face Ingrid. "I hope we can do this again...soon." He reached down beside her seat, picked up the flowers, and handed them to Ingrid. He smiled, and before she could say goodbye or voice any protests, he was gone.

Ingrid glanced over at Frieda with obvious disappointment on her face, causing Frieda to grimace.

"Ah...I am so sorry, Ingrid," said Frieda. "I didn't mean to frighten him away. Who was this handsome man anyhow? I've seen him here a few times, but he has never said anything to me. He seems nice enough."

Ingrid finally smiled as she thought about Frieda and how she would give constant encouragement when it came to her social life. "You must meet people," she often told Ingrid. "You must enjoy life and share laughter with someone special...But, most of all...you need a man!" Frieda had married Rudolph nearly twenty years ago. She was a tiny woman, much smaller than her husband. They were an oddly matched couple, but their affection for each other was unyielding. They spent their lives trying to build a successful business together. At one point, they found themselves almost destitute. However, through great determination and faith, they finally saw their dream come true. Their club, with its nightly shows, had become one of Berlin's most popular escapes. Frieda and Rudolph had two sons, both soldiers. Gustav, the eldest, had been killed at the beginning of the war. They had not heard from Hans, their second son, for over a year. Much of Frieda's graying hair was prematurely brought on by the stress of not knowing where Hans was. Yet she was a stoic woman, barely allowing her emotions to surface. She always seemed joyful. She was a woman of wisdom and hardship. To Ingrid, Frieda was not only an inspiration, but also a fine example of perseverance.

The moment Johann left, Frieda entered the room, her face beaming like a child. "Ingrid," she began, "I have a letter. It's from Hans!" Her eyes glistened with tears. "He wrote it one month ago to tell us he's coming home...in November! That's only..." She stopped and glanced up at Ingrid. "That's only one week from now!"

Ingrid's face lit up at her friend's excitement. "He is?

That is wonderful news!" she shouted out. "Oh, Frieda. I'm so happy. I've never met Hans, but I feel as if I know him... like a brother. I can't wait to meet him!"

"You will like him. He is such a good son to us. This is the best news we have received in a very long time. We will throw a big party for him when he returns."

"When do you expect him?" asked Ingrid.

"I don't know. I just know that he is on his way now. Please, God, let it be true." Frieda closed her eyes and tightly grasped Ingrid's hands as she spoke. "I must go now and talk to Rudy. Preparations must be made!" She turned and pranced away happily.

Once Frieda had gone, Ingrid sat quietly, gazing into the mirror, reflecting on her own past. Suddenly she was hit with a deep ache of loneliness and longing for her own family. Vivid recollections of her father returned. How she missed him. Her thoughts then shifted to Johann Brandt, who so mysteriously appeared, but then disappeared just as quickly. She wondered if she would ever see him again. She yearned for that special someone who would one day bring her into a world of fantasy and ecstasy, someone who could help her forget the real world. All the while it was Johann's image that lingered in her mind.

Before long, the fatigue began pulling her down. Ingrid stood up and headed to her bedroom. All the other performers had already left for the evening. Ingrid made her way up the cement stairwell that led to her bedroom, directly above the club. The air became increasingly chilled as she left the club. *Only a few more steps to go,* she thought. She passed by Frieda and Rudolph's room and saw the light glowing beneath the door. She could hear Frieda's enthusiastic voice muffled through the door as she spoke to Rudolph, most likely still buzzing with the news of their youngest son. Ingrid smiled. She felt comfort in knowing that her two friends were only a few steps away, tucked away in the next room. She felt grateful to have them in her life.

Once she reached her bedroom, Ingrid quickly undressed and climbed into her bed. She curled up and wrapped herself tightly in the surrounding blankets, imagining Johann was lying beside her. That night, Ingrid's dreams were filled with passion and fantasy and when she finally awoke the following morning, she clamped her eyes shut, hoping to fall back to sleep to rejoin Johann in her dreams.

Two days later a young boy with straight blonde hair appeared at the door of the club. "Are you Frau Kaisendorf?" he asked Ingrid, who greeted him.

"No. I am Fräulein Stahl. The Kaisendorfs are in the back room at the moment."

The young boy handed an envelope to Ingrid and said, "This is a message for Herr or Frau Kaisendorf." He turned and scampered away. Ingrid brought the envelope to Frieda, who stared at it for a long moment, hesitating. Finally she took a deep breath and tore it open. The note inside was short. It read:

> *Herr und Frau Kaisendorf,*
> *We regret to inform you that your son, Hans Kaisendorf, is listed as missing in action. All efforts have been taken to find him. We shall keep you informed as events unfold.*
> *Signed,*
> *Fritz Schumacher*
> *Bataillonskommandeur*

Frieda clutched the note in her hand as silent tears flowed freely down her face. Rudolph came up behind her and peered over her shoulder at the note. He placed his hand on her back. Ingrid rushed to Frieda's side and put her arms around her, echoing those same words that she had heard again and again from Frieda herself, "But...there is still hope. We have to believe that."

One week later, as Ingrid sat at a table in the club, reading a book about the history of the Russian empire, there came a loud knock at the door. Frieda was just entering the room with an old stale mop and a bucket, preparing to wash the floor. "Well, Ingrid, are you just going to sit there and ignore the knock until it goes away?" she asked. There was another knock.

Ingrid looked up at her and chuckled. "I'm sorry. This book is so fascinating. I didn't even hear it." She rose from her chair and walked to the door. When she opened it her heart skipped two beats. Johann Brandt was standing there. Their eyes fixed upon each other as they both stood quietly mesmerized.

"Fräulein Stahl," Johann finally said. "My name is Johann. We met the..."

"Yes," Ingrid interrupted. "I remember you." She felt a strong quiver, which began in her stomach and shot down to her thighs.

They continued standing there, gazing awkwardly at one another until Frieda stepped up behind Ingrid. "Are you going to make this handsome, young man stand outside in the cold or are you going to invite him in?" she asked, somewhat amused by Ingrid's ungainly reaction. Frieda recognized Johann from the week before when she had practically chased him off.

Ingrid chuckled and invited him into the club, locking the door behind them.

"Are you dancing tonight?" he asked as he followed her.

"I am," she responded without looking up.

"Are you busy now or do you have time to go for a

walk?" he asked.

Ingrid glanced over at Frieda, who offered her a nod of approval. She then put the book down and followed him out.

Outside, the sky maintained a hazy glow as the sun struggled to pierce through the clouds. The time was just after one o'clock and the air felt chilly. Ingrid wrapped her hand over her shoulder as they strolled down the street. Seeing her discomfort, Johann removed his jacket and placed it over her shoulders, encircling them with his arm to help warm her. She leaned her head toward him, starting to feel more secure by his presence. They continued to walk for another ten minutes, neither one uttering a single word, seeping into each other's private worlds through the light contact that they made.

—⚓——⚓——⚓—

Johann visited Ingrid almost daily, giving her life new meaning and offering her a new sense of calm. Rather than dwelling on the war and her father's death, Ingrid now occupied her mind and imagination with thoughts of Johann, always looking forward to the next time she would see him. Johann fostered hope and courage in her.

One evening he showed up at Ingrid's dressing room carrying a small box. "What's that?" Ingrid asked as she began reaching for it.

"Well, it's supposed to be a gift for you," he answered.

Ingrid's face was shining as she looked at it. "May I open it now?" she asked.

Johann marveled at her childish innocence. "Please."

She fumbled nervously with it, trying to find her way inside without tearing the wrapping paper. Carefully she lifted the outer edges and peeled them backward, acting as if ruining the paper might damage its precious contents. Managing to clear away the paper, she revealed a small, plain, brown box, about five centimeters long. She carefully popped the lid open and gasped at its contents. "Johann..." Her eyes filled with tears. "It's beautiful!" She reached into the tiny box and removed a small golden locket, which dangled from a delicate chain. She threw her arms around his neck and held onto him for a long moment. He kissed her and then took the locket from her hands.

"It's magical," he explained as he showed it to her.

The locket was no larger than a small coin. On the front side a golden wreath of carnations and roses surrounded a tiny ballerina. "She is beautiful!" gasped Ingrid.

"She is you, *meine liebe Ingrid*. But look, there's more." He turned the locket over to show her the back, which had the inscription, *"Meine Liebe Ingrid"* (My Beloved Ingrid). It was almost too small to be noticeable. Johann carefully pressed a tiny lever, concealed on the bottom of the locket, with his thumbnail. The locket sprang open, exposing a tiny portrait of Johann on the left hand side. "The right side is for you. The locket represents the two of us, always side by side, stronger in union than alone. I know we haven't known each other for very long, Ingrid, but I also know that I want to be with you forever. I've fallen in love with you." Ingrid threw her arms around him and Johann drew her body in closely to his.

That night, exhausted from dancing, Ingrid drifted off into a heavy sleep. She slept so soundly that she failed to hear the sirens as they began wailing outside. When she finally did wake up, it was to the sound of an airplane crashing in the distance. She sat straight up, but then the air grew silent again. She waited for a moment before lying back down. She wrapped herself in her blanket and her thoughts drifted back to Johann before she fell back to sleep.

Air raids took place almost nightly at that point, but they were mostly harmless. The club continued to be a refuge for its patrons, who were becoming increasingly weary of the war. However, one night, after another plane nearly crashed into the building during a performance, Rudolph had other ideas. That same night, Ingrid walked down to the basement where she found him shoving boxes into cabinets along the walls that lined the basement. When Ingrid asked him what he was doing, he explained, "Putting the food and drink that's left away for safe keeping." He stopped and turned to face her. "I'm sorry, Ingrid, but we have to close down the club."

Ingrid frowned. She said nothing, but instead turned and left the room.

CHAPTER THREE

NOVEMBER 1943

A sudden, frantic knock came at the door one day. As Ingrid opened it, Johann forcefully pushed his way into the club, nearly knocking her to the ground. He immediately reached out to catch her before she fell, and then slammed the door shut behind him. "I'm sorry!" he gasped, panting out of control.

"What happened?!" shrieked Ingrid.

"I...They." He stopped and struggled to catch his breath. It was raining outside and he was drenched.

"Johann! Please!" Ingrid's concern mounted. "You are frightening me."

"The...the Gestapo is after me! I should not have come here. If they find me here, we could all be arrested or worse. I am so sorry, Ingrid."

"The Gestapo? But, why?"

"I was involved in a plot…" He hesitated. "…a plot to kill Hitler."

"Kill Hitler?!" Ingrid did not conceal her astonishment. "Why? Why would you want to kill the Führer?"

"Why? Ingrid, how can you possibly ask that question?" he asked, taking a hold of her by the arms. "Don't you see what has been happening!? Look around you!" His expression frightened her.

"Yes, I do see what has been happening. We've been getting attacked and the Führer is going to save us. Please, Johann. You are hurting me," she pleaded, attempting to wriggle free from his tight grip.

Johann loosened his grasp and softened his expression. "Hitler is a madman. He ordered the death of thousands, maybe even millions, of Jews and others. Ingrid…" Johann stopped, his eyes fixed on hers. "He is killing my people. The Nazis have taken our homes, our businesses, our livelihoods, and now innocent people are being murdered for no good reason."

Ingrid stood in a stunned silence, staring up at Johann who now stopped talking. "Your people?" she finally managed to say.

Johann nodded. "My mother was Jewish. I didn't want to tell you. I didn't want to put your life in danger. A group of us had a plan on how we might stop this madman, maybe even stop the war."

"You're Jewish?" Ingrid repeated.

Johann carefully searched for the right words. "Half. My mother was Jewish. Five years ago she had been visiting with family in Potsdam when the Nazis forced their way into the house and took them all away. A few days later, when my father tried to find out what had happened, they shot him. The last I heard, my mother had been sent to Sachsenhausen. I can only assume the worst.

"My father had given my mother a necklace when they first started dating. It was a gold pendant in the shape of the Star of David. She never took it off… Not until three weeks before they sent her away. Things were becoming dangerous. I suppose she knew what was in store for her. She ended up giving it to me, and made me promise I'd put it somewhere safe. After they sent her away, I never took it off, keeping it tucked into my shirt where only I knew of its existence … until the day that I was discovered."

"Discovered?"

"Have you ever heard of a man named Karl von Euken?" asked Johann.

Ingrid shook her head slowly from side to side, trying to absorb all the information.

"Von Euken became a member of the Nazi Party about seven years ago. He shared Hitler's ideologies. He is now one of the leading figures in the Gestapo. He is also the only man alive who knows my true identity. As long as he is alive, I will never be completely safe."

"But, how does this man know you?" asked Ingrid.

"They discovered our group during one of our gatherings. One of our members turned out to be an informant. It was late at night when the Gestapo broke through the door. Before we could even react, they had us at gunpoint. Von Euken came up behind his men and ordered them to shoot anyone who even looked like they were Jewish. They killed more than half my men. Then, when the shooting finally stopped, he ordered them to take the rest of us in for questioning. Of course, we knew that our fates were sealed and that we would eventually be executed.

"As they marched us back to their headquarters, three of us tried to run away. They shot one man. My friend and I managed to reach an alley and two men chased us. The street divided and we each ran a different direction. No more than 20 seconds passed when I heard three shots fired. I knew my friend was dead. Then, I heard two very loud gunshots directly behind me. I turned around and found myself face to face with von Euken. He pointed his gun at me. I heard him pull the trigger again, but his weapon must have jammed or something. I ran toward him and managed to knock him to the ground. Before I knew it he had pulled out a knife and we struggled over it. Unfortunately, during our struggle the Star of David fell out of my shirt. When von Euken saw this he froze. He just stared at it, as if it were poison. The man is mad. He became completely delirious. Somehow, I managed to escape. I could hear him shouting after me, though, vowing revenge. How I wish I had killed him when I had the chance."

"So, what happened today?" asked Ingrid.

"About three hours ago von Euken happened to be standing around with several other men when he spotted me walking across the street from where they were. They immediately started chasing me, but I managed to get away."

Ingrid reached toward him and ran her hand across his shoulders and neck. "You're not wearing the Star," she remarked. "What did you do with it?"

"I stopped wearing it the day von Euken discovered it. Now it is hidden somewhere where no one will ever find it..." He paused for a moment then said, "You're wearing it, Ingrid."

"I don't understa...," she began, but then stopped. Johann nodded as Ingrid placed her right hand over her heart in disbelief. She reached around her neck and removed the tiny locket. She stirred slightly, fighting back tears.

"I had it melted down for you," he explained. "I knew that way it would always be in a good place."

"I need to find a safe place to hide," Johann said, once Ingrid had a chance to digest the news. "I don't know where else to go." With Rudolph and Frieda's approval, Johann would end up moving into the club.

Later that evening, Frieda walked up the steps from the basement and into the main showroom, carrying several jars of food. As she passed by the telephone, it rang. Ingrid rushed to her side to take the food from her, allowing Frieda to answer the telephone. "Kaisendorf," she said into the receiver. Ingrid put the food down onto a nearby table. Frieda grew silent and all eyes turned to her. Her face grew pale. "When?" she asked the caller. "Thank you." She hung up the phone and headed toward the stairs to get Rudolph. Before heading up, she turned around and said, "Ingrid, take the food back downstairs."

"What's going on?" Ingrid called out after her.

Frieda stopped only long enough to explain. In a trembling voice she said, "There is an enemy air formation coming. They are saying that it's much larger than usual." Then she disappeared around the corner.

Ingrid stood momentarily in stunned silence. Johann walked over to the window and peered outside. It was still raining and the streets were filled with people. He shook his head, and then followed Ingrid down into the basement where they began to lay out the food. Frieda and Rudolph joined them five minutes later.

They were just finishing up their last few bites of food when the *flak* (air defense cannon) opened up. It was immediately very violent. Rudolph quickly sealed off the entry to the basement. Before long, they could hear the muffled sounds of approaching airplanes, followed by the barking of the *flak*. Then, there was a very different sound. It was the sound of bombs dropping. At first, they were far in the distance, but then they drew closer and closer until it felt as if the bombs were dropping directly on top of the club. Ingrid braced herself for the worst. With every crash, the ground shook violently. The air pressure became unbearable and the noise deafening. The power had gone off and the room grew pitch black. Then the door leading out of the basement shattered and they could hear the sound of breaking glass coming from within the club. While Ingrid, Johann, and Frieda pushed away from the open entryway and pressed themselves up against the wall on the far end, Rudolph fumbled his way to a nearby trunk, where he pulled out two flashlights. The attack continued ceaselessly for more than an hour. When it finally let up, Rudolph reached into a nearby box, from which he pulled out a bottle of Schnapps, opened it, and took a drink. He then passed it around and they each took large gulps. Just when they thought the attack was over, it all began again. It wasn't until about nine thirty that evening that the droning of the planes overhead ceased.

Once silence set in, they made their way out of the basement to assess the damage. The windows around the club were completely shattered. The front door had blown off its hinges and into the club. Outside, people began gathering into a nearby square. Ingrid and Johann approached the group and quickly learned that the greatest danger was yet to come. The wind had kicked up, fueling fires caused by the bombing. The flames were so hot that even the rain could not extinguish them. Ingrid looked around and saw that the sky had turned blood-red in three directions from them. The smoke grew thicker.

They made their way back into the club and began to look around. To their surprise, the room was mostly intact, other than the shattered glass and broken doors. Once again, the sirens bellowed throughout the city, but the planes never came. Now, hearing nothing but silence and occasional voices outside, Ingrid and Johann walked to where a window once was and stared out over the street. They waited quietly until, after nothing more happened, the all clear sounded again. By three o'clock that morning they had all managed to bring their bedding down into the basement, where they wrapped themselves in blankets.

Ingrid found at least a little comfort in having Johann beside her, feeling his warmth as she lay on the cold, hard cement floor with nothing but her blanket and a pillow.

Over the next few days more sirens rang throughout the city, followed by more bombing. Sometimes the damage was not too extensive. Sometimes it was simply a false alarm as reconnaissance planes flew overhead to assess the damage. Ingrid and Johann walked countless kilometers throughout the city hoping to find out the fate of some of their friends. Messages began appearing on the blackened walls of destroyed homes. "Dear Herr M, where are you? We are taking refuge in Potsdam. Everyone in our cellar managed to survive..."

Some neighborhoods were completely destroyed, while others were barely touched. The smoke burned Ingrid's and Johann's eyes. They held dampened clothes, which Frieda had given them, over their faces to allow them to breathe more easily. They also covered their heads to protect themselves from the falling ash.

"You're not concerned that von Euken will see you?" Ingrid asked Johann at one point as they walked by a pile of fallen rubble, which once used to be a home. A young woman sat atop the rubble, expressionless, in shock, staring out at nothing. Her face was covered in soot. She paid attention to neither Johann nor Ingrid. Her entire family had perished beneath the rubble. It was the type of scene that was all too familiar by now. Death and destruction everywhere.

"I doubt that von Euken is thinking about me right now," Johann said, as he turned away from the scene and continued walking.

Meanwhile, Frieda and Rudolph decided to remain at the club which, so far, still stood. They had a supply of food and drink hidden away in the basement and Rudolph was determined to protect it, like a treasure, from potential looters, but none ever came. Every evening, Ingrid and Johann would return to the club, with stories of despair and updates on the damage.

CHAPTER FOUR

DECEMBER 1943

ate one afternoon Ingrid and Johann ventured out to pick up what rations they could. The German food-rationing system required individuals to register their coupons in a given shop. However, the food shop in which Ingrid had registered her coupons had been destroyed a few nights earlier, leaving her with nothing. The telephone was not functional and so they decided to walk five kilometers to where Johann had registered his ration coupons to see if that food shop had survived the bombings. To their relief, it was still standing. They managed to get bread, but there was nothing else on the shelves.

As they began heading back to the club, the sirens bellowed out over the city. People in the streets quickly scattered, ducking into nearby buildings still standing. "Run!" an old man shouted. "Find shelter!" He disappeared through a door leading into a factory across the street. Ingrid and Johann watched helplessly as several more people rushed into another nearby building. Just then, before they had a chance to move, they looked up in horror to see three bombers coming directly toward them, soaring close to the ground.

"Mein Gott!" cried Ingrid as the realization of what was happening sunk in. "Not again!" She clung desperately to Johann as they raced across the street to the building into which they had seen the old man disappear moments earlier. The door was locked. They began racing down the street. The earth suddenly shook below them, sending them both tumbling to the ground as one bomb fell directly onto the building where the old man had sought refuge moments earlier. Debris flew everywhere, one piece narrowly missing Ingrid. They struggled back to their feet. A second bomb hit the same building, while a third landed next to the building.

"We have to find shelter," Johann cried out. Before they could take another step, however, they were overcome by intense heat as the bombs spread into wild fire, forcing people out of nearby buildings left standing. Hundreds of people appeared out of nowhere and streamed past them. Caught up in the mass confusion, they were swept away like a branch in the fury of a raging river. The crowd around them intensified.

Ingrid felt certain they would be smothered alive by the masses in the frantic rush for survival. "Where are they all coming from?!" she shouted. Through the rush she lost her grip on Johann and felt him slip away from her. With all her force, she tried to push in the direction where he last stood, but it was an impossible feat. The crowds were too strong and she found herself being pushed further and further away.

"Johann!" her voice cracked as she screamed out in desperation while the crowd shoved her relentlessly from side to side. She frantically jumped up, catching only a glimpse of him as the crowd continued to push him back. "Johann!" she shouted again. But Johann, who had fallen out of sight, could no longer hear her cries.

As quickly as it had begun, the bombing stopped. Ingrid no longer heard the plane engines. She gazed upward as the crowd around her began to disperse. Suddenly she heard the blood-curdling cries of a woman who sat huddled over a child, holding his tiny, lifeless body in her arms. Half his body had been charred from flames. Ingrid wanted desperately to rush to the woman's side, but no sooner had she taken a step forward then she heard another cry, then another, and another as survivors discovered their dead and wounded loved ones nearby. She began trembling uncontrollably. Where was Johann? Was he still alive? She would have to find her own way back to the club.

When she finally reached the club, nearly two hours later, Ingrid's heart jumped at the tiny spark of hope that Johann might have made it back safely before she did. She rushed through the doorway calling out his name. Nobody answered. "Frieda?" she called out. Still there was no answer. Ingrid fumbled through the dark, knocking over a chair, before she reached the entrance to the basement. She carefully made her way downstairs.

A flood of relief came over her when she saw Frieda and Rudolph sitting around a candle. Frieda saw her first. "Ingrid!" she shouted out. "Look, Rudy! It's Ingrid! When you didn't show up earlier, we started to worry." Then she stopped for a few seconds. "But, where is Johann?"

Tears filled Ingrid's eyes. "I...I don't know. We were separated. I couldn't hold onto him. It...it was impossible. There were so many people. They just came out of nowhere."

They all went upstairs to the bar area, where Frieda assisted Ingrid into a nearby chair. Frieda lit a candle and placed it on the table. Dirt from all the soot and dust created by the flying debris covered Ingrid's hands and face.

"What happened?" asked Rudolph.

Ingrid recounted the events, building up to the moment she lost track of Johann.

"I am sure he is all right!" insisted Frieda. "Johann is a strong man."

"Then why has he not yet returned?" asked Ingrid.

Frieda merely shook her head slowly, not knowing what more to say.

Later that night, Johann still had not returned. Unable to sleep, Ingrid donned a velvety red robe and went into the main room, where she found Frieda and Rudolph sitting quietly.

"I can't sleep," she said dismally. "I'm so worried about Johann."

"Come join us then," Frieda said in her typical maternal tone. There were several burning candles spread throughout the room.

Ingrid approached her friends as they sat quietly at a table. Frieda, preoccupied with her own thoughts, stared out over the empty stage, her expression filled with longing. A round, crystal jar with a white candle burning inside sat in the center of the table. Finally, Rudolph stood up and walked away. The room seemed to come alive as the wavering candlelight flickered its magic, and eerie shadows were cast out in every direction.

"I'm frightened," whispered Ingrid, as she bit her lip to hold back the tears. Rudolph quietly began sweeping, trying desperately to fill his empty time productively. Ingrid did not move. "Things have become so bad, Frieda. What do you think will happen to us?" She turned to Rudolph and snapped bitterly, "Why do you even bother to clean? What is the point?!!" She buried her face in her hands and began to weep.

"The war will pass soon," predicted Frieda. "You will see."

"But how many more of us must die before it ends?" asked Ingrid. "If the bombs and fire don't kill us first, we'll probably end up starving to death. The whole world has gone mad."

"I know, Ingrid. I know. But all things must end sometime," said Frieda. "I see an end to this war. I really do."

"We are losing! Berlin is in ruin! How much worse can it get? So many lives have already been lost." Her voice hardened. "Damned Hitler! Damned Nazis! Damn them all!"

Frieda's eyes grew wide. "Ingrid… This is the first time I've ever heard you speak out like so against the Führer." Ingrid said nothing, but instead gently brought her hand up to her chest, where she could feel the pendant through her shirt. "We have to be strong," Frieda finally said. "We can't just give up. The end of hope would mean the end of everything we've ever worked for." Frieda put her hand over Ingrid's to try to comfort her.

"I just have a bad feeling ...a...a very bad feeling." Ingrid wiped away another tear. She stood up, walked over to the door, opened it, and peered outside. Her expression changed from fear to a moment of solemn acceptance. "It's suddenly very quiet tonight. It's al...almost too quiet." She stepped back, closed the door and locked it, then turned to face her friends.

Suddenly, the sound of the *flak* illuminating the skies replaced the sound of silence. Seconds later, sirens wailed once again across the city.

Rudolph picked up one candle then ordered, "Quick! Put out the candles and get into the basement again!" The three of them hurried around the room, blowing out the candles, and then quickly made their way down the steps, with Rudolph lighting the way with his one candle.

"Johann!" Ingrid shrieked. "What if Johann is nearby

and is trying to get in. I've locked the door."

"Ingrid, don't be foolish," Frieda countered.

"I know it sounds crazy, but what if he's out there? What if he's trying to get in and he can't."

"Stay here," Rudolph grunted as he hurried back up the steps. Not heeding his instructions, the women followed him up to the top of the stairs, where they stood at the entrance of the basement, watching him as he stumbled through the dark room. Their eyes followed the candlelight as Rudolph made his way to the front door. Just as he reached for the lock, however, there was a loud crash and the ceiling caved in on him.

"Ruuudyyyy!" screamed Frieda. She raced to the spot where Rudolph had been standing only seconds earlier.

Ingrid watched in horror as the rest of the ceiling caved in, covering both of her friends. At that same moment, she took a step backward, then tumbled down to the bottom of the stairs, where she blacked out.

—⊁————⊁————⊁—

A little while later Ingrid awoke to the vague images of people hovering over her. Was she dead? No. She could not possibly be dead. The dull ache throughout her entire body was proof of that fact. She felt arms beneath her, carefully picking her up. The world around her began spinning. It was difficult to distinguish what the voices were saying, but, in the midst of it all, she did manage to catch one thing. A man's voice rang out above all the others, saying, "The owners, both are dead..." Ingrid's world blacked out again.

The next time she opened her eyes, Ingrid struggled to sit up. Her head immediately fell back against a pillow. Her eyes scanned her new surroundings. She was in some sort of medical facility where the medicinal smell of alcohol lingered in the air. The room, which contained no windows, was cold and glum. Ingrid heard the moans and cries of other patients. She closed her eyes momentarily. When she opened them again, she was startled by a young woman, in her twenties, standing over her. The young woman had sensitive, expressive eyes. These were eyes that somehow had not yet been hardened by all the surrounding death.

"How do you feel?" the woman asked.

Ingrid struggled to speak. "Wh...where am I?" Her voice was barely audible. The young woman drew her face closer to Ingrid's face so that she could hear her words. Ingrid repeated the question.

"You are in an underground hospital near the Oberbaum Bridge," she explained.

"How long have...have I been like this?"

"They brought you here three days ago. You are going to be fine. The doctors are calling you a miracle because you have no broken bones, only a few scrapes and scratches and several bad bruises. However, you did suffer from a bad concussion."

"The club!" Ingrid suddenly remembered as she attempted to get up. "Frieda and Rudolph...I heard they are dead!"

"I'm sorry... I don't know, but you have to rest," the woman urged as she pushed Ingrid gently back down. "I'll bring you some soup." She left and returned a few minutes later with a bowl of watered-down turnip soup. Gently easing Ingrid's head up with one arm, she fed her with the other. "Eat this. You have to regain your strength."

Ingrid did as she was instructed. The soup tasted bland with nothing but water and a meager portion of turnips. She managed to finish every drop. The woman laid her gently back down and told her once again to rest. Ingrid complied and fell immediately to sleep.

One week later, when Ingrid felt strong enough to stand and walk around, the nurse sent her to an underground bunker. Once inside, a woman led Ingrid to a small room crammed with three-high metal bunk beds. The room was dank and felt claustrophobic with its low ceiling. The woman handed Ingrid a thin blanket and pointed to one of the bunk beds, saying, "The middle one became vacant this morning. You take that." Ingrid nodded. She dared not complain. She knew that acceptance into the bunker was on a first come, first served basis. "You will get two and a half liters of water every day and a bowl of pea soup every other day. Other than that, you are on your own," the woman explained. Ingrid nodded and the woman left.

The shelter was cold, had no natural lighting, and was packed with strangers. Ingrid climbed into her bed, which made a loud screeching noise. She closed her eyes and thought about Frieda and Rudolph. A tear fell from her eye as she rolled over onto her side, facing the wall. Her thoughts then drifted to Johann. How she longed to have her old life back.

CHAPTER FIVE

APRIL 1945

More than a year had passed since Johann lost Ingrid. He thought about her often and how he might have been able to save her. The last time they were together, he had tried desperately to hold onto her hand as bombs plummeted from the skies. Before long the crowd had become too intense and he had lost his grip on her. Johann had then been caught up in the flood of people, being pushed further and further away. Once the crowd had dissipated, Ingrid had simply vanished.

All around there was death and destruction. As Johann began searching the area, he saw a ten-year-old girl sitting in the middle of the street crying. In her arms she carried an infant boy, wrapped in a soot-filled blanket. Johann watched as several bewildered people passed them by without paying any attention.

"Help me," the girl said weakly. Johann approached her, and then crouched down to her level. There was a gash on her bloodied forehead. "My oma. She's dead. I want my mother. I don't know how to get back to my house." Her voice cracked.

Johann hesitated at first, wanting to continue his search

for Ingrid, but then reached into his pocket to pull out a handkerchief. He wiped the blood from the girl's wound then pressed down to try to stop the bleeding. "Here. Hold this on your forehead," he instructed as he gently took the infant from the girl's arms. "What happened to your parents?" he asked.

"Our mother is at home. She's ill right now and so we were with our oma."

"What happened to her... your grandmother?" asked Johann.

The girl simply pointed to where a building once stood, but was now reduced to a pile of smoldering rubble. Unwilling to leave the little girl and her baby brother alone to fend for themselves, Johann spent the remainder of the day escorting the children back to their home. It was late in the evening when they arrived at an apartment building. It was still intact. As if she had been waiting by the window, staring out into the dark, their mother suddenly burst out of the door and raced over to greet her children. She sobbed uncontrollably with relief to be reunited. Just then, however, they heard the *flak* in the distance. "Quickly! Into the cellar!" the mother ordered her daughter. "You too!" she urged Johann as she took the infant from him. "You'll be safe here."

Once inside, Johann settled in for the long night. The next day he made his way back to the club, only to find it mostly in ruins. He saw a shop owner across the street and approached him. "Do you know what happened?" he asked the shop owner.

"I heard they died." The man shook his head sadly, then turned and walked away, leaving Johann alone in his grief.

Now, it was late April, 1945. Johann had managed to obtain a place to live in the partial ruins of a blown-out apartment building, which he shared with five families.

Rumors abounded that the Gestapo was shooting deserters and those men refusing to take up arms in a last ditch effort to save Berlin. Up until now he had managed to keep a low profile, leaving the building only long enough to go find food and tending to a tiny plot of dirt, what he viewed as a measly excuse of a garden.

Johann had used up his last ration card and there was no way to get any others. It was increasingly difficult to find food and Johann was hungry. One day, after trying to cook a miserable potato over a tiny, flicker of a flame for several hours, Johann gave up and took a bite of the half-raw vegetable. It tasted like cardboard and only seemed to intensify his hunger. Just then, though, his thoughts wandered to the club. He wondered if any of the food might still be in the basement, or if someone had already found it. At first, he hesitated, but then he decided to try to make his way across the city to find out. There was little left that he could do. It was almost nightfall when he left his room.

Johann thought he heard artillery off in the distance, but pressed on. Within an hour a group of ten haggard German soldiers intercepted him. The leader of the group, a tall sergeant with broad shoulders, stepped forward and confronted him. "Join us," he ordered. "Hitler has ordered the people of Berlin to take up arms. Fight for the motherland. Soviet forces are coming." Johann could not refuse.

After passing by smoldering ruins and rubble, the group came upon two trucks. One carried weapons and ammunition, while the other carried German citizens, crammed into the back. The sergeant led Johann and his group to the trucks, where another German soldier was busy passing out the weapons. The selection of weapons was sparse. The sergeant handed Johann a rifle and several boxes of ammunition. Johann then joined the other people in the back of the truck.

Staring at one another, nobody in the truck uttered a single word as they drove off. They made their way over and around debris for nearly an hour before arriving at a five foot barricade made up of bricks and broken chunks of old, dried mortar. On either side of the street lay the partial remains of several high-rise apartment complexes. Rubble piled up high on the sidewalks flowed over onto the street.

Once the truck had stopped, three soldiers appeared from within the ruins of one of the buildings and quickly approached them. They ordered everyone onboard to get out. A fourth person, a captain, approached, carrying a large bulky rounded weapon over his right shoulder. "Have any of you ever used a Panzerfaust before?" he asked as he approached the group.

One man, who appeared to be in his fifties, raised his hand and said, "I have never used one, but I have seen them in the news."

The officer nodded and offered a brief demonstration. As he neared the end of his instructions, a German cargo truck drove up alongside the captain. Two soldiers stepped out of the truck and offered a Sieg Heil, then went to the back of the truck, removed a wooden crate filled with Panzerfausts, and brought it to the officer. There was a moment of silence, then one man in the group took a step forward and thrust his right arm up into the air. "Heil Hitler!" he exclaimed with determination in his voice. Another man stepped forward, then another, then a woman, all offering the Sieg Heil and exclaiming, "Heil Hitler!" Johann, meanwhile, who had quietly slunk to the back of the group, said nothing and made no motion.

Two days later Johann was sent to the eastern part of the city, where he worked for nearly 20 hours straight, building up barricades and carrying weapons and ammunition to key strategic locations. The work was grueling and his hands became raw. Instead of attacking from the east, however, the Soviets came up from the south and quickly pushed their way toward the center of the city. The Soviet forces were relentless, sending infantrymen into buildings to clear out any German forces poised to attack the oncoming tanks. Then, once they cleared the buildings, the tanks could safely continue their assault on Berlin.

As word reached Johann's group, they changed their location to fight the onrushing Soviet infantrymen. Along with three other men, one of them a German officer, Johann hid inside an abandoned office building, poised to attack oncoming enemy tanks, Soviet infantrymen stormed the building. Johann heard commands yelled out in Russian as soldiers scrambled through the hallways. Sounds of doors being busted open were followed by a barrage of gunfire. The noise drew closer and closer until three Soviet infantrymen pushed their way into the room where Johann and his three comrades were hiding. Both sides attacked, sending out a barrage of gunfire, which stopped just as quickly as it had started. When the dust finally settled, Johann heard the cocking of a gun right in front of him. He looked up to find himself staring down the barrel of a Tokarev SVT-40. Blood covered the floor, with some of it splattered on the walls. The body of his first comrade lay one meter away. The body of his second comrade was sprawled across the windowsill, where he had tried to escape, directly behind Johann. The body of a Soviet soldier was twisted over a wooden tabletop on the other side of the room. Staring straight into the barrel of the rifle, Johann slowly raised his hands over his head to surrender. The Soviet infantryman stepped up to him, pressed the barrel of his rifle between his eyes, and squeezed the trigger. Johann clamped his eyes shut, but then heard the empty click of the trigger. Seeing his opportunity, he leaped up. The infantryman's eyes grew wide as he pulled back his rifle. He then whipped it around and coldcocked Johann on the side of his head with the butt, causing him to black out.

When Johann finally came to, it was dusk and the streets were quiet. His head was pounding as he struggled to get to his feet. He reached up and rubbed the spot where he had been hit. He felt a large bump. He looked around the room at the lifeless bodies of the first two Germans and noticed that their weapons were gone.

Johann hobbled toward the door to leave, but then something caught his eye – a sliver of army-green material lay toward the back end of a nearby desk. He approached it to get a better look and found the dead German officer's body, jammed behind the desk. Beneath the officer's body lay his pistol, a Luger P-08, which the Soviets somehow had missed. Johann quickly snatched it up and checked to see if there was any ammunition remaining. There were only two rounds left. He tucked the pistol into his pants, further concealing it under his shirt and then left the building.

Johann barely made it two blocks when he saw a group of Soviet tanks making their way up the street toward him. He immediately ducked into the ruins of an old abandoned warehouse, obviously picked over by desperate German citizens. He climbed over several boards, and almost lost his balance before he found an empty dark corner where he could hide. Unable to stand any longer, he lay down and closed his eyes. Utterly exhausted, he was oblivious to the danger that followed him into the building.

"Look, Son, at who we found. It's Johann Brandt, the Jew I've told you about. The Jew who's been living a lie." Johann sat up to find himself once again staring into the twisted face of Karl von Euken. "I knew we would meet again," said Karl.

Beside Karl stood his 16-year old son, Max, with a knowing expression on his face. He had features very similar to his father's. Karl glanced over at his son and declared, "I'm going to show you what we do with filthy Jews who lie about who they are."

Karl approached Johann then kicked him in the stomach. Hunched over in pain, Johann struggled to get to his feet, heaving and gasping from the blow. Karl then shoved his son forward. Laughing, Max swung his foot and dealt a devastating blow to Johann's right knee. Johann shouted out in agony. He grasped his knee with both hands and felt fragments of bone grinding throughout his kneecap. The thought of the shattered bones made his face grow hot as he fought back nausea.

"Stand aside for just a moment," Karl instructed his son, pushing him back gently with one arm.

He swung his foot at Johann's chest. But this time Johann managed to reach out and grab it, yanking and pulling him down with all his force. Maintaining his grip on Karl's foot, Johann struggled to his feet, using his left leg to get up and leaning against Karl's leg to maintain his equilibrium. He was now standing over Karl, who had been completely caught off guard and had fallen with a thud on his back. Karl did not see the pistol as Johann pulled it out from under his shirt, pointed it at him and squeezed the trigger twice. The deafening blasts reverberated throughout the building. Then, the atmosphere grew still. The only sound was Johann's breath, as he gasped for air.

Seeing that his father had been mortally wounded, Max began to shout hysterically. "You filthy Jew! You killed my father!" he cried out. Johann then turned the gun on the youth. "Go ahead, Jew pig! Shoot me!" the youth shrieked rabidly.

Johann stared at Max. His hair was blonde and straight and he had the bluest eyes Johann had ever seen. He was shorter than Johann, but he had a strong demeanor about him.

They stood face to face. It felt like a game of cat and mouse. Johann, with his gun still smoking, realized that he had used his last two bullets to kill Karl. "You might as well kill me now, pig, because I'll never forget your face," Max spat.

"Turn around," ordered Johann.

To his relief, Max relented and slowly turned around. As Johann raised his pistol, Max closed his eyes and sputtered, "I will find y…" The pistol came crashing down onto the back of his head, sending him crashing to the ground.

———※———※———※———

Born in 1929, Max von Euken grew up in Munich, the product of a strict upbringing. His father, Karl, always drove him to succeed. In 1938, after Max's mother died of cancer, Karl was forced to care for him alone. When he was not in school, the boy spent time with his father, learning about the Nazi ways, and his obsession over the regime grew. Two weeks after his tenth birthday, the boy joined the Hitlerjugend.

Max had met Adolf Hitler on one occasion and it was an experience he would never forget. He was only 11 years old when the Führer paid a visit to his school. The headmaster had begun preparation for the visit twelve days ahead of time. Everything had to be perfect, not one thing out of place. Spirits were high, classrooms were scrubbed, and students were groomed to perfection. Caught up in the commotion, it was a frantic time for young Max, but nothing could have prepared him emotionally for Hitler's arrival.

On the thirteenth day, Hitler rode up in a large, black Mercedes. The students were already standing in a line, prepared to catch the first glimpse of the Führer as he emerged from the back seat of the car. To Max's surprise, Hitler was physically unimpressive. He was considerably small for the great powers he possessed. While he walked down the line, the headmaster introduced each boy by name. Max felt his body grow numb and his stomach tense up as they drew closer. Once he finally stood face to face with the Führer, Max swallowed carefully as the headmaster introduced him.

"This is Max von Euken. He shows much promise and is one of our top pupils."

Max immediately threw out his right arm and snapped his heels together, exclaiming, *"Heil Hitler!"* The Führer maintained a cold expression. Max found himself nearly hypnotized by his piercing eyes.

The Führer's expression softened somewhat and he finally smiled. "You will go far," he said before returning the salute and continuing down the line of students. Afterwards, Hitler gave a short but potent speech, reminding the students that they were the next generation. He stressed the importance of the National Socialist movement, how it must be spread world-wide and how the Aryan race would prevail above all others. When he finally left, his words echoed through the boy's mind. Max felt more determined than ever to follow the Führer's great words.

CHAPTER SIX

APRIL 1945

There were many rumors circulating about the approaching Soviet troops. "I heard they are taking over the South," one woman said.

"It's true," said another, "and they've taken Köpenick."

"Did you hear what happened in Wünsdorf?" asked a third. "Someone said they crashed into a church, murdered the men, and took the women." Ingrid listened, but never said anything.

As the end of April neared, rumor turned to reality. One night it was far too quiet. As Ingrid lay in bed, she heard something that sounded like someone running through the shelter. She hopped down from her bunk and made her way to the doorway where she saw several German soldiers running in her direction. One of them stopped and walked to catch his breath. As he passed by Ingrid, she asked him, "What's happening?"

"Soviet forces are now in the square, directly above the bunker." The soldier picked his pace back up. Ingrid watched him until he disappeared around the corner. Her heart began to race. It was really happening. The shelters and bunkers would no longer be safe. Ingrid had heard the many stories of Soviet soldiers taking what they wanted, food, money, jewels, and even women. She did not want to fall victim to any of it, but what could she do? Ahead, down the corridor, she saw two men, huddled together in conversation, sitting around a burning candle. Ingrid approached them.

"What's going on?" she asked. They did not answer. As Ingrid looked more closely, she realized they were not men at all, but women disguising themselves as men. Already dressed in slacks and working shirts, the older woman was busy cutting the hair of the younger one. "Do you really think that will help?" asked Ingrid. "I mean, do you really think the Soviets will mistake you for men and leave you alone?"

"It's worth a try," answered the older woman. "There are too many horror stories not to try." Ingrid did not move as the woman resumed cutting the hair, then stopped. "Look, you're welcome to join us, or not, but don't just stand there and stare." Ingrid simply turned and began walking away. "Wait," the woman called after her. "If you change your mind, we're in the next room down, third bunk from the entrance."

Ingrid left the scene. In a terrified trance, and not knowing what else to do, she returned to her bunk, where she lay down and pulled the covers up over her head.

The following morning Ingrid made her way up the steps to try to see what was happening outside. The smell of gasoline lingered in the air as she emerged into the sunlight. Overnight, it seemed as if the entire world had shifted. There were no more German planes, no more running water, no gas, no electricity, and hardly any German *flak*. All around, Soviet soldiers were wandering around the streets. Ingrid was suddenly startled by the sound of breaking glass, probably one of the last remaining windows in the area. She looked to her right to see two Soviet soldiers climbing through the broken window of one of the few standing buildings. Off in the distance three soldiers were riding bicycles, teetering clumsily as one tried to teach the other two how to peddle. A minute later a large soldier with squared shoulders brushed against her. He grunted slightly as he continued past her. Ingrid immediately noticed that the man was wearing at least five watches on his arm. Once he left the area Ingrid returned to the shelter.

Two days later, while many of the residents were gone from the bunker, Russian soldiers came bursting through the doors. Pointing their rifles at the women, they pushed them in one corner. The Russians began taking whatever item of value that they could from the helpless woman. Ingrid attempted to conceal her locket, the only memory remaining that she had of Johann, fearful that they might take that too. She watched in horror as one woman resisted, was slapped to the ground and kicked in the stomach. Laughing, several Russians randomly chose some of the women and young girls and dragged them away. One of the victims was a young girl who had recently been accepted into the shelter and slept only two bunks away from Ingrid.

Ingrid shriveled back in fear against the cold, damp wall behind her as one soldier reached for her. His face was twisted and crazed, his eyes wild. As Ingrid turned to her side and tried desperately to crawl away, he picked her up by the back of her collar and threw her back down, almost crushing a nearby infant.

"Stop run!" he bellowed out in poor German. "You come!"

He reached down and grabbed her brutally by the shoulder. Just then the door burst open and a Russian political commissar entered the room, his face contorted with rage at the scene before him. He shouted out something in Russian, causing the soldier to let go of Ingrid. The soldiers immediately picked themselves up and scrambled out of the shelter. The room grew silent as the dismayed faces of the women stared at the final intruder. He acknowledged their gazes with a slight nod and immediately left.

Long minutes of silence followed as the women waited, anticipating more abuse, but none came. Later that evening, Ingrid sought out the two women from before. They proceeded to cut her hair short and uneven, and offered her a pair of slacks and a shirt, both of which hung loosely around her body. Lastly, they gave her a flat cap, which she pulled over her eyes. "How do I look?" Ingrid asked.

"I think you can pull it off… as long as you don't talk," replied the younger woman.

Two days later, as Ingrid passed by a group of people huddled together, she overheard one of them say, "It's true! He killed himself."

The women all gasped. "How could he?" exclaimed one of the women.

"How could we ever have followed him?" asked another.

"He's the only reason I stayed in Berlin," interjected a man.

The group grew quiet and Ingrid pressed on. Hitler's death and betrayal fell across many lips as the German people struggled to make sense of it all. One week later a young boy came running through the shelter, shouting in a high pitched voice, "The war is over...Germany has surrendered! The war is over!" Ingrid clasped her hands over her mouth as she fought back tears. They were tears of relief, but also tears from a sense of defeat.

For the first time in days, Ingrid donned her new clothes and cap and left the shelter. Outside, she saw that the Soviet soldiers had settled into makeshift camp sites. One was busy feeding a cow, another was busy shaving, looking into a piece of broken mirror that hung on a light post. Two soldiers had managed to find a bottle of Schnapps and they staggered down the street with it, passing it back and forth. Ingrid watched the two drunken soldiers as one pulled out a pistol and shot a nearby pigeon. Both men laughed, kicking the dead bird several times as they passed. Then, they spotted a young German woman walking hand-in-hand with a German man. The first soldier said something to the second one. Ingrid watched in horror as he smiled, aimed his pistol at the German man, and shot him in the back. As the German woman began to scream, the soldiers rushed to her side, pulled her away from the scene, and disappeared with her into a nearby building. Ingrid turned and quickly made her way back to the shelter.

Just as she reached the entrance, she found herself face to face with six Soviet soldiers. She froze. "Boy, do you live in this shelter?" one asked in good German. He appeared to be an officer. Ingrid nodded without making eye contact. "Stay here!" ordered the man without giving any further explanation.

He said something in Russian to the other soldiers. All but one of the men disappeared into the shelter, leaving Ingrid alone with the one who stayed behind. Ingrid glanced up at him nervously. His face remained expressionless as they waited. Minutes later the group reappeared, this time with several women. The leader gave an order in Russian and the women, including Ingrid, were marched away.

The journey felt long. The soldiers chattered happily, occasionally pointing to something or someone in the streets and laughing. None of the women dared to speak for fear of repercussion. One younger girl leaned over to Ingrid and whispered, "Where do you suppose they are taking us?" Her voice was barely audible. Ingrid strained to hear her. She only shrugged.

The weather was mild with clouds gathering overhead, and it appeared as if it might rain later. After a long walk, the group arrived at a street completely covered by rubble. The women stood, awaiting the soldiers' next move. The leader made a rapid visual sweep of the area before walking toward a small pile of rubble nearby. He brushed past Ingrid, throwing her slightly off balance and proceeded to make an announcement, speaking German well enough to be understood. "You will clear away all bricks and masonry from streets. It's your city. You will make beautiful again!" He then turned to Ingrid. "You. Boy. You push cart." He showed Ingrid a nearby handcart, which the women began filling with the debris.

As they worked, the Russian leader explained in a commanding voice, "Every day you work until no more rubble left in streets. For your work, we give ration card. You have high priority for food." The women stopped working briefly and stared, wide eyed, not answering. "Everyone understand?" He paused a moment and looked through the crowd. "Good. Continue work."

After several hours of the grueling task of pulling the cart back and forth and emptying it repeatedly, Ingrid was exhausted and her hands were bruised and cut. Two more Russian soldiers joined the group, bringing along two loaves of bread. The loaves were cut up and distributed to the women with some sort of strangely flavored water. After a short break, they resumed their work.

When nightfall had finally arrived, the women returned to the shelter. After eating undercooked potatoes for dinner, Ingrid, exhausted from the labor, found no difficulty in falling asleep.

The following morning when she awoke, Ingrid could barely move. She felt as if her body had been run through a grinder. She sat up and gently rubbed her arms and legs, trying to work out some of the pain that had built up through the night, but the rubbing only seemed to further irritate her muscles. She gazed down at her hands. They were cracked and brown, old blood had settled in the crevices. After she got dressed, Ingrid went to the sink and ran her hands through a tiny trickle of cold flowing water. It felt good as she rubbed them gently together. She carefully dried them then headed back to her bunk.

A little later, Ingrid heard a commotion, which prompted her to peer out her room. She watched silently as soldiers gathered up a dozen women and led them away. Nearly half an hour later, as Ingrid was resting on her bunk, another group of soldiers appeared. This time they selected Ingrid with a group of twenty other women and a teenage boy, and led them to a different location from the previous day.

As they began their work, Ingrid found it difficult to move about freely. Her entire body ached, her back in particular. In time, the pain became slightly more tolerable. They were forced to work all day, with only one short break. Rations were barely enough to maintain their energy.

Time passed and the daily rituals began repeating themselves. By now the shelter had become a popular source for the Russian soldiers to come and gather women and an occasional boy to aid in the postwar clearing efforts. Before long the Soviets had taken over the shelter completely. One day they decided that only those women healthy enough for labor and children under 15 were permitted to stay at the shelter.

In time, the work load became lighter and lighter as the surrounding streets were nearly cleared away. Germany could now concentrate on rebuilding. Ingrid thought it would be impossible to recreate Berlin as it stood before the war. Yet she labored on for fear of losing her place in the shelter, kept her hair short, and never spoke to anyone outside of the few people who knew her. She had witnessed too many women who had given up, sent away to fend for themselves on the streets, and others, unwilling to give up, work themselves to death. The shelter was overcrowded, with each room filled to capacity.

One day, a girl appeared and took over the bunk below Ingrid's. The girl, who was barely fifteen years old, struggled to arrange her belongings. She was petite and had dark, shoulder-length hair and a pale complexion. Her large blue eyes sunk in with pronounced circles underneath them. Neither woman spoke until the girl finished arranging her belongings. She then turned and introduced herself. "Hello," she began. "My name is Marlene." Her voice sounded sweet and soft.

"Ingri…" she stopped suddenly. "I mean…"

"Hello," Marlene cut in. "It's all right. I understand."

"Thank you," Ingrid said softly.

Marlene stopped and stared intently at her. "Is it hard? I mean, pretending to be a boy?" She smiled weakly.

"It's harder not to." After another moment Ingrid asked, "Where is your family?"

Marlene shook her head sadly. "Some were killed during the last air raids. My brother was sent to prison for committing acts against the German government. Last I heard, he had been shot for treason. I also have a sister who ran away early last year. I've heard rumors that she has devoted her time to aiding certain war criminals." Her voice trailed off at these last words. She shuddered lightly, but her face remained expressionless.

They both stood there for a moment, each contemplating what to say next. Suddenly, Marlene coughed several times uncontrollably and held her chest.

Once she stopped, Ingrid commented, "That doesn't sound very good."

"I know." Another moment of silence followed before Marlene said, "Tell me what it's like here. Is it as horrible as they say?"

Ingrid shifted her weight to one side and answered, "Probably worse." There was a hint of cynicism in her voice. "We've become slaves to the Soviets. We work every day and they can take whatever they want, whenever they want it – your meager possessions, jewelry, even your body." The girl coughed again. Ingrid shook her head and cautioned, "If you are sick, I suggest you do everything you can to conceal it if you want to be allowed to stay here in this shelter." The girl nodded her head as she struggled to hold back another cough.

Finally Ingrid stood up. "Come. It's almost time to eat." Taking on a maternal stance toward Marlene, she reached out and helped the girl to her feet. They walked toward the entrance of the shelter where three men were distributing food and water. Tonight they would be served a tepid potato soup and a small ration of bread. Ingrid watched as Marlene, who had not eaten anything in two days, devoured her food.

The following day, when the soldiers appeared to gather their workers, Ingrid kept Marlene close, knowing the girl would be safer with her.

"New girl?" asked one soldier, in poor German, when he saw Marlene.

Another soldier stepped forward and said something in Russian as he reached out and caressed the girl's cheek. Marlene turned and withdrew her face. Her eyes became wild with fear. Her reaction prompted the soldier to pull back his hand. "I not hurt." However, Marlene did not feel too reassured. The entire day, as Marlene worked, Ingrid sensed her uneasiness. Marlene did all she could to avoid the stares of the soldier who had previously reached for her.

Later that night Ingrid was awakened by the sound of whimpering. She leaned her head down and saw that it was Marlene. She climbed down from her bunk and crouched beside her. "What's wrong?" she whispered.

"I can't sleep," Marlene sniffled. "I'm so cold." Her face was flush.

Ingrid reached out to feel her forehead. She was burning up. Her skin glimmered as tears streamed down her pale face. "You need a doctor. You have a terrible fever."

Marlene shook her head almost violently. "No," she balked, her voice cracking. "No doctor!"

"But you need one! You are very ill!"

"Have you already forgotten your own warning?!" Marlene lashed out. "They will turn me away. I have nowhere else to go. I will never survive in the streets!"

"But... Marlene... Don't be foolish. Such a fever is dangerous!"

"No." She suddenly stopped and straightened herself up. "I'll be fine. Don't try to force me to go. I just need rest." Marlene began coughing wildly. Afraid to draw too much attention, she buried her face into her blanket to help muffle the sounds. Ingrid finally stood, picked up her towel, and walked away. She returned moments later, having soaked the towel in cold water. By now Marlene had quit coughing.

"Lie back," instructed Ingrid. "This should help cool down your fever."

The girl did as she was told and Ingrid dabbed her forehead lightly with the towel. She then laid it carefully across Marlene's forehead and urged her to get some sleep. Ingrid's warmth and protection were soothing. Before she knew it, Marlene was fast asleep.

As the days passed, Ingrid grew particularly fond of

Marlene. Unfortunately, her condition only deteriorated. Ingrid watched helplessly as the girl grew weaker and weaker from the tuberculosis that she had been fighting for the past several months. That, coupled with a serious lack of nutrition, pulled the girl down. Somehow, though, she managed to hang on to her miserable life and retain her place of refuge in the shelter.

Before long, however, Marlene became too weak to leave her bed. One day, Ingrid sat with the girl for a while. Following lunch, once Marlene had fallen back to sleep, Ingrid felt restless and decided to wander outside to escape the depressing atmosphere of the shelter. Dressed in slacks, an overcoat, and her flat cap pulled down low on her brow, Ingrid headed out. The streets were filled with people, yet she had never before felt more lonely. She observed the heavily clothed people as they scurried about their business. Passing an isolated street, Ingrid observed two men tearing away a large segment of the wooden door to an old church, which had somehow managed to survive the war. Moving closer she overheard one man saying, "There is enough for a few nights of heat!" Ingrid turned and headed toward a more populated area. She eventually came upon a large public building, which had a notice reading, COFFINS AVAILABLE ONLY FOR THOSE WHO DIED OF INFECTIOUS DISEASE. The image of Marlene came to Ingrid.

Berlin was a depressing sight of incredible ruins. Ingrid was thankful for peace, but overwhelmed with the emptiness of the future. Most of her friends and family were either dead or missing. Why did God have to spare her? She could not help but think that it would have been better if she had died along with Frieda and Rudolph during the air raid. Ingrid walked through the streets, shivering and trying to come to grips with reality.

Later that evening when she returned to the shelter, Ingrid saw that Marlene had grown almost lifeless. "Marlene," she said in a near whisper.

Marlene, still lying down on her bed, had become too weak to move. The girl struggled to turn her head and stared at Ingrid. "You have been so kind," she said weakly. Her glassy eyes were sunken in even more and her face pale. "I'm afraid I can't hold on much longer."

Ingrid looked out into the corridor and saw two men approaching. They were carrying a stretcher. She immediately grew frightened. What would become of the girl? Her fear shifted to herself. Once they took Marlene away, they took away Ingrid's sole reason to survive. Who would need her now?

Once the men walked in, Ingrid pleaded, "Wait! Please. Give me a few minutes alone with her." Seeing the desperation on her face, the men complied and walked away. Ingrid reached out and grasped Marlene's hand. "I am here for you. What can I do?"

Marlene smiled. "You have always been here for me. You are the mother I lost. Just stay by my side." Marlene coughed several times. When Ingrid saw blood coming up through the corners of her mouth, she pulled an old torn handkerchief from her pocket and gently wiped her lips. She felt helpless as she watched the girl slipping away from her. "Pl...please don't le...leave me, In...Ingrid." Marlene's whispers were barely audible as Ingrid tightened her grip on her hand to offer reassurance.

Marlene's grip loosened and her hand became limp and lifeless. Ingrid looked into her open eyes and saw that there was nothing there, nothing but a hollow stare on her face. She let go of the young girl's hand and gently closed her eyes shut. "Merry Christmas, little Marlene," she whispered. "You're free at last." Ingrid cried silently.

Winter had set in as Ingrid stood in line to receive a ration of bread. She had been waiting for hours. When the trucks arrived, soldiers began passing out the bread and Ingrid found herself being shoved from side to side by hungry German citizens, unwilling to wait another moment. Feeling too weak to struggle, she was quickly shoved to the rear of the crowd. By the time she finally reached the truck, the rations had all been distributed. She was not alone, though. Other people found themselves with nothing to eat that day.

Ingrid simply turned and walked away. She wandered the streets aimlessly. It was another typically overcast day, which did not help her depression any. She had no desire to return to the shelter where, since cutting her hair, she had stayed mostly to herself, outside of her interaction with Marlene. Instead, she decided to walk and walk until her feet would carry her no further. She wandered through torn-up cobblestone streets, old cracked paved roads, and former business districts, now completely obliterated by the war. Finally, as she arrived by the Spree River, she stopped walking and glanced down into the murky water. Ingrid stood for a long moment, contemplating her future and recalling her past. She leaned against the railing, grasping its cold metal in her hands. Finally, she wept, releasing all the emotion that she had held in over the past months. She wept for all of Germany, for humanity, but mostly, she wept for her own losses. It felt good to let it out and she could feel some of the tension rising off her shoulders.

She began walking again, and nearly an hour later she came upon a familiar street. She blinked several times at all the rubble in her surroundings and made her way slowly through the familiar neighborhood until she reached the old club. Her days of dancing were now just a distant dream. At least three-fourths of the building still stood. Ingrid walked up to what had once been the entrance, but was now merely a gaping hole in the side. She could still make out part of the sign that once hung above the door.

She stepped forward and peered through the debris, where she spotted an old weather-worn photograph carefully wedged between two rocks. She reached down and picked it up. It was the photograph that had always hung in the window, advertising the nightly shows. She saw her faded image standing happily in the center of it and vividly recalled the day the photograph had been taken. It was barely two weeks after Ingrid first arrived in Berlin. She wondered what had happened to all the other performers. Were any of them still alive?

Then, just as Ingrid leaned forward, she felt a hand gently grasp her shoulder. She quickly turned around and gasped. Standing before her was Johann Brandt. He was wearing a brown, wool coat buttoned up to his neck and a pair of black leather gloves. In his right hand he held a dull, brown cane that appeared as if it had warped over time. Tears began to well up in her eyes and they immediately fell into each other's arms.

"Ingrid! Ingrid, *meine liebe*. You are still alive! I almost didn't recognize you. Where have you been? What happened to you?"

Ingrid was overwhelmed with joy, barely able to speak, as she wrapped her arms around Johann's neck and held him tightly. After a long while, she finally pulled away and gazed up into his eyes. "I have been staying in a public shelter," she said.

"I thought you were dead. They told me that everyone here perished," he said.

Ingrid looked down sadly. "Frieda and Rudolph didn't make it."

"Ingrid, I'm so sorry. I know how much they meant to you." He held her even tighter, making her feel secure. "I missed you so much. Not a day went by that I didn't think of you." Johann then reached up and stroked Ingrid's short hair. "But what did you do to your hair?"

Ingrid's cheeks reddened slightly. "It was self-defense against the Soviets. I'm fine. Everything is good now." She smiled. "But what happened to you? Why are you walking with a cane?"

Johann quickly recounted the events that led up to his confrontation with Karl von Euken and his 16-year-old son Max. "My knee doesn't seem to want to heal. A doctor told me that I would probably always walk with a cane. No matter, though. I can still move about quite well." He embraced Ingrid again. "Oh, Ingrid! I am so relieved to find you here, alive and well. I've come here many times. I just didn't want to believe you were dead. And now you are here!!" He pulled away from her. "Come home with me. It's not a perfect place, but it has to be better than the shelter. I have the top level of a small apartment only a few kilometers east of here in Prenzlauerberg. It's missing part of a ceiling and some walls, but I've been rebuilding it."

Without hesitating, Ingrid buzzed, "Thank you. I would like that very much."

"We have so much to catch up on. We'll go pick up your belongings and bring them back with us. Then I'll cook you a feast!"

"How is that possible?" she asked.

"We'll pretend," he answered with a wink.

Later at the apartment, Johann prepared a flour-based meat loaf and boiled potatoes. When Ingrid saw the food she gasped, "Johann! Where did you learn to cook like this?!"

"Radio shows during the war." He walked over to a cabinet and opened it. Inside, Ingrid saw packages of dried milk, dried eggs, wholemeal flour, jars of fruit, olives, and fish. "Do you recognize any of this?" he asked.

"Food from the club?"

Johann nodded proudly. "I actually lived in the basement of the club for several months before I moved here."

"How? It looked like it was destroyed."

"In the back part of the building there is a discrete passage through the debris. No one ever found out about it." Johann grinned proudly.

Looking through the food items again, Ingrid remarked, "I'm surprised there is anything left."

"I had to ration it. I don't ever want to go hungry and so what I can get on the streets, I eat first, and save this for when I truly need it." Johann closed the cabinet. "Let me show you something else." He led her to a door to what was once a bedroom, and opened it. "It's my own personal piece of the country."

Half the ceiling and part of a wall in the next room were missing. With the night air flowing in, the temperature felt cold. "There are some advantages to what the bombs did. This room is now my private garden and farm," Johann boasted. He walked over to the far corner and removed a sheet that had been covering three small cages. One cage was empty while the other two each contained one rabbit. "I hope you like rabbit meatloaf." He grinned.

"Johann! You shouldn't have. Now you only have two left," Ingrid protested.

Johann pointed to the rabbit in the closest cage. "She's pregnant." He then walked over to the center of the room and lifted another sheet. Beneath it there were a few plants struggling to grow. "The sun hits the garden perfectly every morning through there." He pointed upward at the massive opening in the wall and ceiling. After covering up the cages and the garden, they returned to the kitchen.

The apartment felt cold. Johann had managed to patch up a lot of the damage done, but air still flowed in through several smaller holes. There was a kitchen, barely large enough to fit two people, and a small dining area, which was part of the living room. The walls still had their original prewar colors, an off-yellow that now appeared chipped and cracked. At the opposite end of the living room was a tiny bedroom, and off to the left stood a bathroom with a half-size bath tub, although there was no running water in the building to go to it. The apartment smelled damp and slightly musty throughout, much like the odor Ingrid had so willingly left behind at the shelter.

They returned to the table, where Johann pulled out a chair for Ingrid. It was an old cedar table that Johann had obtained from an abandoned, partially destroyed apartment complex a few blocks away.

During dinner Ingrid recounted the events that followed their dramatic separation. After dinner they walked to the bedroom, sat on the bed and continued their conversation. They talked about the Soviet invasion and its effect on the German people. They both expressed their bitterness.

"Germany is our country!" exclaimed Ingrid.

By the time they had ended their conversation, Ingrid was fast asleep on the bed. Johann smiled as he gazed down at her lovingly. He stood up, reached for a blanket and pulled it over her. Gently stroking her short hair, he leaned over and kissed her lightly on the forehead. He turned out the light and eased his way out into the living room, where he eventually lay down on the sofa and fell asleep.

The following morning Ingrid woke up to find the dining room table already set and Johann in the kitchen grilling what little bread remained from the night before. On the stove sat a kettle filled with a bitter ersatz coffee

"Where did you get the coffee?'" inquired Ingrid, as she approached Johann. Sleep still filled her eyes.

"It's a special recipe that an old friend gave me some years ago." He poured her a cup, which she readily accepted. Upon taking a sip, Ingrid grimaced.

"That good?" asked Johann, holding back his laughter. When Ingrid forced a nod, he chuckled. "You'll get used to it. Come. Sit down. Breakfast is ready."

They both sat down to eat. There was neither butter nor jam, but it was satisfying nonetheless. Ingrid watched Johann as he devoured his bread. He had not yet shaved that morning, giving him a light shadow and a more rugged expression. Johann looked up to catch Ingrid smiling at him. "Eat, Ingrid," he urged. "Eat before it gets cold."

Ingrid cooed, "You look so handsome this morning." She smiled. He returned her smile.

"I look handsome every morning," he shot back with laughter.

When they finished their breakfast, Ingrid jumped in to help Johann clean up. She washed the dishes as Johann dried them. They kept the conversation light as they worked. He leaned over and whispered in her ear, "You are so beautiful." His warm breath gently brushed her ear. "More beautiful than anything I know."

She returned his gaze with a smile and reached over to kiss him lightly on the cheek. Johann immediately turned, fully faced her, and began kissing her passionately. Ingrid drew her arms around his neck. He then turned, wrapped his right arm over her shoulders, and led her to the bedroom where they began undressing each other. They both worked feverishly, unable to bear another moment apart, longing to feel their bodies pressed against each other.

Johann's lips gently caressed Ingrid's neck as she threw back her head and closed her eyes. He gently made his way down her pale body, filling her entire being with sensuous kisses. At long last they became one, sharing in a long awaited passion, engulfed in each other's senses. Ingrid and Johann made love that morning, and remained in each other's arms most of the day. They forgot their hunger and went without lunch. They did not want the moment to end. Two weeks later they were married.

CHAPTER EIGHT

NOVEMBER 1946

It was hard to believe that his father had been so brutally murdered, and all Max could do was to stand by helplessly as it happened. His desire for revenge seemed to grow stronger with each passing day.

Max von Euken, now seventeen, lived on the second level of a tiny two-story complex, where living conditions were grim. The building lay in partial ruin, its windows having all been blown out by bombs, and had no electricity. Inside the building the air was dank. Four other men, acquaintances of Max, occupied the lower level of the building. The men were all former associates of Max's father, Karl. Holding Karl in such high regard they offered to lodge Max, which he gladly accepted.

Max had only two things on his mind, to avoid being discovered by the Soviet forces who had invaded his city, and to seek revenge for the murder of his father. While many members of Hitler's regime had already been apprehended, others had managed to flee Germany. Obsessed with the past, Max committed himself to remain in Berlin until he could find his father's murderer.

In the building Max felt trapped, unwilling to go

out into the streets, fearing that his family lineage and connections might come back and haunt him. He shared a room with a young woman named Sabine Vogt, for whom he had no affection, but who served a purpose. Sabine took care of his sexual needs. She also ran errands for Max and the other men. It was convenient, for she never roused suspicion. She was able to come and go from the building. Sabine was still a teenager. During the war she had lost contact with all members of her family. She was petite with long, straight black hair and an ashen complexion. She was timid and soft-spoken.

As Max, his thoughts preoccupied with the past, gazed out of the window one day, Sabine came up behind him and placed her hand on his shoulder, startling him. He jumped, causing her to quickly withdraw her hands.

"I'm sorry, Max, I didn't mean to startle you," she said meekly. Max tilted his head and looked up at her, forcing a smile. He was grateful for all that she did. However, he found himself repelled at times by her dark hair. Too closely resembling a Jewess, she served as a constant reminder of his father's death. In a darkened room, however, it didn't matter.

Sabine watched him for a moment. Deep down, she knew he did not care for her the way she cared about him, but she would resort to anything to capture his affection. "I've prepared something special for dinner tonight," she informed him. He raised his eyebrows slightly. "I've prepared a potato soup, but not just simple potato soup. I found someone on the street who was selling ham. You will like it."

"You found someone who was selling meat?" he asked.

"Black market," she answered.

"How did you pay for it?"

"I traded my watch."

Max shook his head then turned away, refusing to be too friendly for fear Sabine would expect more from him. Over the past months he had grown accustomed to his solitude. He wondered if he would ever be free to walk the streets again.

"I have to get out of here," he muttered.

"You will."

"And what makes you so sure?" He became slightly agitated.

"I just feel certain of it," she answered.

He finally turned to her, reached over, and grabbed her by the shirt with one hand and pulled her toward him. "How can you stand there, with your smug little attitude, and tell me that? I see you come and go every day. Nothing stops you from leaving this... this... hell, which has become our prison! This apartment isn't even suitable for animals!"

Caught off balance, Sabine fell to her knees. Max had never been overly friendly toward her, but this was the first time he had actually ever displayed any physical force toward her.

She looked into his eyes and stammered, "I...I might be able to help you."

He tightened his grip, pulling her face close to his. "How?" he asked. His breath surged up her nostrils.

"I can't say now, but… well… I have a plan."

"What kind of plan?"

Sabine did not answer. Instead, she leaned away from him and suggested, "Just trust me and let me do a few things first."

"You do that," Max snorted.

Sabine struggled to get back on her feet and then brushed herself off. "Give me a week," she said. "In the meantime let's eat. The food is getting cold."

Max stood up and followed Sabine into the dining area.

—※———※———※—

A week later, just past midnight, Sabine returned to the apartment after having been gone nearly the entire day. She clutched a small brown backpack in her right hand. She approached the bed, reached down, and tugged on Max's shoulder, trying to awaken him from a deep sleep. When he finally opened his eyes and saw her, he sat up and blinked several times. He appeared somewhat dazed.

"What are you doing?" he whispered harshly.

"Come. It's time," she whispered back without offering an explanation. This time she exuded confidence, something that was somewhat startling to Max. Overcome with curiosity, he did not object. He stepped out of bed, slipped into his trousers, and put on the same light brown shirt he had worn the previous day. "Don't you have anything darker than that?" Sabine asked.

Max stopped and stared at her, blinked a few times, then asked with a hint of skepticism, "Do you have a real plan?"

"Of course I do!" she snapped.

"What is it then? Tell me!"

"Not now. Just come with me… and hurry up! There's no time to waste." Max stopped insisting and did as she instructed. He walked to his closet, pulled out a black shirt and put it on.

"You'll also need a warm jacket," she told him. "It's cold out and we have a long walk."

"What? You don't have a Mercedes waiting outside?" he smirked while reaching for a jacket in the closet.

"Much better," she said, ignoring his comment.

They headed east. Barely five blocks away from the apartment, they spotted two soldiers standing in the corner of a crossroad. The men were smoking cigarettes and speaking to one another, not paying particular attention to their surroundings. Sabine and Max quickly ducked behind the remains of an old building that had once been a drugstore. Max felt his pulse beating at a furious rate, the adrenaline coursing through his body. He closed his eyes and took several deep breaths, trying to calm his nerves. Max and Sabine stood completely still, waiting for a break. The air was chilly, causing their breaths to form a fine mist each time they exhaled.

After what felt like half an hour, but was really only ten minutes, the two soldiers finally left the area, allowing Sabine and Max to continue their journey. A few short blocks away from their final destination they came across three more soldiers. Once again Max and Sabine ducked behind a building.

The air grew still. They could hear nothing except for the three soldiers, who were caught up in conversation, laughing and joking. The soldiers began walking in their direction, prompting Max to take a step backward to avoid from being seen. In doing so he stepped on a wooden board, which cracked beneath his feet. The soldiers' expressions became serious and they stopped laughing.

"Chto takoye? Kto tam idyot?" The soldiers drew their weapons and cautiously walked toward where they had heard the sound. *"Otvet'tye! Kto eto tam idyot?!"* Their voices grew sterner.

A trickle of sweat made its way down Max's neck and his breathing became labored. Had they been discovered? What were they saying? Then he felt something brush up against his leg. He glanced down to see a black cat at his feet. Just as the soldiers walked closer, Max instinctively reached down and picked up the cat, then gently tossed it out into plain view, startling them. They immediately pointed their weapons at the animal. Then, once they realized it was merely a cat, they began laughing. *"Tol'ko koshka, no ochen' opasnaya Koshka!"*

Once the soldiers walked away, Max breathed a sigh of relief. "That was too close," he muttered.

"Come. We're almost there. It's just around the corner," Sabine said, and they pressed on.

Max looked around at his surroundings. The entire area lay in ruin. "But there's nothing here," he noted.

"Trust me," urged Sabine.

They walked three more blocks until reaching what before the war had been one of the premier hotels of Europe. It was a magnificent four-story building set in eighteenth century architecture. Now, however, the walls were visibly cracked and looked in some places as if they were barely holding up the building. It appeared completely abandoned. The front door and all the windows on the first level were boarded shut. "We've arrived," Sabine informed Max. "This is it."

"This is it?" Max looked bewildered. "What? Are we moving in or something?!"

"There is a man inside who can help you. Come on! Follow me."

Sabine's mysterious actions were beginning to wear on Max's nerves, but he complied. They walked quickly around to the other side of the building until they reached the only entrance that had not been boarded shut. Sabine knocked slowly three times on a cracked wooden door. She then followed up with two knocks in rapid succession, then two more slow knocks. Within ten seconds the door swung open. An old, disheveled man with gray hair nearly reaching his shoulders and a long, unkempt gray beard that dangled four inches below his chin greeted them. His clothing was dark and shoddy, and it appeared as if he had not changed them for a month. His pants were torn in several areas. When he saw Sabine, he smiled a toothless grin.

"Did you bring the goods?" he asked her. She removed her backpack, opened it, and pulled out a bottle of schnapps. The old man turned his attention to Max, whose eyes grew wide upon seeing the bottle.

"You must be Max," he said happily as he took the bottle. "Come in. Come in. I've been expecting you." His breath reeked of neglect. He motioned them both to follow him. "Close the door behind you." The old man leaned over and retrieved a rusty lantern that had been sitting on the floor in a corner across from the door. "Come this way." He led them through various empty corridors until they reached what had once been a splendid restaurant, patronized by some of the wealthiest Europeans before the war. The room had been stripped of everything of value by looters during and immediately after the war. Remnants of pink and blue wall covering were all that was left behind.

They proceeded past the restaurant and through the grand ballroom. On par with the rest of the hotel, that room was empty too. The only item left behind was a large and once magnificent chandelier, hanging nearly ten meters in the air, now covered in dust and silt. They made their way through the hotel, twisting and turning every which direction like rats in a maze. It was not long before Max became disoriented. They finally stopped in front of a closed door. The old man reached for the door handle and opened it. Inside, there were several empty hangers suspended from a tattered wooden bar. Max refrained from asking any questions. The old man bent down and, kneeling on one knee, reached across the floor and pulled up a hidden panel. Beneath the panel was a secret stairwell that disappeared deep into the bowels of the hotel. The old man set the lamp to one side and ushered Max and

Sabine down the stairwell as he closed the closet door and replaced the floor panel behind them. He escorted them down nearly two flights of stairs. A minute later they reached the bottom.

"Where are we?" asked Max.

"This is my sanctuary," answered the old man in a giddy tone. "I am the keeper of this great hotel. This is where I stayed when our city was bombed. This is where I stayed when the looters broke into the hotel. This is where I hide and where I work. Few people know about it. I am the king of the hotel, buried in its bowels." He laughed hoarsely then stopped. "Enough. Let's continue."

Pathetic, Max thought. "How long have you lived down here?" he asked.

"Many…many… years, actually. You see, the building was built two centuries ago by an architect named von Friesen. Ten years after the construction was completed, the story goes, von Friesen went completely insane and decapitated everyone in his family right before jumping to his own death." Sabine cringed at the details of the story. The old man leaned toward Sabine. "I believe he must have been the only one who knew about this special hideaway." Sabine stepped back, unable to bear the stench of his breath. "I discovered it, quite by accident one day, when I dropped a coin and it rolled beneath the closet door. I need my coins… every one of them is important to me. Even now. I searched and searched for it and ended up finding the secret passageway instead. When I first saw this place it looked as if nobody had been down here for over a century." The old man squinted and pointed to his head proudly. "So I kept a close eye on it, and after I saw that no one came near this place, I gradually began moving all my things down here. You see, I was a poor man with no proper place to sleep, and since I was the head caretaker of the hotel, I decided it would be most fitting for me to live here. You must agree! No?" The old man chuckled with delight at his idea.

"I suppose," mumbled Max. He rolled his eyes as he turned away from the old man.

The room was small. Shelves filled with semi-modern equipment covered cracked stone walls. There was an unkempt mattress tossed to the side. Tattered blankets were strewn across it haphazardly. In the center of the room sat an antique mahogany table with four chairs around it. The overwhelming odor of sweat and wet cement lingered in the air.

"Sit down," instructed the old man. Max and Sabine complied as he reached for some items on the shelves.

"This is a beautiful table," commented Sabine. "Did you get it from the hotel?"

"Everything here is from the hotel," he answered smugly, "even all my equipment."

"What is all that?" asked Max, pointing.

"Why, it's equipment to make you new identification papers. You're going to become a new man!"

"And this is costing only one bottle of vodka?" asked Max somewhat surprised.

The old man flashed him another toothless grin then glanced over at Sabine. "Actually, that is only half the price. This bottle only covers the cost of the photography. There will be another payment due once the documents are handed over."

Once he finished assembling all the equipment, the old man reached for a bag and removed a large bulky camera and an old rusty, slightly bent tripod. After taking three photographs of Max, the old man disassembled the equipment and informed them that the documents would be ready in one week. "Have Fräulein Vogt pick them up for you. It's not safe walking around the streets without proper identification."

"We'll be back," said Max.

"No! The girl comes alone! Now leave… Both of you. I'm tired and would like to sleep." The old man led them to the back door, where they quickly slipped out and headed back to the apartment. Neither Max nor Sabine uttered a single word during their journey home.

A week later Sabine returned to the hotel alone as instructed. The old man had been expecting her. He quickly led her through the corridors and once again into the depths of the hotel. Once inside, he reached into a rusty basket located on one of the center shelves and removed a small, brown leather billfold, inside of which contained a new identification card with Max's new name on it. "Did you bring the goods?" he asked. Sabine reached into her bag and took out another bottle of schnapps. The old man took it and looked down for a moment, contemplating. He scratched his tangled gray beard then finally looked up at Sabine.

"This will not be enough," he growled.

Sabine felt the panic begin to surge within her. "I don't understand," she exclaimed. "This is what we agreed on."

He shook his head. "Perhaps you misunderstood me." He took a step toward her. Sabine's heart began pounding at a more rapid rate. "Do you really think that all my services would be worth a mere two bottles of vodka? My work is worth much more than that, especially when you are trying to buy your life back." He flashed a toothless grin, which made her shudder.

"I don't have anything more. I don't think you understand how difficult it is to get this. Please!" Sabine began pleading, knowing how much Max's life depended on her.

"Do you have cigarettes?" asked the old man. Sabine shook her head slowly from side to side. "Food?" Again, she shook her head. "Surely you must have something." He stepped toward her, backing her into a corner. He reached out and caressed her cheek. His old hands were rough and calloused, his long nails stained and filled with grime. "Do you have anything?" he asked softly.

Sabine, frightened by what was happening, closed her eyes and shook her head. She bit her lip, fighting back tears as the old man began stroking her long black hair. "I am certain," he began, carefully choosing his words. "I am certain we can think of some form of payment. Something that would not be too difficult for you to get, something that… say… you have in your possession this very instant."

"Please, Sir. You are old." She could now hear the rhythm of her pulse pounding in her ears.

He laughed. It was a vulgar laugh. "Oh… my. You have insulted me. Besides, old men deserve a little satisfaction too. Don't you agree?" He reached over and placed the schnapps on the shelf next to her. Then he reached out and clutched her head firmly between his two hardened hands. Leaning over, he began kissing her lips, drooling with each breath he took. His stench was overpowering. She shoved him away, causing him to lose his grip on her. His bewildered eyes were fixated on hers.

"I can't!" she gasped.

"Very well," he stated candidly. "Then you find someone else to help you."

"But I know no one who can."

He shrugged his shoulders. "Then I suppose your friend will eventually be caught. Too bad for him. Do you know what they do with people like Max?" Sabine did not answer. "They put a bullet through their worthless skulls!" He thrust his face one inch from hers. She felt his rank breath each time he exhaled. He then stepped back and turned away from her. "Just go away."

"Wait!" she exclaimed. "I..." He turned to look at her. "I'll do whatever it takes."

"I knew you would come to your senses." He smiled as he reached for her arm. He shoved her to the mattress and pushed her down. Sitting next to her, he placed one hand firmly behind her neck and began kissing her on the lips. She closed her eyes. It was all she could do to keep from seeing his image, but there was nothing she could do to alleviate the stench. He slowly made his way down her neck. His beard was coarse and sticky. She kept her eyes closed as he began tugging at her blouse. Struggling to unfasten it, he ripped off several of the buttons. She did not move, making the task of removing her clothing even more difficult for him. Realizing this he stood up and ordered her to undress. She did as he said, slowly and reluctantly stripping down to her brassiere and panties.

"Everything," he ordered harshly.

She looked up at him. "I can't." She began to weep. He then reached out and took a firm hold of her brassiere. Yanking it, he broke the clasps in back.

"I don't have all day." He became agitated. Finally Sabine complied and slowly removed the remaining articles of clothing.

Seeing her plump ripe breasts he found himself quickly aroused. She was so perfect, so pure and innocent, every man's dream, his reality. He reached for her breasts and began squeezing them, one in each rough hand, violating her. He was hurting her, emotionally and physically, scraping her tender flesh. Leaning over he kissed her on the mouth once again. She fought back the nausea, fearful she would get sick and vomit at any moment. This could not possibly be happening to her. But it was.

He then pushed her back onto the bed and lay on top of her. Pinning her beneath him he reached down and struggled out of his trousers. He sat up for a moment to push them over his feet. Sabine gasped. She found him to be repulsive. The old man kept his shirt on as he lay back on top of the young girl. She squeezed her eyes shut as he forced her legs apart with his bony knees. Sweat poured from his body, as he ground his bony hips against hers. He finally pierced through her, thrust three times and, before she knew it, was finished. Out of breath, he lay on top of her.

Finally, after a few short moments, he sat up and informed her, "That is all. Take your papers and leave."

Sabine quickly dressed and ran out. She managed to remain somewhat calm on the way home, but once she reached her building she began shaking violently. Outside her front door she fumbled through her backpack to find her keys when Max opened his door and saw her standing there. She stopped and stared at him, fighting back her emotions.

"I...ah...I have your new identification," she informed him. She desperately wanted to run and hide somewhere, but instead handed him the billfold.

"I'm free. I'm a free man!" he beamed, his enthusiasm mounting as he looked at his new paperwork. He read his new name aloud. "Max Schmidt. My name is now Max Schmidt." Then he looked at Sabine and saw that her blouse was ripped. "What happened to you?" His voice was filled with indifference.

"I don't want to talk right now."

"Sabine..." He stepped out of the way and Sabine entered the apartment. Max jumped behind her and closed the door as they disappeared into the room. "What happened, Sabine? Tell me."

Unable to control herself any longer, she finally broke out into gasping sobs. "He said the schnapps wasn't enough payment for the papers. He said he wanted more."

"I don't understand."

She peered into his blue eyes, her face red, swollen, and wet from tears. When Max saw her expression he realized what had happened. He instantly felt ill, not because she had been violated, but rather because she cared so much about him that she would go to such terrible lengths to help him.

⸺⼁⸺⼁⸺⼁⸺

The days rolled on, turning into weeks and eventually months. Postwar conditions were grim. There was no work, no money, and mass starvation, as there was very little food. Eventually Sabine resorted to selling sexual favors to soldiers for food and cigarettes. Several times a week she traveled to the Brandenburg Gate, where she partook in the flourishing black market. Seeing her actions as his own gain, and having gotten used to Sabine's daily activities, Max did nothing to try to stop her.

Despite Sabine's efforts, however, they were both still hungry, forcing Max to try to find other measures to acquire food. While masses of people were fleeing the Eastern sector, Max Schmidt continued to stay, feeling more of a sense of security with his new identity. He never grew too fond of Sabine but he learned to appreciate her and all that she had to offer. Finally, he figured it was about time he contributed something to their meager lives. They had to survive.

Max decided to pay a visit to Soviet headquarters. The building, which had miraculously survived the air raids, was surrounded by a ten-foot fence, whose top was covered in barbed wire. The building had previously been used during the war by the Nazis to manufacture weapons. The Red Army immediately seized control and took it over upon entering Berlin.

As Max approached the building, two armed Soviet guards stepped out in front of him. *"Stoi!"* one of the guards exclaimed as he jammed his machine gun against Max's chest.

"I've come to speak to someone in charge," Max said. However, none of the Russians knew German. "I need to speak to someone in charge," he repeated. One of the guards then grabbed him by the collar and threw him face first against the fence. Twisting his arm behind him, the soldier held Max tightly, while the second guard checked him over carefully for weapons. "What are you doing? Are you insane?" Max's voice became desperate.

"Zatknis!" the first guard said firmly.

"I am here to help you, you ignorant swine," growled Max as they pressed his face into the fence.

Suddenly he heard a voice behind him. "How can you possibly help us?" asked the stranger in perfect German. "You are barely a man."

Satisfied that Max was not carrying any weapons, the two guards loosened their grip and allowed him to turn around. He came face to face with General Ivanov, a powerful man, both physically and influentially. Max felt himself immediately intimidated by the imposing stranger.

"I asked you a question," snapped the general. "I don't have time to waste."

"My name is Max von Eu, I mean Max Schmidt," he immediately corrected himself.

"I know who you are, young von Euken," said the general. "Now tell me why you are here." Stunned, Max could only stare. "We are not stupid, boy. We have files. If you were your father, Karl, we would have captured and shot you long ago, but fortunately for you, you are not."

"Are you going to arrest me?" asked Max.

"Don't flatter yourself. You are not worth our efforts," the general said in a deep and penetrating voice. "Let's go inside the building where we can have some privacy."

As they entered the building, Max gawked at the interior, which was beautifully decorated in earthy tones, with a floor covered in a red oak wood. They walked up a long spiral stairway, its banister coated with pure white marble, to the second story, where they entered the general's office. He motioned Max to take a seat while he sat down behind his desk.

"Would you care for something to drink, Max?" asked the general.

"No, thank you," he replied, trying to act confident.

"Are you certain? We have vodka," tempted the general. Max accepted. The general stood up and walked to the back of his office where he removed a brand new bottle of vodka from behind a bookshelf. He poured some into two shot glasses, handed one to Max then returned to his seat. "Now, let us talk." He softened his voice, making Max even more uneasy. "What can you do for us?"

"I would like to offer some assistance, which you will probably find invaluable," Max said, carefully choosing his words.

"What kind of assistance?"

"I know a lot of people, shall we say...ah, traitors... potential traitors."

"Go on."

"I personally know some of the war criminals you seek."

"And what do you plan to get for all of this?"

"I'm hungry and I'm tired of living my life in a trash pit."

The general sat quietly for a long moment, studying the

young man who sat across from him. Could he be trusted? What were his true motivations? "Continue," the general finally said.

"To start, I know where you can find four Nazi criminals, hiding, this very moment, as we speak." Max's heart began pounding through his ears. The general sat back in his chair and folded his arms. He maintained a grim expression. "Trust me, General. I can make your efforts so much simpler. I can blend in."

"And what is to stop me from having *you* arrested?"

"Other than my not being worth your time in arresting me?" quipped Max. The general did not respond and Max cleared his throat, growing serious again. "Common sense, General. I know a lot of people. If you were to have me arrested then you would be missing out. If we cooperate, I could make you a very popular man in the Soviet Union."

The general thought for a moment, weighing each side of the situation. He scratched his chin then said, "Very well. Now tell me where I can find these four men."

Triumphant, Max sat back in his chair and began to speak.

That same night, Max and Sabine awoke to a thunderous crash downstairs as Soviet troops smashed through the door of his father's four unsuspecting former colleagues. They heard shouting and peered out their window to see their four comrades being hauled away in trucks. Max felt a pang of guilt as he watched the truck drive away, but that guilt went away as he thought about how the general would repay him.

CHAPTER NINE

1946-1947

Johann and Ingrid had been married for less than one year when Europe was hit by a particularly harsh winter. In Berlin the snow fell heavily. Scores of people died as a result of the freezing temperatures and starvation. All around, the smell of death lingered as bodies lay decaying beneath the rubble of the ruined city. There were even rumors of wolves appearing in Berlin, attracted by the scent.

Despite having patched up as much of the building as he could, Johann's apartment was bitterly cold. Due to an increase in the crime rate, Johann grew exceptionally protective of Ingrid, doing everything he could to ensure she never had to venture out alone. Often he stood in long food lines in the freezing cold weather for hours on end. Having spent vast amounts of time outside, Johann eventually succumbed to frostbite, losing two of his toes. By day Johann sacrificed his own body so that Ingrid might be able to stay indoors and survive. By night he would wrap himself tenderly around her so that she could stay warm. Having no more food reserves remaining, Johann and Ingrid were forced to go days, and even weeks, without a proper meal.

Constantly covered in a hazy gloom of never-ending clouds, it had been weeks since Berlin had seen clear skies, but eventually the snow began to melt as warmth settled in. The trees began budding and once again birds reappeared and the smell of lilacs filled the air. The winter beating was over.

One afternoon, while Johann was away in search of food and work, Ingrid decided to take a walk. She could not resist the sun's rays as they stroked her skin through the window. She quickly changed into her dark blue dress, walking shoes, and an old, dark gray overcoat. She then covered her hair with a black scarf and left the building. Once outside, she took a deep breath and threw back her head to greet the afternoon sun. There was a breeze and the air was cool and brisk.

The streets were filled with people. Everywhere there was the sound of relief and happy chatter. Ingrid walked and walked until she came across a dumping site used by the Soviets. Inside, among the piles of rubbish, she saw a group of people picking through the garbage in hopes of finding anything edible or something that might be used as fuel. A woman came across half a potato and several old leaves of a cabbage, which had turned brittle with time. Ingrid saw the woman hand the items to an old man. A short distance from them another man found a cigarette butt and, smiling triumphantly, placed it in his pocket.

Saddened by the misery surrounding her, Ingrid pressed on, hoping to shake the images from her mind. Later, she came across a long line of people waiting for their daily rations. Ingrid thought of Johann, as he was probably standing in one of these lines.

Realizing that the club was located only a few blocks away, Ingrid's focus changed and she decided to go see what remained of the building. Upon reaching it, she saw that none of the rubble from buildings on the street had been cleared. She quietly approached the spot where the club once stood and bowed her head in silence for a moment to honor her two friends who had perished during the air raid. Just then she spotted some writing neatly etched onto the side of a partial wall where the entrance once stood. She took a step forward and bent down. The note began: "Mama und Papa…" Ingrid gasped as she read it. It was dated only two months earlier. Hans was alive! The note read that he would wait by the cross section of Stralauer and Warschauer Streets, close to the river, on the first day of every month for the next two years or until he could find his parents. Ingrid raced back home as quickly as she could, eager to share the news with Johann.

Two days later, on the first of April, Ingrid and Johann made their way to Stralauer and Warschauer Streets, where they hoped to find Hans. However, when they arrived there was no one on either side of the street except for two women, caught up in conversation. They decided to cross the street and walk along the Spree River, keeping a close eye out for Hans. Having seen his picture only once, Ingrid tried to conjure up a memory of what he looked like.

Hours passed and they still saw no one. Ingrid and Johann continued to wait. "Maybe we missed him already," suggested Johann. With each passing hour, they began to lose faith. It was rapidly approaching six o'clock and they could not stay much longer. Finally, at six thirty, they turned and silently walked away, both feeling a deep sense of defeat.

"Well, there is always next month," said Johann, hoping to console his wife. Ingrid did not comment.

They walked silently through the street, each lost in his and her own thoughts. The only sound that seemed to stand out was the sound of their footsteps and the tapping of Johann's wooden cane. Then, just as they picked up their pace, a young man dashed past. Ingrid stopped cold and glanced back as he disappeared around the corner. "Johann," Ingrid began in a shrill voice, "do you suppose that could be Hans?" They turned around and headed back to the meeting point to find the young man, out of breath, appearing despondent. He stood there momentarily then glanced down at his watch. Shaking his head in frustration, he began to walk away. Ingrid and Johann stopped walking as the young man headed in their direction.

As he passed by, Ingrid called out, "Hans?" He stopped suddenly. "Are you Hans Kaisendorf?" she asked.

He whipped around and faced her. "Do I know you?" he asked cautiously.

"No, but I know of you," replied Ingrid. "My name is Ingrid. I was a friend of your parents."

"Ingrid… Ah yes… Ingrid." He repeated the name several times. "I've heard all about you." The young man shifted uncomfortably and continued, "Do you know where my parents are? Has something happened to them?"

Ingrid looked down and woefully said, "I'm so sorry, Hans, but your parents… They were both killed during the war."

"That can't…" Hans began shifting his weight uncomfortably from side to side. He pressed his lips tightly together, biting down on them, trying hard to fight back the tears. "No, that can't be," he said. His voice cracked. He ran his hand nervously over the side of his head, grabbed ahold of his hair and tugged. "Why? How?"

Ingrid's eyes filled with tears as she stood helplessly watching his agony. "I'm so sorry, Hans." She reached out and touched his shoulder.

"What happened to them?" asked Hans.

"The club collapsed on them during an air raid. We were all inside when it happened. It happened so fast. They didn't suffer."

"You were there too?" he asked.

"I was, but when the building collapsed, I fell down the stairs into the basement. I really don't remember much."

Johann stepped forward and suggested, "We ought to be heading back. Nightfall is almost here. Hans, why don't you come home with us and have dinner?"

Hans forced a smile and thanked them. "But I couldn't possibly impose."

"I insist," urged Ingrid. "Your mother and father took me in when I needed a home. I want to do it for them… to repay them somehow."

Together they headed toward the apartment. The sun descended quickly over the horizon and nightfall came. By the time they returned home, it was dark.

That evening, sitting around the dinner table, Ingrid and Johann discussed the past events with their guest. "My parents were very fond of you, Ingrid," said Hans. "They wrote about you in many letters. You really enriched their lives."

"I loved your parents very much. They helped me in more ways than you could possibly imagine. They were very special people and I miss them terribly."

"What have you been doing since the war ended?" asked Hans.

"Well… we were married last year," replied Ingrid as she leaned into Johann and squeezed his hand.

"Congratulations," he said softly before lowering his head.

"I'm sorry," Ingrid said. "This must be so difficult for you." She paused for a few seconds and then asked, "Where have you been staying, Hans?"

"Anywhere I can find. The last place was a shelter not too far from here."

"Are you alone?" she asked.

"Yes," he answered.

"Then you must come stay with us," insisted Ingrid.

"Oh, I don't know."

"It would be an honor, not an imposition," said Ingrid. "Stay at least until things begin to settle down and you find something better. Certainly this is better than any shelter or the streets."

"I can't argue with that. This is very kind of you. Thank you."

"So, Hans, tell us what happened to you," said Ingrid. "We received a telegram, shortly after your letter, saying that you were missing in action."

"The Soviet forces came in through Poland, and by the time they caught up to my unit we were too weak to fight back. They killed many of my comrades. I got shot in the leg. They kept me prisoner for more than a year after the war ended, but finally let me go, and I returned to Berlin." Hans shook his head with disgust. "It was all so senseless... all so senseless. Why did it have to happen? If it weren't for this war, my parents would still be alive today."

The very next day, Hans packed his few personal belongings and moved into the tiny apartment with Ingrid and Johann.

CHAPTER TEN

SEPTEMBER 1947

In time, the residents of Berlin began to settle, though living conditions had not improved much. Food was still scarce and production and employment remained at a standstill. Ingrid and Johann decided to stay in Berlin, where they both labored to fix up the apartment as best as possible, collecting what they could from the streets. They knew that living standards could only improve. Johann continued his daily ritual of searching for odd jobs and food. Finally, one day he managed to find steady work in a factory that manufactured railway parts. Shortly after that he persuaded his supervisor to employ Hans.

Meanwhile, Ingrid decided to pursue an opportunity to give dance lessons to young children. Her dream became a reality some time later, when she managed to open up a tiny studio nearly four kilometers from the apartment. Each day, trying to avoid the massive confusion plaguing the train systems, Ingrid made her way on foot to the studio.

Not long after Ingrid had opened the studio, a haggard, young woman walked in and took a seat near the entrance while Ingrid was giving a lesson. Ingrid acknowledged her with a nod, but continued teaching the class. The young woman sat quietly, soaking in the atmosphere, until the end of the lesson, when Ingrid finally approached her. "You are an amazing teacher. Is this your studio?" asked the woman.

"Thank you," replied Ingrid with a smile. "Yes. I'm Ingrid Brandt."

The stranger's face was dirty and she looked as if she had not had a proper bath in weeks. She had long black hair that hung loosely, knotted in several areas. Her eyes were weak and drawn and her nose was narrow, with a slight protruding curve. She wore a loose-fitting black overcoat, which appeared sloppy and two sizes too large. Her brown leather shoes were obviously too large for her feet. In a word, she appeared awkward.

"May I help you with something?" inquired Ingrid politely.

"Yes, I would like to join your studio," responded the stranger with hope in her voice. Her innocence in the way she said this was staggering.

Ingrid softened her voice. "What is your name?"

"Mitzi. Mitzi Freiwald."

Ingrid thought for a moment then asked, "Mitzi, how old are you?"

"I'm twenty-one," she answered.

Ingrid scratched her neck and said, "I…Well, I'm sorry. These classes are designed for younger students. Do you have any kind of background in dance?"

"I've danced before, Frau Brandt," said Mitzi, urgency building in her voice.

"Have you? When?"

"I started when I was eight years old." Seeing Ingrid's reluctance she continued, "Please, give me just one chance. All I ask for is a place to continue my dancing. I miss it so." Her voice cracked and faded away.

Ingrid finally gave in. "Very well. After my last class

you can give me a demonstration of what you can do." By now the students for the next class had already arrived and they were sitting patiently on the floor along the wall.

"Oh… thank you! Thank you!" exclaimed Mitzi.

"Don't thank me yet," cautioned Ingrid. "Call it an audition."

Mitzi spent the next two hours watching intently as Ingrid worked with her students. She was impressed with the rapport Ingrid had with them. Ingrid was stern and critical, yet compassionate with an uncanny way of making the students laugh. Mitzi liked Ingrid immediately. Once the last class had ended and Ingrid had said goodbye to all her students, she turned to Mitzi and nodded. "You have my full attention," she said.

"May I first warm up, please?"

Ingrid smiled and replied, "Of course. I have some paper work to do. I'll be at my desk. Just let me know when you are ready."

Ingrid turned and began walking away when Mitzi asked, "Frau Brandt, if I may, could I please bother you for some music?"

Ingrid stopped and turned to face the young woman again. "Is there anything in particular that you like?" she asked.

"Whatever you have available will be fine, thank you."

Ingrid walked to the phonograph sitting near the entrance of the studio, pulled out a disk, and then read its contents. "Do you like Tschaikovsky?" she asked.

"What dancer doesn't like Tschaikovsky?"

"How about a number from Dornröschen?"

"Oh yes," replied Mitzi enthusiastically. "That would be absolutely perfect! Would you happen to have the Adagio. Pas d'action?" she asked.

"I do," answered Ingrid, smiling.

Ingrid sat down and began to work but stopped momentarily to watch as Mitzi sat on the floor and pulled off her old brown leather shoes. Her socks were dark and torn. She hesitated a moment, and then removed her socks. Her feet were blackened with dirt. There was something intriguing about the way she moved. Her appearance was clumsy and foul, but her movements were graceful. Ingrid continued to watch as the woman stretched out thoroughly. When she was finally ready, she turned to Ingrid. "I'm ready," she announced.

"Very well." Ingrid stood up from her desk, but then looked at the woman's bare feet. "Do you have any dance slippers?" she asked. Mitzi shook her head, feeling somewhat embarrassed. Ingrid smiled reassuringly. "What size do you wear?"

"Thirty eight."

Ingrid reached down into her desk and removed a pair of dance slippers, which she always kept as a personal backup. "Here, try these. They should fit you just fine."

Mitzi approached Ingrid and took the slippers from her hand. She then stopped and said sadly, "But, Frau Brandt, I could not possibly wear these. My feet are so dirty."

Ingrid smiled reassuringly. "It's fine. Put them on."

Mitzi sat back down on the floor and proceeded to pull on the shoes, meticulously lacing each one around her tiny ankles. When she stood up she looked rather awkward. There was a deep contrast between her dark and soiled dress, the dirt on her body, and the pink ballet slippers.

Ingrid walked over to the phonograph, carefully removed the record from its sleeve, and then placed it on the turntable. "Are you ready?" she asked.

Mitzi took a deep breath and closed her eyes momentarily, nodded at Ingrid, and smiled nervously. "Yes," she answered.

When the music began to play, Mitzi's body suddenly transformed. Ingrid held her breath as she watched. Before her was the most pathetic, yet most beautiful young woman she had ever seen. Mitzi moved in perfect rhythm and grace. She was a true dancer in the purest sense. Once the number was complete, Ingrid stood there dumbfounded, silently staring at her. She cupped a hand over her mouth in shock as her eyes filled with tears. This had been perhaps the best display of dance that Ingrid had ever witnessed.

Seeing her tears, Mitzi rushed up to her. "Frau Brandt, did I do something wrong?" she asked innocently.

Ingrid closed her eyes, trying hard to fight back her tears. How could so much talent be lost in such misery and squalor? She shook her head slowly from side to side and replied, "Mitzi it is nothing you have done. I'm sorry. I'm tired. I should be getting home now."

"Frau Brandt? May I join your studio then?"

"Of course. I would be honored to have you join us."

Before she left the studio Mitzi handed Ingrid the slippers she had borrowed. Ingrid took them, but then, glancing down at the young woman's dirty feet suggested, "Why don't you keep them. I already have a pair."

The following day, when Ingrid arrived at the studio, she found Mitzi waiting quietly by the front door. "You're two hours early," Ingrid cheerfully informed her as she approached.

"I know, Frau Brandt," replied Mitzi, "but I'm eager to get started."

As she opened the door Ingrid asked, "Mitzi, how would you like to be my assistant dance coach?"

"Oh yes! YES! You would let me?! That would be so wonderful! I'll work hard every day. I promise! You won't be disappointed!" Mitzi jumped at the offer.

"Then we have a deal!" Ingrid patted Mitzi on the

shoulders as they entered the studio.

During her first day, Mitzi spent time getting acquainted with the young students in each class. Ingrid supervised the lessons, but it was Mitzi who walked around constantly, carefully correcting each student's position. When she saw a student struggling, she pulled her aside and worked with her until the student felt comfortable with the steps. She was devoted and attentive to each child. With her careful guidance, their postures and legs became straighter and their arms more graceful.

When they broke for lunch, Mitzi took advantage of the opportunity to work on some of her ballet steps. She walked over to the phonograph. "May I?" she asked Ingrid, pointing to the collection of records.

"Please. Please. My studio is your studio."

"Thank you," said Mitzi as she reached for a record and placed it on the phonograph. The sound of static filled the room, followed by piano music. Ingrid watched in silence as the young woman made a series of pirouettes and practiced her leaps and turns. Within twenty minutes, however, the blood drained suddenly from Mitzi's face and she fell against the wall.

Ingrid immediately rushed to her side. "Are you all right?" she asked.

"I'm sorry. I don't feel quite well enough to go on."

Concerned, Ingrid asked, "What happened?"

Mitzi looked away a moment then replied, "I'm so hungry."

"Come! Sit down with me. You need to eat. You can have some of my lunch." Ingrid guided her to her desk, where she had laid out a slice of bread and a jar of preserved apples. "Why don't you come to my house and join us for dinner tonight?" she suggested.

"Oh, Frau Brandt, I could not possibly..."

"Yes, you could possibly," interrupted Ingrid. "Do you have somebody at home waiting for you?"

Mitzi stared down at the ground. "No."

"Then I must insist!" said Ingrid firmly. "You can meet my husband, Johann, and our friend, Hans. I know they would both enjoy meeting you too."

"But, Frau Brandt, I cannot possibly put that extra burden on you. Food is scarce."

"Don't be silly."

Later that day the two women left the studio. "Oh, one last thing," said Ingrid just before reaching the apartment. "Please stop calling me Frau Brandt. My name is Ingrid. Next, let's also drop all formalities and start using *'du'* with each other."

"Thank you Fra… I mean Ingrid."

Ingrid prepared boiled cabbage, potatoes, and bread for dinner. Just as the meal was nearly ready, Hans came rushing through the door, carrying something wrapped in butcher's paper. "Ingrid! Johann! Look what I have!" he exclaimed gleefully. Then he saw Mitzi, who was busy setting the table. "Who are you?" he asked abruptly.

Mitzi said nothing and barely looked at him, feeling self-conscious by her unkempt appearance.

"Hans. This is Mitzi," replied Ingrid as she walked out from the kitchen and into the room. "Mitzi is my new assistant at the studio."

"Oh… Well…How do you do?" asked Hans politely.

"So what did you bring home," asked Johann, who had just sat down at the dinner table.

"Just a moment, Johann," said Hans. "Ingrid, may I speak with you for a minute?"

"Certainly," she replied.

"In private," he insisted. They both disappeared into the kitchen where Hans asked Ingrid somewhat sternly,

"What is she doing here?"

"I invited her to have dinner with us."

"Why?" he asked, sounding like a spoiled child.

"Hans! What is the matter with you?" snapped Ingrid somewhat irritated by his sudden change of attitude.

Hans revealed to Ingrid what he had brought home. Inside the paper were three small pork chops. "There is not enough here for four people. There is barely enough for three. Look at how small they are!"

"Then she can have mine," said Ingrid without any hesitation.

"You're insane."

"Oh come now. Stop your nonsense. Sometimes sacrifices have to be made. We have plenty of food for everyone tonight."

Hans shook his head disapprovingly. "Sometimes I don't understand you, Ingrid. You are too kind for your own good. You could starve to death because of it."

"Perhaps, but," She poked her index finger into his chest and said austerely, "where would *you* be without *our* charity?"

Hans softened his tone and answered, "You're right, Ingrid. I'm sorry." He leaned over and kissed her cheek. "I don't suppose we can wash her first?"

"Hans!" snapped Ingrid angrily.

"Sorry." Hans immediately backed down.

That evening, during dinner, Mitzi talked about her past. She came from an affluent family in Berlin. She had been dancing for as long as she could remember, starting her formal training when she turned eight. Once the war broke out it became increasingly difficult to continue her classes on a routine basis. She had just auditioned and won the role of Swanilda in *Coppelia* when the war intensified and the production was canceled.

Mitzi only had one brother. He had been killed while fighting the Soviets as they crossed the Polish border into Germany. Her parents had also been killed during the war when several bombs hit their home. Mitzi happened to be at a friend's house when it happened. When she returned home she found it completely demolished, with everything she ever owned buried beneath the deadly mass. She managed to find shelter in one of the subways, which had been converted into a shelter. Unfortunately the station was destroyed during an air raid. Again she managed to survive. She tried an underground shelter, but was turned away due to a lack of space available. She then shared an overcrowded, partially demolished warehouse with others, being afforded no privacy. Soon, the war had ended and the Soviets had seized control over part of Berlin, including the warehouse.

Over the past two years Mitzi had often slept among the ruins of partially destroyed buildings, constantly moving from one location to another. On two occasions she even spent the night with two different soldiers, a British one, then a Russian. After the second encounter she was gripped by shame and nearly jumped to her death into the Spree River. She was afraid and desperately confused. However, something held her back. Two days later she was walking past Ingrid's studio, half-starved, when she caught a glimpse of the class of young dancers taking their lesson inside. That was when she decided to enter.

Ingrid, Johann, and Hans all sat quietly captivated. When she stopped talking, Ingrid asked, "But how did you manage to dance as well as you did yesterday? You were starved, you poor girl."

"When you love something as desperately as I love to dance, it's easy to forget." She spoke softly, bringing her hands to her heart in an emotional gesture. "The music is my energy. I truly believe that I could be gravely ill, but if anything were to postpone my death, it would be the dance and music. Do you understand?"

Ingrid nodded her head silently and smiled. She *did* understand. Even Hans softened his attitude toward Mitzi after that. When they finished eating dinner, Ingrid cleared the table and washed the dishes while Mitzi dried and put them away. "You might as well stay the night. I don't want you going back out into the dark," Ingrid insisted as she cleared away the last of the dishes.

Once everything was washed and put away, the four of them sat around the tiny living room while Johann read a portion of the Thomas Mann novel, *Buddenbrooks*, aloud. The story depicted the social decline through three generations of an upper-class family similar to Mann's. Completely engrossed in the book, Johann read non-stop for one hour. When he finally looked up from his book, he saw Ingrid, Hans, and Mitzi all fast asleep on the sofa. He shook his head and thought, *it must be the dinner. Thomas Mann is one of my favorite authors. It can't possibly be the book.* He smiled to himself.

He leaned over and nudged Ingrid's shoulder. "Come to bed," he whispered. Ingrid yawned, stretched, and then followed him into their bedroom. Before crawling into bed, she brought two blankets into the living room. Hans awoke to find her preparing an area to sleep on the floor alongside the sofa.

"I'll sleep there," he told her in a near whisper. He stood up and carefully turned Mitzi's body so that she was lying fully on the sofa. "Give me one of those." Ingrid handed him a blanket, which he placed over Mitzi, who never even stirred.

"Hans," whispered Ingrid. She kissed him on the cheek. "Thank you."

The following morning they awoke to the sound of raindrops tapping gently against the window. Mitzi sat up and looked around at her new surroundings. It took her a moment to realize where she was. She could not recall the last time she had slept so well. For the first time in over three years she felt a sense of security. When Ingrid walked into the living room and saw Mitzi sitting up she went and sat beside her.

"Johann and I talked for a long time last night," Ingrid began, "and we both agreed that you should come and live here with us. I know the apartment is small and it's far from perfect, but we can easily make room for one more person."

Mitzi's eyes began to fill with tears. "Oh, Ingrid!" She reached over and hugged her. "I don't know what to say. How can I ever thank you?"

"You already have." Ingrid patted her on the back. "Come, let's get you cleaned up." Ingrid led her to the bathroom, where she had already prepared a bath for her. She pointed out the soap, shampoo and brush, and gave her a towel. She left, then returned a few minutes later with a change of clothing. "These are mine. You are a little smaller than I am, but I think they may still fit you well enough."

After Ingrid departed, Mitzi stepped into the tub. It was small, but the clean, warm water felt marvelous. She scrubbed herself completely from head to toe, then stepped out onto a white towel on the floor. The water, which was now a murky gray color, swirled down the drain. She donned the clothing Ingrid had given her and spent ten minutes completely combing out her matted black hair.

When she emerged from the bathroom, both Johann and Hans stopped and gawked at her. Hans whistled, nodded his approval, and exclaimed, "Much better!" His expression caused her cheeks to redden.

They all sat down to a breakfast of Johann's ersatz coffee and grilled bread. Shortly after breakfast the two men left for work while the two women headed for the studio, where they planned out the lessons for the day. Once Ingrid was satisfied with the outline, she turned to Mitzi and announced, "I have a surprise for you, Mitzi." She walked over to the phonograph and began thumbing through her collection of records. When she found what she was looking for, she said, "Close your eyes," as she placed a record on the turntable. Mitzi kept her eyes closed as the record crackled throughout the studio. When the music began, it sent an immediate shock up her spine.

"It's the Waltz from *Coppelia!*" she gasped. Her body immediately began to sway to the music. She closed her eyes and a smile lit up her face. She moved her head in rhythmic gestures. Ingrid took hold of her hands. "Let's dance it!" she urged as she led Mitzi to the center of the studio. She then pushed off and exclaimed over the music, "Follow my lead!" She began calling out various movements in French. "*Temps de cuisse dessus. Sissonne ouvert, chassé passé croisé. Brisé dessus.*" With each movement Mitzi followed in near perfect rhythm, becoming more and more a part of the music. They concluded the number with a series of *pirouettes* followed by a magnificent *entrechat*. Finally, both women landed by the barre. Ingrid laughed as Mitzi tried to catch her breath.

"I must be getting old," quipped Mitzi.

"Then I am in serious trouble."

"Perhaps we can teach that number to the older students," suggested Mitzi as she stood up from the barre.

"There's one slight problem," Ingrid sputtered, still catching her breath.

"What?"

"I'm not certain I can remember what we just did!"

They both laughed.

Mitzi found the classes to be even more invigorating that day. The older, more advanced girls caught on rather quickly to the new routine that they were presented. Ingrid enjoyed the break as Mitzi demonstrated each step.

Once they reached the end of their final class of the day, Mitzi asked if she could practice for another hour. Ingrid agreed and allowed her to use the studio before they headed back to the apartment.

Their routine remained unchanged over the next month, and even though winter was setting in, neither woman ever grew weary of their daily walk together to and from the studio. Ingrid was pleased that she had a friend with whom she could converse during the long walk home. Time seemed to pass more quickly. Their conversations usually bordered along the same two topics – their hopes and dreams for the studio and their expectations of the students.

One day they discussed the possibilities of holding a recital for students' families and friends. "The studio is not large enough," Ingrid remarked sadly. At that moment, they were passing by Treptower Park, which gave Ingrid an idea. "Mitzi," she began, as she stopped and faced the park, "do you suppose it would ever be possible to have a recital out here in this park?"

"It's a little cold, don't you think?" quipped Mitzi.

"No, Mitzi! I'm talking about when it gets warmer. I'm talking about next summer."

"It's a little odd, don't you think?"

Ingrid ignored Mitzi's comment and continued. "We could have a small stage set up right over there." Ingrid motioned with her hands to an open area in the park. "And the people could sit over there in that area." She motioned to another area, fully envisioning the entire setting. "I'm sure the parents would support it." Ingrid became increasingly excited at the idea.

Mitzi stroked her chin then looked at Ingrid. "I suppose anything is possible," she said. The women discussed the idea for the duration of their walk to the apartment.

"What about music?" asked Mitzi.

"This is a good point." Ingrid thought for a moment then suggested, "We could have a small orchestra or even a quartet or something. There are plenty of musicians who would love to have an opportunity to play. Anyhow, I'll take care of all the planning and you take care of preparing our little dancers."

The sun set, chilling the air even more. By the time they reached the apartment the last of the sun's rays had buried themselves beyond the horizon, and the city grew dark.

CHAPTER ELEVEN

MARCH 1948

Several months had passed since Ingrid and Mitzi had first discussed the possibility of holding a recital. Ingrid decided to finally take the plunge and sent a request to the Ministry of Culture. In the letter she stressed the idea that the recital was intended to boost morale during tense political times. Nearly two months later, as Mitzi was demonstrating various dance moves to the advanced class, three Russian officers walked into the studio. Ingrid froze, fearing repercussion from her request. Mitzi immediately stopped dancing and headed toward the phonograph, but was stopped by one of the officers who shook his head and smiled. She hesitated only for a moment, but then continued with the lesson. The men watched intently for the last fifteen minutes of class.

Once the class had ended, Ingrid stepped up and clapped her hands three times, dismissing the students. The two women stood side by side as the officers approached them. Their expressions remained unchanged as they spoke. "You wish to put together recital for parents?" asked the first officer in broken German. Ingrid nodded nervously. His expression softened and he smiled when he noticed her anxiety. "Please, we only come to speak." Ingrid remained silent. "This is very good, how you work with these students. Some are good." He stopped a moment, carefully searching for the right words. "But, you cannot dance in park." He paused. Then, seeing her disappointment, he continued. "Theater better. You should use old theater in Lichtenberg. It seats more than 1000 people. Would be good?"

Ingrid was speechless. "How...? May we?" Ingrid gasped.

"We make happen for you," he said.

"Tha... thank you! Thank you very much!" Ingrid said, catching her breath.

"In Russia, ballet is beloved. Maybe we come to your show?" he suggested. "This would be nice."

"Certainly. Absolutely. Of course!"

The officer turned to Mitzi and asked, "What is your name?"

"Mitzi," she answered. "Mitzi Freiwald."

"Where did you learn to dance?"

"I was a Brzezka pupil."

He raised his eyebrows. "Tatiana Brzezka?" he asked.

She nodded. "You know of her?" she asked surprised.

"Indeed. Now I understand," he said. "Good day to you both." The officers headed out.

Ingrid's eyes danced with excitement. Once the men had departed, both she and Mitzi shouted out with delight. Ingrid then stopped suddenly, stared at Mitzi, and asked, "You were a Brzezka pupil?" When Mitzi smiled and nodded Ingrid asked, "But why didn't you tell me that?"

She shrugged her shoulders and answered modestly, "You never asked."

Tatiana Brzezka was the daughter of Elena Brzezka, who founded the Brzezka Dance Academy in Germany. Up until the war, Elena, a former student of Russia's Imperial Ballet

School, worked for the Imperial Russian Ballet. She ended up fleeing to Germany during the Russian Revolution and eventually opened up her own studio in Berlin, where she taught classical Russian style ballet. Her daughter, Tatiana, adopted her methods and rose to become a prima ballerina and then eventually one of the foremost dance instructors in Germany. After she was killed during the war, the school closed.

With the production now becoming a reality, Ingrid began informing the parents as they dropped by the studio. Excitement filled the air as the news of her plans spread quickly throughout each class. However, there still remained the problem of music. A small phonograph hardly seemed to be a good answer. To Ingrid's amazement word reached the streets and various musicians began to appear at the studio. They were eager to find an opportunity to play their instruments. Nearly a dozen arrived, one after another, over the next month. There were several violinists, a cellist, two trumpeters, two flutists, a tuba player, an oboist, and even a pianist.

Not only did musicians show up, but so did dancers – women, men, girls, and boys. Ingrid was gaining celebrity status in and around Berlin. People reached out to offer anything they could. Many felt deprived of their rich culture through the devastation of the war. Mothers lined up to enroll their children in Ingrid's classes, with hopes of offering them a brighter future. Before long, what had originally been planned as a small, private recital now turned into a major production. It was beyond anything Ingrid had ever imagined possible.

Winter was ending in Berlin and the snow had completely melted away, leaving nothing but a chill in the air. Once again, tiny buds began to appear on the trees. Soon spring would arrive.

Now, with eleven talented musicians and a variety of dancers ranging in age, Ingrid had everything she needed for the production. She and Mitzi spent many hours finalizing the program, deciding on the music, and tweaking the choreography to the point of exhaustion. They held auditions for key soloists. Ingrid had already planned to have Mitzi dance a primary solo. The auditions drew dozens more dancers to the studio.

Ingrid was particularly impressed with a young dancer named Peter. "I have an idea," she told Mitzi one day after everyone had already left the studio. "How about doing the pas de deux from the third act of *Coppelia* with him?"

Mitzi gasped at the thought. "I was supposed to perform *Coppelia* but was never..."

"I know," interrupted Ingrid. "You already told me." They both smiled. "In fact, I'm hoping that this recital will attract enough attention so we can maybe next put on the full production." She paused a moment then continued, "How would you like to portray Swanilda or Coppelia? This can be our next project."

"Oh, Ingrid! I would be so honored." Mitzi took a deep breath and closed her eyes to fight back the tears.

By March, Ingrid and Mitzi were spending up to 13 hours a day at the studio, arriving each morning by seven o'clock and not returning home until after eight o'clock in the evening. The hours were grueling, and Ingrid found herself becoming gradually worn down, until one day she fainted during one of her classes. A hush fell over the class as Mitzi rushed to her side. When Ingrid regained consciousness moments later, Mitzi halted the lesson and closed the studio for the day to bring her to see a doctor.

Several hours later both women returned to the apartment, driven by a staff member from the hospital. Ingrid insisted all the way home that they should not close the studio.

"The doctor said you need rest," insisted Mitzi with obvious cheer in her voice. She led Ingrid to the sofa so that she could lie down until Johann arrived.

"Mitzi, I'm fine. Stop this mothering." Ingrid sat down on the sofa. "You act as if I have some terrible disease. This is silly."

Mitzi ignored her and explained, "I'm going to run a few errands before Johann and Hans return." She then coaxed Ingrid onto her back and leaned over and kissed her on the forehead. "I'm very happy for you," she said just before leaving the apartment.

An hour later, Johann arrived to discover Ingrid fast asleep on the sofa. He immediately grew concerned to find her home so early. Softly, he crept to her side, where he startled her with a gentle peck on her nose. Ingrid opened her weary eyes to see him standing there staring down at her. She stretched her arms, yawned, and rubbed her eyes.

"*Meine liebe* Ingrid," he cooed. "Why are you home so early?" He crouched back down as he spoke.

Ingrid reached out and wrapped her arms around his neck, drawing him in closely. She buried her face into his neck then whispered in his ear. "I have good news. I saw the doctor this afternoon."

Johann pulled away and looked at her face, his concerned eyes searching for an explanation. "You're smiling," he remarked. "Ingrid. So what did the doctor tell you?"

"We're going to have a baby!" Johann was motionless for a moment. Once the words sunk in, his smile widened. He reached down and kissed his wife passionately, holding her tenderly in his arms.

"When?" he asked with glee.

"In November," she responded.

The following morning, as they ate breakfast, Mitzi

suggested that Ingrid stay home and rest. "I can take care of the classes today," she said eagerly. "You need to be strong for your baby."

Ingrid began to protest. "I agree with Mitzi," Johann chimed in as he reached out and took a hold of Ingrid's hand.

Finding herself outnumbered, Ingrid relented, adding, "Fine, but I won't stay home *every* day! There is too much to be done."

"Fair enough," agreed Johann.

The lessons ran smoothly. After she returned home, Mitzi gave Ingrid a complete rundown, even demonstrating some of the new steps they had worked on. Ingrid was pleased. Thereafter, Ingrid went to the studio only every other day.

One day, having a free afternoon, Hans decided to meet up with Mitzi at the studio. It was getting late and he knew he had to hurry. The studio light was still illuminated when he walked up to the window and saw Mitzi, alone with Peter, rehearsing their pas de deux. Hans quietly opened the door, crept inside unnoticed, and sat down to watch the two dancers rehearse. Together they danced in a moving adagio to the deep melody of strings. Peter picked Mitzi up with amazing ease and carried her high on his shoulders before setting her down carefully. She kneeled before him then rose on point and pirouetted gracefully into his arms, where once again she was lifted, caught, and held across Peter's knee. He turned her in arabesque.

Hans' heart unexpectedly began racing. Soon the routine came to an end and all he could do was to stand up and fixate on the woman across the room.

Peter noticed him first and asked pleasantly, "Is there something we can help you with?"

Then Mitzi turned and saw him. "Hello, Hans," she

said cheerfully. "What are you doing here?"

"I was passing through and… well, I thought we could walk home together."

"I'd better go," said Peter. "I'll see you tomorrow afternoon, Mitzi." He leaned over and kissed her on the cheek, causing Hans to cringe.

Once Peter had gone, Hans turned to Mitzi and said lightheartedly, "I'm jealous." She looked up at him and smiled.

It was a chilly evening. They walked in silence for several blocks. Hans was the first one to finally break the silence. "I knew you could dance, but I didn't realize how well." Mitzi blushed modestly, but did not answer. "I mean," he continued, "I knew you could dance but I never thought ... well, I..." He struggled to find the right words. "It was like watching an angel," he finally blurted out. She looked up at him as they walked. He kept his eyes on the ground, slightly abashed, but hesitant to hold back his feelings. Feeling the heat rise to her cheeks, Mitzi turned away, struggling to suppress a smile.

They continued the rest of the journey in silence, each lost in thought. From that day on Hans made it a point to race to the studio after work as often as possible so that he could watch her rehearse, and then accompany her home. Their friendship blossomed.

When May finally arrived, the dancers were jittery with excitement, anxious to show off their hard work and talent. The recital was now only one month away. Hans devoted every free hour he had to spreading news about the upcoming performance. He asked a friend to create and print 200 flyers, which he and Mitzi posted wherever they could.

"Why did you make so many copies?" she asked.

"I'm hopelessly optimistic," he replied.

As time passed, Mitzi found herself thinking more and more about Hans and their newfound friendship. She loved the way he walked, the way he talked, and especially the way he smiled. She yearned for more than just friendship, and she sensed that he felt the same way about her. Yet he never made a move to confirm her belief. She grabbed a pillow from the sofa and held it closely when suddenly the door swung open. Startled, she jumped out of her self-induced trance and threw the pillow onto the floor. It was Hans. Mitzi's face reddened.

"Hello. Where are the others?" he asked.

"They are both still out," she answered. "Ingrid is probably still at the studio."

"You didn't teach today?" he asked.

"I did. But I left early to run a few errands. Besides, there is no class tomorrow, but we'll still be spending the day there. Ingrid and I need to do some work in the morning, and then I want to rehearse during the afternoon."

Hans watched her thoughtfully then asked, "May I come and watch?"

"Of course!" Her face lit up at the thought.

The following morning, as Ingrid and Mitzi set out for the studio, Hans called out, "I'll see you this afternoon." Once outside, Ingrid remarked, "You've been spending a great deal of time with Hans lately."

Mitzi did not respond at first. Finally she asked, "Ingrid, how long did you know Johann before he finally kissed you?"

Astonished by her friend's abruptness, Ingrid gasped, "Mitzi!"

"It's a simple question," said Mitzi.

"Yes, but I never realized you were that fond of Hans before."

"I wasn't. Well ... hm ... actually I was… am. You see, I don't think he ever really liked me in the beginning… and so I kept my distance."

"What makes you say that?"

"Little comments he would make. I got the feeling he resented my being there at the apartment at first. Let's face it, would you be happy if some stranger appeared out of nowhere and suddenly you had to share what little you had with him?" Ingrid merely shrugged. "Now, however, Hans' feelings have changed toward me."

"In what way?" Ingrid asked.

"One day he showed up at the studio and offered to walk me home. He watched me dance and told me that he enjoyed it, and since then his entire attitude has been vastly different toward me."

"You like him, don't you?" said Ingrid smugly. Mitzi smiled and blushed. "He certainly is handsome," Ingrid teased. Mitzi smiled then blushed again. Ingrid chuckled. Mitzi seemed remarkably innocent at times.

At the studio the two women immediately went to work preparing for the recital, carefully rehashing the final details. Just before noon Hans showed up, carrying a small paper bag from which he withdrew four sandwiches. All three sat around Ingrid's desk and devoured their lunch. During lunch Hans announced that he had quit his position at the factory.

"But why, Hans?" asked Ingrid stunned. "Why would you quit a good job?"

"I've found something else, something better," he answered.

"Doing what?" asked Mitzi.

He turned to her and answered, "I'll tell you when the

time is right. For now, let's celebrate a new life together." He reached into his bag and removed a small brown and yellow box of fine Swiss chocolates. Both women gasped when they saw this. He opened the box and removed the first piece.

"Hans!" Ingrid gasped. Chocolate was a rare treat. "You have answered the dreams of a pregnant woman!"

"Then perhaps you should be the first one to taste one of these," he suggested.

"I certainly won't be the one to refuse such an offer! After all, never keep a pregnant woman waiting too long for her chocolates!" she quipped.

They all laughed.

"Open your mouth, Ingrid, and close your eyes," he instructed, "and you shall have a nice surprise."

Ingrid did as she was told and Hans placed the morsel in her mouth. She gasped with obvious delight, savoring the sweet, creamy chocolate as it melted slowly in her mouth.

"*Mein Gott,*" she sighed. "It's almost more pleasure than I can handle!" She clasped both hands over her heart in melodramatic gesture. "We must be careful. I don't want to lose the baby... Do you have any more?"

"Mitzi's next," said Hans.

Mitzi watched patiently, amused by Ingrid's reactions. Hans turned to her. "Mitzi, Open your mouth and close your eyes," he whispered seductively.

Hans placed the morsel of chocolate on her tongue. She closed her mouth around it, savoring the deep sweet flavor as it coated her tongue and trickled down her throat.

Ingrid stood up and announced, "Enough fun for one day. I think I shall return home and spend some time with Johann. Thank you so much, Hans, for your kindness and generosity." She reached over and kissed him on the cheek.

Before Ingrid left, Hans called to her. "Wait," he said.

He removed one more morsel of chocolate and walked up to her. "This is for the baby Brandt." Ingrid cheerfully accepted his generous offer before leaving the studio.

Mitzi headed over to the phonograph, where she rummaged through the stack of records beside it until she found the right one. She placed the disk on the turntable and began to play the music. It was the deep melodic tune of Beethoven's Moonlight Sonata. She often enjoyed doing her preliminary warm-up to this music. For the next two hours, Hans sat back completely absorbed by her dance practice.

Later, Mitzi rearranged all the records and covered up the phonograph. She then turned to Hans. "Are you ready to go home?"

He smiled and slowly stood up, feeling completely relaxed. He picked up the box of chocolates, removed one more and offered it to her.

"You deserve one more for giving me such a wonderful private performance," he said.

She kept her eyes open as he brought the chocolate to her mouth, then stopped short of her lips, holding the morsel directly beneath her nose. The sweet aroma filled her nostrils making her mouth water. She opened her mouth in an attempt to grab the chocolate, but Hans pulled it back playfully. They both laughed as he brought the candy back beneath her nose and pulled it away once again, teasing and tantalizing her with it until she lunged forward and caught it between her teeth, almost biting his fingers.

"Oh… That was close," he mused. He then watched in silence as the morsel disappeared. "How was it?" he asked.

"Mmmm. Wonderful."

"Close your eyes once more," he instructed.

"Oh, Hans, I shouldn't have another."

"Just close your eyes."

No sooner did Mitzi close her eyes than she felt his lips pressing hard against hers. Afraid he would stop if she opened her eyes, she kept them tightly closed. She drew her arms around his neck, bringing him as closely as possible. They stopped and gazed hard into each other's eyes, neither one willing to move.

"I don't ever want to lose you, Mitzi," he said before kissing her again. Together they ambled home, savoring each other's company.

That night, once everyone had gone to bed, Mitzi called to Hans. "Would you like to join me?" she whispered. Hans did not hesitate and quietly slipped under the covers beside her.

The political atmosphere in Berlin had grown thicker. Ingrid and Mitzi feared that any turn of events might force them to cancel their production. Then, just when they thought the political situation could not get any worse, rumors of the occupying forces trying to create a separate West German state were all over the streets of Berlin.

Hans had left early one morning to escort Mitzi to the studio before heading off to work himself. With only two classes running that day at the studio, Johann insisted that Ingrid stay home. Mitzi was quick to take his side. Ingrid did not balk much, happy to spend extra time with Johann.

Later, as they sat down for some soup, Ingrid said, "I heard the people in the West are worse off than we are. Do you think this is true?"

"I don't know," responded Johann.

Before he could say anything more, Hans rushed through the door. "I cannot believe this!" he exclaimed, slamming the door behind him. Ingrid and Johann watched him as he plopped down onto the sofa and folded his arms.

After several seconds Johann finally spoke. "Are you

going to tell us what this is about, Hans?"

Hans shook his head. "They've stopped the trains and blocked off all transit routes going into the western part of the city. It's really happening. They're not letting anyone pass. I don't see how I can possibly work now."

"How long will the roads be closed?" asked Ingrid.

Hans merely shook his head. "I was told to wait three days and then to come back to work. Hopefully they will know more by then, or maybe they will open the streets back up."

Two days later, the hum of aircraft could be heard in the distance. Hans raced out the door with Mitzi to see what was happening. Three hours later they returned with the news of what they saw: airplanes dropping goods to West Berliners.

"They can't possibly keep it up," Ingrid chimed in. "The Americans and British are sure to leave." She sighed. "Maybe it would be easier that way."

Hans shook his head slowly, but said nothing.

The air drops would continue at a steady pace for nearly a year. While it impacted Hans' work, Ingrid and Mitzi managed to keep the dance studio alive. Despite a handful of dancers who would not be able to perform due to the blockade, the show would still go on. After months of rigorous rehearsals and preparation, the big day had finally arrived. Feeling a good bit of anxiety, Ingrid had barely slept the night before. She, Mitzi, Hans, and Johann all woke up especially early.

The recital was not until seven o'clock that evening. However, both men decided to take the day off so that they could be on hand to provide assistance for any last minute preparations.

The theater could seat up to 1200 people. Ingrid knew that they would have no problem finding seats for all the families and friends of her students, especially since some of the Western participants would not be attending.

As Ingrid stood on the darkened stage peering out over the auditorium, she experienced an overwhelming feeling of *déjà vu*. It felt like only yesterday when she herself graced the stage in front of thousands of spectators. Everybody loves a grand production. Perhaps one day her productions would draw in thousands of people. Suddenly, someone placed a hand on her shoulder, startling her. She turned and saw Johann.

"You look sad, Ingrid," he noted. "Why so sad on such an exciting day?"

She smiled somberly and answered, "I was just remembering ... remembering how things were before the war..."

Johann drew his arms around her. "I'm very proud of you," he said. "You have come a long way since the war ended. You've given hope to so many young people."

She straightened up, took both his hands into hers then guided them to her belly. "I can't wait to see her," he said, smiling.

Ingrid cocked her head to the right and asked, "How do you know it's a she?"

"Anything that beautiful has to be a she." His eyes danced as he spoke. They stood there for a moment, allowing the reality of a baby coming into their lives to sink in. "We'll call her Andrea," he said. "Do you like that name ... Andrea?" he murmured against her neck.

"Andrea," she whispered back. "Andrea. It's a beautiful name, but what if she's a boy?"

Johann chuckled, and rested his chin on her shoulder. "Then we'll call him Johann. Johann the second." He chuckled again. "But she won't be a boy."

The floodlights came on abruptly, startling them both

and illuminating the entire stage.

"Hey you two!" They heard Hans' voice bellow out through a loudspeaker sitting on the edge of the stage. "Who gave you permission to stand on this stage!" They both laughed. As they walked off, Hans illuminated them with a light blue spotlight, tracing their movement until they disappeared out of sight.

The dancers and musicians began to arrive at two o'clock for one final dress rehearsal. Ingrid's nerves felt wildly out of control and her stomach was tense. This would be the first time that the dancers actually danced on the stage. All previous rehearsals were held in Ingrid's small studio. Nevertheless, each participant was determined to make the production a success. Hans, with his natural creative ability, assisted inside the lighting booth. Johann stayed close by Ingrid's side as she provided last minute directions. They sat together in the center orchestra, in the eighth row, where Ingrid could have a full view of the stage and where she could best communicate with the dancers. Once the rehearsal commenced, Ingrid was careful not to overdo it, wanting key dancers to be rested and alert. They spent the next two and a half hours finalizing their moves and becoming accustomed to their new surroundings.

Ingrid clapped her hands three times loudly together in her usual fashion and exclaimed, "You have one hour to make your personal preparations!"

Johann began heading toward the front of the theater when he saw Hans hastening toward him. His eyes were wild and excited. "Johann!" he exclaimed. "We need you right away in the ticket booth!" Once they reached the ticket booth, Johann's eyes grew wide. Despite pouring rain outside, a line of people had built up and was beginning to wind around the building. There was nearly an hour to go before the first dancers would light up the stage.

"Run and get Ingrid, and tell her we are going to need anyone who is available to serve as an usher," instructed Johann. "Then come right back."

Fifteen minutes before the curtain rose, every seat was occupied and people had begun lining the aisles. When Ingrid walked outside the rain had subsided into a mere drizzle, and there were still people standing in line. "Ladies and Gentlemen," she began nervously. "Unfortunately, there are no seats left in the theater. We did not anticipate such a big turnout." She paused a moment as a murmur of disappointment passed through the crowd. Then she said, "If you would still like to see the recital, we will try to provide some additional chairs. If we don't have enough chairs, you are welcome to stand in back of the theater." She then hurried backstage to where the dancers were gathered.

"How many people are out there?" Mitzi asked her.

Ingrid grinned and answered, "We have somehow managed to fill every seat! People are literally standing behind the back row!!"

The curtain rose a few minutes late. Mitzi waited patiently backstage. She took several deep breaths to try to rid herself of her growing anxiety. Her duet with Peter was imminent. Ingrid approached her. "How are you feeling, Mitzi?" she whispered.

"Nervous."

Ingrid put her hands on Mitzi's shoulders and said, "You'll do great. You are my best dancer."

Mitzi swallowed. "It's time," she declared as she crept quietly onto the stage and took her place behind the line of girls, being careful not to be seen by the audience. Peter began dancing first, appearing from the other side of the stage. He pranced about, looking as though he was searching for something or someone. As the music unfolded, the dancers moved to each side, exposing Mitzi in her white flowing dress. Once she began to dance, she completely left behind her fears and inhibitions and became totally immersed in the melody. The audience sat silently, savoring the number up until its final moments. At the end she received a standing ovation.

After the recital Mitzi ran back and flew into Hans' arms. "You were brilliant," he exclaimed. "I am so proud of you! The audience fell in love with you!" He kissed her passionately.

Ingrid scurried about backstage, congratulating her dancers on a fine performance, when Johann came up behind her. "There are two Russian gentlemen who insist on seeing you. They are waiting by the stage wing."

Ingrid hardly recognized the Russian officers who had visited her at the studio. They looked different, now dressed in dark suits and ties. "The performance was ... how do you say ... magnificent, Frau Brandt," said the first Russian in somewhat broken German.

Ingrid flashed them a genuine smile. "I'm so pleased you could make the performance," she said, feeling more confident than she had been during their first encounter.

"We would not miss."

The second officer glanced around then inquired, "And where is Fräulein Freiwald?"

"She is in her dressing room," answered Ingrid.

"Do you suppose we see her to offer congratulation?" he asked.

"Wait here one moment please."

Ingrid returned moments later with Mitzi, who had already changed clothes. "Mitzi," began Ingrid, "you remember these gentlemen, don't you?"

"Certainly," she answered as she extended her hand to greet them. "How good to see you."

The first officer handed her a bouquet of flowers. "That was remarkable performance," he complimented. He then turned to Ingrid and asked, "Frau Brandt, do you plan further productions?"

"Yes, as a matter of fact," she answered. "I've promised Mitzi that we would perform *Coppelia* next." She winked at Mitzi.

"If Fräulein Freiwald is to perform lead, then when you plan, contact us. We arrange you to perform in State Opera," he declared.

Ingrid's heart began beating wildly with excitement. All her dreams were finally becoming a reality.

※────※────※

Ingrid's and Mitzi's names spread across Berlin at an unprecedented rate. Before long, mothers lined up outside the studio to enroll their children. The classes quickly filled up. With help from various families and officials, Ingrid eventually opened a larger studio just up the street. The studio was twice the size, consisting of two large adjacent classrooms with a door separating them. It used to be two apparel shops that stood side by side. The windows were large, allowing ample lighting on sunny days to flow into both rooms. To the rear of one classroom there was a private office where Ingrid could take care of all administrative matters, or simply go lie down for a bit in a sofa, which sat directly in front of her desk. It was perfect.

By late September, due to her doctor's persistence, Ingrid had stopped teaching classes. The weather grew colder and her belly became so swollen that she now could make the trip to the studio only once a week. On one of those days, as Mitzi was giving a lesson, she heard Ingrid call out her name. "Mitzi! Mitzi!" Her voice became increasingly frantic.

Mitzi rushed into the office and found Ingrid sitting on the floor in a puddle of water. "I think my water broke," said Ingrid as she gazed up at her.

—⊬— — ⊬— —⊬—

Ingrid's cries could be heard from across the hall of the hospital. Johann paced the floor feverishly, hoping the pain and agony would come to an end. Nearly seven hours later the cries died down and before he knew it, a young nurse came out to inform him, "It's a girl. You have a beautiful baby girl!" Johann covered his face and wept, releasing the tension that had built up over the past hours.

They named the baby Andrea.

CHAPTER THIRTEEN

1948

In a few short months Max had already turned in fourteen war criminals. With each criminal came rewards. It became a dangerous ritual, but his identity as an informant was never realized.

Eventually, however, he became weary of his routine and focused his attention on turning in purveyors within the Black Market. He spent the first month carefully scouting all areas in the vicinity of the Brandenburg Gate, where the black market was prevalent, taking meticulous notes on all visible activity. He then would infiltrate their operations. Max possessed a knack for gaining people's trust. Once he earned their trust, he would send word to the general, but only after he took what he could. The authorities would then stage a sting operation, which usually resulted in the capture of individuals.

Max's growing thirst for increasing challenges prompted him to go after one of Berlin's most notorious and sought-after criminals – a man, simply known as Kai. Max became obsessed and completely focused on the idea of turning Kai over to the Soviets. Kai's shrewd business tactics and connections helped him to earn more than twice what most of his competitors earned and many people believed that he was untouchable.

One gray and dreary day, Max headed to the Brandenburg Gate. Once there, after walking four blocks, he turned into a long alley that ran parallel to the main street, where black market activities were prevalent Although traveling between the East and West had now become more restricted, many Western smugglers still had free access into the Soviet sector, and they came into the ill-famed Feifergutten Alley to sell their goods.

Prepared to bribe anyone who might lead him to Kai, Max carried a pack of American cigarettes and some money in his coat pocket. He walked down the alley once, taking thorough mental notes on his surroundings. The air was thick with the pungent odor of rotting trash. Two small boys scurried past Max, kicking a tin can back and forth. Several meters ahead, standing in the shadows of a doorway, Max saw a disheveled old woman staring at him as she smoked the end of a cigarette butt. He walked past her, then stopped to peer back. The old woman had disappeared into the partially destroyed building. Max suddenly had an idea. He approached the doorway where the old woman had been standing and knocked on the door. There was no answer. He waited a moment before knocking again. Finally, a young boy, who looked like he was about 12 years old, answered the door. He was exceptionally thin, his cheeks sunken in. His brown eyes were glossy and drawn, with deep, dark circles below them.

"Yes?" he said in a high pitched voice.

Max hesitated a moment. He disliked children and was reluctant to deal with them. He flinched uncomfortably then asked, "Is your mother home?"

"I don't have a mother," answered the boy. His face remained expressionless.

"How about your father?"

"I don't have a father either."

Max took a deep breath, his impatience mounting. "Grandmother?" he guessed.

"You want to speak to *Oma*?"

Max blinked twice and forced a smile. "Yes, let me speak to your *Oma*."

He watched silently as the boy scampered off and disappeared into the dark building. A moment later the old woman came to the door. Her round face was gray and wrinkled. Her nose was flat and entrenched with large porous marks. She waited for Max to speak first.

"Eh ... hello," he began. "My name is Max Schmidt and I'm looking for Kai." He waited for a reaction.

The old woman finally spoke. "What do you want with Kai?" Her hoarse voice cracked.

Max thought quickly. "I want to do business, of course."

She exclaimed, "Don't know him!" then slammed the door in his face.

Max, refusing to give up, knocked again. There was no answer. He knocked louder this time. Then he exclaimed loudly, "I can pay you!" But still there was no answer. "Damn old, senile woman!" he muttered before stepping away.

Suddenly the door opened again. Max turned to see the little boy standing in the doorway. "How much?" asked the boy in his high pitched voice.

"Hm?" Max raised his eyebrows.

"How much will you pay? *Oma* wants to know."

"How about two cigarettes? They're new, right out of the package," offered Max.

The boy darted back into the dark building. Max could hear him shouting, "*Oma*, he has new cigarettes!"

A moment later the woman reappeared. Max repeated the question. "Will two cigarettes do?"

"Do you have any money?" she countered.

He removed the cash from his back pocket and offered her two large bills. The woman looked down distastefully at the money. "That paper is useless to me."

Max, growing increasingly impatient, removed more money from his wallet.

"As I said, that is useless to me," she repeated.

"Why did you ask then? Besides, you can still trade it in!" He clenched his teeth, fighting back his anger.

"Cigarettes," she snapped. "I want twelve packs of cigarettes and four bottles of Russian vodka."

"Are you in…" Max gritted his teeth, then continued, "Very well. I'll bring them to you in several days," he lied. "Now where can I find Kai?"

The obstinate old woman shook her head. "Goods first!" She slammed the door once more. This time he walked away.

Max tromped down the alley, all the while cursing the old woman under his breath. He looked around wondering where he might turn next. Up until this point all he knew was that Kai owned one of the surrounding shops, but which one? He looked up in time to see two men, carrying boxes, disappear through one of the doorways. He immediately picked up his pace to reach the spot where he had seen them.

Now, standing before a battered wooden door, Max raised his fist to knock. However, before he had a chance, he heard the high pitched voice behind him. "You really shouldn't go in there," warned the voice. Max swung around to see the young boy, from earlier, standing before him in the middle of the street. "I can help you though."

"Did *Oma* send you?" asked Max, feeling somewhat skeptical.

"She doesn't know I'm here."

Max bent down to the youth's level. "So, where can I find Kai?" His voice was gentle.

"I don't know."

"Forget it then." Max stood up and began walking away.

The youth tore after him. "No! Wait! I can still help you," insisted the boy. Max stopped, turned around and faced him. "I don't know where you can find this man, but I do know where you can begin your search."

Max knelt down once more in front of the youth. "Where?" he asked.

Pointing to a nearby bakery, the boy said, "You should start in there."

Max stood back up and pulled a small amount of money from his pocket. "Will this be enough?" he asked.

"I'd rather have the two cigarettes." Max smiled and gave them to the boy. "Oh… there's one last thing, but it will cost you more," added the boy. Max rolled his eyes impatiently. "It's the password to get in."

"Password?"

"Yes."

"How much?" asked Max.

"The whole pack."

"The whole pa…?!" Max clenched his teeth to hold back his anger. He refused to be outsmarted by a mere child. "What's to stop me from going there? Now I know where it is."

"You need the password," insisted the boy confidently.

Max analyzed him a moment, then said, "Very well. Tell me what you know."

"The pack first."

Max clenched his teeth. "Fine." He pulled the pack of cigarettes from his pocket and handed it to the boy, who shoved it into his shirt.

"Ask for Fräulein Vogel. Then tell her, 'I am here to see

the sparrow.' She will take you into the back where all the good stuff is."

"That's it?"

"Yes," answered the youth.

Pointing to the first shop where he had seen the two men entering earlier Max asked, "What is in there?"

"The competition." The boy grinned. "They hate each other."

Max loosened up a bit and smiled. "But how is it that you know so much?"

"I'm small. I hear a lot and people don't pay any attention to me."

Max patted the youth on the head and flashed him a genuine smile. He thanked him then headed toward the main street.

"One last thing!" the boy called out as he chased after him.

Max stopped and turned around. "I thought you said that was it," he said, rolling his eyes.

The boy continued, "Yes... well. Could you bring me an apple, please?"

Max grinned then pressed on without answering his question.

Once he reached the entrance of the shop Max noticed a sign hanging in the window. It read *Out of Rations*. He ignored the sign and entered the shop. Inside, he was greeted by the overwhelming odor of freshly baked bread, but the shelves were empty. Behind the counter a woman in her mid-twenties swept the floor. She was fairly attractive, with shoulder length blonde hair. Sitting on the counter behind her, an old radio crackled the music of Chopin. Off in the far corner a tiny parakeet squawked noisily at the intruder. The woman stopped sweeping when she heard the sound of the old cow bell dangling from the door handle. She watched quietly as Max entered.

"Good afternoon," began Max pleasantly. "I wish to see Fräulein Vogel."

Leaning against her broom, the woman stared at him a moment then replied cautiously, "I am Martha Vogel."

Hoping his information was accurate he took a breath and said, "I am here to see the sparrow."

She scratched the back of her neck and raised her eyebrows. Then, pointing to the boisterous little parakeet she said, "There is no sparrow here… just a parakeet." She turned her back to him, then continued sweeping.

He stopped smiling and took a deep breath. His jaws became rigid. He felt betrayed, and worse yet, outsmarted by a mere boy who had robbed him. He was at a loss for words but decided to continue the game. He snapped, "Stop playing with me. That is no sparrow."

The woman, half smiling, pressed her chin up into the air and asked, "Who sent you?"

Max searched desperately for an answer then finally blurted out, "Kai sent me."

She immediately lightened up. "Oh… well then. You meant the wild sparrow." She stood with one hand on her hip. Max felt as if she were mocking him. He nodded his head in affirmation. She leaned her broom against the counter and instructed him to follow her.

Together they walked through a door, leading into a darkened storage room. Martha reached up, fumbled in the dark, and pulled a small chain that turned on a light, barely bright enough to illuminate the room. Max blinked several times, trying to adjust his eyes to the new darkness. Crates and boxes, filled with various goods, were neatly arranged on the floor, which was lightly covered in a dusting of flour. He could see various shuffle footprints in the dust.

"So," Martha said as they stood amidst all the

merchandise. "How do you know Kai?"

Max's mind began racing again. He had to be careful. He could not afford to lose this one. "Eh... actually," he began, "I never met Kai. I met a friend of his at a party one night. He... ah... we spoke of special merchandise such as yours and... Well, you see, I used to have a shop of my own, but was forced to give it up for reasons I'd rather not go into." Max looked down sadly as he played his role.

"Hmm... Who was the friend?"

"Ah... Zimmermann." He made up the name. "Herbert Zimmermann."

She thought for a moment, scratching the corner of her forehead. "Herbert Zimmermann. I don't believe I've heard of him. But then again, he has many friends and even more acquaintances. Is there anything in particular that you want?" she asked.

Relieved, Max exhaled slowly as his heart began pounding with excitement. He had walked into a regular gold mine! One shelf was lined with fruits and vegetables. There were apples, cabbages, and potatoes. There was even a can of pineapple.

"Pineapple!" gasped Max.

"That has already been promised to a patron."

"Everything over there has been promised." She pointed. "However, the rest is available."

Max saw some European chocolates, various bottles of Russian vodka and French wine. There was even a bottle of Irish whisky. Most predominant, however, were the stacked boxes, marked *US Army*. Many were filled with American cigarettes and real coffee.

"We have a few more goods in the refrigerator," Martha informed him. "We have butter and even some sausage."

Max was amazed as he observed the quantities of items. He had seen many black market operations, but his mind could hardly fathom the operations that could result in what he saw concealed in these premises. He reached out and picked up an apple. It felt slightly grainy. A closer look revealed a dusting of fine white powder clinging to it.

"What is all the white powder?" he asked.

"Flour," she explained. "We are a bakery, after all."

He nodded.

Once Max had made his purchase, Martha led him to a rear entrance of the store, where he discreetly exited. Back in the alley he spotted the youth and called out to him. As the young boy scampered over to him, Max reached into a bag and removed an apple.

"Here. You earned it!" He tossed it to the boy.

Seeing this, the youth's face lit up. He caught the apple and quickly scurried away, disappearing into the building.

Later, Max returned home in a particularly good mood. That evening for dinner Sabine cooked Polish sausage, potatoes, and carrots and baked apples for dessert. They topped it off with pure Swiss chocolate morsels, which Max chose to wash down with Russian vodka. The alcohol quickly went to his head and he found himself becoming aroused as he watched Sabine cleaning the kitchen. He crept up behind her and wrapped his arms around her waist, pressing his male hardness against her hip. She turned around to meet his embrace. Unwilling to wait another minute, he leaned over and picked her up, bringing her to the bedroom. He closed the door quietly behind them.

━╫━━━╫━━╫━

Max spent most of the week planning his strategy to get Kai. The case was too valuable to jeopardize with any rash decision or quick actions. It could take weeks, even months, but Max was determined to not only lead the Soviets to

Kai but also expose his entire operation, which had grown into a black market empire. He decided that his first step would be to befriend Martha and to win her trust. He was convinced that once he was able to penetrate this barrier, she would lead him to Kai.

A week later Max revisited Martha's shop. This time there was a long line of people standing outside, waiting to purchase bread. Max decided to hold off, allowing the line to dwindle down before making his move.

When the last of the customers had finally cleared out of the shop, Max entered. The cow bell banged against the door. Martha and another woman working with her, looked up from behind the counter. Recognizing Max from the previous week, Martha was much more receptive. She smiled warmly. "Good afternoon," she said. Max glanced over at the other woman. "This is Bertha. She works during our busier days."

"Good afternoon, Bertha." He hesitated a moment, not knowing whether to proceed.

"We are all out of bread and waiting for more to bake. Perhaps there is something else that you'd like?" Martha nodded at him.

"Ah," Max looked upward toward the noisy parakeet. "He is a fine bird."

Martha smiled cunningly and said, "Do you like birds? We have a wild sparrow in back. Would you care to see him?"

He approached the counter and said in a beguiling voice, "I certainly would."

Martha suddenly felt aroused as Max looked deeply into her eyes. "F-Follow me, please," she stammered. Max followed her into the rear storage room. He smiled to himself, knowing he had won Martha's trust.

Max visited Martha's shop weekly, trying to acquire as

much as he could before pressing her for information about the operations. Just as he was ready to make his move, he received word that General Ivanov demanded his presence at Headquarters the following day noon.

The next day Max showed up at Soviet Headquarters. When he announced his appointment with the general, the guard picked up the telephone and said something in Russian. Five minutes later the general appeared and escorted Max into his office. This time he did not offer any cigarettes or alcohol and his expression was stern. Max shifted uncomfortably in his seat. The general closed the door and sat down behind the desk.

"Do you know why you are here?" he finally asked.

Max shook his head slowly from side to side.

The general pulled out a cigarette and lit it. Taking a long draw and holding in the smoke, he leaned back in his chair. He was silent for a moment then said, "I'm not happy, Max." The smoke emptied from his mouth as his eyes narrowed.

Max stared at him bewildered. "What's the problem?" he spouted nervously.

The general took another long drag on his cigarette, again holding the smoke deep in his lungs for a moment before releasing it. He finally said, "It's been nearly two months. We haven't heard a word from you. What are you doing? Have you forgotten about our agreement?" He stopped and examined Max, who did not respond. "What is going on? Hmm? Are you growing soft on us?"

Max sat straight up in his seat. "Forgive me, General," he said, "but I've been working on a very important case. It is probably the largest black market operation in all of Berlin. It's just that... I need more time. There is absolutely nothing I can do about that."

"You're running out of time."

Max starred at the general, blinking several times. "What do you mean?" he finally asked.

"I have a feeling that by this summer, the black market will cease to exist. So, if you have something for me, I suggest you give it to me now." He leaned forward in his chair and continued in a calm voice. "So, what can you tell me about this case?"

"Nothing…nothing yet," answered Max. "It's a very different kind of case. It goes far deeper than arresting shop owners. This time I intend to give you distributors. Beyond this, though, I cannot say…at least not yet… not until I find out more."

The general narrowed his eyes and asked sternly, "Why should I trust you?"

"Because you have a lot to gain by trusting me, and I have everything to lose if I'm wrong," answered Max with conviction.

"I think you are about to dry up," the general snapped. "I'll tell you what. You have one week and that is it!"

"One week?! I need at least one month," Max snapped back. "General, you have no idea of the wealth of goods you will get once we close on this."

The general thought for a long moment before agreeing. "Very well, but after one month, you'd better have some impressive results. There will be no second chances."

Max released his breath. Tomorrow he would begin to close in on Kai's operations somehow.

⁂

The following day, cool but sunny, drew crowds of people out into the streets. Max made his way to Martha's shop. When he arrived at the bakery he saw that the line to purchase bread once again extended out into the street. He watched from outside while contemplating what to do next. Finally he entered the shop and walked straight to the front of the line.

Martha was alone, her forehead glistening in sweat. She glanced over at Max. "You can't just come to the front of the line like that," she said sternly. She scurried about, behind the counter, attempting to fill each order. Despite having prepared the dough the night before, she was overwhelmed. She stopped only long enough to wipe the sweat off her brow. The white apron around her waist was encrusted with old remnants of dough and dusted with flour. The air inside the shop was stagnant and hot from the ovens and the people.

"Where is Bertha?" asked Max.

"Bertha is sick today," she answered without stopping. Seeing that Max was not moving, Martha snapped, "You have to go to the end of the line."

Ignoring her order, Max made his way behind the counter.

"Wh…?!" Martha began to protest. "What are you doing?!"

"I'm going to help you," he insisted. "I can take care of the bread in the oven."

Martha did not have to think twice before reaching into a drawer and pulling out a clean apron. "Here," she said, tossing it to him. "Put this on."

Max complied then began working. To Martha's relief, the line began moving much more quickly. Nearly three hours later, as the last of the customers left the shop, Martha wiped her forehead then fell back against the counter. She let out a loud sigh of relief and slid down to rest on the floor. Max looked down at her and began to laugh.

"How can I thank you for all your help?" asked Martha as she stared up at him.

"Have dinner with me tonight," he answered without hesitating.

She closed her eyes and leaned her head back. "I'd love to but now I have to prepare the dough for tomorrow's bread and clean up my shop. It will take me about four hours "

"Let me help you then," insisted Max.

Martha smiled and nodded.

Max cleaned up the shop while Martha prepared the dough for the following day, separating it into even quantities and placing it into various steel bowls to rise. At nearly seven o'clock, they were finished with the work. Martha suggested going back to her home for dinner.

"I live with my father and he is rather dependent on me when it comes to cooking," she said laughing. Before locking up the shop, Martha vanished into the back to retrieve a black leather jacket.

"Do you have a jacket?" she asked. "It'll be chilly out." Max shook his head. She disappeared once again into the back, only to reappear a moment later carrying a blue knit smock. Max began to protest but Martha insisted.

She locked up the shop before they headed out. A short distance away they came across a faded red bicycle. Much of its paint was chipped away. Martha bent down to unlock it. She then pushed the handlebars in Max's direction. He peddled the bicycle with her sitting on a bike rack behind him.

She lived on the outskirts of the city in a brick house that had somehow miraculously been spared during the war. It was surrounded by dense shrubbery. The house stood at the end of a cul-de-sac. Despite the cold temperature, Max's forehead was wet with perspiration. They both hopped off the bicycle and entered the house.

Inside, a blue and yellow Emile Galle lamp, etched with marguerites, illuminated the rustic entryway. Martha picked up a note lying on the table beside a lamp. "It doesn't appear as if you will be meeting my father this evening," she finally said. "He has some business tonight."

"Tonight?"

"Yes, he keeps very busy with his work," she said quickly. "So, what would you like for dinner?" she asked, changing the subject.

"You mean I have a choice?" he marveled in jest.

Martha settled on preparing fish and potatoes. They drank white wine and topped off the meal with a slice of warmed apple tart that she had prepared for her father the day before. To Martha it was a typical meal. To Max, despite his position with the Soviets, it was a meal of luxury. Once they finished eating, Martha directed Max to the living room while she cleared the table.

When she had finished working in the kitchen, she joined Max in the living room, where she sat beside him on the sofa. Max appeared pensive as he watched her. "What are you thinking about?" she asked him.

Max smiled and answered, "I'm thinking of how peaceful it feels to be sitting here with you. This is a wonderful home."

"Yes," she said, taking in a deep breath and slowly exhaling. "We live like royalty compared to everyone else."

Max found her rather appealing, warm, and friendly. However, he also sensed an invisible barrier between them. Hoping to chisel his way through that barrier, he inched up closer to her. "Has anyone ever told you how beautiful you are?" he asked with a sweet sincerity in his voice.

"Ahh," she began to stammer. "Not lately."

"Well, you are," he said gently, gazing at her through provocative eyes. He reached out and stroked her cheek. Suddenly the front door opened and in walked a middle-aged man. He was tall and thin with graying hair.

Martha's father greeted them both but raised his eyebrows and asked, "Who is your friend, Martha?"

"Hello, Father," she said, jumping to her feet to greet him. She kissed him on the cheek and asked, "How was your day?"

"Very good," he answered without taking his eyes off Max. "Who is your friend?" he repeated the question.

"This is Max," she answered happily. "He is a friend of... a friend of... ah..." She looked at Max and asked, "What did you say his name was?"

Max crumpled his forehead in question. "Who?" he asked somewhat confused.

"Why, your friend who said he was a friend of Father?"

Shocked, Max grew wide eyed and his stomach felt as if it was about to leap into his throat. His search was finally over. Kai was Martha's father.

"What's the matter?" she asked. "You don't look too well."

He had wanted to find Kai but did not expect him to fall so blatantly into his lap. Unprepared, he quickly straightened up and cleared his throat. "I'm sorry." Keeping his eyes on Kai he said, "It's just that I haven't been feeling too well lately."

"Would you care for something to drink?"

"No, no. I'm fine. I really must be getting home now. I have a lot of work to do tomorrow." He headed toward the door.

Martha followed him. She opened the door for him and walked outside to see him off. "Are you certain you are all right?" she asked. "You're acting rather peculiar."

"Yes," he answered. "Thank you for a memorable evening."

"Will I see you again soon?" she asked.

"Sooner than you think," he answered. He leaned over

to give her a quick kiss on the cheek before leaving.

It was nearly midnight by the time Max returned home. Sabine sat alone in the dark living room, waiting for him to return. When the door swung open she jumped up and rushed toward it.

"Where have you been?" she snapped.

He grabbed her roughly by the arm and, placing his face directly in front of hers, exclaimed, "Do not ever, ever question me like that again!" Then he let go and stomped off into the bedroom. Sabine did not pursue him. Instead she stood there like a wounded animal, trying to make sense of his reaction. When she saw that the bedroom light was out, she went to join him in bed. She lay beside him, longing for him, but knowing he would never truly be hers, never care for her the way she cared for him.

Three days passed before Max returned to Martha's shop, armed with an explanation for his odd behavior the other night. This time he intentionally arrived later to avoid the rush of people purchasing their bread. Upon reaching the shop he watched through the window from outside. Martha slipped into the back room, accompanied by an elderly couple while Bertha busily swept the floor. Moments later, Martha returned. Max walked into the shop. He greeted the two women as he approached Martha.

"Can we talk?" he asked quickly.

"Not now, Max," she answered coldly as she began wiping down the counters with a soiled, damp cloth.

He watched her for a moment then said, "I am here to see the wild sparrow."

She looked up, but only momentarily, and then continued her work. Growing agitated, Max removed a stack of money from his pocket.

At that moment, they were all startled by an armed Soviet policeman who entered the shop. Max quickly tucked the money away into his rear pocket. The atmosphere grew tense as the man wandered about freely, carefully surveilling the area. His face was rigid. "Who is in charge here?" he asked in good German.

"I am," answered Martha quickly.

"Show me your rations list," he ordered.

She reached into a drawer, removed a stack of papers and handed it to him. He quickly thumbed through the documents then handed them back to her.

"You made two hundred loaves of bread today?" he asked. She nodded silently. "Are you receiving sufficient supplies?" he asked.

"I could always use more...," she answered.

"We'll see what we can do. That will be all for now." He departed as quickly as he had appeared.

Martha continued her work, acting as if nothing had happened.

"Do they come in here often?" asked Max.

"More often than I would like," she answered without looking up. "They promise us more supplies but never deliver." She finally looked up at him. "They give us only so much. Then they come around to ensure that we are not making any personal profit from it. Basically, they want to make sure we're not doing anything illegal." She finally let out a partial smile and rolled her eyes.

Bertha disappeared through the back door. Once they were alone Max turned to Martha. "I wanted to apologize about the other day," he said, choosing his words carefully. "I was... I was not completely honest with you." He looked downward, feigning remorse. "This man, Herbert Zimmermann... he is not really a friend of Kai. He had never even met Kai. It's just that I was afraid you wouldn't allow a mere stranger in to buy your goods. Of course, the thing is that...well... once I met you, I found myself attracted to you and for some reason... I can't explain it... when I came face to face with your father..." He paused for effect. "Well, I just got nervous. I can't explain it. Do you understand?" She shook her head slowly. Max's mind raced for a more believable explanation. Finally, reaching over the counter and taking her hands into his, he blurted out, "I'm in love with you, Martha, and I was scared. Once I realized Kai was your father, I was afraid that I would not be good enough for you. I'm not a wealthy man, but I would like to get to know you better... if you will give me a chance." He stopped for a moment, then stared into her eyes and pleaded, "Please, give me a chance. That's all I ask, just one chance." She pulled her hands away from him and averted her eyes. Max was moving too quickly. Seeing her apprehension he backed away. "I'm sorry," he whispered.

Bertha returned from the back room carrying a large bag of flour, which she dropped onto a table, sending a cloud of white dust into the air. She carefully tore the bag open, spilling some of its contents onto the floor. Max watched her clean up the mess. He became impatient.

"May I speak to you... outside?" he finally asked Martha. Without answering she followed him out the front door. "Look," he said, once the door had closed behind them. "Why must this be so difficult? I said I was sorry."

"There's one problem." Martha paused a moment. "My father is suspicious."

"Of what?" he asked, feigning ignorance.

"In case you were not aware, what we are doing here is not necessarily the most legal thing." Her answer tasted of biting sarcasm.

"All I ask is for an opportunity to get to know you better. I don't care about your father." He paused briefly, then reached over and took her right hand into both of his hands and continued tenderly, "All I can do anymore is think about you... your smile... your beautiful face... the way you look... the way you talk. You're always on my mind." His voice sang with a sweet sincerity, causing Martha to loosen up a little.

"Come back in three days. In the meantime, go home and cool off." Bringing her hand to his lips he kissed it and thanked her several times before departing.

— ✳ — ✳ — ✳ —

When Max returned to Martha's shop, there were only three weeks remaining before he had to report back to the general. He had to move quickly yet cautiously. He reached the bakery in the late afternoon, just when Martha was wrapping up her business. After waiting patiently for her to finish her work, he invited her to join him for a walk.

Over the course of two hours Martha warmed up to him. She talked about life with her father since the end of the war. She talked about the challenges of running the bakery. However, just as Max began probing about the black market, she ended the discussion.

"Why are you so interested in the details of our operations anyhow?" she finally asked.

"I want to be a part of it," he answered, hoping she would take the bait.

"Why?"

Max thought a moment. "Isn't that obvious?" he finally stated. "Why wouldn't I want to take part in such an operation?"

"Hmmm." Martha pursed her lips. "If you want more information, you'll have to speak with Father," she responded blandly.

"I don't think he likes me much," Max said. "I suppose it's not important. There are other ways to earn a living."

Martha raised her brow but said nothing.

Before they each went their separate ways Max turned to Martha and asked, "Would you care to join me for dinner tomorrow evening… at my home?" His blue eyes penetrated hers one last time.

"Tomorrow I'm expecting a very important delivery."

Max's heart jumped at the information. "What time?"

"It's generally late in the evening. So, I won't likely be going anywhere," she responded.

"Maybe I can come by and pick you up afterwards?"

"No." Her answer was abrupt.

"How about dinner the following night?" he persisted.

"Uh….Maybe. I don't know. We'll see."

That night when he returned home, Max found Sabine asleep on the sofa. He slammed the door loudly, jarring her out of a sound sleep. He disappeared into the bedroom, slamming the door behind him. Sabine felt tense and saddened. She hesitated just long enough to see the bedroom light go out beneath the door. She crept silently into the room and stumbled over Max's clothing. Quietly folding back the covers on her side of the bed, she carefully slipped in beside him. He did not utter a single word, lying with his back to her. She felt cold and wanted desperately to reach out and wrap her body around his, but did not dare. A single teardrop rolled down her cheek and onto her pillow.

The following morning Max announced that he would be late again that night. "Don't wait for me," he said. Sabine did not respond. "Actually," he continued, "I need you to find somewhere else to go tomorrow night. I need the apartment for an important meeting."

"But… what of me?" she finally asked. "What am I supposed to do? Where am I supposed to go?"

"You need to figure it out. This is really important," he

snapped before slamming the door behind him.

Later that evening Max headed to Feifergutten Alley. He arrived one hour before the scheduled delivery was to take place at Martha's shop. The wind had picked up, making it feel even colder than it actually was. With his hands tucked deeply in his pockets, he walked down the alley, which by now was nearly deserted. As he approached the shop he spotted the young boy, who had assisted him in the beginning. The boy was sitting alone in his doorway.

"Good evening," called out Max as he approached the boy.

The boy's scrawny face lit up and he jumped to his feet. "Good evening," he exclaimed.

Max joined the boy on the step and together they sat silently, side by side, for a minute. "Do you know anything about special deliveries at Martha's shop?" asked Max.

"Do you have any cigarettes?"

Max chuckled and reached into his pocket. "I only have one left," he said as he placed it into the boy's outstretched hand.

"There's a big gray truck that goes to the bakery every other week," began the boy confidently. "Tonight's the night. I think it'll be here in about another hour. The truck comes from over there..." The boy pointed upward past the shop, "...and drives down the street. Inside the truck they have these large sacks of flour for making bread, but it's not really flour... if you know what I mean." The youth grinned.

"How do you know it's not flour?" asked Max.

"I just know!" he answered, pompously pointing to himself with his thumb and winking. "I know everything that goes on around here!"

At that instant Max spotted a large black Mercedes making its way through the alley. The vehicle rolled along slowly, carefully avoiding several parked cars and a handful of garbage canisters set out in the street. Max stood up and stepped back into the doorway to avoid being seen. The boy followed his lead and stepped behind Max, who watched silently from around the corner of the doorway. The Mercedes stopped just short of Martha's shop and two men exited the vehicle. Max recognized the older man as Kai, but he did not recognize the driver.

The youth whispered, "That's Kai. He doesn't usually come here during delivery. This must be a big one."

"Who's the other man?" asked Max.

"I don't know, but I sometimes see him driving the truck."

Both men slammed the doors to the vehicle and disappeared into Martha's shop. Nearly twenty minutes later Kai reemerged and drove off alone in the car. Max ducked deeper into the shadows as the car swept past the doorway where he was hiding with the boy.

A gray delivery truck appeared down the alley nearly twenty minutes later. Max looked at his watch. The truck was early. He watched as the driver walked around the truck to the back door of the shop, where he knocked several times. Martha answered the door moments later. Max could hear their voices but was unable to make out their words. The driver and the first stranger unloaded what appeared to be large sacks of flour and brought them into the shop. Afterwards they climbed into the front of the truck and began driving away.

Max's mind began racing. "I need to find a way onto that truck," he whispered. "But how?"

"This will cost you a whole pack of cigarettes," whispered the boy as he jumped out in front of Max. Before Max knew what was happening, the youth darted out onto the street, where he began skipping about playfully, causing the truck to nearly hit him. The vehicle came to a screeching halt directly in front of where Max was hiding.

"Off the street!" exclaimed the driver angrily as he stuck his head out of the window. "Are you trying to get yourself killed?!"

The youth hesitated a moment as Max stole into the back of the truck. Once Max was onboard, the boy stepped to the side and allowed them to pass. As the truck drove off he saw Max throw him an enthusiastic wave of approval.

Large sacks of flour, stacked one upon the other, filled the back of the delivery truck. Max, carefully kneading one of the sacks with his fingers, thought he felt something hard on the inside of it. *That explains the flour all over the storage room,* he thought. One thing caught his eye. Each sack had a different color-coded tag with no writing on it. Somewhere there had to be a list with addresses matching each color. Suddenly the truck stopped and Max heard the two front doors open, then slam shut. His heart began pounding through his ears as he jumped behind a stack of sacks with orange tags on them. He felt the truck list to one side as the two men jumped into the back. One man spoke with a very thick Slavic accent. The other man was German.

"What does it say on the list?" asked the German.

"Orange," answered the Slav. Max froze completely. Despite the cold snap in the air, he could feel sweat begin trickling down his temple. He held his breath and balled his hand into a tight fist, ready to come out swinging.

"Wait a minute," said the Slav. "I read it wrong. We need green. Orange is the Heinersdorf delivery. That will be next."

Relieved, Max slowly let out his breath and remained still as each man grabbed a bag and jumped down from the truck. When the men had gone inside a building, Max looked down and spotted the delivery notebook on the floor. Just as he began reaching for it, he heard the voices of the men as they reemerged from the building. Max quickly jumped back into his hiding place.

The two men talked and laughed as they hopped back into the truck to retrieve more sacks. Once they had left again, Max peered back out. This time the notebook was gone. He gritted his teeth in frustration. A moment later they returned. They started the engine and drove off.

Remembering that the next stop was for the orange-coded tags, Max moved behind a large pile of sacks with blue- and yellow-coded tags. After nearly twenty minutes the truck pulled over and both men descended once again. Max's eyes grew wide as he saw an arm reaching out in front of him, nearly touching his face, to grab and pull down a sack.

The next time Max peered out from his hiding place he saw the list lying on the floor. There was no time to waste. He leaped out and picked up the notebook. Luck played in his favor. There were three carbon copies below the original. Hopefully they would not notice that one was missing until he was long gone. Max quickly ripped out one of the carbon copies before hearing the voices of the two men reemerge from the building. He quietly put the notebook back down and returned to his hiding place. The men grabbed several more sacks then once again disappeared into the building. *This might be my last opportunity*, he thought, and jumped out of the truck and ran around the corner of the building, carrying with him a copy of the delivery schedule.

With over two weeks left before his deadline, Max decided to pursue Martha further before going to the general. The following day he returned to the shop and invited her to his home for dinner. He had left specific instructions with Sabine to have a meal prepared for eight o'clock and to be out of the apartment by then. Hoping to quell her objections, Max explained that this was necessary for his job and promised that he would make it up to her by spending more time with her after his assignment was complete. Sabine complied and spent the afternoon preparing a dinner that he had only to warm up. Max rushed off to the shop where once again he invited Martha to join him for dinner. She accepted his offer.

"Your father won't mind?" he asked impassively.

"I mentioned it yesterday. He said he would manage. He has some urgent business to take care of."

"Urgent?"

"Well, yes, to my father it's urgent. He said something about some missing paperwork. He's very particular and likes to keep everything in order and to have everything accounted for."

"Oh… I see. So, I hope you are hungry tonight," Max said, changing the subject.

"Ravenous!"

"Good."

By the time they returned to his home, Sabine was gone and the table was set, including two long-stem white candles, which Max lit just before going into the kitchen. Martha looked around the living room and spotted a photograph of Sabine hanging on the wall. "Who is the girl in the photograph?" she asked.

Max emerged from the kitchen and replied, "Oh, her? She's my sister. She lives in Leipzig."

"She is very beautiful."

"Yes. She is."

"Do you live here alone?" she asked a moment later as she sat on the sofa.

"Generally," he answered. "Sometimes my sister will come and stay."

"She's not married?" she asked.

"No, though she would like to find a husband," he replied, returning to the kitchen.

After warming up the meal, they sat down at the dinner table. Martha complimented Max repeatedly for an outstanding meal. "You'd think you had a business better than my father's," she quipped. After dinner they both sat on the sofa trying to learn more about each other. Finally Max reached over and kissed Martha on the cheek.

"What was that for?" she asked, somewhat surprised.

"That's to say thank you for coming. It gets very lonesome here by myself," he answered gently. He stared at her, saying nothing. Tilting her head forward she leaned over and kissed him softly on the lips. He responded immediately, taking her into his arms. They kissed passionately for several minutes with mounting intensity. He stopped and peered into her eyes. "Go with me into the bedroom," he whispered, his voice deep and husky. Throwing caution to the wind, Martha did not object and Max swept her up into his arms. She held onto his neck as he carried her through the door. He placed her gently onto the bed. Yearning for him she pulled him toward her. He lost his balance and fell down next to her. They both laughed then continued kissing, consumed with a furious hunger for one another. She wrapped her legs around his waist, holding him closely. He began unbuttoning her blouse, kissing his way down toward her navel. He reached around her waist and unzipped her skirt, pulling it down over her hips. Next he pulled down her scanty lace panties until she lay completely naked. Wrapped up in his own fury, he tore away his own clothing. Unable to hold back any longer, he quickly mounted her, reaching a disappointing climax.

Afterwards, as they lay there, he whispered softly in

her ear, "I'm sorry. It's just that it's been so long..."

"Sh..." she interrupted. "Don't worry about it."

They both fell asleep, wrapped in each other's embrace, where they would remain for the rest of the night.

—————

It was pouring rain outside. The cold, damp night air penetrated Sabine's body as she sat, shivering behind a pile of rubble at the train depot. The floor was hard and cold. The old stone wall behind her reeked of urine, but it was all she could do to keep out of the wind and rain. She had nothing to keep her warm but her long black overcoat. On her head she wore a brown scarf, which at least helped a little. She looked around and saw several other people sleeping. Most had some kind of blanket, but she was not as fortunate. She moaned softly to herself, cursing Max beneath her breath for his cruelty and cursing herself even more for allowing this to happen.

—————

Three days later Max returned to the bakery. As he entered the shop, Martha looked up and smiled. It was getting late and she was down to her final group of customers. Once all the customers had left, Max stepped up to the counter. However, before he had an opportunity to say hello, the door swung open. A group of five young men in their late teens entered the shop. "We are here to see the wild sparrow," exclaimed the oldest, paying little attention to Max.

Seeing the group, Martha smiled and informed them, "You'll have to wait your turn. This gentleman is first."

Wanting to spend more time with Martha, Max stepped

back and said, "No, go ahead. I'll wait."

The young men thanked Max, shuffled past him, and followed Martha into the back room. However, one of the men suddenly stopped and stared hard at Max. "Hey, don't I know you from some place?" he asked.

"Come on, Wolfgang!" called the others. "We haven't got all day!"

Wolfgang stood still for a moment trying to recall where he had met Max. Then his eyes grew wider. "Yes, I do know you." His voice remained low and calm. He pointed at Max with his right hand. "You're that swine who turned my father in!"

"You don't know what you're talking about," replied Max, gritting his teeth and trying to remain calm.

"Hey, fellows!" called out Wolfgang. They peered out from the back room.

"This is that pig who turned in my father!" The urgency grew in his voice. "Why did you do it? Aren't you a German like the rest of us? Aren't you trying to survive too? Just tell me, you filthy traitor!"

His friends reemerged to see what was going on, Martha coming up behind them. They all approached Max and formed a circle around him, cornering him against the display cabinet.

"What is going on here?" demanded Martha. Her expression was filled with a deepening concern.

"This boy seems to have me confused with someone else, Martha. He doesn't know what he is talking about," insisted Max. A trickle of sweat dripped down his back. He was trapped.

"You lying pig!" exclaimed Wolfgang, who lunged forward and grabbed Max by the collar. "My father would be a free man today if it hadn't been for you!"

"Get this creature off of me!" exclaimed Max as he tried

to push the boy away.

Suddenly there came a knock at the back door. Martha rushed over to answer it. Kai emerged along with the German delivery truck driver. The two men were alone. Seeing the scuffle in the shop they both lunged forward to pull the boy off Max. At that point Max broke free and scrambled out the front door.

Turning quickly to Martha, Kai asked, "Wasn't that your friend?" Martha stood speechless, her eyes wide.

"He's an informant!" sputtered Wolfgang, trying to regain his composure. His face was red with anger.

"What?! Are you sure?" asked Kai, dismayed.

"He turned my father in!"

Kai glanced over at his partner. Before Wolfgang could utter another word, Kai and his partner were out the door and racing for their vehicle. The tires squealed as the driver put all his weight on the gas pedal. The vehicle skidded momentarily, knocking over a trash can, until it regained traction. They raced down Feifergutten Alley until they reached the end of the street. Glancing down the main street Kai spotted Max running off to the right. "Over there," he shouted out.

Max glanced behind him and saw the Mercedes in hot pursuit. His pulse was racing and the adrenalin flowing as he quickened his pace. He ran two blocks, then tore down a narrow deserted alley. When the car reached the entrance of the alley, it screeched to a halt and both men jumped out to continue their pursuit on foot. Halfway down it they stopped and looked around at their surroundings. Max had completely vanished.

"What do we do now?" asked the driver, gasping for air.

"We have to find him," replied Kai, who was bending over, trying to catch his breath. "He could ruin everything."

Suddenly they heard a noise coming from a nearby

dumpster. Putting his index finger up to his lips, Kai motioned with his head to the driver before quietly tiptoeing toward the dumpster. The driver pulled out a knife as they approached it.

Realizing his hiding place had been compromised, Max leaped out and ran right past Kai, who then tore after him. Max had barely run five meters when the driver lunged at him, knocking him to the ground. There was a momentary scuffle as he attempted to escape, but he was quickly subdued by the driver, who now stood behind him holding the knife to his throat. Both men were gasping for air.

"Move a millimeter and I'll cut your throat," the driver growled. Max froze.

Kai paced back and forth for a moment, contemplating what to do next. Finally he turned to Max and asked him, "Is this why you ran out of my house so quickly two weeks ago?" Max said nothing. "Answer me!" demanded Kai in a calm but authoritative voice.

"I… I am not an informant," Max finally stammered.

"You're not very convincing. Why would you run away, then, if you don't have anything to hide?" asked Kai. "When were you planning to turn us in? And, oh by the way, where was my daughter all night three nights ago? I ought to kill you for that alone." He lowered his voice to a soft growl. "By the way, you wouldn't happen to know anything about a missing delivery document, would you? Seems it just vanished." Max remained silent. "I'm very disappointed. Martha spoke so highly of you too. She actually had me convinced that I could trust you. Not only are you a menace to my business, but you're also breaking my daughter's heart. You don't deserve to live." Bringing his face close to Max's, Kai stared directly into his eyes, waiting for an explanation. None was offered. "I don't want to kill you but I will if I have to." His voice softened. "What are your plans?"

"I don't have any plans," replied Max.

"You don't. Why do I find that hard to believe? Have you sold your soul to the Soviets? Aren't you a German like us?"

"Let's just cut his throat here and get it over with!" insisted the driver.

Kai shook his head. "No. Let's not be too hasty," he responded. "I'm a businessman, not a murderer. Who is your contact?" Max did not answer. "Listen, Max, I don't want to hurt you. Help me out here."

Max looked up toward the sky, then back down at Kai. "Why should I help you?" he asked.

"Why? I'm a very wealthy man. What do the Soviets pay you? I can pay you much more than they will ever pay you," said Kai confidently as he scratched his pointy chin.

Max twitched uncomfortably. "What's the catch?" he asked, leery of Kai's offer.

"I'm not sure we should do that, Boss," interjected the driver, who still held Max in his strong grip. "He knows too much."

"Why not?" asked Kai, who now had a faint smile on his face. "Think about it. Having him on our side could keep the Soviets, as well as the German police, off our backs."

"I'm not sure I understand," said the driver.

"We pay him much more than the Soviets do and his job is to keep them off our backs."

"And how will he do that?"

"Oh come on. Why is this so difficult for you to understand?" Kai laughed then continued. "He can lead them away from us. For one thing, maybe he can lead them to some of the competition."

"Have you lost your mind?" objected the driver. His voice cracked. "What's to keep him from turning us in?"

"Money and access to a lot of goods. That's all he is after. Isn't that right, Max?"

Max nodded his head slowly, astonished at the turn of events. Kai instructed the driver to release him. "Nobody can know of our arrangement," he told Max. "Especially not my daughter. Oh, and one more thing: Martha is off limits! Now do we have an agreement?"

Max sprung to life. He reached out and enthusiastically shook Kai's hand. "I think we can work well together," he said to Kai.

"I have a name for you. Several shops down from Martha operates a powerful black marketeer. His name is Sebastian..."

The driver stood by nervously as Kai offered Max a complete description of Sebastian's operation. It would be one of the last busts General Ivanov's men would make. Three days later, as political tensions grew, the Soviets closed off all access leading into the western sector, offering Max a chance to distance himself from the general's grip and a way in with Kai. Two days later, the roar of airplanes would fill the air off in the distance, dropping goods beyond Kai's reach. However, not all was lost. Kai had other resources, including deep reserves hidden away. They would last for months, and his operations would continue, albeit at a slower pace.

CHAPTER FOURTEEN

JANUARY 1949

After several weeks' absence from the dance studio, Ingrid showed up, proudly carrying her two-month-old baby girl in her arms. Andrea was large for her age, with rounded cheeks that practically concealed her eyes when she laughed or smiled. Ingrid jumped back into her work, bringing Andrea along to the studio nearly each day.

Meanwhile, Ingrid and Mitzi began planning their next production, *Coppelia*. They worked closely together, planning all the details. After Ingrid received approval for the production, the women got to work spreading the news and holding auditions.

With word that Mitzi Freiwald would play the lead role in the performance of *Coppelia*, tickets disappeared quickly. Having originally scheduled five performances, Ingrid and Mitzi added three more. This time a complete orchestra provided the music. After each performance Mitzi enjoyed a standing ovation. Through their tireless efforts Ingrid had reached celebrity status as a teacher and Mitzi was being touted as a prima ballerina.

Three months later, Ingrid, Johann, Andrea, Mitzi,

and Hans moved into a two-story house on the outskirts of Berlin. Ingrid and her family occupied the lower level of the house, while Mitzi and Hans occupied the upper level. Just days before their move into the new house, Hans confided in Mitzi his plans to leave the Soviet-run sector. "Come with me, Mitzi," he urged. "We are a divided country and I want to be on the other side. We can build our lives together with more freedoms."

Mitzi stared at him incredulously before responding, "But Ingrid and I have too much invested in the studio. I couldn't possibly just leave her like that."

"Ingrid will be fine," he insisted. "She has a wonderful reputation. Her studio will continue to thrive with or without you, Mitzi."

She looked down. "I don't know. I don't think it's so bad here anymore. We've done well," she proclaimed stubbornly.

"Your success is because of your dedication and hard work, Mitzi!   Besides, look at our city! It's still in ruin! People still struggle and there's never enough food for most." Hans began to raise his voice.

"Stop it!!" Mitzi struggled to regain her composure. "Besides, how can you be so sure I would do as well if I were to leave Ingrid and the studio? She is the foundation of the business."

"Mitzi, you're not only good. You're great! People don't love you because of the studio. They love you because you can dance... with or without Ingrid's studio!"

"No, Hans, I like my life the way it is."

Hans stopped and glared at her, frustrated by her obstinacy. "The only reason we have been doing as well as we do is because of the black market," he finally confessed.

Mitzi stood and stared awkwardly at him. "I...I don't understand," she finally said.

Frowning, Hans pressed his lips tightly together and dropped his head, shaking it slowly. Pushing his hands deeply into his pockets he muttered, "I'm sorry, Mitzi. I didn't want to tell you..."

"Tell me what?"

"I don't want to lose you."

"Hans?" she stepped toward him. "You're scaring me."

He finally explained, "Do you remember when I quit my job at the factory? I never told you the complete story. You see, I do drive a delivery truck but there's more." He took a deep breath. "What I do could possibly jeopardize your position here in Berlin... at least as long as we're together."

"What? Wh...what are you saying?"

"I work for a man named Kai. He is an important man and very successful in the black market. He's so successful that even the Soviet blockade couldn't destroy his empire. Last year I drove the goods that we got from the Americans, British, and French across the borders. Now, of course, over the past months things have slowed, but we still manage to get some things from Russians and even for the Russians. It's extremely dangerous, Mitzi. The scale is so large that the authorities would probably kill us all, or put us in prison for a long time if they knew about it. It's dangerous, but the rewards are endless. That's how we're able to eat the way we do. That is why you are dancing instead of digging through piles of garbage and rubble with everyone else. That is how our small family has managed to stay somewhat shielded from the aftermath of the war."

Mitzi turned away, shaking her head. She sighed softly and said, "What was I thinking?" Hans stared at her inquisitively. He saw that she was now half smiling. She hit the palm of her hand to her head and said, "I should have known. Nobody has that much around here!" Her laughter grew. "And here I thought... 'Wow! He must be the most talented delivery man in all of Germany!'" By now tears filled her eyes from laughter.

"Ah... I'm sorry, but I really don't quite see why this is funny." He looked at her awkwardly.

She finally straightened up and cleared her throat. "You're right. It's not funny." She struggled to refrain from having another outburst. Her expression caused Hans to suddenly lose his own composure and begin laughing.

"So, you're not angry?" he asked cautiously.

"Why would I be?"

"Ahhhh… because it's dangerous? Because I was never completely honest?"

Then she suddenly grew serious. "Oh, Hans, I'm not angry. I'm just… just a bit concerned. I don't want to lose you either. I love you so much."

"Come away with me, Mitzi." He reached out and gently took hold of her shoulders. "It's not too late. I know how we can do it. We can move to the American side or maybe even out of Germany all together. I have a contact who can help us get set up. You will be happy… and successful! I promise you."

She stopped smiling. "I'm sorry, I just … can't," she responded solemnly. "Everything… everything I have ever worked for is right here. They take care of us here. I know you don't agree, but that's how I feel. And besides, I can't abandon Ingrid. Not now. Not after everything she has done for me."

"The Soviets are not our friends. You're nothing but a financial asset to them."

"Don't be ridiculous."

"You'll never be able to enjoy the true benefits of all your hard work and talent. If we move away, you'll have so much more! *We* will have so much more. What's wrong with a little independence? Come with me, Mitzi, to the

West. Here, you will always be held back."

Mitzi did not respond at first, nor did she move. She simply stared down at the floor and shook her head, unwilling to meet Hans' eyes with her own. Finally, she looked up and said softly, "Hans, I can't go, but I hope you will reconsider and stay with me here. Despite the risks, I'm in love with you. I'm willing to live with the risks that your work brings. But as I said already, I can't... I won't leave." Hans stared at her for a long moment before turning and walking out the door.

That night, as they lay in bed, Hans tossed and turned, unable to shake the thoughts of their earlier conversation from his mind. He had to choose, and he had to do it soon. The following morning, when they both awoke, Hans came forward with his decision. "I've decided to stay," he announced. Mitzi flew into his arms and kissed him wildly.

"Oh thank you, thank you, *thank you*! I prayed to God last night that you would come to your senses!"

"Come to *my* sens...?! Oh never mind." They kissed for a long time.

⸺⸺⸺⸺⸺

Life's routines went on as usual. Johann continued working at the factory, Ingrid and Mitzi spent countless hours working at the studio, and Hans became more deeply involved in the black market. Everything seemed perfect, almost too perfect. It was the summer of 1950 and German citizens all around were still suffering from the fallout of the war. Balancing on a fine wire, with the economic and political strife remaining unresolved between the East and West, something had to give.

CHAPTER FIFTEEN

SUMMER 1950

ax was with Martha, helping her to prepare her storage shed to receive their next delivery, when someone knocked three times at the back door. "That must be our delivery!" exclaimed Martha. They never wasted any time on delivery days. Everything had to be carefully timed, and the quicker the delivery could be executed, the less dangerous it was for everyone involved. When Martha opened the back door, the delivery driver had already climbed into the back of his truck.

"Hello," Martha called out to him cheerfully as she approached the truck. "Are you alone today?"

"Yes I am," he responded.

"How many bags of flour do you have for me?"

"Seven," he answered without looking back at her.

"Good. That's more than usual." She turned and called out to Max. "Max, would you mind assisting us with this delivery? We are short one man."

"Certainly."

The deliveryman was just climbing down from the truck, carrying a large, brown, twill bag over his right shoulder. Max approached and extended his hand. "Hello,

I'm Max Schmidt."

Balancing the bag on his shoulder, the man extended his right hand. "Pleased to meet you. Hans Kaisendorf here." They laughed and joked while they unloaded the truck.

"So, Max, are you coming to the party tomorrow?" asked Hans as they each carried the last two bags through the back room.

"Party?" Max glanced over at Martha, who was busy rearranging goods on the shelves inside the storage room.

"Oh. Sorry, Max," she began. "I forgot to tell you. My father is throwing a party at the house tomorrow. You are invited. You can also bring a guest."

Max arrived at eight o'clock. When Martha opened the door to greet him, his eyes grew wide. She wore a revealing blue silk evening gown. "He... hello, Martha," he stammered, barely able to speak.

"Good evening, Max," Martha greeted him. She then turned to the young woman with him. "And who is your guest?"

"Oh..." he hesitated. "Her? This... is Fräulein Sabine Vogt."

"How lovely to finally get to meet you. I saw your photo. You are even more beautiful in person."

"W...why, thank you," responded Sabine, somewhat taken aback.

"Max tells me you are from Leipzig," remarked Martha. "Are you just visiting or are you here to stay?"

"I... eh..." Sabine glanced over at Max, who shifted uncomfortably from one side to the other. "I think I might as well just stay." Then she reached for Max's hand and held it in both her hands.

"Well, how lovely to see that you are so close to your brother."

"My brother?" Sabine half smiled. "Oh, yes. My brother"

She immediately released his hand.

At that moment Max put his arm around Sabine. "Yes," he interjected. "I don't know what I'd do without my little sister. We don't have anyone left but each other." He squeezed her arm so tightly that she winced slightly. "Isn't that true, Sabine?"

"Yes, it is, kind brother. Sometimes I wish we were even closer. But there has been so much distance between us," Sabine responded.

Martha smiled, and then stepped to the side. "Won't you both come in?" she said. Sabine handed her an apple tart that she had made earlier in the day, and they entered the home.

"I baked this for you. I hope you like it," Sabine said to Martha. "It's an old specialty from Leipzig."

Martha thanked her, took the tart, and carried it into the kitchen.

"You never told me she was so beautiful," said Sabine to Max, who continued gawking at Martha as she disappeared into the kitchen. Max said nothing, taking in the party atmosphere. Nearly 100 people, mostly members from Kai's underground organization, were there. The air was thick with the smoke from cigarettes that Kai had set out. A variety of food, such as shrimp, pork, sausages, apples, pineapples, and chocolates, had been smuggled in for the event. There was also an assortment of beer, wine, and schnapps to choose from. Laughter and endless chatter filled the house as the guests mingled, becoming acquainted with one another.

Max finally snapped out of his spell when Kai approached them both from behind. "Who is this lovely young lady, Max?" asked Kai as he put his arms around them both.

Before Max could answer, Sabine extended her hand

and said, "Pleased to meet you. I'm Fräulein Sabine Vogt, the sister from Leipzig."

Kai raised his eyebrows in wonder. "I never knew you had a sister, and a lovely one at that." Kai took Sabine's hand and brought it to his lips. "Very nice to meet you."

Sabine, who had quickly thrown herself into the role of Max's sister from Leipzig, was enjoying the attention from Kai, despite their age difference. Max then turned to Kai and said, "Tell me something, Kai. Does Martha have a boyfriend?" Sabine cringed at his question.

"Why would you ask, my friend?" Kai asked with a hint of cynicism.

Max leaned toward Kai and told him, "I find Martha to be absolutely beautiful."

"Kai tightened his hold around Max's shoulders. "Max, my friend. Touch my daughter and you'll regret the day we ever met. I thought we already had this discussion before." He continued to smile. "Come and let me introduce you both to some of the other guests."

Max and Sabine followed Kai into the living room. As Kai began introducing them to various other guests, someone caught Max's eye. He leaned over to Kai and whispered, "Who is that woman standing over there? She looks familiar."

Kai turned to see to whom Max was referring. "Why, that is Fräulein Mitzi Freiwald," he answered. "She is here with Herr Hans Kaisendorf, one of my delivery men. Come. I'll introduce you. Excuse me, Fräulein Freiwald," Kai said as they approached. "Someone wishes to meet you." Max stepped forward. "This is Herr Max Schmidt. Max, I'd like to introduce you to Fräulein Mitzi Freiwald." They both shook hands. "And this is… ah… I'm sorry. I did not catch your name."

"Fräulein Sabine Vogt," said Max.

"From Leipzig," added Sabine snidely.

At that moment Martha approached the group and interrupted, "How would you two ladies like to escape with me for a bit? I could use some help in the kitchen."

Both Mitzi and Sabine followed her willingly, leaving behind Kai, Hans, and a very disappointed Max.

"Actually," began Martha, once they entered the kitchen. "Outside of my bakery, I almost never get to speak to other ladies and I thought this would be a good opportunity to get away and talk about something a little more interesting than the business. With my father's work, it seems that we are always surrounded by his men, and the only topic of interest to them is the business."

Sabine was silent at first, suddenly intimidated by her surroundings and feeling somewhat inadequate. Eventually, however, Mitzi and Martha managed to draw her out.

"Do you work?" Mitzi asked Sabine.

"No," she answered, somewhat embarrassed. "And you, you're a dancer, aren't you?" Mitzi nodded confidently. "I've never seen you perform, but I've heard about you in the news."

"You'll have to come to a performance," suggested Mitzi.

"Oh, that would be simply splendid!" Sabine's eyes lit up at the idea. Max rarely took her out, preferring to venture out on his own.

Mitzi then said, "Why don't you come by the studio some time and meet some of my friends."

"This is a lovely tart, Fräulein Vogt. Would you mind cutting it for our guests?" interrupted Martha. "We can put it out with the other food."

"It would be my pleasure," replied Sabine.

In the next room, Kai had stepped away as Hans and Max engaged in deep conversation.

"So, how long have you been working with Kai?"

inquired Hans.

"For just over one year now." Max took a long drag on his cigarette.

"How is it that we've only met the one time?"

Max thought for a moment then replied, "I don't get too involved with the actual business. Right now you could say… well, I'm more of a messenger."

Hans frowned at first, then softened his expression and shrugged slightly to indicate he understood, even though he did not. "You're lucky. Kai's is a difficult organization to join," he said.

"How did you join the operation?"

"Actually, it was through a mutual friend," Hans explained. "At the time Kai was just starting out and he needed drivers. When my friend told me about all the benefits, it was hard to turn down. I quit my job at the railway factory, and the rest is history. How about you? How did you get on with Kai?"

Max smiled and replied, "I had something Kai wanted."

"What's that?"

"A grand scheme. It was a way to put ourselves above the competition."

"How?"

"Ah ah!" Max shrugged smugly and quipped. "That's classified information." He smiled shrewdly, waving his cigarette in Hans' direction.

Moments later the three women emerged from the kitchen, carrying platters of *hors d'oeuvres*. "It looks as if they've become fast friends," noted Kai waving his hand toward the three women as he came up behind Max and Hans.

Max spent most of the evening speaking and drinking with Hans. They had one thing in common. Both were eager to reach out beyond legal limits to better their lifestyles. By the end of the party, they were both feeling the effects of the alcohol.

"What do you say we get together some time, Hans. You're a good man," sputtered an inebriated Max with his arm around Hans' shoulders.

"Let's meet at Martha's on the next delivery date. Maybe you can come and help me carry a few loads. Then we can meet the girls for a drink afterwards."

At half past midnight the guests began to file out. Hans and Mitzi were among the last to leave. Once they were out the door, Mitzi stepped up beside Hans, who staggered slightly from side to side as he walked. "It's going to be a long trip home," she said wryly.

The cold air nipped at their faces as they walked through the streets toward the train station. The clouds seemed unusually close. "It looks as if we might get some snow tonight," Mitzi observed.

Hans was excited about having made a new friend. "What did you think of the party?" he asked.

She looked over at him and smiled. "Kai seems like a very charismatic man, and his daughter is absolutely charming."

"Max and I are planning to meet after work in a week and a half for a drink. You and his sister should join us."

Mitzi cringed slightly and shrugged. "Hans," she began reluctantly, "his sister seemed very nice but there's just something I don't like about Max."

"What do you mean?"

"Well, I don't know exactly what it is but… I just don't trust him. If I were you, I'd be careful."

"Don't be ridiculous. Max is a great man. Besides, you didn't spend that much time with him, so I don't think you're qualified to make such negative comments."

"Hans, you should have seen the way his sister was

acting all night. I noticed that whenever we were in the same room with Max, Sabine's expression changed. It seemed that she would look over at him constantly, but would never make eye contact with him. I mean, as soon as he would look over, she immediately turned away. It was almost as if she was afraid of him. I don't know. It just seems that if they are so close, then why would she be like that?"

"Maybe she's just shy."

"Shy? Of her own brother? That's even stranger." At that moment she looked upward and chanted, "Oh look, Hans! It's snowing!" As the snow fell, it began to leave a sparkling white mask across the city. Peace filled the night air.

A week and a half later, as planned, Hans met up with Max at Martha's shop. The delivery took less than five minutes to complete, with only three bags deposited on this particular day. After spending a few more minutes visiting with Martha, Max joined Hans for his remaining deliveries. Afterwards, the two men dropped the truck off and headed to Victor's, a quaint little bar where the locals could buy a mug of cheap, room temperature beer.

Sabine met up with them. As soon as she walked through the door, Hans jumped up and kissed her once on each cheek. Max simply shook his head and frowned.

"Where's Mitzi?" she asked as she sat down beside Max.

"She couldn't join us today. She had extended rehearsals," explained Hans.

Sabine's disappointment was apparent.

The three of them sat at a small, round mahogany table pressed up against a dirty window where they could watch people passing by. A few minutes later the waitress, a robust woman in her late fifties, walked over from behind the bar. "Ah, I see your company has finally arrived," she said with a hearty voice. "Would you care for some more beer?"

They ordered three more beers and continued their conversation. Sabine did not care much for beer, but sat there and sipped it slowly anyhow while the two men exchanged stories. She quickly grew bored, wishing Mitzi had shown up. The conversation seemed endless. After nearly forty minutes of complete silence, she finally spoke up and asked about Mitzi.

"She's doing quite well," responded Hans. "Say, why don't you and Max come to her next production? We'd love to see you there. She's a remarkable dancer!"

"So we've heard," commented Max. "I would love to see her dance!" Sabine's expression brightened.

The trio lingered at the pub for nearly two hours. Before they departed, Hans reminded them again about Mitzi's upcoming performance.

⸻ ✳ ⸻ ✳ ⸻ ✳ ⸻

December came quickly and Ingrid rushed about the theater feverishly, preparing the last minute details for the Nutcracker Suite. Johann opted to stay home to care for Andrea, who had become far too active and had to be constantly watched.

As always, the show was a success and Mitzi received her usual standing ovation. Following the production, Mitzi retreated to her dressing room. A few minutes later there came a knock at the door. She opened it and burst into laughter. Before her Hans stood in an awkward pose on his toes, holding his arms high above his head and carrying a long stem rose between his teeth.

"Hans," she laughed, "you really are too much at times.

How dare you mock my talent!"

Hans laughed and stepped into the dressing room.

Moments later another knock came at the door. It was Ingrid. "There's someone who wants to see you," she told Mitzi.

"Who is it?"

"I believe he said his name is Max." Mitzi's mood quickly changed as she rolled her eyes. Seeing this Ingrid continued, "I'll tell him you're busy."

As Ingrid turned to leave, Hans interjected, "No, I'll go talk to him. Max is a friend and associate of mine." He leaned over and kissed Mitzi before heading out the door.

Mitzi sat back down in front of the mirror and began removing her make up. After an awkward pause, Ingrid asked, "You don't like Hans' friend, Max? Who is he? What's wrong with him? He seemed nice enough."

Mitzi stopped working momentarily. "There's just something that doesn't feel right about him. For one thing I don't like the way his sister acts when he's around her. There is something that I just don't trust about him, but I can't seem to pinpoint it."

There was a knock at the door. "I'll get that," Ingrid said as she reached for the doorknob. Hans had returned with two other people who stood behind him. "Good! You're still here," Hans said when he saw Ingrid. "Ingrid, I would like you to meet two friends. This is Max..." Max stepped up and greeted Ingrid with a handshake. "Max, this is Frau Ingrid Brandt, our *maitresse des productions* and also the owner of the dance studio." He then turned to Sabine. "And this is Max's sister, Sabine."

As Sabine stepped out of the shadows into full view, Ingrid felt the blood rush out of her face and her jaw dropped. Her expression was clearly that of shock. "*Mein Gott!*" she gasped. "You look identical to someone I had met five years ago in one of the shelters."

Sabine raised her brow. "Oh? What was her name?" she asked as if she were expecting a particular answer.

"Marlene."

Sabine grew very still. "You met Marlene?"

"You were related?" asked Ingrid.

"Yes… yes... Marlene was my twin sister."

"*Mein Gott!*" shrilled Ingrid. "I don't believe it!" Ingrid shook her head and finally allowed a smile to appear on her face. "Marlene was your sister," she repeated. "She was such a brave girl."

The women stopped talking momentarily as Hans and Max stepped out of the dressing room.

"I have a few things to do before leaving. Max is going to help me. That way you women can get acquainted," said Hans. "It appears that you have a lot to discuss anyhow."

As soon as the men left, Ingrid began recounting the story to Sabine, of how she had met Marlene in the shelter in 1945. Sabine listened intently, savoring every detail of her twin sister and shedding a few tears in the end.

"Thank you for being there for her. I miss her so much," Sabine sniffled as she wiped away a final tear. "She was so strong…the stronger of the two of us. I can't tell you how many times we switched places. I once had a boy pursue me. I was about ten years old. He would not leave me alone until I agreed to play with him. I dreaded it so much that Marlene took my place. I'm still not sure what happened, but he never spoke to me again after that!" Sabine chuckled at the recollection. "Whenever I needed help, whenever I needed to be stronger... Well, we would simply trade places. People never knew the difference. Marlene knew how to get out of difficult situations much better than I did."

Ingrid listened, acknowledging Sabine's descriptions of her sister with a sympathetic nod. Sabine wrapped up the conversation. "It truly was a pleasure to meet you, Frau Brandt," she said timidly.

"Indeed. Perhaps next time you can meet Johann, my husband."

"I would like that." Just then someone knocked at the door. Ingrid opened it to find Hans and Max waiting patiently.

"Sabine," said Max, "we have to get going." Turning to Ingrid he nodded. "It was a pleasure to meet you, Frau Brandt."

Mitzi jumped up and suggested, "Oh, Sabine, if you aren't too busy during the day, why don't you come by and visit us at the studio this week?"

"Thank you, Mitzi. I'd be thrilled. I've been meaning to come by earlier."

Max grabbed Sabine by the arm and they departed.

When Ingrid arrived home with Hans and Mitzi, she found Andrea fast asleep. Ingrid crept softly into the tiny bedroom and approached Andrea's bed. She gazed down at her daughter for a long while.

Johann was still awake, reading a novel, when Ingrid entered their bedroom. "How was the production?" he asked, peering over his book at Ingrid.

"It was absolutely perfect," she answered as she began shedding her clothing. She stepped into the bathroom to wash up before crawling under the covers beside him. "Turn out the lights," she whispered into his ear.

"But I'm not tired," he cooed.

"Who said anything about sleep?"

He quickly put the book aside and turned out the light.

✳———✳———✳

Sabine sat alone in the café, where she had planned

to meet up with Max. She quietly stared out the window, watching the heavily clothed people as they hurried by. Snow covered the ground. She grew impatient, and then noticed an old poster advertising the Nutcracker Suite with Mitzi's photograph. Sabine's mind drifted back to the evening Max brought her to the ballet to see the performance.

"Excuse me... Excuse me." Sabine was suddenly jolted from her trance by the young waitress standing beside her. "Excuse me," she said once again. "Are you Fräulein Sabine Vogt?"

"Yes, I am." Sabine perked up.

"You have a telephone call. Please follow me."

Sabine followed the waitress into the tiny kitchen where she was handed a telephone. She spoke in a low voice. "Max?" she began. "Where are you?"

"Sabine, I can't get away now. I'll see you at home later this evening."

"Oh." She paused for a moment then suggested, "Max, I think I'll drop by Frau Brandt's dance studio this afternoon."

"Fine." The line went dead.

A short while later Sabine showed up at the studio. Upon seeing her, Mitzi, who was in the midst of teaching a class, smiled and waved, then pressed on with her lesson. Minutes later Ingrid stepped out of the office, carrying Andrea. At the end of her lesson, Mitzi took Andrea from Ingrid and then broke away from the crowd, signaling Sabine to follow her into the back office. They closed the door to the office and both women sat together on the sofa.

"She is so beautiful," chanted Sabine as she reached across to touch Andrea's knee. "Is she yours?"

"No." Mitzi squeezed Andrea gently in her arms. "She belongs to Frau Brandt. This is Andrea. We call her Andi."

"May I hold her?" Sabine asked eagerly.

"Absolutely. She might get upset if you don't."

Sabine reached across and gathered the child into her arms, placing her on her lap. "So your name is Andrea."

"Andiii!" cooed Andrea happily.

"So you *do* have a voice! Fine. Then Andi it is. That's a beautiful name. Do you always bring her to the studio?" Sabine asked.

"Yes. Otherwise there's no way we can do this. Ingrid refuses to leave her with strangers."

"What do you do, then? Do you take turns watching her?"

Mitzi nodded. Just then, Andrea reached up and grabbed Sabine's nose. She then pulled her hand away from the nose, opened her hand, gazed at her bare palm, and began laughing.

Mitzi chuckled. "She has your nose. Give her back her nose, Andi! You know you shouldn't be taking people's noses without their permission!"

Andrea reached up and pressed the invisible nose back onto Sabine's face, making her audience laugh.

"Unfortunately we had to cut back some of our classes recently because it's become too challenging to try to watch Andi and teach at the same time."

Sabine thought for a moment, then suggested, "What if I were to watch Andi for you."

"Oh, I don't know," Mitzi hesitated.

"Why not? I could come here and watch her while you and Frau Brandt concentrate on the students."

Mitzi thought for a moment then said, "That would be a wonderful idea, but it's a huge commitment!"

Sabine beamed at her idea. "It wouldn't be a problem. I don't work and I'd really like to have something more in my life to fill my time productively."

"You don't think Max will mind? I mean, I don't know

if we would be able to really pay for your time."

Sabine cringed at the mention of Max. "I..." She hesitated a moment then continued, "Max is never home, and when he is... he's not exactly the kindest person." Her voice trailed off.

"Do you mind my asking you a personal question?" Mitzi asked. Sabine shook her head. "Why do you let your brother have such a hold on you? It seems a little bit odd."

"He's... he's actually not my brother..." Her voice trailed off.

Unswayed by her response, Mitzi asked, "Do you love him?"

Sabine took a deep breath. "I don't know if it's love or insanity. I don't know why, but... Oh, I oughtn't talk about it. I don't like burdening people with my problems."

"It's no burden. I'm here if you ever do want to talk." Mitzi smiled and changed the subject. "I'll speak with Ingrid after class to see what she thinks about you helping out with Andi."

"Oh thank you!"

Forty minutes later, they heard the familiar three claps of Ingrid's hands, followed by the cheer and laughter of young voices as the students scampered off to greet their parents. All that was left was the sound of Ingrid's footsteps as she walked to the office. When Andrea saw her mother, she struggled to climb down from Sabine's lap and scampered over to greet her. Ingrid swept the toddler up into her arms. "My little Andi," Andrea pointed happily to Sabine and to everyone's delight, squealed, "Sabeeeed."

"She's taken quite fondly to Sabine," noted Mitzi. "In fact, Sabine has offered to take care of her while we teach, and..."

Ingrid immediately shook her head and interrupted, "No."

"Ingrid, you really ought to think about it," Mitzi shot

back. "We would be able to accommodate even more students if you were freed up a little more. It's not like you wouldn't see her throughout the day."

"I can do it here, Frau Brandt, so you'll always be close by," Sabine interjected. Her eyes locked with Ingrid's. "Andi is simply wonderful to be around and I enjoy being here. It would be such a great pleasure."

Ingrid's eyes wandered from Sabine to Mitzi to Andrea, who sat high in her arms and back to Sabine again. "Well… I suppose we could try it for one month."

CHAPTER SIXTEEN

OCTOBER 1952

Johann showed up unannounced at the studio one day. As he walked into the office, he saw Sabine sitting on the floor with Andrea, who was now almost four years old. The child sat proudly inside of a box, pretending it was a house. When she saw her father, Andrea toppled out of the box and ran to greet him.

"*Papi! Papi!*" she called out.

Johann dropped his cane and gathered the child into his arms, giving her a giant bear hug and a kiss on the cheek. She squealed with delight as his coarse whiskers brushed against her tender cheek. She wrapped her small arms around his neck.

"How's my little Andi?" he asked in an almost childlike voice.

As she stood high in his arms Andrea gasped, "*Mami* said I can start dancing soon!"

"Oh did she now? And do you think you are ready to learn?" Tiny wrinkles gathered around his kind eyes as he smiled at her.

"*Ja!* I've been ready for a long time."

Ingrid stood up from the sofa, where she had been sitting,

and greeted Johann with a kiss before taking Andrea from his arms. As she held her daughter, Ingrid asked her if she really thought she was ready to begin taking classes. "It's a lot of work, Andi," she explained. "Are you ready for all that? Dancing is not a game. It's a way of life."

"I'm big now!" Andrea said with such a confident attitude that it made everyone in the room laugh.

"Ingrid, may I speak to you in private?" said Johann. Sabine took this as a cue to leave, took Andrea from Ingrid, and left the office. Johann turned back to Ingrid. "We might be seeing some more difficult times in the days ahead," he began.

"What's going on?" Ingrid inquired.

"Well, the Russians continue to clamp down. This time they are creating some kind of security zone to stop people from leaving." He paused a moment before continuing. "I can't help but think that maybe we need to consider getting out before it's too late."

Ingrid looked around at her surroundings and shook her head slowly. "But Johann… We've put so much into this."

"I know. It's just that… well, I was talking to Hans earlier today. They've been tightening the Communist rule over the Soviet sector. People are fleeing in large numbers to the West. They are taking away our rights. Last year they took away any chance of earning more money in our jobs. Ingrid, it could be only a matter of time before they take over your studio. Germany is no longer ours and I just don't know how much longer we can go on like this."

"Can we discuss this later, Johann? I have so much to do right now. We have the next two classes starting in a few minutes." Johann said nothing and began heading toward the door. "Johann," Ingrid called out. He turned. "Is this the only reason you came here?"

"People are getting antsy. I've been hearing rumors that

there could be a rebellion at any time. I want to make sure you're staying safe. That's all." He turned and left the office, brushing against Mitzi as he left the studio.

"What was that all about? Is everything all right?" Mitzi asked as she joined Ingrid in the office.

"Johann is worried," Ingrid replied. Still carrying Andrea in her arms, Sabine approached the door to the office. Ingrid shook her head and continued, "I've never seen him react this way, Mitzi. He's talking about us leaving." Sabine stood back and listened to the conversation from outside the office door.

"What are you going to do?" asked Mitzi.

"I don't know."

"Hans and I had talked about leaving some time ago."

"And?"

"I couldn't do it… and then Hans changed his mind." They both smiled. "Don't worry. Things will work out."

"Come. We have more classes to teach," said Ingrid before walking out of the office, right past Sabine.

⸻✶⸻✶⸻✶⸻

That evening, in the bathroom of their apartment, Sabine stood in front of the mirror slowly combing her long black hair. Meanwhile, Max lingered in the living room, thumbing through the newspaper. "Max," she called out from within the bathroom, "have you ever thought about having children?" When he did not respond she stepped out into the living room. She stood there for a moment, quietly watching him. He continued reading the newspaper. "Max, are you listening?" she finally asked. There was some hesitance in her voice.

He finally put his paper down and rolled his eyes. "Don't be absurd, Sabine," he blasted.

"But we've been living together for the past few years. I just thought that…"

"What does that matter? Time means nothing," he interrupted before going back to his newspaper.

"I just thought…"

He put the newspaper down and interjected, "You just thought! You just thought! Sabine, that's your problem! You're always trying to think!"

"Max…" Her voice trembled slightly. "Why must you be so cruel all the time? What have I ever done to hurt you?"

"Leave me alone. I'm trying to enjoy the quiet," he ordered before returning again to his newspaper. Sabine stared at him until he looked back up at her. "Why are you staring at me? Stop staring at me!"

Feeling a sudden touch of defiance, Sabine decided to push back. "Ingrid's husband doesn't have full use of his leg, yet he is a wonderful father."

"Ingrid's husband. Ingrid's husband," he said mimicking Sabine. "What is it with you and these people? Ingrid's crippled husband has nothing to do with anything. I have two well-functioning legs, but it does not make me want to share a child with you."

Sabine glared at him as he continued reading the newspaper. "He's not crippled," she finally spouted.

"You just said…"

"He walks with a cane. That does not make him crippled."

Suddenly they heard shouting in the street and Max rushed to the window. In the street below, two soldiers had pinned down a teenage boy, who was now lying on his stomach. "What's going on down there?" asked Sabine as she came up behind him.

"They're arresting a boy," he responded as he pushed aside the curtain to get a better glimpse of the situation.

Sabine shook her head and said, "Things are getting

worse. Maybe we should consider leaving too."

"Huh? Leave too?"

"Johann talked to Ingrid today about leaving…"

"Sabine, you know damn well I can't leave. At least here I have a purpose and…" He stopped and fixed his eyes on her.

"What?" began Sabine. "Why are you staring?"

"Johann," Max muttered beneath his breath. He wrinkled his forehead. "Johann?"

"Ingrid's husband."

Max's eyes grew wide. "Johann," he repeated the name. "Ingrid's last name is Brandt, is it not?"

"Yes, but…"

"Which means that her husband's name is also Brandt."

"Obviously, but…"

"What does this man look like?"

"Why does this make a difference?"

"Just answer the question!"

"He is… is an older gentleman," she stammered slightly. "He's probably about Ingrid's age… a little taller than you, has dark hair, with some gray and he walks with a cane."

"What's wrong with his leg?" The scene of his father kicking Johann in the knee was still vivid in his mind. "I need you to find out what happened to him. But no matter what, under no circumstance are you to mention my name or my interest in him to anyone. Do you understand?" When she did not respond immediately he repeated, "I said, do you understand?!"

"Yes!" she shrieked, staring at him as if he had lost his mind.

He shoved her backwards, almost knocking her down, then stopped and glared at her. His piercing eyes and hair-trigger temper frightened her. Then he caught himself and stopped, stepped toward her and put his arms around her tenderly. "I'm sorry," he apologized. "I don't mean to frighten you." He reached over and kissed her on the lips. "Please find out these things for me. I'm sorry." His voice trailed off.

The following day, when Sabine arrived at the studio she asked Mitzi, rather inconspicuously, why Johann walked with a cane. The answer was simple. Johann had been attacked by a mad German Nazi who broke his knee.

"Did he know the man?" asked Sabine.

"Johann doesn't like to talk about what happened, so I don't ask," Mitzi answered. She was sitting on the hard tile floor of the studio office, helping Andrea into her leotard, and did not look up as she spoke. It was the little girl's first ballet lesson and she was so excited that she would barely sit still long enough for Mitzi to finish dressing her. "Come on, Andi! You are driving me insane," Mitzi urged. "Your class is starting very soon and the other girls are already here. You're going to be late." Finally, when Andrea stood still long enough, Mitzi was able to finish helping her into her leotard. She brought her out into the main class, where Ingrid had already lined up the other students. She resembled a doll with her bright blue eyes and golden hair, which had been pulled back into a tiny bun. The pink leotard emphasized her slim physique.

Ingrid kept the class simple, sticking with basic techniques. Mitzi and Sabine watched from the sideline, both smiling and trying to hold back their laughter at times. "She is going to be a prima ballerina one day," Mitzi whispered to Sabine. "I can feel it in my heart."

CHAPTER SEVENTEEN

JANUARY 1953

Max returned to the Soviet Headquarters. Upon entering the office he saw that the general was deeply engaged in a telephone conversation. He could not understand what he was saying, but his face was twisted in anger. Several minutes passed before he slammed the receiver down. Max braced himself, but when the general finally noticed him, he immediately regained his composure and softened his expression. He stood up and walked around the desk to greet Max, firmly shaking his hand.

"Max, Max! How have you been? It's been a while since I've seen you."

"Very well, thank you," Max responded. "I'm surprised you're still in Berlin."

"Yes, well there is ongoing work here." The general motioned toward a chair before he walked up to his bookcase, opened it, and removed a bottle of Stolichnaya. He poured some into two shot glasses and offered one to Max. "I'm very pleased with you, Max," he said as he stepped back behind his desk and sat down. "I only wish everyone were as cooperative and useful as you have been.

Granted, things have slowed down considerably."

"Thank you." Max smiled as the compliment soaked in.

"So tell me, young Max, what brings you to my office today?"

"There is someone I need to question." Max hesitated a moment then continued. "But I need men and weapons."

There was a moment of silence. The general put his drink down. "Weapons? This is an odd request, don't you think? Why would you need weapons and men? You are not the Stasi, Max. Your job is simply to give us information and we take care of the rest."

Max leaned back in his chair and explained, "General, this is very important to me. It's a rather delicate situation and must be handled with extreme caution. This case is not like any of the others."

"What makes it so different?"

"I can't tell you. Not yet. You will just have to trust me." When he saw the general's skepticism he continued, "Actually, I'm not one hundred percent certain it's the same man. I need to be certain before I move on to the next steps. I'll need to question him... I'll need the men to back me up. That's all."

The general took a deep breath and said, "Max, I'm completely confused. You're sounding a bit crazy right now. I can't just start sending out men and issuing guns for you to do as you please. That's absurd!" He stood up and poured more vodka into Max's glass. Max threw the clear potent liquid down his throat in one swift shot. His eyes suddenly grew wide and began to water as he coughed and wheezed, causing the general to laugh. Max struggled to regain his composure.

Just then a woman peered into the office through the door. "Comrade General. Our guests will be arriving soon," she informed him. "May I please access the storage cabinet?"

General Ivanov nodded, then motioned for the woman to enter his office. She walked over to a large wooden storage cabinet and began rummaging through it as he continued his meeting with Max.

Through the corner of his eyes Max noticed the woman pulling out various items from the storage cabinet: a carton of Camel cigarettes, two bottles of Stolichnaya, an assortment of European chocolates, and several watches. She put the items into a bag and left the office.

"Another drink, young Max?" asked General Ivanov.

Max shook his head, then inquired, "What kind of guests do you give watches to?" Their eyes locked and the general simply smiled and reached for his own glass to fill it with vodka. That's when Max noticed a Mickey Mouse watch on his wrist. "Nice watch. Which one of my leads earned you that?" he asked boldly.

"Max, where I get my goods is of no concern to you."

"It is if I am providing the information that leads you to these goods," Max answered blandly. The general simply stared at him. "General, why do I have this suspicion that you are breaking the law?"

The general raised his brow at Max's boldness. "I could have you arrested or worse, Max. Be very careful. You're playing with fire here."

"You won't though," retorted Max. "I'm too crucial to your personal comfort. Besides..." Max chose his words carefully. "I am about to bust open the mother lode of operations. General, you will be able to retire on the goods you will get from this one. You have my word. You won't be disappointed."

"What do you want, Max?"

"Two men and weapons."

"You can have two men, but I have to draw the line at weapons. *They* will be armed, not you."

"This is a dangerous operation," snapped Max.

The general shook his head and suggested, "Why don't you just give me the information that you already have and let us take it from here."

"I can't do that. There's not enough information to give you and I've already won over their trust. I just have a few more steps to take."

"Whose trust?"

"You'll just have to see, General. I will make you a rich man once I solve this one!"

General Ivanov shook his head slowly then muttered under his breath, "I must be crazy." He looked at Max and announced, "Very well. You will have them."

CHAPTER EIGHTEEN

FEBRUARY 1953

he power was down as Sabine walked through the empty studio toward the office in back. The door to the office was closed. Outside, dark clouds hovered low in the sky, making the room even darker. Suddenly, she heard the front door behind her open. She whipped around to see the shadow of a man cautiously entering the building. As he approached her, she could tell immediately who it was.

"Max!" she exclaimed, surprised to see him there.

"Shhh!" he snapped.

Sabine stared at him as he reached out and touched her chin. She said nothing.

"Where is everyone?" he whispered.

"I don't know. They might be in the office over there," she responded nervously as she pointed to the back of the room.

"Why don't you go and check," he said, softening his voice.

Sabine felt a surge of trepidation as he said this. "Why are you here?" she asked.

"Go into the office and don't tell them I was here," he

urged, ignoring her question. He then reached across and kissed her on the lips before beginning to head back outside. She did not question his final request and headed toward the rear of the room.

As she opened the door to the office, she did not notice Max as he changed his direction, veered right, and quietly slipped through the door into the adjacent classroom, closing the door behind him.

Sabine saw Ingrid sitting quietly on the sofa inside the office. On the desk, two small candles burned brightly. Ingrid always kept spare candles around the studio, as well as around her home, for emergencies. Andrea, now four years old, seemed unaffected by the power outage. She sat happily at her mother's feet, playing with her doll. Mitzi sat behind the desk in front of Ingrid, planning their next production in her notebook, where she had been keeping a record of all her choreography since she first met Ingrid.

As Sabine stepped into the office, Ingrid looked up and smiled. "Is someone with you?" Ingrid asked. "I thought I heard you talking."

Sabine shook her head reluctantly. "No," she responded. "I… I was just thinking out loud." She stood for a moment, fidgeting with her hands.

"Sabine, is something wrong?" Ingrid asked.

"I..." She stopped a moment, searching for the right excuse. "I've really no place to go right now and the weather is bad."

Ingrid accepted her explanation without question and invited her into the office to join them. She moved over to the far left of the sofa, allowing Sabine to sit down. Sabine continued fidgeting. Her fingers were intertwined. Ingrid watched her intently then glanced over at Mitzi, who also noticed her unusual behavior.

"Sabine," Ingrid broke the silence. "Is there something

wrong? You seem to be nervous."

"Nervous?" murmured Sabine. She stopped fidgeting temporarily. "I'm sorry. No. I'm fine."

Ingrid glanced back at Mitzi, who remained silent. Then Sabine began fidgeting once more, looking away from Ingrid, whose eyes were now fixed upon her again. "Sabine?" Ingrid said, maintaining her stare. Andrea, oblivious to her surroundings, continued playing with her doll. "Sabine!" Ingrid repeated the name with growing concern.

Finally Sabine turned back and looked at her. Ingrid saw that her eyes were wide, her face wild with fear. "I... I have a feeling you may be in danger... You may all be in danger and..."

"What... are... you... talking... about?" demanded Ingrid, enunciating each word. Mitzi sat straight up in her chair. Her voice retained its usual calmness.

"Max..." Sabine paused a moment. "I think he wants to hurt you."

Ingrid leaned toward her. She came so close that Sabine saw the reflection of the candlelight burning in her eyes. "Max? Max who?"

"Max Schmidt," Sabine answered, "but actually that's not even his real name. His real name is Max von Euken."

Ingrid felt her blood grow cold and her body numb at the mention of his name. She did not conceal her astonishment and immediately stood up. Andrea stopped playing and looked up at her mother. The tension in the office escalated, causing the child to stand up, walk over to her mother and put her arms up. Taking her cue, Ingrid reached down and scooped up the child. "Are you certain?" she asked as she began pacing the floor with Andrea wrapped around her.

"Yes, I'm certain." Sabine hesitated then continued, "I helped him to change his identity a few years ago."

Ingrid stopped pacing the floor and glared at Sabine.

"You?! Then it's true what your sister said about you. I had forgotten! How stupid could I be?!" Ingrid stomped her right foot. "You really *have* devoted yourself to helping Nazi war criminals." When Sabine did not respond Ingrid turned to Mitzi. "We need to get to the police."

"But Frau Brandt..." Sabine interrupted desperately. "You don't understand. He was here ... only moments ago!"

"Wha... What are you saying?" The pitch of Ingrid's voice went up with increasing alarm.

"I don't understand. What could he want with you?"

"Johann!" gasped Ingrid, realizing he was due to arrive soon. "We must warn Johann! We need to keep him away from here! How could you do this, Sabine?! We trusted you!"

"I didn't do anything. I didn't know! You have been so good to me. Why would I..."

Just as she said that they heard the front door of the studio slam shut. The all grew still. Mitzi leaned over and blew out the candles. Ingrid's heart began beating at a furious rate as she peered out the office door to try to see who had entered the studio. She breathed a sigh of relief when she saw Hans and no one else. She rushed out to him. Mitzi followed closely behind.

"Thank God!" Ingrid gasped. "Hans, where is Johann?"

"He'll be here in twenty minutes." Hans was smiling until he noticed Ingrid's expression. "What's wrong?"

"Johann is in grave danger. We must warn him. There is someone who wants to hurt him."

"What? Why would anyone want to hurt Johann?" asked Hans astonished.

"There is no time to explain. I need you to find him and warn him. Keep him away from the studio." She glanced at Mitzi. "And take Mitzi with you. I don't think Max will harm either of you. It's Johann he's after."

"Max?" Hans asked bewildered. "Max Schmidt? My

friend Max?"

"I'm afraid so. It's not even his real name. His real name is Max von Euken."

"I know that name." He scrunched his face and scratched his forehead.

"His father was Karl von Euken," continued Ingrid.

"The Nazi! That's it! But why would Max want Johann dead?"

"Johann killed his father at the end of the war."

Hans was speechless. He looked over at Mitzi, who could only shake her head disapprovingly at him, never having trusted Max from the moment she first met him.

"Please, Hans, we have no time to waste. He's somewhere out there now," Ingrid pleaded.

At that moment, Mitzi stepped in. "We'll do whatever we must, Ingrid."

She grabbed Hans' arm and began pulling him toward the door. "Be careful when you leave. Act normal, and lock the doors on your way out," Ingrid urged.

"What about you? You shouldn't stay here," Hans said.

"Someone needs to stay here in case Johann arrives. Go quickly. We'll be fine."

They both left the studio, leaving Ingrid behind, alone with Andrea and Sabine.

Holding Andrea in her arms, Ingrid watched from the window as her two friends disappeared around the corner. Her heart was beating wildly. She heard Sabine's footsteps behind her and turned around to face the young woman.

"Would you like me to take Andi for a while?" asked Sabine meekly.

"No!" Ingrid hissed in a chilling voice, causing Sabine to shrink back. Ingrid swiftly brushed past the bewildered young woman and marched back into the office. Barely had she reentered the room when she was startled by Sabine's shrill voice blasting out Johann's name. Ingrid put Andrea down and darted back out into the classroom.

"What's wrong?" she asked in a panic as she pushed the young woman to the side and peered out the window. Outside, off to the right, she saw Johann making his way toward the studio. Ingrid unlocked the door. "Johann!" she called out.

He stopped walking. His expression suddenly changed when he saw someone came up from behind Ingrid and reach for her.

"So, we meet again," growled Max. He wrapped his arm around Ingrid's neck, withdrew a knife from his pocket, and brought it up to her cheek. "I always knew we would." Seeing Johann's confusion Max blared, "Don't you remember me?" He paused for a moment, allowing the recognition to settle in. "That's right! You murdered my father."

"Let her go," Johann demanded. "She has nothing to do with this."

Ingrid struggled to free herself, but Max tightened his grip around her neck, causing her to gasp for air. Johann took two steps toward the studio, but was quickly seized from behind by two other men, each wearing trench coats and carrying a pistol. They began to shove him toward the studio door. Ingrid felt herself being pulled back into the building. Max then swung her around so that she was facing Sabine. Ingrid felt a stinging blow to her back as Max brought his knee up sharply, thrusting her forward into Sabine. The door slammed shut behind them, rattling the walls around them. Max continued pushing Ingrid forward to the back of the studio and into the office. Ingrid finally came to rest, shoved up against the wall.

"Sit down and don't move," he growled, shoving her onto the sofa. Stunned, Ingrid blinked several times, trying to readjust her eyes to the dark room. Max left the office and returned a moment later with Andrea who, by now, was screaming.

"Shut her up," he ordered as he pushed Andrea up against her mother. Ingrid bent over and swept the shaken child up into her arms, pulling her onto her lap.

"Sh... sh... Do not cry. Everything will be all right." At that instant they were startled by a thunderous crash in the main studio followed by Johann's protests.

"Silence!" Max bellowed as he stormed back out of the office.

Ingrid heard a brief scuffle. "Don't move, Andi," she whispered as she placed her on the sofa. She took Andrea's tiny face into her hands and kissed her on the forehead before stepping away. Andrea sat there wide eyed and in shock.

Ingrid crept up to the doorway of the office and peered around the corner. She saw Johann lying on the floor in the center of the dark studio. She watched in horror as he struggled to pull himself back up onto his feet, receiving blow after devastating blow from Max's foot. Outside, the two men stood by, looking away from the studio. By the forth blow Ingrid rushed out of the office, toward Johann. "Johann!" her voice cracked as she called out in desperation. Hearing her screams, the two men rushed inside to intervene. The first man managed to get between Ingrid and Johann, catching her in his arms. She struggled to free herself, bringing her knee up sharply into his groin. The man released her and bent over in pain. Ingrid managed to take several more steps toward Johann, but was quickly subdued by the second man who immobilized her by twisting her arm sharply behind her back. Screeching out in pain, Ingrid felt as though her arm was about to snap. Max finally stopped dealing blows to Johann, who lay on the floor practically immobile. He approached Ingrid and swung his arm at her face, dealing her a sharp, back-handed blow, knocking her further into the second man's arms.

"Why?" she managed to ask in a raspy voice as a drop of blood crept out of the side of her mouth.

Sabine stepped forward and attempted to voice her protests. "Max, she has done nothing."

At that moment Max backhanded Sabine squarely in the jaw, knocking her to the ground. "Shut up, whore!" he shouted out. It was all Sabine could do to avert her eyes from his own delirious eyes.

Frightened by all the noise, Andrea struggled down from the sofa and peered out the door of the office. Stunned, she dropped to her knees, clutching the wall of the doorway. *"Mami… Papi."* She began crying. Just as Max raised his arm to deal another blow to Ingrid, Johann heaved himself up onto his feet. He staggered toward Max, who stood with his back to him. A deafening shot echoed throughout the studio and the room grew still. All eyes turned to Johann, who dropped to his knees, clasping his chest with his hands.

"Johann!" Ingrid cried out hysterically as blood began spilling out from between his fingers. He gazed up at her one last time before toppling over onto the floor. The air grew eerily still. Appearing stunned, Max took several steps toward Johann's body, stopped, then turned to the man who had fired the shot.

"You weren't supposed to do that! I wanted him alive!" Max said, struggling to maintain his calm.

"General Ivanov said we were to ensure your safety under all circumstances. He was coming toward you," explained the man.

The second man slowly approached Johann's body and stared down at him for a long moment. "This is not good," he muttered. Then he spotted the German steel cross ring on his middle finger. "Ah. What have we here?" He crouched down, lifted up Johann's lifeless hand, and began twisting off the ring.

"Wha…? What are you doing?" asked Max.

"I'm taking a souvenir to give to the general," answered the Russian.

"Let me see that," demanded Max. The Russian handed the ring to Max, who looked it over. "It's completely worthless… just like Johann's life."

"Good!" The man stood up and snatched the ring out of Max's hands. "Then you won't mind if I take it. I know the general would like it."

"Be my guest," muttered Max. He then instructed the man to check on Andrea. "This wasn't supposed to happen," he muttered again to himself, sounding like a madman.

"Max." Sabine stepped up behind him, placing her hand on his shoulder. He swung around and struck her in the face, sending her to the ground.

"Woman! You have betrayed me!" he turned on her unexpectedly.

"How...how have I betrayed you?" she stammered, staring up at him.

Max kicked her in the ribs and shouted out, "You've grown soft! You have no spine! You like these people and you question my will. That is betrayal!" He turned to one of the men and demanded, "Finish her off."

"This is not what we have been assigned to do," objected the man.

"The general will question why you killed Herr Brandt when I specifically said that we would not do this!"

"I must insist that this is not correct pro..."

Max stepped up to the man and thrust his face toward his, glaring into his eyes. He pointed to Johann's lifeless body. "And do you suppose that was standard procedure? Do you know what will happen to you if I tell them you murdered this man in cold blood?"

"It wasn't in cold blood," retorted the man.

"Look! He is not even armed." Max stopped for a moment to allow the information to sink in. He then softened his voice and continued, "Now, do as I tell you. She is a witness and can only ruin your career. I thought your kind never left any witnesses anyhow."

"Max, please. No," came Sabine's futile pleas as the man raised his pistol and pointed it at the helpless young woman. He hesitated a moment.

"Shoot her!" Max blazed into his ear.

"Max!" came Sabine's final plea. She looked up into the eyes of the stranger just as the deafening shot echoed throughout the studio. Sabine suddenly felt a deep piercing pain go through her chest followed by another bullet through her head as she fell with a deep look of despair upon her face. Ingrid turned around. Her head began to spin. The room began swirling around her faster and faster, her expression filled with horror and pain.

Suddenly, Andrea felt someone pick her up. It was one of the men.

Ingrid glanced back and saw Andrea. "Please. Let my child go," she pleaded. Then, "Close your eyes, my child. Close your eyes." Her voice quivered. But it was too late. Andrea had witnessed everything. The child tried to struggle, but the demon man was too powerful for her.

Max suddenly grew quiet as he paced a few times near Johann's body. He then instructed the two men to lock the doors and bring Ingrid and Andrea into the back office. A minute later the five of them were standing in the office. "Do you have any matches to light these damned candles?" he growled at Ingrid. He then addressed the two men. "Could you please give us some privacy?" They stepped back out of the office, bringing Andrea with them. Max leaned toward Ingrid and whispered, "I like to see my subjects before I kill them."

"You'll never get away with this," Ingrid hissed.

"Who's going to stop me? I have friends in high places."

"You are nothing but despicable murderers."

"Where are your matches?" he asked again, ignoring her last comment.

"Top drawer," she answered without looking at him. Her mind raced as she tried to devise an escape. How could she get past these men? How could she get Andrea out to safety?

Max opened the drawer and removed a white box of matches and lit the candles. Pleased with himself he sat in Ingrid's chair and propped his mud-soiled shoes onto the desk. He reached into his jacket and withdrew a large cigar. Bringing the cigar up to his nose, he took three long whiffs then said, "Ahhhh… It's delectable." He then leaned forward toward the lit candle and puffed several times on the cigar to light it. The smoke quickly filled the air. "Frau Brandt, what shall we do with you?" he said, clicking his tongue. "It's a dangerous and sinister world we live in. Have you ever read a newspaper? Or are you too busy lost in your dancing?" Ingrid did not respond. "You ought to read the newspaper. Did you know the Russians have taken over part of our country? They even got rid of the Nazis." He smiled. "Well, at least some of the less fortunate ones." He laughed, but still Ingrid did not reply, causing him to become irritated. "Did Johann know how to please you? Was he a real man? I heard Jews were quite small. Is this true?" He stood, stepped up to her, and sniffed her head. "I can smell him on you." More silence. "Maybe you'd be happier with the smell of a real man on you." He reached out and stroked her hair.

"You are repulsive!" snapped Ingrid. "I'd sooner be dead!"

"Ah! She still speaks. There is life underneath all that." Ingrid did not reply. "What did you ever see in the Jew anyhow?" he asked. Ingrid remained silent.

Max began pacing the floor. "Do you know what I heard?" His gaze pierced through her. The reflection of the flickering candle danced in his eyes. "I was told that the best way to affect a woman is through her child? Is this true?"

Ingrid hissed, "Leave her alone!"

"Only if you dance for me." Ingrid's body was frozen as she fought back tears. "I said dance, Jew lover! You are a dance teacher, which means you know how to dance. So now I would like to see what you can do."

"Why don't you just kill me instead?" she finally said.

"How about if I kill that child of yours first?"

Suddenly, Ingrid lunged at him, grabbing Max by the hair. She threw him off balance and they both went toppling to the ground toward the doorway. Hearing the crash inside the office, one of the two men rushed to the door, but with Ingrid and Max blocking it, he could not open it enough to see what was happening inside. "What's going on in…"

"Leave us," Max ordered. "I'm fine. She tried to attack me. I have her under control now." Max struggled to keep from getting hit by Ingrid's flailing arms.

"It doesn't sound that way to me, Herr Schmidt," the man said, trying to push through the door.

Max ignored him then reached up and grabbed Ingrid's arms and rolled over on top of her, pinning her to the ground. "That was a huge mistake," he hissed. His right eye began twitching from a drop of perspiration that dripped into it. He was breathing hard and Ingrid could smell alcohol on his breath, as he straddled her with both of his legs. He leaned over and kissed her on the cheek as she struggled to try to free herself. She finally managed to free one hand and swung fiercely at his face, hitting him squarely in the jaw. Stunned, Max sat up and began beating her mercilessly on the face. Ingrid could taste her own blood as her lip split.

Then, he began ripping at her blouse, tearing off the buttons. Finally, with one strong tug, he tore her blouse open, exposing her breasts. She screamed out in pain, this time from him beating her head against the floor.

Suddenly, Ingrid heard Andrea's voice screaming, *"Mami! Mami!"* The world began to collapse around her as the second man had managed to push open the door, and now had the child in his arms.

In one last desperate effort, Ingrid lashed out and dug her nails into the tender flesh of Max's face, tearing a one-inch gash into his right cheek, barely missing his eye. Max drew back, screeching in pain as he drew his hand over his cheek and stumbled backwards.

"You'll pay dearly for this!" he shrieked hysterically. He turned to the man who was holding Andrea and ordered in a hallowing voice, "Take the child out somewhere and dispose of her!"

Ingrid began screaming hysterically, "Andi! Nooooo!" She attempted to crawl toward the door but was dealt a heavy blow with Max's foot to her side. She bent over in pain as her ribs cracked below her. He dealt another heavier blow to her face then ripped off her skirt. As he brutally climbed atop her, they heard a shot fired outside. Ingrid could feel her own life slipping away from her. Then, finally there was relief as her eyes closed… and her world turned black.

CHAPTER NINETEEN

FOUR DAYS LATER

"**S**he is a beautiful child."

"She won't speak, though."

"Why not?"

"The man who led us to her told us that she had been through a lot. He told us her mother and father were both killed in an attempted robbery."

"Such a tragedy." The doctor shook his head sympathetically as he examined the child. "Look at her eyes, so striking, yet terrified!"

Little Andrea sat in the doctor's office on top of a hard, bare table.

"What will you do with her?" inquired the doctor.

"My husband and I would like very much to take care of her."

"Do you know anything about her?"

"Not really. I was hoping you might be able to help us, though. The man informed us that we must change her identity immediately."

"Why? Whose child was she?" the doctor asked with a puzzled expression.

"The child belonged to Frau Ingrid Brandt," answered

the woman with a deep sigh.

The doctor did not conceal his astonishment.

Four days earlier little Andrea was sitting helplessly, bound in the clutches of an evil man, forced to witness the beating of her mother. She attempted to free herself, but her struggle was in vain. The man's grip was much too firm, giving Andrea no opportunity to evade him. She had never seen such panic on her mother's face. What was happening was incomprehensible. Why would anyone want to hurt her parents? After a terrible struggle in the office, the man took Andrea into the main studio where the other man waited, and they then carried her out of the building.

Once outside, the man holding Andrea withdrew his pistol. Andrea began struggling and screaming. She bent down and bit down into the fleshy part of his hand. The gun went off. In anger the man fired one more round into the ground, causing Andrea to flinch and let out a shriek.

"Get her out of here before someone comes," the second man told the first. They placed her into the trunk of a vehicle and slammed the door down, leaving her cold and trembling in the tight, dark space.

Andrea heard the engine start and felt the vehicle begin rolling. She lay trapped in the trunk for a long time before it finally came to a complete stop. When the man, who was now alone with Andrea, finally opened the trunk again, he reached in and picked her up. At first she tried to struggle, but he was too strong. He carried her into an abandoned building nearly completely demolished by the war. Once inside, he placed her on the floor and bound her hands and feet with a light cord. He then stepped back and raised his pistol. Andrea began to cry. The man stood there, motionless, with his weapon pointed at the helpless little girl. As he looked into her eyes he began to falter. Overwhelmed with shame and sorrow he slowly lowered his pistol and took a deep breath. They stared at one another for a long moment. "Aaaahhhh!" he suddenly shouted out in anger and frustration as his fist crashed into the wall beside him. He turned and stormed out of the building, slamming the door behind him without saying another word. She heard his car door open and then close again. The man returned once more, just long enough to drape a blanket over her before he left for good.

Andrea was alone in the cold, unfamiliar place, afraid and tense. Shadows filled the room and she had no way to hide from them. The rope that bound her feet and hands cut into her tender flesh, and she felt weak with hunger and very cold. The only good thing in her life was missing – her mother and father. Andrea imagined she was once again tucked deeply into her mother's protecting arms, feeling the warmth of her body. Closing her eyes, she could see Ingrid and Johann gazing down at her. Andrea finally fell asleep.

When she woke up the next morning, Andrea felt someone removing the cord from her wrists and legs and several more warm blankets being draped over her. Then came the sound of a woman humming softly behind her. "*Mami?!*" she inquired. She opened her eyes, hoping to find her mother. Instead, she found herself in the same room, face to face with an unfamiliar woman. Andrea sat up and stared at the stranger without saying a word.

Suddenly, the door behind the woman swung open and Andrea saw a silhouette enter the room. When she saw that it was a man, she began scooting herself backwards, pushing away from him. Before she knew it, she had backed into a corner.

"Don't be frightened," said the woman, as she carefully approached the child. "What is your name?" she asked as she knelt down in front of Andrea. "We're going to help you. Tell us your name." Andrea did not answer, nor did she take her eyes off the man who now stood behind the woman. "You'll come with us," the woman said softly. "You can't stay here." Andrea did not move. Finally the woman reached across and picked her up. Dazed and confused, Andrea did not resist.

"I hope this isn't a mistake," grumbled the man standing behind her.

"Don't be so cruel, Walter," reprimanded the woman. "Can't you see she is already hurt and frightened?"

Softening his tone, the man knelt down beside the woman. "My name is Walter and this is my wife, Hanna." Andrea stared at him, her expression frozen.

"You'll come home with us," said Hanna. "We'll take care of you."

Walter and Hanna Spangenberg brought Andrea to their home and told friends, neighbors, and acquaintances that she was their niece, whose mother had recently passed away.

They led a somewhat secluded life. Hanna was tall and lanky with dangling brown hair and Walter was a simple and hard-working man. Every morning he would awake before five o'clock, eat a quick breakfast of hardened bread and bitter ersatz coffee, and then ride his bicycle nearly ten kilometers, crossing the border into the Western sector, where he worked in a large factory, polishing brass pipes. Rain, snow, or shine, his routine never changed.

⊹——⊹——⊹

It had been over two weeks since Walter and Hanna

had brought Andrea home. Still, she never uttered a single word. She never even cried. At times, she would pass her time sitting quietly, staring out the apartment window. Other times she sat huddled in a corner, watching Hanna as she worked around the house.

"I know you are upset." Hanna shook her head solemnly. "But you can't be silent for the rest of your life," she insisted. Her gentle eyes swept over Andrea. No matter how much she tried or prayed, she saw no improvement in Andrea's mental condition.

One week later, they made an appointment to see Klaus Molsenger, an old family friend who worked at the headquarters for the Sozialistische Einheitspartei Deutschlands (SED). As they approached the building, two armed guards stopped them. "We have an appointment to see Herr Klaus Molsenger," explained Walter.

"One moment please." The first of the two guards walked to a small telephone inside the building while the second guard watched Walter and Hanna closely. Hanna put her arm around Andrea, drawing her in closely to her side.

A few moments later a thin man, wearing a small goatee, arrived. After shaking hands, he escorted them through a long corridor and up two flights of stairs. When they reached his office, he opened the door and motioned them to enter.

"Sit down over there," he instructed as he shut the door. He quickly took his own seat behind the desk and lit a cigarette. Once they were alone, he immediately relaxed. "I'd offer you one, but I know you don't smoke," he said, smiling. "It's been a long time. What brings you here?" He then glanced over at Andrea. "And who do we have here?"

"We want to know if you have any information about someone," Hanna answered, ignoring his last question.

"Who?"

Seeing Hanna's reluctance, Walter cut in, "Do you know anything about Frau Ingrid Brandt."

"The dance teacher?"

"Yes."

Klaus leaned back in his chair and studied them for a moment. "What is your interest in her?"

Walter hesitated at first, then began, "Klaus, you've been our friend for many years. Please keep this information to yourself. This child... This child, as you know, she is not ours..."

"Ingrid..." Klaus interrupted, and then stopped. He stared at Andrea. "Is this her child?" He looked from Walter to Hanna to Andrea and back to Walter again. His expression filled with comprehension. "You have her child? What are you doing with her child?"

"Klaus, we need your help."

"Walter, my friend, you need more than my help. You need a doctor to examine your head! What is going on here?" Klaus looked at Andrea again and decided to continue the conversation in private. "Let's step out for a minute," he told Walter. As they went out into the hallway, Andrea peered up at Hanna. They both sat quietly, listening to the low murmur of the conversation on the other side of the door as the two men discussed Andrea's future.

Ten minutes passed when Walter re-entered the office and sat beside Hanna. He stared straight ahead, not looking at her, and explained, "He's going to try to help us. It shouldn't take too long." They sat in silence, waiting.

Nearly fifteen minutes later Klaus returned, carrying a small folder tucked beneath his arm. "I found this file," he said as he sat down at his desk. He opened the folder and placed it in front of him and began to read. "It says here that the child's name is Andrea and..." His eyes narrowed.

"Ehhh…"

"What?" Hanna and Walter said in unison as they leaned forward. "Well, according to this, the three of them were killed in an accident." He looked up at them.

"The three?" questioned Walter.

"Well… yes. Andrea and both her parents," he explained.

"Does it say how they were killed?" asked Hanna.

"All it says here is that it was an accident. It doesn't tell what kind of accident."

Hanna shook her head disapprovingly and asked, "Does it say anything else about the child?"

"She was born in 1948. This would make her four years old. She'll be five in November." He scratched his chin and looked up. "What is it that you want from me?" He shifted uncomfortably in his seat.

Hanna glanced over at Walter before stating, with some urgency, "We need to get some type of identity for our new child. We… we can't possibly turn her over to the authorities. There is nothing…no telling what will happen to her. Who would write such a lie … and why?"

Klaus considered it a moment then said firmly, "My friends. I think you are both making a very big mistake. I have to recommend that you turn her over to the proper authority. There's no telling who's behind this!" Klaus stopped and glanced at the three visitors sitting across from his desk. "I don't know what else I can do for you," he grumbled.

"But, Klaus," exclaimed Hanna. "What will happen to the child if you don't help us? Look at her. She is so young. What would you prefer? You would seriously prefer that we turn her over to the authorities? How do we know whether or not we're putting her in danger?"

After a brief pause, Klaus shook his head slowly from side to side and said, "I hope I don't live to regret this."

"Then you'll help us?" asked Walter.

Klaus nodded his head. "I'll try," he answered. They all stood up and walked to the door. "I shall create a record for our little Andrea Spangenberg and bring you some papers when I have them. We'll keep her first name as is, but we should probably change her place of birth to Dresden to be safe."

"Oh thank you! Thank you so much!" exclaimed Walter and Hanna, as they shook Klaus' hand. They left the office.

It was dark outside. The wind howled through the branches of the trees, tossing the leaves about violently. Andrea found herself standing alone in the street. Everything appeared massive – the buildings, the streets, the few parked cars around her. Suddenly she heard a bone-chilling scream. It was a familiar scream. She followed the piercing sound as it grew louder and louder, almost becoming deafening. Her body became paralyzed and her breathing labored. Before her she saw the image of her mother, hunched over on her knees. The woman looked up and saw Andrea. Her arms came up, reaching, reaching. But something held Andrea back. She struggled to free herself from the invisible force, but her struggles proved to be futile. Then, in the corner of her eye Andrea saw him, a faceless man, cloaked in black. He began marching toward her. He was floating, yet Andrea heard his footsteps grow louder and louder until the sound was too unbearable. Then, he reached out for her, and as he did she saw the image of a cat begin to emerge from the back of his hand. The cat turned into a lion with fire in its eyes. Andrea opened her mouth to scream but nothing would come out.

"Andi, run!" echoed the haunting voice of her mother. It sounded like a thousand voices, trapped inside a chasm. "Andi, run or the lion will kill you!"

Andrea clamped her eyes shut…

"Andrea! Andrea! Wake up!"

Andrea opened her eyes to find Hanna bent over her, shaking her shoulders to try to awaken her. Andrea's face was drenched in tears as she came to, relieved that it had only been a dream, but terrified by the lingering images in her mind.

"You poor girl," whispered Hanna softly as she brushed Andrea's golden locks of hair away from her face. "You were having another one of your nightmares." Andrea said nothing. "Go back to sleep. I'm with you now." Hanna continued caressing Andrea's hair until she dozed off once again.

For many months Andrea experienced the same recurring nightmare, causing her to dread going to sleep. Each night Hanna would sit by her bedside, gently caressing her hair, soothing her back to sleep. Often Andrea awoke to the sound of her own ghastly screaming. She would be drenched in a puddle of sweat, tears flowing freely. Deprived of her own sleep, Hanna was exhausted, spending long hours awake with Andrea, consoling her time after time.

After three months the nightmares began to occur less frequently. Yet, Andrea still refused to speak, isolating her emotions from the rest of the world around her. Hanna and Walter grew increasingly concerned. One evening, after Andrea went to bed, she overheard them arguing in the kitchen.

"You can't continue like this!" exclaimed Walter.

"Like what? I'm fine."

"No, you're not. You're exhausted. Andrea needs help and we can't provide that for her. We're not doctors! She needs special care!"

"What are you saying?" asked Hanna. There was a

moment of silence. "Are you saying we give her up?" More silence. "And do what with her... institutionalize her? She's just a child. She's been through a lot. She just needs time." There was a pause. "I need her!"

There was another pause, and then Walter spoke. "If we don't see more of an improvement soon, we won't be able to keep her. What are we going to do with a child who refuses to speak and might never fit in with society?"

Andrea drew the covers over her head as she lay alone in the dark. Now she felt even more isolated.

The following evening, Hanna, Walter, and Andrea sat down for dinner. Hanna had prepared a steaming casserole of cabbage and potatoes, with a meager portion of chopped pork. Andrea's stomach growled as she reached for her fork and slowly began to eat.

"Where did you get the meat?" inquired Walter with a hint of surprise in his voice.

"*Mutter,*" Hanna replied, putting a forkful of cabbage into her mouth.

"*Mutter?*" Walter repeated somewhat surprised.

Hanna smiled, "She said she got it from her neighbor."

"We should have invited her to dinner then."

"I tried, but she is not feeling well again."

"Well, perhaps we can bring her some food later," suggested Walter.

"I'm sure she would like that."

During the next ten minutes they ate in an awkward silence. Hanna finally looked toward Andrea and gave her a hearty smile. "Andrea, it's good to see you eating so well this evening."

Andrea looked up from her plate and smiled for the first time. Then, when she had finished the last bite, she opened her mouth, "M...may I pl...please have more?" she said, holding out her plate.

Hanna and Walter stopped eating. Hanna brought her hand to her mouth, trying to hold back any emotion. Her face lit up as she answered with contained enthusiasm, "You certainly may, Andrea." Her voice quivered. "You certainly may."

"*Mami and Papi* called me Andi."

"Andi. Yes. Andi." Andrea passed her plate across the table and was served another generous portion of steaming cabbage and potatoes.

Later that evening, carrying the pot of food, they walked five blocks to an apartment building. They knocked on the door, and waited in silence until an elderly woman answered. "*Mutter*," Hanna said as she reached over and kissed her mother. "The food was wonderful. We brought you some. Have you had dinner yet?"

"Ach, *Schatzi*, It's good to see you," Hanna's mother spoke with a gentle, but wheezy voice. "No. I'm not too terribly hungry."

"You need to eat." Hanna removed the lid from the pot. The food was still warm as she scooped two spoonfuls out onto a plate and handed it to her mother. "Eat while the food is still warm, *Mutter*."

Ignoring her daughter's urging, Viktoria turned her attention to Andrea, who stared wide eyed at her, and smiled. She then turned to Walter. "When are you going to take your family and leave this terrible place?"

"Now, you know we have this same discussion every time we see you, and my answer never changes. We'll leave as soon as you agree to leave with us."

"And you know I can't do that. My health is failing" Viktoria walked slowly over to the table and put her plate down. She was frail and shaky, her fingers twisted from years of arthritis. "Besides, this is my home. I've lived here far too long to leave. God spared my home and I'm not going to abandon it now." She looked at her daughter, who stood nearby with her arms folded together. "Hanna, I can take care of myself. You should go before it's too late."

"I won't leave you, *Mutter,* and there is no sense in discussing this any further."

"You are stubborn," sighed Viktoria. "What about Andrea? Why not leave for her sake?"

"Andi," interjected Andrea.

"I beg your pardon?"

"I'm called Andi."

"Andi?" Viktoria looked at the child for a moment before agreeing, "Well then, Andi it is." She then leaned forward, took a bite of her food, and smiled to herself.

CHAPTER TWENTY

SEPTEMBER 1958

Over five years had passed since Hanna and Walter had taken in Andrea. Now, nine years old, Andrea blossomed as the harsh memories of her past faded. She even gained a reputation in school for her outspoken nature, which did not always bode well with her teachers. Andrea's school was conveniently located less than half a kilometer away from their apartment.

The air was brisk but pleasant. This was the first year that Andrea walked herself to school without Hanna, insisting that she was too old to be escorted by her mother.

Once she reached the school, Andrea stopped and stared up at the familiar massive, gray, stone building standing before her. She never much cared for school. The routine was rigid at times, and she was often bored by the daily lessons. For a brief moment she contemplated running back home. At the last moment, however, she followed the other school children, making her way to her classroom. She felt a bit of apprehension as she opened the door. The teacher had not yet arrived. Most of the students were already seated at their desks and she sat quietly in her chair with her hands folded together.

Five minutes later the door swung open and in walked a middle-aged woman with a grim expression. Upon seeing her the students immediately stopped talking and jumped to their feet, standing at attention beside their desks. *"Für Frieden und Sozialismus, seid bereit!"* (For peace and socialism, be ready!), she finally said.

The students then responded in near perfect unison, *"Immer bereit!"* (Always ready), then brought their hands to their foreheads.

The teacher smiled and made a motion with her hand for the students to sit down. She marched over to the chalk board and wrote her name. "Frau Straufenberg." Her voice cracked slightly as she enunciated each syllable. Her mere presence caused the students to remain silent. She had gray hair, pulled back into a severe bun and her eyes were deep and penetrating with tiny wrinkles. Her face was blotchy and uneven. Her dark green and black dress hung below her knees.

Most of the students had already heard stories about Frau Straufenberg from her previous students. Andrea slumped down in her chair as she watched the teacher. "Don't slouch at your desk. Sit up, Young Pioneer," snapped the teacher when she saw her. Andrea disliked her immediately, but quickly obeyed. "I am assuming that by now, most of you have become Young Pioneers. Of course, this year you move up to Thälmann Pioneers. As a Thälmann Pioneer, you need to be good examples for the younger students. This year you will be learning a lot about Ernst Thälmann. You will also start your Russian language training with a class every Wednesday. This is going to be a very exciting year for all of you."

As the teacher spoke, Andrea glanced around the room to see who was sitting nearby. She recognized all but one petite blonde girl who sat directly in front of her. Her name was Christa Ernst. She was shy and kept to herself. She looked like she was a little younger than the rest of the students in the class. Andrea and Christa did not speak much to one another during the first week of school. It was not until the second week, during lunch, that their friendship began to take root. On that day the students were served a small portion of bland ground beef with a serving of boiled potatoes and two pieces of overcooked carrots. Andrea finished her food quickly then noticed Christa picking reluctantly at her carrots.

"What's the matter?" Andrea asked, keeping her voice low.

"I don't like carrots," Christa answered, flicking the carrots around in her plate.

"You'd better eat them, or else you'll be punished."

"I don't care. They make me feel sick," Christa sulked.

Andrea quickly scouted her surroundings then stabbed one of Christa's carrots with her fork and placed it into her own plate.

"Are you crazy?!" whispered Christa. "You could get into a lot of trouble!"

Andrea looked around and, proud that no one had noticed, grinned and countered smugly, "They'll have to catch me first." She stabbed her fork into the second piece of carrot on Christa's plate and began eating it.

"Do you really like those things?" asked Christa.

"No, not really. They don't have any taste. They're boring." Andrea giggled.

"Wow! How can you eat them then?" They both giggled then stopped suddenly as the headmaster stood up and announced the end of lunch.

After that, the two girls became inseparable.

"Sunday it is a special day for the German Democratic Republic!" beamed Frau Straufenberg one morning in early November. "Who can tell me what day it is?" she asked the classroom. One boy raised his hand enthusiastically. "Dieter," she called upon him.

Dieter stood up beside his desk, cleared his throat, and exclaimed proudly, "It's our nation's birthday, Frau Straufenberg!"

"Very good," commended the teacher. "And why is this important?"

"Because it's the day we were freed."

"Excellent." Frau Straufenberg took two steps back and studied the children for a moment. "Leading up to Sunday, we are going to have a wonderful week. Tomorrow, we will have a guest from the Soviet Union who will come and speak to you about the war. He is a true Soviet hero. The day after that there will be a parade, and all Pioneers will be able to walk in it. Please be sure to wear your Pioneer colors for the parade." Andrea raised her hand. "Yes, Andrea?"

"What if we don't have a blue neckerchief?"

"You have time to get one," the teacher answered curtly. "Now, let us begin with our lesson."

Three days later Andrea sat in the school auditorium with about 500 other students. Christa sat beside her. They all eagerly awaited the guest speaker. Finally, a Soviet officer walked through the audience of children. He stood tall, proudly wearing his uniform, with medals lining his chest. He stepped up onto the stage toward a chair. "Let's welcome General Ivanov," announced one of the other teachers, and the auditorium erupted in applause.

General Ivanov stood in front of his chair for a moment, looking out over the crowd of cheering students. *"Für Frieden und Sozialismus, seid bereit!"* he called out.

As if it was rehearsed, the students in the auditorium

responded with a resounding *"Immer bereit!"* then brought their hands to their forehead.

"Seid bereit!" the general called out again, but this time even louder.

Once again, the students responded with, *"Immer bereit!"* followed by a salute.

"Seid bereit!" the general said one last time, but this time he cupped his ear with his hand and leaned into the audience as if to tell them to speak up.

"IMMER BEREIT!!" came one last response from the students, prompting the general to smile broadly.

"You are all wonderful Pioneers!" he said as he sat down. "I am pleased to have been invited here today to speak with you. It is always the biggest pleasure to talk to the youngsters of this great nation. You are the next generation. You are the future."

General Ivanov began pacing back and forth along the platform. "During the Great Patriotic War I helped to gather information on the Nazi regime in an operation that would eventually lead to their downfall..."

Andrea sat quietly and listened to the general's story. She found herself mesmerized by the man, who stood tall with a commanding presence. After his speech the teachers gave their students an opportunity to approach the platform to meet the general. Andrea felt reluctant, but found herself being dragged over to the platform by Christa. The two girls stood patiently until they reached the front of the line.

"And what is your name?" General Ivanov asked Andrea, who stood closest to him.

"Andi," she replied.

Then, just as he reached out to shake her hand, she caught a glimpse of a silver colored ring with a cross, identical to the one her real father once wore. The sight cit nearly took her breath away. Her eyes grew wide. Seeing her expression change, General Ivanov asked her, "Is there a problem?"

"I… I." She stopped, then pointed to his ring. "Your ring…"

"My ring?" The general looked down at his hand. "Ah yes. This was a gift from one of my men," he answered. "Why?"

"I don't know," Andrea muttered. "I just wanted to know. It's pretty." She changed her tone.

"As a matter of fact," he went on, "It once belonged to a criminal."

"A criminal?"

Just as the general was about to say something else, the teacher stepped up beside them. "Andrea and Christa, you've spoken to General Ivanov long enough. Head back to class now," she ordered. Christa quickly pulled her friend by the arm and they left the area together.

"What was that about?" asked Christa, once they left the auditorium.

"I didn't like him. He's a bad man and a liar. I know it."

"Are you crazy, Andi? What's wrong with you?"

"I don't want to talk about it." Andrea ran ahead toward her classroom, leaving Christa behind.

That evening Hanna invited Viktoria to join them for dinner. Andrea kept mostly to herself and barely spoke a word as they all sat around the table. Seeing the child picking at her food, Viktoria reached across the table and tapped Andrea's plate three times with her finger nail. "What's wrong, girl?" she asked.

"Nothing," replied Andrea without looking up.

"Don't lie to *Omi* Viktoria," she said. "I can tell when something is wrong. I might be old, but I have a lot of experience." She smiled warmly. "When you hurt, it makes me hurt. You can talk to us."

Andrea finally looked up and took a deep breath. "I..." She stopped, then pushed her soup away. "I'm not very hungry."

"Eat your soup," ordered Walter.

"I don't like it. It tastes like water," complained Andrea.

"Andi!" snapped Walter. "Apologize to your mother for your insult!"

"She's not my mother and you're not my father! My mother and father are both dead, and I'm sick of pretending all the time!" Andrea threw down her spoon and ran to her bedroom."

"Andi!" Hanna shouted after her before the door slammed. "Walter, can you please go talk to her?"

Viktoria put up her hand and cleared her throat. "Let me try," she volunteered. She slowly pulled her frail body up off her chair and made her way to Andrea's bedroom. She knocked gently on the door. When there was no answer, she turned the door knob and found it was not locked. "Little Andi... May we talk?"

"Go away." Andrea's voice was muffled. "Leave me alone."

Viktoria hesitated for a moment, but then approached the bed where Andrea lay with her face buried in her pillow. The old woman sat beside the girl. "Did you know that I once had a son?" she finally began. "He was my first born." As the old woman spoke, Andrea stopped crying and looked up at her. "His name was Heinrich. He was very strong and handsome and quite funny. You would have liked him. At 18 he became a soldier in the German Army. One year later he was killed by the Russians during World War I, when Germany and Russia went to war. That was about 40 years ago and I can still remember how much it hurt to hear the news of Heinrich's death." She paused a moment and wiped away a tear. "Of course, you never really heal completely when you lose a child. After grieving for nearly two years, I found out I was pregnant with my second child… Hanna. Now, while one child can never, nor should ever replace another child, Hanna brought joy back into my life and gave me a new purpose. She gave me the will to continue." Viktoria paused for effect before continuing. "After Hanna and Walter were married she found out she was pregnant. She gave birth to a baby girl."

Andrea sat up. "Where is she now?" she asked.

"Who?"

"Their daughter," Andrea answered.

Viktoria paused for a long moment, took a strained breath, and continued, "Anna was only four when she died at the end of the war, like so many other people. It was hard watching Hanna suffer through her sadness. For three years I thought she would never get over losing her child. She did recover somewhat, but she was never the same until… Well, do you know what really saved my daughter from her eternal sadness?" Andrea shook her head. "A special little girl came into her life. This little girl was about the same age that Anna was when she died. She came into all our lives actually." Andrea pointed to herself and raised her eyebrows in question. "Yes," continued Viktoria. "You. I truly believe you saved my daughter's life and I will always be grateful to you for it."

"*Omi*," Andrea said as she gazed up at Viktoria.

"Yes, *Schatzi*."

"Sometimes it really hurts… knowing that I will never see my real parents again."

"I know, Andi. I know, but you can't let it slow you down or destroy you. Your parents would not have wanted that." Viktoria sat beside Andrea, put her arm around her shoulders, and nodded her head. They sat together quietly.

"*Omi,*" Andrea broke the silence. "I saw something today."

"What did you see?" asked Viktoria as she continued to hold the child around the shoulders.

"A man from the Soviet Union came and spoke to the students in our school. I think he might have stolen my father's ring."

Viktoria's eyes grew wide with astonishment. "This is a strange observation. What makes you say this?" she asked.

"I don't know. He had on a ring that looked just like the one my father wore. I kind of remember that after my father was killed, one of the bad men took it off his hand. I think the general today was wearing the ring."

"You can't be too certain, Andi. It could have been a ring that looked like your father's. Not all rings are different, you know."

As Andrea sat quietly, memories of Johann holding her in his lap played through her mind. She would pick at her father's fingers, spinning the ring around, and push her fingernail into the small, green notch in the front of the ring. "*Omi.*" She broke the silence once more.

"Yes, *Schatzi.*"

"Why do you always seem so sad, and why do you tell *Mutter* and *Vater* that they should leave you?"

Viktoria looked down at the child, kissed the top of her head, and responded, slowly and carefully choosing her words. "I don't want any of you to leave me. I only want you to be happy."

"Why wouldn't we be happy here, near you?"

"Well, things are very different here than they were when I was younger."

"But the Nazis were bad people," observed Andrea, recalling her lessons from class.

Viktoria smiled and shook her head slowly. "I'm talking about times before the Nazis…"

"But, what about…"

Viktoria put her hand up in a gesture to stop Andrea's next question. "*Schatzi*, you ask too many questions. Why don't we go back and finish up with our dinner?"

They both walked back out to the dining area where Andrea apologized to Hanna and Walter, neither of whom had moved from the dinner table. She then approached Hanna and hugged her. Despite making amends with Hanna and Walter, however, Andrea could not shake from her mind the thoughts and ill-feelings she harbored against the general.

—+———*———+—

That Friday, Christa scampered over to Andrea, who sat alone outside on a step. "Andi! Andi!" she cried out. "Are you ready for the parade?" She stopped in front of Andrea and stared at her. "Why aren't you wearing your Pioneer outfit?" she asked.

Andrea reached out and picked up a small rock lying beside her shoe. "I don't have a blue neckerchief." She tossed the rock in front of her and frowned.

"What's wrong, Andi?" Andrea stood up, and began walking away. "Hey!" Christa called after her. "You're acting weird."

Andrea turned around. "It's a stupid parade and I don't want to walk in it. I don't want to be a Pioneer either. I hate the color blue!"

"Andi! Stop it! Do you want to get into trouble?"

"They said we don't have to do it if we don't want to."

"But why don't you want to? It's going to be so much fun!"

Andrea pressed her small lips together. "Can you keep a secret?" she asked.

"I'm great at keeping secrets," bragged Christa.

"Promise. You can't tell anyone!" insisted Andrea.

"I promise. I won't."

"Fine. I'll tell you then." Andrea sat back down on the step and pulled Christa down with her. "You know the general who came to talk to us the other day?"

"General Ivanov?"

Andrea nodded her head and continued, "Well, I think he was wearing my father's ring."

Christa crinkled her forehead. "Huh!? Why would he be wearing your father's ring?"

"Someone killed him and stole it."

"Someone killed your father? When?! I just saw you with him. What happ…?"

"No," interrupted Andrea, "I mean my real father."

Christa cringed. "I don't get it." She shook her head.

"A few years ago some bad men killed both my mother and father. Hanna and Walter, they're not my real parents."

"Really? And… But you think the man from the other day did it?"

"I don't know. I just don't know. All I know is that he was wearing my father's ring and I think he must have stolen it. He must have!"

Christa scratched her head. "So what are you going to do now?"

Andrea thought for a moment before answering, "I don't know. I only know that I don't want to be a Pioneer because that man wants us all to be pioneers and so it has to be bad to be one."

As the school year progressed, Andrea drifted further and further away from the daily extracurricular routine of the Pioneers. She even began to question the world around her. One day during her social studies class, when Frau Straufenberg was giving a lesson on socialism, Andrea raised her hand.

"Yes, Andrea?"

"Frau Straufenberg, if this socialism is so great, then why do so many people seem so unhappy? Are people happier in the West?"

The teacher was taken aback and turned around momentarily to hide her astonishment. Christa sat straight up in her seat, afraid of what would happen to her friend, while Andrea leaned over discretely and poked her in the back with her pencil, giggling at her own boldness.

The teacher then turned back around and answered, "I have great faith in my government. You must learn respect for one's country! As I have said in the past, at the end of the war Germany was divided in two. They created the *DDR* so that we could have equality and so that we can live in peace without being interrupted from the hard wall of money that comes with capitalism. Capitalism is the way of life in the West. Because of this capitalism, there is a lot of unhappiness in the West. There are beggars in the street, people starving. Do you understand? And this is why we have socialism… to be protected from this bad type of life."

Andrea shook her head. "If this capitalism is so bad and socialism is so good, then why do people want to change things here?"

The teacher pursed her lips and looked hard at Andrea, who stared back smugly, holding back a grin. Frau Straufenberg's tone grew stern. "Andrea, people who want to change things are merely ignorant. Don't… fall into that trap." When Andrea's smile disappeared, the teacher's expression softened. "You are still young. You will understand in due time," she said with a partial smile, which Andrea did not return.

When the school day had concluded, Frau Straufenberg dismissed the students, then stopped Andrea on her way out. "Andrea, I'm warning you. Don't ask such questions. Otherwise, you will find yourself facing the headmaster, and you know what happens when students go to see her," she said with a renewed sternness. Andrea shrunk back.

"I... I only wanted to understand, Frau Straufenberg," Andrea stammered, her voice growing weak as she looked up at the teacher.

"These are not the types of questions you need to be concerning yourself with. You are too young. Your job is to just learn and to trust our lessons."

"I only wanted to know why people seem unhappy," Andrea pressed back.

"I'm sorry if this is how you see it," the teacher responded.

"They kill people, don't they?"

"Who?"

"The Soviets, like that general who came here last year."

Frau Straufenberg's eyes grew wide at the child's comment. "Andrea, you will be punished for such comments!" her teacher promised. "What has gotten into you?"

"The men in trench coats are bad. They don't care who they kill!"

"Wha...?"

Andrea turned around and bolted out the door, ignoring her teacher's shouts.

She ran through the hallway, out the main entrance, and right past Christa. Her friend called out to her, but Andrea did not respond, too upset to hear anything.

When she arrived home she ran straight into her bedroom, slamming the door shut behind her. Hanna went to check on her. She opened the door and entered the room.

"What's wrong, Andi?" she asked concerned. Hanna

approached Andrea's bed and sat beside the weeping child. She laid her hand on Andrea's heaving back, hoping to console her. "Andi, what happened? Please talk to me."

"Nothing is good," sobbed Andrea. She buried her face into her white pillow, soaking it with her tears. "I don't ever want to go back. That school is bad! They like bad people."

"What are you talking about? Andi, please, tell me what happened." She suddenly heard a knock at the front door. "I'll be back," she whispered.

Hanna walked through the living room and opened the front door. It was Frau Straufenberg. Her expression was hardened and grim.

"Yes?"

"Hello. I am Frau Straufenberg, Andrea's teacher. Do you have a moment?"

"Oh, please do come in," said Hanna as she opened the door fully. The teacher entered the living room and sat on the sofa, across from Hanna. "Would you care for something to drink?"

"I am only here for a few minutes." Her voice was icy and piercing.

"What can I do for you?"

"We need to discuss your daughter, Andrea. There seems to be a problem with her at school."

"A problem?"

"Yes, you see, lately she has been disrupting the class and defying me during lessons. This must come to an immediate halt or there will be trouble... and I'm not talking about trouble for just her."

"I... don't... think I understand," Hanna said somewhat bemused.

"I was giving a lecture on our government when your daughter began asking insolent questions as to question the validity of our rule."

"I don't think I'm quite following you," Hanna said politely. "What exactly did she ask?"

"She wanted to know why so many people would feel a need to leave the city if the government was so wonderful," the teacher answered.

"She is only being curious."

"Frau Spangenberg, it is not the question she asked, but rather how she asked it."

"I see." Hanna tightened her lips, and then said, "I do apologize for her behavior. I'll have a talk with her."

Frau Straufenberg stood up and brushed herself off. Then, in a cold and piercing tone said, "I suggest you do." She took three steps toward the door then stopped and turned to face Hanna. "If she doesn't straighten up soon, I'll be forced to turn you in."

"I don't understand."

"It is quite obvious that she is being taught improper values here at home. I suggest you change her opinion... and soon." She stomped out the door.

Hanna stood speechless for a minute then went to rejoin Andrea in her room. Andrea had stopped crying and was sitting up on her bed.

"I'm sorry, *Mutter*," she said softly to Hanna.

"Did you hear our conversation?"

"Yes." Andrea looked down.

"This is a fine school. If you don't believe in everything they teach you, it's all right, but please try not to defy the teacher again. If you have questions about anything like that, then come to me." Hanna reached out and stroked Andrea's cheek, wiping away a final tear.

Andrea nodded her head in agreement.

From that day forward, Andrea merely took notes when necessary, just enough to pass her exams, and refused to allow the ideas to penetrate her mind. She knew that there was a reason so many people were running, but she could not understand, nor did she try to anymore.

CHAPTER TWENTY-ONE

AUGUST 1958

ugust break was one week away. During recess, Christa came running toward Andrea, nearly knocking her to the ground.

"Hello, Andi!" she panted out of breath.

"Why are you so happy today?" asked Andrea, attempting to recover her balance.

Ignoring her question, Christa spouted out, "Are you going to try out to be in ballet next year?"

Andrea felt her heart sink as she sat down on a stone step behind her and began sulking.

"What's the matter, Andi?" Christa sat beside her friend.

"Frau Straufenberg told me I'm not allowed to," she answered solemnly.

"What!? Why not?"

Andrea stared down at the ground as she spoke. "Because I'm different. Because I'm not a Thälmann Pioneer, like you. Because I ask too many questions. Because they don't like me."

"That's ridiculous!" snapped Christa. "You should still try out. You're probably the best person. I mean, look at you."

"I wish I could take lessons with you, Christa. My mother was a great dancer. She started teaching me before she was killed..." She stopped.

"We're talking about your real mother, right?"

"Right."

"Oh good. Because I can't imagine your mother now being a dancer... and besides, she's still alive!" They both laughed. "Why don't you try out anyway? The worse they can do is say no."

"I don't think the teacher will let me out of the classroom, but I'll try."

Later that day two women and a man got out of a sedan and climbed up the steps of the school. The headmaster greeted them and escorted them to the school auditorium. Moments later the voice of the headmaster came over the loud speaker. "As you probably know by now, today you have a unique opportunity to audition for ballet school for next year. For those of you interested in learning how to dance, please assemble at this time in the auditorium."

Andrea watched as several students, including Christa, stood up. One by one they approached Frau Straufenberg, who handed a student pass to each child. Andrea hesitated for a moment then rushed up behind her friend.

"Good luck to you," the teacher said as she handed Christa her pass. Andrea approached the teacher, smiled, and held out her hand as the teacher glowered at her. "Andrea, I thought we had already discussed this. You are not eligible to audition. Return to your seat."

"But..."

"Now!"

Andrea stopped smiling, pressed her lips tightly together, and fought back tears. She returned to her desk, where she sat down, glared at the teacher, and refused to participate for the duration of the class.

Within 45 minutes, all but Christa and one other girl had returned to the classroom. Half an hour before school ended both girls returned with a wide smile. Once the bell rang, Andrea leaped up and grabbed her friend by the arm. "Well?" she squealed. "What happened? How was it? Did you make it? Tell me everything!"

"I don't know," Christa chirped, "but I feel good about it. I think we'll find out next week."

As Christa and Andrea walked through the hallway toward the school exit, Andrea demanded more details about the auditions. Christa explained, "It was really kind of strange. Some of us were asked to copy certain steps, and others were sent away without even getting a chance to dance."

"What do you think they were looking for then?" asked Andrea, who now turned to face her friend.

"One girl, Gretchen from the other class… they told her she had a perfect neck."

"A perfect neck?" Andrea laughed, and scrunched her face. "What's that supposed to mean?"

"They like long necks," replied Christa. "The more you look like a giraffe, I guess, the better you're supposed to dance!" Both girls laughed.

"How funny!" Andrea brought her hand up to her mouth. "I never noticed that Gretchen looked like a giraffe! What about you?" She then pushed Christa's hair to the side. "What kind of neck do you have?" Christa lifted her head high and stretched her neck as far up as it would go. Andrea also lifted her head high and stretched her neck as far up as she could. "How about my neck?" she giggled. "Do you think I look like a giraffe too?"

Christa's eyes grew wide. "Wow, Andi!" she gasped "Your neck is longer than that Gretchen girl's! And look at your arms!"

"What's wrong with my arms?"

"They're so long."

"So now you are saying I'm a monkey with a giraffe neck?!"

"No, I'm saying you should've been able to try out. You're perfect."

Andrea smiled confidently, lifted her arms to the sides, and pointed one toe outward. "I told you my mother was a dancer. She was the greatest dancer in the world!" She then sprang forward. "She taught me to do this when I was little."

Christa suddenly grew serious. "Andi, you do really look like a dancer. You're beautiful. You would have been the first one they chose."

The girls were so caught up in their conversation that neither one noticed the three dance judges who now stood by the black sedan, watching them intently. The taller woman leaned over to the others and said something before walking toward the two girls. "Excuse me. You are Christa, right?" she said, startling them.

"Yes," Christa answered confidently.

"And who is your friend?" the woman asked.

"Andrea Spangenberg," Christa answered.

Andrea leaned toward her friend and whispered, "Who's she?"

"She gave us our audition," Christa whispered back.

"We would like to talk to you," said the woman.

Andrea raised her eyebrows and pointed to her chest. "Me?"

"Yes, you." As the other two judges approached, the woman stated, "I don't recall seeing you at the audition today?"

Andrea shifted her weight from side to side nervously. "I wasn't there because Frau Straufenberg told me I couldn't go," she answered.

"Who?"

"That's our teacher," interjected Christa.

Ignoring Christa, the woman ordered, "Put your arms out again and lift your head as high as you can." Andrea did as she was instructed. "Now bring your stomach in and push your shoulders back." The woman smiled. "Why did your teacher tell you that you couldn't audition?"

"I..." Andrea hesitated as she relaxed her stance. "I'm not a Pio..." She stopped. "She says that I'm too different."

"What's your name?" asked the man gently as he stepped up.

"Andrea Spangenberg."

The woman pulled out a small notebook and annotated the name. "And your teacher's name again?"

"Frau Straufenberg," Christa volunteered the information.

"Listen to me, Andrea. Don't be a fool. Join the Pioneer organization. Go to their next meeting tomorrow. We will be back in one week. I expect to see you when we return. Good day."

"What just happened?" Andrea asked her friend once they were alone.

"No idea."

Andrea raced home, the excitement in her mounting as she drew nearer to the apartment. She burst through the door and rushed to her bedroom, nearly knocking over Hanna, who was standing in the middle of the living room.

"Andi!" Hanna called to her as she regained her footing.

Andrea hurried over to her dresser and pulled open the bottom drawer. "Where are you? Where are you? Where are you?" she muttered to herself as she rummaged frantically. She opened the next one. "Ahhh..... Where is it?!" she began to raise her voice in frustration. She then slammed the drawer shut before opening the next one.

"What are you looking for?" she heard Hanna ask behind her.

Andrea swung around and exclaimed, "Where is my white blouse? I need my white blouse!"

"Have you checked the closet?"

"No. Will you check it for me… PLEASE?!!"

"Andi, stop being so frantic." She opened the door and pushed the small stack of clothes to the right. Hidden within was a small white blouse. "Is this it?" She held up the garment.

"Yes!" she exclaimed. "Now I need my blue neckerchief."

Hanna raised her eyebrows. "Have you had a change of heart?"

"No," snapped Andrea, "but it's the only way they will let me dance."

"Let you dance?"

Finally finding her blue neckerchief, Andrea plopped down on her bed and let out a big sigh. "Yes…" Hanna sat down beside her as the girl recounted the events that led up to her brief encounter with the three judges.

One week later, Christa and Andrea were informed of their official acceptance into dance school.

With the beginning of the new school year came the beginning of her ballet training. On the first day, having pre-arranged it with Hanna, Christa's mother met the girls at school. "Now, pay close attention. This is the way you will be going every day," she told them as she led them to the train station, and eventually to the *Staatliche Ballettschule Berlin*, where they would begin their ballet training.

Andrea's eyes grew wide. "That's the school!" she

exclaimed upon seeing the large, white four-story building with many windows.

A thin woman met them at the entrance. "Good afternoon," she said, "and welcome to the *Staatliche Ballettschule Berlin*. My name is Frau Gelbenstein. I am one of the instructors here." Her eyes danced from Andrea to Christa as she spoke. "Every day you will report here at this time. You will receive several hours of dance instruction. You will learn classic ballet the first hour and a half. This will be followed by other dance classes, repertoire and variation. Today you will be fitted for your leotards and get checked in. After that we will have time to go over some basics. We have some strict rules and policies that you must abide by."

Frau Gelbenstein was a graceful woman in her early forties, with dark hair and an ashen, almost ghostly, complexion. Andrea looked up to her immediately. She would become her primary ballet instructor.

Andrea quickly made new friends at the dance school. Christa, however, remained her closest friend. As time passed, the weather grew cold and damp. It was November. During recess one day, as they sat on a bench in the courtyard behind the school, Andrea announced her birthday to Christa. "My birthday is coming up soon," she said enthusiastically, "and my parents said I can have some friends at home."

Christa's eyes grew wide with excitement. "That sounds like fun!"

Andrea nodded confidently. "Well, you know, ten is a very important age."

"Why?"

"Because, it's the day you turn two digits old." She laughed out loud. "Will you come?" she asked.

"When is it?"

"Next Saturday, after school."

"Oh." Christa lowered her eyes and frowned, seemingly disappointed. "There's a meeting for the Pioneers. You should go too, you know."

"It's my birthday, Christa." Andrea frowned. "I'm not going. Can't you miss it just this once? They probably won't even notice you're gone."

"My parents want me to go."

Andrea became sullen and hung her head low. Then she sat up suddenly. "Why don't you ask your parents if you can miss the stupid meeting. It's only this one day."

"Well… I don't know. Let me think about it." When it was time for their next class both girls jumped up and ran back into the building.

The following weekend Andrea and Hanna rushed around the apartment making final preparations for the party. Once everything was in place, 15 minutes prior to the expected arrival of Andrea's guests, Walter brought out a medium-sized wrapped package. Andrea immediately scrambled to his side. "Is that my present?" she asked.

Walter smiled broadly and replied, "Actually it's a special gift from Medwin."

Andrea's eyes lit up. "*Vom Westen!*" she exclaimed. "This is the second time we've gotten a package from the West!" Medwin was Victoria's little brother, who lived in Bavaria. While Andrea had never actually met him, she knew all about him from Victoria's many anecdotes. Andrea put her hands gently around the package and smelled it. "You can tell it came from the West by the way it looks and smells," she said dreamily.

"Go ahead and open it before your friends arrive," urged Hanna, who had walked up behind her.

Andrea carefully folded down the edges of the package and then reached inside. First, she pulled out several packages of chewing gum. *"Kaugummi!"* she cried out. "There's enough here to share with the girls!" Also in the box she found chocolate, nail polish, a jar of peach preserves, a brush, several hair ties, and a doll dressed in a white tutu. "She's beautiful!" Andrea gasped, hugging the doll.

There was a knock at the door. Andrea raced over to answer it. It was Christa. Upon seeing her friend, Andrea gasped enthusiastically, "Your parents let you come!?"

"Yes, but it took some convincing."

"How did you get them to agree?"

"I told them that ten was a very important age. After all, it's the first day you are two digits old! How could they say no?" They both laughed.

By two o'clock all five girls from Andrea's various classes had arrived. The room was alive with laughter and squeals of delight. They indulged in chocolates and chewing gum, and had Hanna paint their fingernails with the nail polish. Andrea received an assortment of gifts, including a kaleidoscope, a knit hat, a coloring book, crayons, and a book of paper dolls. Andrea beamed, reveling in all the attention. Walter handed her the final gift. Both Hanna and Walter looked on eagerly as Andrea tore away the crimson paper, revealing a plain yellow box. She reached in and removed the lid, then froze. Inside the box was a pair of pink pointe shoes.

"My first pointe shoes!" Andrea squealed as she kissed the shoes and held them closely.

"Your teacher contacted us and told us that she thought you would be ready to dance *en pointe* in only a few more months," explained Walter.

"This is the best birthday ever!" Andrea beamed.

The months passed by and Andrea became completely immersed in her dance classes. There was nothing she enjoyed more. On too many occasions in her morning classes, learning about socialism and the history of the Soviet Union, her mind would easily drift to ballet. "Andrea! Pay attention. If you don't, you will be writing a ten-page report on Otto Grotewohl!" the teacher once warned. After school Andrea and Christa always raced each other outside to the train station to go to the ballet school.

One day, while riding the train, Andrea picked up a newspaper that had been left behind by a passenger. On the second page there was a large photo of Otto Grotewohl. "Who is that ugly man," Andrea asked blandly.

"Shhhhh! Be careful what you say!" hissed Christa.

Andrea took out a pencil and began drawing a mustache and beard on the photo. "I think he looks better this way," she joked.

"Stop that! You're going to get us in trouble, Andi!" Christa whispered harshly. Seeing that the woman sitting across from them was watching, Andrea immediately closed the newspaper and grinned at her.

After a moment of silence, Andrea whispered, "Have you ever been to the Western side?" Christa shook her head no. "I wonder if it's as bad as they say?" Christa shrugged her shoulders. "My *oma* wants us to move there," continued Andrea.

"Are you going to?" asked Christa.

"No. My parents want to stay close so that they can take care of her."

Although Andrea had never had an opportunity to visit, she spent hours daydreaming about the forbidden Western zones. Some of her peers in school spoke of visits they had made to the West. She was always intrigued by their stories. One day before Andrea's eleventh birthday, after learning that classes were cancelled, she grabbed Christa by the arm and began pulling her along the sidewalk.

"Where are we going?" squeaked Christa.

"Just follow me."

Christa succumbed to the peer pressure and together they stole away on the S-Bahn. They got off near the border on Friedrich Street. The air felt cool and crisp, but the sun shone through scattered clouds, warming the city.

"My parents will never allow me out of their sight again if they ever find out what we're doing," gasped Christa as they approached the border.

The girls stopped abruptly. Up ahead two guards were checking the identification papers of four young men.

"Maybe this isn't such a good idea, Andi," said Christa.

"Oh, come on! Don't be so scared. People cross over all the time!"

When Andrea spotted a large group of visitors approaching the border on foot, she had an idea.

"Come on, Christa. Follow me and don't say a word." She grabbed Christa by the hand and yanked her across the street to join the group of Germans on the other side.

"Please have your papers available for the border guards on the way out," a man's voice rang out from the front of the group.

"Pull out your student pass," whispered Andrea to her bewildered friend.

"Andi, I'm not sure..."

"Oh, come on! Trust me."

As they drew closer and closer to the border, Andrea noticed the guard off to the left fumbling through his pockets. She latched onto Christa's arm and began veering toward the preoccupied guard. The two girls whirled right past the man, each waving a paper in front of him as he continued fumbling through his pockets.

"How'd you do that?" gasped Christa.

"It's easy. All these guards are idiots," Andrea replied without conviction in her voice.

Before they knew it, they were on the other side, walking through Tiergarten. Andrea turned around and saw the Brandenburg Gate. "Look Christa!" she marveled. "It's so different looking at it from this side, don't you think?" They continued through Tiergarten, where families lined the sidewalks, enjoying afternoon strolls. They snickered past lovers sitting on benches. They stopped to watch an elderly woman beneath the trees feeding bread crumbs to a gaggle of greedy pigeons.

"It's all so … so… different…so happy. I knew it. I knew it couldn't be a bad place!" said Andrea. Before they knew it, nearly two hours had passed and they had traversed the entire Tiergarten.

They eventually came across a large deserted construction site. "What do you think it is?" asked Christa.

Andrea took note of a small sign in front of the building. "It says here that it is the Deutsche Oper," she said dreamily. "Let's look around," she insisted.

"Andi, I don't think that's a good idea," Christa balked, hoping to change her friend's mind.

Andrea ignored Christa's pleas and began making her way through the shell of the building. Not wanting to be left alone, Christa followed closely behind.

Once inside, the girls found a doorway leading to an unfinished auditorium. The air smelled of wood and cement, the walls were incomplete, and there were no seats yet installed. Andrea leaped up onto the stage area and gazed out over her surroundings. "I'll bet a million people will fit in here!" she exclaimed loudly. Christa stood there, watching her friend in silence. "Come on up here." Andrea motioned Christa to join her up on the stage. "Let's dance!"

Christa reluctantly jumped up onto the stage and stood by the edge, while she continued to watch Andrea, who was now leaping across the unfinished stage.

Suddenly they were both startled by a man's voice. "Hey! What are you two doing in here?" the voice rang out.

Andrea, who was in mid-leap, nearly toppled over as she came to an abrupt stop. Both girls turned to face the voice. A young man stepped out of the shadows and jumped up onto the stage.

"I asked you a question," he asserted firmly.

"I... I... ah...ah..." Christa began fumbling for her words, not knowing whether she should run or scream.

"I... I know it was wrong to come in here but I couldn't help it. This place is wonderful! We're leaving now," blurted Andrea. She turned and began walking away. Christa jumped to her side.

"Wait!" he yelled after them. They both froze, and then turned to face him again. "You're not from around here, are you?" The girls looked at each other nervously.

"No... I mean yes," answered Andrea, not knowing what to expect next.

"What brings you here, from the Soviet sector? Where are your parents?"

Andrea and Christa looked at each other, confused.

"But... but... how did you know where we came from?" asked Christa, trying to maintain her composure.

"It's so obvious."

Andrea folded her arms and straightened her back, not taking her eyes away from the stranger. "How?" she asked boldly.

"By the way you both dress. They only dress like that in the Soviet sector."

"What is that supposed to mean?" asked Andrea.

"You're too young to wear such dreary clothing," he

answered, referring to Andrea's black overcoat and dark brown shoes.

"What do you mean dreary?" Andrea felt hurt. "You're not very kind."

"How did you get here?"

"We walked," answered Andrea.

"You walked? All the way here?" He did not hide his astonishment.

"Mm hmm." Andrea nodded her head with renewed pride.

"Well, you ought to think about getting back. It's going to be dark soon and you don't want to be crossing through Tiergarten at night."

Just then Christa gasped, "Oh no! What time is it?"

The stranger looked down at his watch and answered, "It's almost eighteen hundred."

"Our parents are going to kill us!" she squealed.

"You're right. You're in serious trouble." He laughed at their predicament.

"I think we should get back right away," fretted Christa. "Our parents are probably looking for us by now." They turned and began walking away.

"Wait," the young man called after them. They stopped once more to face him. "I'll make you an offer," he began, carefully choosing his words. "I've been trying to reach a friend in the East. If you take a note to him, I'll give you a ride to the border in my car."

Andrea thought for a moment. "I'm not sure." She cringed.

"Come on," he urged. "It could save you some valuable time, and the sooner you get home, the less trouble there'll be."

Andrea thought for a moment then said, "Yes. We'll do it."

"Andi!" shrieked Christa.

"Oh, come on, Christa. We're already in enough trouble."

"And whose fault is that?" snapped Christa. She shook her head and frowned. "My God! My parents are going to lock me in my bedroom for a month!"

The young man chuckled, and then escorted them out of the shell of a building and to his vehicle, which both girls climbed into. He got behind the wheel, started the ignition, and drove off with a screech.

"So, how many people will fit in the theater?" Andrea asked after a while.

"Close to two thousand," he answered smiling with pride.

"Are you one of the men building it?"

"I'm one of the men in charge," he answered.

Once they reached the border he wrote something down on a piece of paper and folded it. He scribbled the name and address of his friend on the outside.

"He is not far north of here. When you get a chance, drop this note off to him. Thank you and good luck," he said, handing the note to Andrea.

"We won't be able to get it to him right away," Andrea informed him.

"As long as he gets it by the end of the month, everything should be fine."

Andrea tucked the note deeply into her pocket. The girls hopped out of the car and thanked the young stranger before he sped away. The sun was rapidly descending beyond the horizon. The girls' hearts skipped nervously as they headed to the border toward two armed guards.

"How are we going to get past them this time?" asked Christa. "I don't see any large groups crossing over."

Andrea took a deep breath and, without removing her eyes from the two border guards said, "We'll just show them our student passes again. It worked the first time!"

"Andi, I don't think that'll work this time." Christa's voice trembled.

"Why not?" Andrea finally looked at her friend. "Think about it. What will they do? Not let us go home? We're only children." She smiled, hoping to ease Christa's nerves, yet she was equally terrified.

"Halt," exclaimed one guard. "What are you two girls doing?"

"We're going home," answered Andrea matter-of-factly.

He looked around. "Where are your parents?" Andrea pointed toward the north.

"What are you two doing wandering about like that? Don't you know it's dangerous? Show me your identification papers."

Andrea and Christa handed him their student passes. He analyzed them for a brief moment then let out a hearty laugh. "Here, Fritz," he told the other guard. "Look at these." They both stood there laughing when Andrea spoke up.

"What's so funny?" she snapped.

"You crossed over with these?" he laughed as he waved the cards in the air.

Both girls nodded simultaneously.

"Wait here," he instructed. Then he turned to the other guard. "Make sure they don't go anywhere. If they do, you have my permission to shoot them." He laughed as he disappeared into a small shack. Minutes later he motioned the girls to join him inside. "Come on. Hurry up!" he called out. Inside, he instructed them to sit quietly on a wooden bench against the wall. Too terrified to protest, the girls followed his order. He closed the door behind them, leaving them alone in the darkened room. Christa was ashamed she had allowed her friend to talk her into this excursion and Andrea was ashamed she had gotten caught.

Half an hour passed when they heard Walter's familiar voice ring out angrily through the air. "Where is she?" he demanded.

"Walter, it won't help matters to be so angry." It was Hanna's voice.

Andrea and Christa leaped up off the bench as they heard the sound of several footsteps shuffling outside the shack. The guard opened the door and allowed Walter and Hanna to enter.

"They're all yours," he smirked. He turned to the girls and said sarcastically, "Good luck!"

Walter's face was red with anger. "Andrea," he began, refraining from lashing out at her, "you are punished for a year!" He turned and walked out, brushing past Hanna.

"Come on," sighed Hanna. "Let's go home. We'll escort you home too, Christa."

The girls followed in silence, glancing at each other only momentarily. They made their way to the S-Bahn and sat quietly the entire trip home. They first walked Christa home, watching her as she entered her building, then returned to their own apartment. Andrea could only assume the worst and hope she would not lose her best friend. Once they reached their own home, Hanna, maintaining a calm façade, ordered Andrea to go to her room.

The following day, after threatening Andrea with removing her from her dance classes, Walter consented to allow her to continue on the condition that she never repeat such a stunt again. Andrea agreed.

Two days later, as both girls left school to go to the *Staatliche Ballettschule Berlin*, Andrea reached into her coat pocket. "What's this?" she muttered to herself as she removed a semi crumpled up piece of paper. She crinkled her nose as she looked more closely at it. "Oh no!"

"What is it?" asked Christa, trying to look over

Andrea's shoulder.

"It's the note that we are supposed to deliver. I'd completely forgotten about it."

"What does it say?"

Andrea read the note aloud. *"It's going down November 7. Meet me at planned destination."* She looked up from the note. "It's signed *Rolf.*"

"He didn't look like a Rolf," said Christa. Andrea tapped her face with the note and continued with a puzzled expression, "That's very strange. What do you suppose *'it'* means?"

"I don't know," replied Christa, scratching her head.

"Well, *I'm* going to find out."

"Andi!"

"What?"

"I think you ought to throw the note in the garbage and forget all about it. We got in enough trouble already for doing what we did."

"I can't," Andrea said stubbornly. "A promise is a promise."

"When do you think you'll be able to do it? Tell me that."

"Quit treating me like a baby," Andrea snapped. "I'll do it during lunch one day at school."

"Have you gone crazy?!" Christa's eyes grew wide. "You're not allowed to leave the school until it's time to go to dance class!"

"I know, but when else can I do it?" Andrea found herself growing irritated by Christa's nervous attitude. "Besides, this place is not that far from school. We can do it during lunch. No one will look for us then."

"We? I'm not going with you. If my parents found out, I'd never be allowed out of the house again! They already don't trust me anymore. Big surprise, huh?!! And I can't do it after ballet either because my parents expect me to come home immediately after! If I'm even five minutes late, they are practically hanging on the doorstep until I show up!"

"Fine! Don't come! Be that way!" Andrea's voice had gone up an octave.

"Stop shouting at me, Andi!"

Andrea lowered her eyes. "I'm sorry. I'm just tired of the way everybody treats me these days. I get it at school. I get it at home. And now you're mad at me. Everybody hates me." Andrea tossed her head back and said, "Listen, you don't have to come with me if you don't want to. I'll understand. But don't tell anyone. Promise?"

"I promise," replied Christa.

"Thank you." Andrea realized she would be on her own this time.

***

It was drizzling rain outside when Andrea planned her move. At eleven o'clock, as the students lined up for lunch, both girls slipped away into the bathroom. Once inside, they made a quick sweep of the area to ensure that they were alone. Andrea headed toward a small window. "Let me try something," she said. "Get on your hands and knees." Andrea grasped Christa's shoulders and began pushing her downward to the floor.

"Wait a minute!" shrieked Christa as she stood up straight. "I'm not going to let you stand on my back with your dirty shoes. What will people think when they see me walking around with footprints on my back?"

Andrea laughed then removed her shoes. "Is that better?"

Christa rolled her eyes then crouched down on her hands and knees. Andrea stepped up onto her back and reached up toward the window. As she strained to open it, however, the window was stubbornly sealed shut by years of rust and neglect. Andrea pushed and pushed. Despite her efforts, the window would not budge.

"This is really making me angry," growled Andrea, her face turning red with frustration and strain.

"Try hitting the handle," suggested Christa.

"Good idea."

Andrea began tapping the metal bar on the side of the window, first lightly, then with increasing force. Again, the window would not budge. She decided to give it one final whack, which caused the window to shatter. Andrea lost her balance and fell on her back, landing beside Christa. *"Autsch!"* she shouted out in pain, clamping her eyes shut.

Christa quickly sat up, with a dazed expression on her face. Still on her back Andrea perched herself up onto her elbows. Just then a voice rang out behind them. "What is all the noise here? What is going on?" They looked up to see Frau Straufenberg standing over them. "Have you both gone mad? On your feet!" she bellowed. "You do realize you could be expelled from the ballet school!"

Andrea and Christa scrambled to their feet. "There... there was a large spider on the window," began Andrea, wide-eyed. "I was afraid it would bite someone if I didn't kill it first."

"Rubbish!" exclaimed the teacher. "Pick up your shoes. You're both in serious trouble!"

Andrea picked up her shoes and, before she could put them on, found herself being led out by the arm by Frau Straufenberg to the office of the headmaster. To everybody's surprise they were not expelled from school. However, from that moment on, they were watched closely.

There was one week remaining before the deadline to

deliver the note. Andrea had become obsessed with the idea. She had to act quickly and cautiously, and she could not afford to be caught. She decided to make her move on a Wednesday, knowing that neither Hanna nor Walter would be home during school that day.

After the first class, Andrea feigned illness, complaining of nausea to her teacher. Touching her forehead the teacher said, "You don't have a fever."

"I don't feel well," whined Andrea. "May I please be excused to go see the nurse?"

"Andrea, there is nothing wrong with you," the teacher insisted.

Just then, Andrea began making gagging noises. "Oh no!" she exclaimed. She grabbed her mouth with one hand as she rushed over to the trashcan beside the front door. She fell to her knees and held the trashcan tightly, placing her head inside. Seeing this, the teacher rushed to her desk, wrote a pass, and sent her on her way. Andrea rushed off to the nurse's office. Before entering, she cleared her throat, shook her head, fluffed her hair with both hands, and then changed her expression to a more sullen one. The nurse, a frail aging woman, greeted her at the door and instructed her to be seated. "What is wrong?" she asked.

"I don't feel well all of a sudden," explained Andrea. "Maybe it was something I ate, but I feel like throwing up." She clasped her stomach and cringed for effect.

"Let's check your temperature," suggested the nurse as she turned around and reached into a nearby drawer, removing a thermometer.

Seeing this, Andrea leaped up and began wailing, "I need a bathroom! I'm going to be sick!"

The nurse rushed her across the office and into the bathroom. Once inside Andrea turned, excused herself then closed the bathroom door behind her, leaving the stunned nurse outside. She stepped up to the toilet, stuck her finger down her throat to help her create a perfect gagging sound. After several minutes she flushed the toilet then exited the bathroom, patting her mouth with her handkerchief. "Please forgive me," she said to the nurse. "I don't know what's wrong. May I please go home now?"

"Certainly," replied the nurse sympathetically. "Is your mother home?"

Andrea nodded her head, sighed, and wrapped her arms around her stomach, gazing downward. "I don't live very far from here. I'll be fine," she said.

The nurse hesitated at first. "Very well," she finally said. "Just make sure you go straight home." She wrote up a special pass and sent Andrea on her way.

Next stop, Wolfgang, Andrea thought as she skipped away from school in the opposite direction from that of her home. The address on the paper brought her to an old gray warehouse located in an industrial neighborhood. As Andrea neared the building she saw several men driving cranes and loading boxed merchandise into trucks in front. After a moment of hesitation, she approached one of the workers.

"Excuse me!" she called out to the stranger. "I'm looking for Herr Wolfgang."

The man pointed through a large entrance on the side of the building. Andrea thanked him before disappearing into the building. Inside, she saw a young, heavyset man with a black flowing beard.

"Excuse me," she began. "But could you please tell me where I can find Herr Wolfgang?"

"That's me," he replied. "What do you want? Shouldn't you be in school, little girl?"

Ignoring his last question, Andrea said, "Herr Wolfgang, I am here to deliver a very important note to you from …

eh… Herr Rolf." She handed him the letter.

He smiled at the young girl then uttered patronizingly, "So, now they are sending children to do their dirty work!"

Irritated by his comment, Andrea's eyes narrowed. "I'm not a child," she insisted sternly.

He read the writing silently then glanced back at Andrea. "Is that all?" he asked.

"Yes," she answered disdainfully.

He reached into his pocket, pulled out some change and handed it to her. "Good, then get out of here."

Ignoring his order she stood up on her toes trying to see the note. "What's the note for?" she asked.

"It doesn't concern you," he replied, folding it back.

"Well, I did risk my life to bring it to you," she said matter-of-factly. "The least you can do is tell me what it's for." She put her hands on her hips and shifted her weight to one leg.

"This is not for children. Off with you!"

"Are you trying to leave the Republic?" she finally asked.

"No! Now go away!"

"Then who is?"

His face grew red with impatience. "Listen, you! Stop asking questions or you might get hurt. Now leave!" He pointed toward the exit.

Andrea left without any further questions.

CHAPTER TWENTY-TWO

AUGUST 1961

Viktoria's health took a turn for the worse. She refused to seek medical attention, proclaiming that life would be better on the other side. She was bedridden, with Hanna spending most of her days tending to her, trying to coax her into eating and drinking. Viktoria would occasionally take one or two bites, then simply smile at her daughter's insistence.

"Ahhhh… *Schatzi*," Viktoria said one day when Hanna and Andrea were visiting her. "I don't know why you must be so stubborn."

"What do you mean, *Mutter*?" asked Hanna, who sat in a wooden chair beside her mother's bed.

"You need to leave, my little *Schatzi*." She smiled at Andrea. "You should not be raising Andi here. She deserves so much more. Show her what Germany really is. I have lived the life before the Nazis came. They are gone now, but we are ruled by another force. We are puppets of the Soviets. People are leaving the city every day. That should tell you something. The government could crack at any moment. You must leave before it's too late."

"Shhhh shhhh, *Mutter*. Everything is going to be fine

here in the Republic. You need to get better, and I need to be here for you, to help you," Hanna retorted. She cleared her throat and smiled confidently. "Besides, Walter has an important job on the other side. They can't stop him from working. That would be foolish. If they did that, then they would have to find him another job, along with countless many others, and I seriously doubt they're prepared to do that. Now get some sleep. Everything's going to be all right." Viktoria smiled, closed her eyes, and dozed off to sleep. "Come," Hanna whispered to Andrea. "Let's go back home. I have to cook dinner."

Exactly one week later, following his usual routine, Walter woke up at four o'clock in the morning, quickly ate two pieces of grilled bread, and drank half a cup of ersatz coffee, then scrambled out the door. He was in a hurry to get to work. His company had an especially large order of brass pipes that were needed for a new construction site, and all the employees were asked to show up extra early to meet the deadline. The sun had not yet risen when Walter hopped on his bicycle and peddled out.

By the time Walter reached the usual border crossing, the sun was just beginning to appear over the horizon. As he drew closer to the border, however, he immediately noticed that something was wrong. Several people were raising their voices in anger. Just then, an elderly German man walked past Walter and muttered, "They've closed the streets." Walter stopped peddling and put his feet down on the sidewalk to catch his balance. He watched the man walk away in disbelief, but, nevertheless, he decided to approach the border to cross. Walter removed his identification paper from his pocket and approached the guards. "Go back to your home," one guard ordered. "There will be no more crossing."

"But I have to work!" Walter pleaded.

"You will have to get another job. If your job was located in the American sector, you are no longer employed there." The man turned away to address another bewildered man hoping to cross over the border.

"But… this is not right. My job needs me," urged Walter.

"This is not my problem, and it is no longer your problem either. Now, leave the area," demanded another guard.

Walter left the area, as he was instructed, but rather than returning home, he rode his bicycle to a different exit point. Along the way he saw the barbed wire stretched across the city, practically chopping the city in half. When he realized that there were no other exit points that he could take with his bicycle, he peddled to the train station, left his bicycle locked up out on the sidewalk and hopped on the train. Finally, when that did not work either and he was turned back, he returned home, completely stunned by the morning's events.

Walter startled Hanna as he entered the apartment. "Walter! What are you doing home so early? I thought you had a big job today at the factory." Walter said nothing. Instead, in a trance, he walked over to the dining room table, sat down, buried his face in his hands, and began to weep. Seeing this, Hanna rushed to his side. "What's wrong?! What happened?"

Once Walter had managed to compose himself, he explained, "We have become prisoners of the city."

"What?! What about your job?"

"They told me to find a different job."

Two days later, East German authorities began constructing a wall, dividing the Soviet sector from the Western sectors. One week after that, Viktoria passed away.

ow 17 years old, Andrea had blossomed in both beauty and talent. Both she and Christa were preparing to graduate from the *Staatliche Ballettschule Berlin*. One day the dance instructor explained to Andrea's class that as part of their graduation repertoire a panel of judges from the *Deutsche Staatsoper* would come and test each student. The test would serve three purposes. First, it would be a test of skills, necessary to graduate. Second, the top dancers would go on to audition for various parts in a revival of *Coppelia*. Finally, it was part of a hiring process to see who would qualify to work for the *Staatsoper*. The classroom broke into a low murmur as Frau Gelbenstein made the announcement. When the students were released from school, she called out to Andrea.

"Will you wait for me outside?" Andrea asked Christa.

"Of course!" answered Christa.

"Andrea," began the instructor with a serious tone. "Many of the graduating class will have an opportunity to work for the *Staatsoper*, mostly performing in the *corps de ballet*. However, we believe that you are good enough to land a lead role. This means you will have to devote extra time to your dance.

"I… I don't have much time left… with school and homework and meetings."

"You will." Her instructor smiled. "The director will be contacting your school to work out an arrangement. We would like to groom you for the lead role of Swanilda."

Andrea's heart skipped a beat. "Oh, thank you!"

"There is one more thing, Andrea."

Andrea swung around. "Yes, Frau Gelbenstein?"

"There is one other student in your graduating class who will be groomed as well. I believe she also goes to the same school as you do."

"Who's that?" asked Andrea.

"Gretchen, from the other class. Gretchen Schnidler."

"Gretchen?" Andrea cringed. They had an ongoing rivalry, which began the day they were both first selected to attend the dance school.

"Yes. Is there a problem?"

"No, Frau Gelbenstein." Andrea forced a smile. "Will we both be working together then?"

The dance instructor smiled and replied, "No, Andrea. We want you to work separately. I will be coaching you and Gretchen will be with Herr Eichmann." Andrea frowned. Herr Eichmann was one of the top dance instructors in the school. "Don't worry," Frau Gelbenstein insisted. "You will have just as much of a chance as Gretchen."

"Thank you, Frau Gelbenstein." Andrea nodded her head then darted out the door to rejoin Christa, who had been waiting outside, eager to find out the details of the conversation.

Over the next few months, Andrea left school two hours early every day and caught the train to go to the Ballet School. The work was grueling, but Andrea never slowed her pace, determined to win the lead. She knew the competition for the role of Swanilda would be fierce. On the day of the test Andrea and Christa decided to take a lengthy detour by the *Staatsoper*. As they walked down Unter den Linden, several young men stopped and whistled at them. Andrea held herself erectly and proudly, fully absorbing the compliments. Then, feigning aversion, she turned to Christa and exclaimed, "How rude!"

"Oh! You enjoy it!" teased Christa.

"But I still think it is rude!" A slight blush came to Andrea's face as they both giggled and walked on.

Just then, two young boys raced toward them. Before Andrea could step out of their way in time, they whirled past her, knocking her bag of clothes out of her hands and spilling the contents onto the ground. Andrea shouted after them, shaking her fist. "Stupid idiots!" she scowled beneath her breath.

As Andrea bent over to retrieve her belongings, a young border guard, who happened to be walking by, stopped to assist. He smiled as their eyes met. Andrea felt a strange sensation deep in the pit of her abdomen as their eyes locked. Then, as they both stood up, he stood tall with perfect military bearing. He gazed back at Andrea. Finally he handed Andrea her ballet slippers. She looked downward bashfully toward the ground, and mumbled a slight, "Thank you," as she took hold of the shoes.

Afraid they would be late for their test, Christa began tugging at Andrea's arm, saying, "Come on, Andi. We have to hurry." Andrea snapped back into reality and took off.

"Wasn't he just magnificent?! I've never met anyone like him before!" Andrea marveled as they quickened their steps.

"I would hardly say you met," Christa countered with a smirk. She then asked, "So, are you ready for the test?"

Andrea nodded her head. They both walked the

remainder of the way in silence, each preoccupied with her own thoughts.

As expected, the test was rigorous. A panel of judges stood by, waiting to select the most talented dancers of the group, while also grading the rest of the group for their final evaluation. One by one the judges called each dancer in to a private studio to demonstrate their newly prepared routine. Outside the studio the room was buzzing with excitement. Christa was the third girl to test. When she was called, she peered back at Andrea for reassurance and threw her an expression of apprehension before disappearing through the door. When she returned, Andrea rushed up to her friend to hear the news.

"I did horribly," she muttered in obvious self-pity. "I might graduate, but I doubt they will ever hire me."

Andrea patted her friend on the back, saying, "You can't think that way. There will be other opportunities if this one doesn't work out for you. Do you want to talk about it?" Andrea asked.

"No. But I do hope you make it, Andi. You deserve it!" They both smiled.

"Thank you."

Just then, Andrea heard her name being called.

"Toi toi toi!" Christa called out sincerely. Andrea acknowledged her friend's words with a grin before disappearing through the doors.

Once inside the next room, Andrea boldly faced a panel of mostly unfamiliar faces and confidently introduced herself. "My name is Andrea Spangenburg and today I will be dancing the first act variation from *Giselle*." She could hear her heart pounding. Eventually, when the music kicked on, Andrea quickly dismissed her fears. At the end of her routine she gave a quick curtsy to the judges and retreated from the room.

Christa met her as she walked through the door. "So!" she exclaimed. "How did you do?"

Andrea shrugged. "I'm not sure. But I feel pretty good about it."

Then it was Gretchen's turn to be called in. After her test, she felt equally enthusiastic about her efforts. Andrea overheard her telling a friend, "Not only am I going to be hired, but I'm certain they already think I'm perfect to be Swanilda!"

A little later the instructor entered the room and addressed the anxious girls. "We've almost completed our selection process, but first we need to see Christa and Stefani. You will go into the room and be judged on several chosen steps."

Christa's eyes grew wide as she stood up, barely able to contain herself. Christa and Stefani disappeared through the door. They came out ten minutes later, both with a sober expression. Christa walked up and stood beside Andrea, but said nothing. Frau Gelbenstein emerged from the room and scanned all the eager faces.

"The judges have already made a decision, but first I would like to congratulate each one of you. These tests are never easy, but you all did well. Our judges have selected three of you to become permanent members of the *Staatsoper*." Andrea and Christa locked their arms together in anticipation." They are Gretchen Schnidler, Andrea Spangenberg..." Andrea felt Christa's arm tighten around hers. "...and Stefani Waldorf."

Christa's shoulders slumped down and she loosened her lock on Andrea while a murmur went through the room. "I'm so sorry," Andrea whispered.

Frau Gelbenstein put her hand up to calm the class. "Quiet, please. The rest of you will have other chances. This is just a first step. The three girls who were selected, however, will go on to audition for *Coppelia* in three weeks."

⊹ ⸺ ✳ ⸺ ⊹

Three weeks later, Andrea made her way to the auditions, which were scheduled to begin at six o'clock that evening. She entered a small building situated beside the main auditorium. At the entrance a thin gentleman with a dangling black mustache met her. "What is your name?" he asked. His tone was resonating.

"I'm Andrea Spangenberg."

He handed her a small yellow sheet of paper with the number 38 in bold black ink and four safety pins. "Attach this number onto the front of your leotard where it is clearly visible," he instructed.

Andrea's heart began racing wildly as she made her way toward the rehearsal stage. The room was bright. Some of the other dancers were already there, stretching and warming up. After putting on her ballet shoes and finding a spot on the wooden floor to put her belongings, she walked up a few steps and onto the stage. Gretchen was off to the side of the stage, stretching and appearing overly confident. Andrea's eyes narrowed as she watched her competition, her adversary. Gretchen looked up. They made eye contact, both freezing momentarily. Andrea quickly averted her eyes.

"Let's get started," came a woman's voice. Andrea did not see her, but the voice seemed to come from a long balcony in the room. The dancers grew still as the man who had greeted Andrea at the door walked up the steps and onto the stage. "Good evening," he said with a distinct Russian accent. "My name is Vadim. I am a choreographer. For the next hour we will be going over several steps and movements. It will be rigorous and you are all expected to keep up." His voice sounded cold and demanding.

There were approximately fifty girls on the stage. Vadim quickly found his spot center stage. He nodded to a woman sitting at a piano nearby. "Begin!" he said with a nod.

The sound of the piano began filling the room. It was a slow movement. Andrea did not recognize the tune. Vadim led the dancers through a series of common steps. As time passed, the steps became increasingly challenging. Andrea could feel the sweat trickling down her neck as she struggled to maintain the pace. By now Vadim was calling out step after step, "arabesque, fouette, pirouette..." Andrea found the pace ridiculous, without any real order.

By the time all the dancers had passed through the front line, she was exhausted. After nearly an hour, Vadim stopped and he instructed the dancers to stand by. He walked down the steps, heading toward the back of the room, where a woman had been observing the dancers. Andrea could not hear their conversation.

"So, Mitzi," he began. "What do you think?"

Mitzi Kaisendorf ran her long, slender fingers through her dark, shoulder length hair, which by now was streaked with gray. "There are some fine dancers in the group," she answered in a soft voice. "I've managed to narrow it down to these five." She pulled out a piece of paper with the five numbers written on them.

Vadim took the paper and analyzed it carefully. "Good choice," he agreed. He walked back up onto the stage. "If I call out your number please remain here. The rest of you, thank you very much for your time. "Numbers three, ten, twenty, twenty four and thirty eight."

Andrea's eyes grew wide at the mention of her number. She glanced around to see her competition. Number three, Gretchen, stood in front of her. The dancers who had not been selected quickly cleared the stage, leaving behind the five eager young women with expressions of disquieting hope.

Young men began making their way into the rehearsal auditorium for the next round of auditions and Mitzi's voice rang out, from the back of the room, with great authority. "Take a break. We'll continue where we left off in fifteen minutes. Get a drink of water and catch your breaths."

Andrea opted to remain on stage, where she practiced several steps that had caused her some difficulty during the first round. Within ten minutes she was startled by three loud claps, followed by an authoritative voice. "Let's get started!" Mitzi's voice reverberated throughout the auditorium.

Vadim returned to the stage. "We don't have much time left." His mustache twitched. "In the next half hour, we will test each one of you individually."

Each dancer was required to dance a variation that they had just learned. Mitzi watched offstage. She was rather impressed with number three, Gretchen, as she danced each step to near perfection. Gretchen, despite being new, would be difficult to beat.

Before Andrea knew it, it was her turn to take the stage. As she began to dance, Mitzi suddenly stopped taking notes and leaned forward, watching Andrea intently. Once the number ended she sat in silence, staring at the young girl before her.

"Mitzi. Mitzi, have you decided." Vadim's voice startled her out of her trance.

"Hand me the list of names, Vadim," she ordered without taking her eyes off Andrea, who stood alone on stage, awaiting her next instructions.

He handed her the notebook. She scanned down the page. "Hmm, Andrea Spangenberg. Date of birth - November 5th, 1948." She stopped. "Wow. How ironic," she muttered softly.

"What is?" asked Vadim, hearing her words.

Mitzi smiled and leaned back. "Number thirty eight just reminds me so much of someone I knew years ago. It's uncanny, the similarities."

"Are you sure it's not her? You seem disturbed, as if you've seen a ghost."

"Impossible. She died… along with the rest of her family." Mitzi shook her head.

"I see." Vadim hesitated a moment then pressed, "So, what do you want to do next? Have you reached a decision? We need to start soon with the next set of auditions otherwise it's going to be a long day."

"Not yet," Mitzi responded. "How about you? What are your thoughts?" she asked him.

"I'm torn between numbers three and ten," he replied dryly.

Mitzi glanced down at the list of names, "Gretchen Schnidler," she said softly. "I've never seen her before." She looked back up at Vadim. "What do you think of number thirty eight?"

He nodded his head quickly and replied, "She's quite good, but her lack of experience shows through." He cleared his throat and continued sternly, "and you would be wise to not select someone simply because she reminds you of an old dead friend."

Mitzi raised her eyebrows and pressed her lips together. "You can be so callous in your wording sometimes, Vadim," she shot back. "I don't know why I choose to work with you."

"Because I'm the best in Russia and you are the best in the *DDR*. We are an ideal team. Besides, there would be no revival without me," he smirked.

Mitzi shook her head, then instructed Vadim to call the rest of the finalists back onto the stage. She then walked up the steps onto the stage and addressed the group.

"You all did an excellent job today. We will be casting the leads along with their understudies. You'll each be hearing from me within the next week, either through your dance instructors or by telegram." She turned and left the area.

—⊁————⊁————⊁—

The next seven days proved to be agonizing for Andrea. The following week, during her last dance class, the director of the ballet school entered unexpectedly. He smiled broadly as he put up his hand. "I have an announcement to make. Gather around. I received a telephone call from Frau Kaisendorf, the director of *Coppelia*," he began. Andrea felt a jolt of energy race through her body at the words. She braced herself for the results. He continued, "I am proud to announce that one of our very own students will dance the lead role of Swanilda." He turned and looked at Andrea. "Congratulations to Andrea Spangenberg."

The class broke out into a loud applause. Andrea stopped breathing, her heart seemingly palpitating spasmodically. It was a dream-come-true. She struggled to remain calm, feeling as if she would burst at any moment. The director handed Andrea a piece of paper that had written on it the date, time, and location of her first rehearsals. The remainder of the class was a blur to Andrea.

Later on that day, when Christa caught up to her friend, Andrea latched onto her forearms and exclaimed, "Am I dreaming, Christa?!"

After quieting down, except for her heavy breathing, she ducked behind Christa. "There's Gretchen Schnidler," she pointed out as she peered over her friend's right shoulder.

Christa turned around and sneered, "I'll bet she's crazy

with envy right now."

"Well, I'll try not to be too cruel," said Andrea. "Perhaps we should make the last week a special week. We'll call it, 'Be Kind to Gretchen Week.'" They both laughed and headed home, half walking, half skipping before each turned off into her respective street, waving to one another as the distance between them grew.

CHAPTER TWENTY-FOUR

JUNE 1966

ndrea's first day of rehearsal came quickly. She had already graduated from dance school and now she dreamed of one day becoming a principal ballerina. After dressing and eating a light breakfast, she kissed Hanna and darted out the door.

"Andi!" Hanna called after her.

"I have to go, *Mutter*! I don't want to be late!"

She took off down the street to catch the S-Bahn. Unfortunately, in her haste, she caught the wrong train, causing her to arrive late. Vadim stepped up behind her and tapped her on the shoulder. "Never never never arrive after me again," he hissed. "You've missed the warm up. Now hurry up and join the rest of the group."

Andrea's face turned red. "I'm sorry," she gasped. "It won't happen again."

"It had better not," Vadim threatened. "You are the lead, and therefore critical to this entire production. If you miss the warm up, you risk injury. If you are injured, you hurt the production."

"Vadim, lay off," came Mitzi's voice as she stepped away from the group and approached Andrea. "It's just the first day." Mitzi whisked Andrea away and off to the side.

"I'm… I'm truly sorry about being late, Frau Kaisendorf," Andrea repeated. "I got on the wrong train somehow."

Mitzi smiled. "Calm down, Andrea. Vadim was born uptight. He can be pretty head-strong too, but we really need him for this production. You're going to be working with him one on one a lot, so you might as well get used to him now."

Andrea nodded quickly. "I understand."

Over the next few hours Andrea worked with Vadim to learn about her character and some of the movements. His temper was short and he was easily irritated. By the end of the morning she was physically and emotionally exhausted. After lunch, she returned to the studio. Vadim was off in the corner laughing and joking with Leah, dancer number ten from the auditions. Upon seeing Andrea, he walked up to her.

"Are you ready for round two?" he asked with a forced grin.

"Yes, I am." Andrea glanced up at Leah, who shook her head slightly, then turned away and began warming up for the next round of rehearsals.

Over the next few weeks Andrea spent countless hours working with Vadim, one on one, trying to perfect each step and memorize her routines. While she looked forward to the rehearsals, she often dreaded having to endure his harsh criticism. Then one day, unable to withstand it much longer, she lashed out at him. "What is your problem?!" she exclaimed. "Why is everything that I do wrong to you?!"

"Swanilda should not have been yours. Plain and simple," Vadim spouted out. "There! I've said what I've wanted to say since you were selected."

"Wha…?" Andrea stood in stunned silence.

Vadim bit his lower lip. "You are a fine dancer, Andrea.

However, you were not the best fit for the role. We need a more experienced dancer for the part."

"And who would that be?" asked Andrea somewhat sarcastically. "Leah I suppose?"

"As a matter of fact, yes. Leah has been performing solos for five years now. She does not need much prompting on what to do next."

"So… so why did I get the part then?"

"I had nothing to do with it. Our dear director chose you. Just focus better!" He stormed out of the room, leaving Andrea feeling perplexed and angry.

A few minutes later Mitzi returned. "Where's Vadim?" she innocently asked.

"Frau Kaisendorf," began Andrea, "I can't work with him anymore."

"What? What's going on, Andrea?"

"He hates me. It is so obvious."

"Vadim doesn't hate you. What makes you say that?" Mitzi raised her eyebrows in astonishment.

"He does nothing but criticize me," explained Andrea.

"That sounds like Vadim. So, if that's the case, then he hates everyone."

Andrea's lips puckered. "He doesn't hate Leah! He told me that I shouldn't be in this role. He's obviously angry that Leah is not dancing the part and he's taking it out on me!"

"I see." Mitzi thought for a moment, trying to find the right words. "Andrea, I awarded you the part because of everything about you: your talent, look, grace, and determination. Don't ever stop believing in yourself because of one person's ideas. There's more that goes into making a great dancer than just raw talent. Besides, I'm the director and therefore it's my decision. I believe in you and you were the best choice for the role." Mitzi paused before continuing. "You know, someone once gave me a chance and without her I wouldn't be here today." She took a deep breath and swallowed. "So stop worrying about it and let's get started again. How about if I work with you for a while, and give you a break from Vadim? You both probably could use a break."

"Thank you."

⸙

Summer flew by quickly. Busy with her rehearsals and too tired for much else, Andrea had little contact with Christa or any other friends outside of those she made in the dance company.

One day, as Andrea headed out the door, Mitzi stopped her. "You have a birthday coming up, don't you?" she said.

"You have an amazing memory, Frau Kaisendorf," remarked Andrea.

Mitzi let out a soft chuckle. "Why don't you come over to my house this weekend? We can celebrate. You can meet my husband. Besides, I have a dress I'd like to give to you. It no longer fits me and it would look lovely on you."

"I'd like that very much!" Andrea gleamed at the suggestion. She had grown quite fond of Mitzi. Oddly, there was something distinctly familiar about her, but she could not put her finger on it.

"Shall I invite Vadim as well?" Mitzi asked with a mocking grin. Seeing the look of horror on Andrea's face, she smiled. "I'm kidding."

They both laughed.

⸙

A few days later, as planned, Andrea found her way to Mitzi's house. A man answered the door. "Ooooh," he said, seemingly startled. "You must be Andrea." He stood in the doorway staring at her for a minute, wide-eyed. It was an awkward moment for Andrea.

"Um… Yes. That's me," Andrea responded. "It's nice to meet you. You must be Herr Kaisendorf."

As Andrea tried to peer over his shoulder and into the house, Mitzi came up behind Hans and eased him to the side. "Hans," she said, "don't be rude. Let our guest in."

"Sorry!" he gasped, coming out of his temporary trance. "I didn't mean to be rude. It's just that…" He stopped himself. "Please. Come in!" He took a step backward and Andrea walked past him, staring at her surroundings.

Andrea was just about to comment on the house when Mitzi spoke up. "Andrea, would you like something to drink?" she asked. "How about some soda or some tea?"

"I…I would love to try soda. I've never had any before."

"I'll have one too, Hans." Mitzi grinned as Hans disappeared into the kitchen.

He returned a few minutes later, carrying two filled glasses. He then stared again at their guest. "It's simply remarkable," he said, shaking his head slowly without pulling his eyes away from Andrea. "If I didn't know better, I'd say Ingrid rose from the dead."

"Who?" asked Andrea as she took a sip of her soda.

"Oh. Ingrid was a dear friend of ours. She changed my life," explained Mitzi. She stood up and walked over to a nearby oak table, picked up a framed picture, and handed it to Andrea. The child in the picture was almost four years old. Mitzi pointed to Ingrid in the picture. "Here is Ingrid. You look just like her… well, except a little younger of course; And that's Johann, her husband, and that…" she pointed to the little girl in the photo, then looked up at Andrea to see that her face had turned pale. "Andrea? What seems to be…?"

"I remember...," Andrea muttered. Her voice was barely audible.

"Excuse me?"

"I ...remember...when they took that picture." Her voice quivered and her eyes grew watery as the recollection flooded her memory. Mitzi and Hans froze, their eyes wide at what was unfolding before them. "I didn't want to wear that dress. I wanted to wear a different one instead because that one was too big, and so I remember being very angry, but *Papi* knew how to make me stop being angry. He told me I was prettiest in that one." Lost in the moment, Andrea ran her finger over the image of the dress.

Mitzi glanced over at Hans, then back at Andrea. "Andi? You're Ingrid's Andi?" She brought her hand to her mouth and grew silent as tears began to trickle down her cheeks. "But...they said you died... along with your parents."

Andrea bit her lip, trying to fight tears. "I... No. I didn't." She looked at Mitzi. "It was you who was always there helping my mother, wasn't it? You and Hans... you both lived with us... in this house," she said as she pointed to the ground.

Hans' eyes drifted back and forth between the two women before he finally spoke. "It seems that we have a lot to talk about," he said.

As he said this, Mitzi reached out and, taking Andrea into her arms, embraced her tightly. "I can't believe it's you!" she gasped. "I can't believe it. I'm so sorry I didn't find you sooner! I'm so sorry. I'm so sorry." She pulled away and gently took Andrea's face in her hands. "If I had just known you were still alive..."

The three of them sat together, with Mitzi not wanting to let go of Andrea's hand. Hans sat across from them, unable to tear his eyes from the girl. Finally, Andrea opened up and told her story. Over the next hour Mitzi and Hans sat there completely mesmerized by the account of what happened – the struggle at the studio, how she had been taken away from Ingrid, and how she ended up with Hanna and Walter. As Andrea neared the end of her narrative, she commented, "It's funny. I didn't really recognize you, but the way you move and the way you clap and the way you work with us and… Well… It was just as *Mami* used to clap and teach. Those three claps, so concise and constant. I've never forgotten that. I almost forgot what she looked like, but I never forgot the clapping." Her voice faded off with these last few words. "Would you mind telling me more about my parents? Do you have more photographs?"

Mitzi hopped off the sofa and headed into her bedroom. She reemerged moments later carrying two large photo albums and sat back down beside Andrea. "I put these two photo albums together after your parents were killed," she explained. She opened the first album. "In this album you'll find many pictures of when you were a baby. I had dedicated it to you." Andrea took the album and began thumbing through it page by page. "This is your mother when she was pregnant with you. She's teaching a class in this photo. This is your father holding you when you were only two weeks old." Andrea smiled as certain memories set it. She remembered Johann walking with a cane and how she had once hidden it from him, hoping he would stay home that day. She recalled receiving numerous kisses from both her father and mother as they would tuck her in for the night. She recalled her mother's arms holding her tightly.

"This second album is to honor your parents' lives." One of the first pictures she came across was torn and faded. It was a picture of Ingrid dancing in a cabaret. There were several photographs of the piles of rubble in the streets and of bombed out buildings. As she turned to the fourth page, on the left hand side was a portrait of her mother. Across from it, on the right, was a portrait of her father.

Andrea stared for a long while at the photos, running her fingers across them several times. She pointed to the locket that was clearly visible around Ingrid's neck. "I remember that locket so well," she said. "My mother wore it all the time. I don't ever remember seeing her without it. She called it her secret locket. She said it had a hidden door. One day I surprised her by figuring out how to open it. After that I kind of remember her calling it her 'not so secret locket.'" Andrea smiled and closed her eyes. She recalled playing with the locket, opening it from time to time to see the two tiny photographs displayed inside.

Mitzi leaned over to Andrea and placed her hand on her shoulder. "Why don't you keep these albums. It's the best keepsake I can offer you."

"Both of them?" Andrea gasped.

"Absolutely. They belong to you."

Fighting back tears, Andrea reached for Mitzi and gave her a big hug. Once she managed to gather herself, she asked. "What happened to you… after…" she hesitated, "… after my parents were killed?"

Mitzi took a deep breath. "You were very young the last time I saw you. You were only four. On that last day Hans and I left the studio to go find your father to warn him about the danger. We searched the streets around the studio before returning home. We couldn't find him anywhere. When we saw that the house was empty, we decided to go back to the studio. It was a very frightening time. As we came around the corner, we saw a man dressed in an overcoat leaving the building. He got into a car and drove away. When it was safe, we went into the studio. We turned on the lights and looked everywhere. There was nobody there. We saw two spots in the middle of the floor that looked like someone had tried to clean up a mess. It was a brownish, reddish color. I knew it was blood. It was horrible! We called the police. They told us that they would conduct an investigation and that we should go home." Mitzi stopped. She reached into one of her pockets for her handkerchief to dry her eyes. Then she resumed her story. "The police did not allow us to return to the studio for three days. Naturally we feared the worst but hoped for the best. On the third day the police came to the house." Her voice became strained and shaky. "I was so angry when they told us that you, your mother, and your father had all been killed. They called it an accident. I tried to argue with them, but they just shut us up. They never told us more than that, no matter how much we begged. Of course they were lying. I knew there was no accident. Before the police left, one of them pulled me to the side and told me to forget everything I had seen at the studio, otherwise they would see to it that we would lose everything. I've never felt more helpless in my life. There was nothing I could do, nowhere to turn, and no one to confide in." She looked up at Andrea, who listened sadly as the story unfolded before her. "I'm so sorry I couldn't save your parents." Her voice cracked.

"Had you been there, they would have just killed you too," Andrea said softly.

Mitzi nodded and wiped away more tears.

"But why did you stay here all these years?" Andrea asked. "I mean here, in the *DDR*?"

"We tried to go to the West, but the government made it impossible. They watched us for at least three years, maybe even longer. I stopped paying attention." She paused for another moment and took a sip of her drink. "They ordered us to continue on with our lives. I wanted desperately to give it all up, but Hans made me realize that your mother would have preferred for me to keep the studio alive. She was such a gift to so many children, and many dancers depended on me. Why should they be punished? So, as painful as it was, I continued. I did it for the students. But, especially, I did it for your mother. Ingrid had given me back my life by bringing me into her studio when others would have thrown me out the door. It was my way of repaying her. Of course, after they built the wall they closed down our studio and offered me a position with the *Staatsoper*. It's not quite the same, but they do take good care of us and there's not much more I can do about it at this point. I'm a bit too old to be jumping over walls."

That night, when Andrea returned home, she said nothing to Hanna and Walter about the evening. She went to her bedroom and placed the albums beneath a stack of books in a dark corner of her closet.

⸻ ✳ ⸻ ✳ ⸻

Andrea sat in her dressing room, staring into the mirror, while the makeup artist tugged and pulled at her hair. Suddenly a knock at the door startled her. "Come in!" she called out.

The door opened and Mitzi peered in. "How are you doing?" she asked with a raised brow. "Are you ready for your debut, Swanilda?" She smiled.

Andrea groaned. "I can't stand it. I'm so nervous I can't even think."

Mitzi entered the dressing room and stepped up beside Andrea. "You'll do great." She watched for a minute as the makeup artist pulled the last bit of hair up and secured it with several bobby pins. "I'll put the last one in." The makeup artist nodded and left the room.

Mitzi stepped up behind Andrea and placed her hands on her shoulders reassuringly. "You know, Andi, you mustn't let your nerves get a hold of you like this. Rehearsals for the past week were practically flawless, and at this point there's nothing more we can do. So, it doesn't make sense to get completely stressed out." She then reached across, picked up a bobby pin, and proceeded to push it into Andrea's hair. "I like to put the last bobby pin in for good luck. It's kind of an old superstition. If I put the last one in, the production will hold well together." She placed her hands on Andrea's shoulders and they both looked into the mirror. "Now you don't have to worry about anything. You look lovely. Everything will be perfect."

"Promise?"

"Andi," Mitzi tapped Andrea on the back and turned to leave. "Showtime is in half an hour."

"Mitzi, thank you for allowing me to have my own dressing room. It's a real honor."

Mitzi winked and answered, "Get used to it. I never had to share after I met your mother. You're going to be a prima ballerina." She left the dressing room, closing the door behind her.

Andrea gazed into the mirror and smiled to herself. A prima ballerina. Nothing could please her more than hearing Mitzi say those words.

Andrea's performance as Swanilda was lauded as one of the top performances in years. Each night she enjoyed a standing ovation. She enjoyed the attention and dreaded closing night, but looked forward to future dance productions.

CHAPTER TWENTY-FIVE

DECEMBER 1967

Andrea found herself walking alone one night after staying out late with friends. The air outside was freezing. The few lights that were lit cast black and gray shadows throughout the area, filling Andrea with a sense of trepidation. She decided to take a shortcut, which took her past a section of the Wall and through a deserted neighborhood still in partial ruin from the war. Few people ventured in this area, as it served as a grim reminder of both the city's past and present. Andrea stopped and glanced up at the old bullet holes that still filled the building beside her.

"Halt!" A man's voice suddenly cut through the night, startling her. She looked ahead in time to see two dark figures, carrying rifles, heading her direction. They were approximately one hundred meters away.

In a panic she turned and began to run. The two figures immediately took off after her. Her heart raced. As the men gained a distance on her, Andrea suddenly realized that she was only one block away from Christa's apartment. With one final burst of energy she raced toward the large brick building and crashed through the wooden door. She raced up three flights of stairs to Christa's familiar red door.

"Open up!" she shrieked as she pounded on the door.

The moment she saw the door knob begin to turn she reached down, twisted it, and pushed her way inside, knocking her bewildered friend to the ground. She slammed the door behind her, then leaned against it. Her lungs were burning from the cold air.

"Wha...?" Christa began, still dazed by her friend's abrupt entrance. "Why don't you come in?" Christa said sarcastically. "Why are you out on a night like this, Andi? Oh, and by the way, nice to see you after so long."

Andrea grasped her chest with her right hand, trying desperately to catch her breath. "I... I'm sorry, Christa," she gasped, out of breath.

"What happened?"

"I... There are some men chasing after me. Where are your parents?"

"They're off visiting relatives. But why would anyone be after you?"

"I don't know. I was walking home and..."

Just then they heard the muffled sounds of footsteps, followed by sharp banging in the passageway. They both strained to listen.

"We're looking for a woman who was seen running into this building," said the first voice.

"I heard some shouts," a woman's voice answered. "They came from over there."

The girls ceased talking and stared at the door, afraid it would crash open at any moment. Within seconds a sharp knock came at the door. "Open up! Open up now!"

"*Mein Gott! Mein Gott!* I've got to hide," Andrea whispered out of control. She scrambled around the living room before dashing into Christa's room where she took refuge in the closet.

"Open up by order of the police!" a man's voice shouted on the other side of the door.

Fearful that they would break down the door, Christa decided to open it. She found herself pushed backward as two uniformed border guards forced their way into the apartment. "What is going on?" she asked, quite frightened.

"Where is she?" asked the first man.

"Where is who?"

"Are you alone?" he asked.

"Yes."

After a brief pause, the first guard ordered the second one to search the home. "I'll stay here and watch the door."

The atmosphere grew still as the second guard wandered through each room finally ending up in Christa's bedroom. Andrea caught a glimpse of him through a tiny crack in the closet door.

Using the tip of his rifle, he carefully lifted the knit blanket hanging loosely down the edge of the bed. After peering beneath the bed, he turned and stared at the closet. Andrea held her breath as he approached. The door opened slowly. Trapped, she froze with fear, and then their eyes met.

Without taking his eyes away from her, he shouted out, "Sergeant!" He opened his mouth to say something else, but then stopped suddenly, slowly backed away, and shut the closet door just as the sergeant entered the room.

Andrea's heart was pounding.

"Did you find anything?" inquired the sergeant.

"No. I'm starting to think she did not come into this apartment. Let's go check the others before she gets away."

Andrea swallowed carefully.

"Did you look under the bed and in the closet?"

"Yes, Sergeant. The woman next door must have been mistaken. After all, she was quite old. Her hearing is probably not reliable."

"Sorry for the intrusion," they said to Christa while departing.

Hearing the door slam in the living room, Andrea emerged from Christa's room, soaked with perspiration. She stepped over to the sofa, plopped down, and stared at the floor.

"What happened?" asked Christa as she stepped up to her friend and sat beside her.

"I…I'm not sure," replied Andrea, trying to gather her thoughts. "He saw me but didn't turn me in. I don't know why. Maybe it's a trick."

"I've seen him before. He looked very familiar," remarked Christa.

"I know. So have I."

"In any case, Andi, you can't leave now. It would be too dangerous."

"You're right. *Mutter* will be worried, but I can't risk trying to get home right now."

Over the next hour, they both sat on the sofa in the living room, chatting about what just happened and how Berlin had been changing, when they were interrupted by a light tap at the front door. Andrea immediately dashed to Christa's room and shut herself up inside the closet. Christa opened the door to find the second guard standing alone. He removed his hat.

"I'm sorry to disturb you, Fräulein, but may I please come in for a minute?" he asked. Seeing Christa's reluctance he explained, "Nobody is in trouble. I'm here on my own. I just wanted to see… eh, was that your friend or your sister? You know, the one who was hiding in the closet. Would she happen to still be here?"

Christa leaned up against the door and stared cautiously at the man. "You're that guard we ran into awhile back, who helped my friend pick up her things after some boys knocked them out of her hands, aren't you?"

"Yes." He smiled, happy that she remembered him. "May I come in? Is she still here?" Christa opened the door reluctantly and he entered. Overhearing their conversation Andrea emerged from the room. The guard stopped speaking, stared at her, and extended his hand. "My name is Erich Köhler. I believe we've met before," he said gently.

Andrea shook his hand without removing her eyes from his. "Yes. On Unter den Linden," she confirmed. A smile finally appeared on her face.

"So, what is your name?" he asked.

"Andrea... Andrea Spangenberg."

They both sat on the sofa and spoke as Christa disappeared into the kitchen to prepare some tea.

"How old were you when you started dancing?" Erich asked once her friend left.

"Ten," she answered.

"So that makes what, ten...eleven years?"

"Nine."

"Ah! You're nineteen! So young!" he teased.

Andrea quickly changed the subject. "How about you? Have you been a guard for very long?"

"No. Not really. When we met that first time, I had been working for less than a month." His expression became thoughtful.

Andrea hesitated and then asked, "Have...have you ever had to shoot anybody?"

"Andi!" Christa scolded as she walked in on the conversation. "Don't ask questions like that."

"No, I've never shot anyone, and I hope I never have to." Seeing Andrea's expression, the guard suggested, "Let's change the subject."

Christa set a tray down on the coffee table and poured

three cups of a chicory-based ersatz coffee. They talked for another ten minutes and then Erich stood up. "It's late. I should leave you ladies," he suggested. He turned to Andrea, who remained seated. "May I see you again?"

"I would like that," she cooed as she stood up. "I don't live here, though. I live several blocks away."

"You're not thinking of walking back home now, are you?" he asked, suddenly concerned. "Perhaps I could escort you there. You'd be safe with me."

"That sounds like a splendid idea," beamed Andrea, relishing the idea of being alone with him.

"Andi," began Christa with obvious concern in her voice. "I really think you should stay here. It's late and..."

"I'm fine," Andrea insisted.

During the walk back to Andrea's house, Erich asked her numerous questions about her dance career. Andrea enjoyed his attention. Before they knew it, they had reached her home. She turned to Erich, who stretched his neck to gaze upward at the apartment complex. "Thank you for walking me back," she said.

"It was a great pleasure." His eyes twinkled. "I really would like to see you again. Do you have a telephone? Perhaps I could call you and we could do something," he suggested.

"Well, ah… we don't have a telephone, but…" Andrea thought for a moment then said quickly, "Do you want to see me dance? I can get you a ticket some time."

"I would like that. Are there any shows coming up soon?" he asked eagerly.

"Not right away, but…" Andrea's mind raced. "If you're not working Sunday afternoon, come by my house," she blurted out. She turned and hurried away. Erich stood by and watched her as she disappeared into the building. Once she was completely out of sight, he took a deep breath, smiled, turned, and walked away.

Sunday afternoon there was a loud knock at the door. As Andrea reached for the door knob, Walter stepped up behind her. "*Vater*, please don't embarrass me," she insisted. She then snapped on a smile and opened the door.

Erich stood patiently on the other side, holding two daffodils in his left hand. "For a moment I was afraid I didn't have the correct apartment," he said with a boyish grin. Andrea felt her knees grow weak at the sight of him. He looked different without his uniform. He reached out and handed Andrea the flowers. "These are for you."

Forgetting Walter was still standing behind her, Andrea's smile grew. As she took the flowers, she felt Walter discretely poke her in the back with his index finger. "Ch… Erich, I'd like you to meet my father." She turned sideways in the doorway so that both men could meet. "*Vater*, this is Erich."

Erich extended his hand. "I'm pleased to meet you, Herr Spangenberg," he said as he shook Walter's hand.

As Walter invited Erich into the apartment, Andrea began to try to coax him back outside. "But we should go," she insisted, worried that Walter or Hanna might say or do something embarrassing. She took one step outside.

"What's the rush?" Hanna called out from across the room. "I would like to meet this fine young man as well."

Reluctantly, Andrea stepped back inside and led Erich to the sofa. "This is my mother. *Mutter*… Erich," she relented before plopping down beside him onto the sofa. Hanna and Walter sat down in front of them.

There was an awkward silence before Walter finally spoke up. "So, Erich, tell us about yourself. How old are you? What do you do for a living?" He stared intently at the young man.

"I'm a…" Erich began to answer.

"Student," Andrea blurted out. Erich's eyes grew wide and he stopped talking and stared at her. "Yes, he is a student at the university," she continued.

"Interesting," Hanna nodded approvingly. "Which university?"

"Eh…" Erich hesitated.

"*Humboldt-Universität,*" Andrea chimed in quickly.

Hanna and Walter glanced over at Andrea then refocused their attention back to Erich. "What are you studying?" asked Walter.

"Well, I…" began Erich. "Various topics."

"Various topics?" asked Hanna. "What kind of topics?"

"Physics!" Andrea blurted out. "He's going to be a great scientist one day!"

"Really?" Hanna nodded her approval, raising her eyebrows. "How lovely."

"I suppose," Erich nodded uncomfortably.

"How old are you, Erich?" asked Walter.

Erich scratched his head and looked to his side at Andrea.

"He's twenty years old, *Vater,*" she answered. "Now, may we please leave and stop this interrogation?"

"Andi!" Hanna finally snapped, "It would be nice if you would let Erich speak." Ignoring Andrea's last question, she turned her attention back to the young man. "Why did you choose physics?"

"Well, eh…"

Andrea began to open her mouth, but was silenced by Walter who put his hand up into the air and raised a finger as if to say *wait!* Andrea closed her mouth and shrunk back into her seat.

"I'm a great admirer of Albert Einstein," he said, finally jumping into his new role.

"Very nice," said Hanna.

"He was a family friend before the Nazi's took over," he continued.

"Really?" asked Hanna, straightening up in her chair.

"Yes. He is the reason I do what I do today."

"How nice," gasped Hanna, "to have had such a wonderful role model in your life."

"Well, I met him when I was very young. My parents still talk about him today."

"I think we should be leaving now," Andrea chimed in as she hopped up from the sofa.

Erich stood up as well and excused himself. "It's been a pleasure meeting you both. I'll make sure Andrea does not stay out late."

Walter stood and extended his hand, which Erich took into his own. "Nice meeting you, Erich. Good luck in your studies too."

"Thank you, Herr Spangenberg."

They both headed for the door and made a quick exit. Once outside, Erich tossed Andrea an inquisitive look. "Physics?" he spouted. "The one topic I hated most in school."

Andrea apologized. "Sorry. I just didn't know what else to say."

"What's wrong with being a guard?"

"Nothing, of course, unless you are my Father." Andrea rolled her eyes.

"Your father does not like us?"

"He blames the Soviets and the guards for losing his job."

"I see."

They both grew silent as they passed two buildings

that still bore the scars from the war twenty years earlier. Andrea finally broke the silence. "Do you think they will ever restore these buildings?" she asked.

"I imagine they'll restore them eventually. I just don't know when."

"My grandmother often told me about how beautiful this city used to be before…" She stopped.

"Before what?" he prodded knowingly.

"Never mind."

They walked for a while before catching the S-Bahn. In the train Erich turned to Andrea, smiled, and said, "By the way, I'm 24, not 20."

"Oh… Sorry."

After a short ride and a brief walk they reached a small restaurant. Andrea's eyes scanned the room as they stood in the entryway. "It's quite fancy," she pointed out.

"You're not uncomfortable, are you?" he asked, turning to her.

"Oh, no," she lied.

"Good. This is one of my favorite cafes. I don't think it's too fancy, but it is definitely good! They have the best schnitzel in all of Berlin." He stopped, "Eh… are you allowed to have schnitzel?"

"Yes! Of course!" Andrea laughed. "Do I look like I can't?" she waved her hands over her waist.

"No no. Absolutely not." Erich straightened up. The host motioned for them to follow him and pulled out a chair for Andrea. "We can sit here by the window and watch the people walk by."

Andrea noticed a painting of the Brandenburg gate hanging on the wall. "Have you been there?" she asked. As she stared at the poster, she sensed Erich's eyes on her.

"Been where?" he asked.

"You know, the western occupied zones," she replied.

"On several occasions, when I was a boy."

"Hm."

"You?" he asked.

"Once," she answered. "We were young. Christa and I went there to explore before the Wall came up." She took a breath, looked across the table at Erich, and rested her chin on her knuckles.

"You seem bothered," remarked Erich.

"It's beautiful, isn't it?" she added, ignoring his last statement.

"It certainly is," he answered as he watched her.

"Do you enjoy working as a guard?"

"It's all right for a job. Do you enjoy your work as a dancer?" he asked.

Andrea perked up. "Oh yes. I love everything about dancing!" Andrea hesitated, then asked, "Do you believe in what you do?"

"In what I do? What do you mean?"

"Do you believe in your work as a guard?"

"Oh, yeah, yeah." Erich straightened up and cleared his throat. "Of course I do." They both suddenly grew quiet. Erich finally broke the silence. "What are you thinking?" he asked.

"I'm thinking… I'm thinking that sometimes I wish I were a bird so that I could just spread my wings and go anywhere I wanted to."

"With your grace you could dance across any border," he cooed.

"How would you know I'm graceful? You've never seen me dance," she said smiling.

"I can tell by the way you walk and move." He reached across the table and took her hand into his, causing Andrea to sit straight up.

"Your hands are cold," he remarked.

The warmth of his hands felt good. Andrea took a deep breath and gazed back at the poster. She quietly recalled when she and Christa crossed over to the West and explored. What would have happened had she never returned? Of course, she was too young, but what if another family had taken her in? Surely, her life would be much different than it was today.

When the waiter finally approached, they both ordered schnitzel with potatoes and a beer. "Something is disturbing you," Erich noted. "I can tell."

Andrea began fidgeting with her fingers. "If you could go anywhere, where would you go, Erich?"

He thought for a moment then answered, "I would like to see Italy or Spain. What about you?"

"Those would be nice, but America would be my first choice."

"Why?"

"I don't know. I've heard stories about it. I heard someone call it the land of opportunity. Maybe mine are simple, childish dreams but I can't help but to think about it. Someone once told me that anything can happen there. It's like magic there."

"Well, if I ever can, I'll take you to America," Erich said sincerely.

"I suppose it doesn't hurt to dream."

Their food finally arrived. They grew quiet as they ate. Erich was right. It was the best schnitzel that Andrea ever tasted.

Andrea began seeing Erich more and more frequently after that. Whenever he was not working he would meet her at the *Staatsoper* and escort her home. On weekends, if he was working, Andrea would intentionally pass close to his post to catch a glimpse of him as he stood his watch. Other days they would spend time in a park or at their favorite restaurant eating schnitzel and watching pedestrians pass by on the sidewalk.

—⊁———⊁———⊁—

Mitzi cast Andrea in the lead role of Juliet in *Romeo and Juliet*, a move that, despite Andrea's progress and growing reputation, completely enraged Gretchen, who felt she had been cheated out of another role.

"I feel like some of the other girls are beginning to hate me," Andrea confided in Mitzi one day.

"Don't worry about it, Andi. They don't see in you what I see," explained Mitzi.

"I'm afraid you're just biased, Mitzi."

"Seriously, I'm not biased at all. You have it, Andi," she said firmly. "You have that special something that will one day come out and turn you into a world-class dancer. I have no doubt that you will be our next prima ballerina, and I am doing everything I can to harvest that. You are good enough to play Juliet." She reached out and stroked Andrea's hair, adding, "You will have to dye your hair dark though."

Andrea began to laugh. "Fine! Absolutely. Are you sure you are not just doing it for my mother?"

"I promise you that I am not. However, I will admit that it's nice to be able to have that extra push. Ingrid or no Ingrid, you are the next big thing."

"Thank you."

One day, several months later, as Andrea was walking home from rehearsals, Erich swiftly came up behind her and grabbed her hand. Andrea jumped. When she turned and saw him, she gasped. He was wearing his uniform, which was in disarray, and stumbling slightly. His eyelids were at half-mast. Clearly, he was intoxicated. He reached around her and took her into his arms. He reeked of alcohol. Andrea pushed him back slightly and glared at him.

"What are you doing here dressed like that… and what is *wrong* with you?!" she exclaimed. Some of the other dancers from the production were exiting the building, followed by Mitzi, who waved to Andrea. "You have to leave now, Erich. I don't want to be seen with a drunken guard. My reputation is important."

"I need you, Andi," he proclaimed. "I need to be with you right now."

"Andi!" Mitzi called out. "Is everything all right?" She began walking toward them.

"Erich, please leave," begged Andrea in a hoarse whisper. "Come back tomorrow when you are sober… and not in uniform!"

"What's wrong with my uniform? It's only a job. It doesn't define me." He slurred his words.

Before Andrea could respond, Mitzi caught up to them. "Who is this?" she asked with concern in her voice. "Andi? What's going on?"

Andrea cringed. "Everything is fine. Mitzi, this is Erich. He's just a friend."

"Oh yes. I have seen you come by here on many occasions," Mitzi said to Erich. "I didn't realize you were a border guard. I've never seen you in uniform. Well, at least I think that's the uniform. What happened to you?"

"I'm sorry," began Erich, "but I really need to speak with Andi… alone."

"I'm fine, Mitzi. I'll see you tomorrow. Erich will walk me home."

"All right, then," said Mitzi reluctantly. "You both have a good evening. I'll see you early tomorrow, Andi. We have a lot to cover for next month's production."

As Mitzi walked away, Andrea turned back to Erich. "I

can't believe you showed up in this condition, Erich. What's come over you? I've never seen you like this before."

"I'm sorry," he said somberly. "It's just that..." He stopped. "Let's walk. My head is spinning and I might fall down if I stand still too long." They began walking and he continued. "My brother was arrested this afternoon," he finally admitted.

"Your brother? I'm so sorry, Erich. What happened?"

"He and several others had been trying to dig their way out of the Republic. Someone turned them in."

"What's going to happen to him?" Andrea asked, clearly surprised by the news and outwardly sympathetic.

"He was remanded in Leipzig."

"Then what?"

"Normally he would get one to two years. It could be more. I'm afraid... What if he doesn't make it out alive. These are terrible places."

"Oh no, Eric. I don't know what to say." They walked for another block before Andrea spoke again. "What about the others who were with him?"

"I don't know."

"How old is your brother?" Andrea asked.

"He turns 18 next month." His lower lip began quivering uncontrollably. "I've killed my little brother," he said.

Andrea reached around and wrapped her arms around his neck. They stood there for a long moment, embracing, his face buried in her shoulder. The street was completely deserted. After a long silence, Andrea heard Erich's muffled voice say, "And now there's one more problem."

Andrea pulled away slightly to see his face. "What's that?"

"I can't see you anymore," he said as he reached up and pulled her arms away from around his neck.

Andrea took a step backward. "I... I don't understand," she stammered.

Erich shook his head. "When something like this happens, they punish the family, and I'm afraid they might punish you as well. I don't want that to happen. I mean, they've already started watching me and if they see us together…"

Andrea stood up straight and glanced around at their surroundings. "I don't see anyone here now."

Erich smiled and wrapped his arms around her again. "Well, maybe not every moment, but often enough."

"Do you have any reason to hide?" Andrea asked, almost joking.

Erich drew his lips close to Andrea's ear and whispered, "I'm leaving the Republic. I have a plan."

Andrea's eyes grew wide with a kind of childish excitement. "Then just take me with you!" she whispered back with a contained excitement.

⸺⊹⸺⁕⸺⊹⸺

By the time Andrea and Erich reached her apartment it was past ten o'clock. They stopped in front of the building and Erich faced her. "Are you sure you're up to it?" he asked. "It could be dangerous."

"Not as dangerous as trying to climb over the wall," she added.

"That's true." He leaned over and kissed her gently on the lips. They kissed for a long while. The alcohol was still strong on his breath, but he felt good to her. "I love you, Andi," he murmured as he pulled away from her slightly and gazed down into her eyes. "I really do love you. We are going to have a wonderful life together."

Just then she saw the curtains move upstairs in her bedroom window. The lights were turned off. "Oh no," she grumbled. "I think my parents were watching us. I have to go. Good night, Erich." She gave him a last peck on the cheek before scampering away.

Only the living room light was on when she crept in through the front door. As she closed the door behind her, Walter met her at the entrance, his expression stern and unforgiving.

"Where have you been?" he demanded.

"I... well, out... with Erich," Andrea stammered, startled by his sudden appearance.

"We've been worried about you," he noted. "It's late. You never said you would be out this late."

"It's not that late, *Vater*," Andrea refuted. "Besides, I'm grown up now. I have a job."

"As long as you are living in our house, you will live by our rules!" he snapped. Andrea clenched her teeth together, trying to hold back her anger as she watched him. She did not respond. "Since when did the physics student decide to become a guard?" Walter asked.

Andrea hesitated before answering. "Not long ago," she replied meekly. She braced herself for the backlash.

"Andi, I think you are lying," Walter said firmly.

"I..."

"You are not to see him again."

"Whaa...?" Andrea stood there dumbfounded. "You can't forbid me to see him, *Vater*. We haven't done anything wrong," she protested.

"He is the devil!" Walter shouted. "Besides, this is not a hotel, Andi." He reached around Andrea and locked the front door. "You can't just come and go anytime you want to, especially not without telling us first. We are still your parents, and as long as you live here you will be home when you are supposed to, and certainly not this late at night."

"Really, *Vater*. I'm fine. I'm able to handle it. I..."

Walter cut her off. "No!" he snapped. "You're too young

and that's the end of it."

"Just like that?" Andrea glared at him. She quickly rushed to her bedroom, nearly knocking down Hanna who had been standing around the corner listening in on their conversation. Andrea slammed the door behind her.

The following day, when Andrea was finished with rehearsals, she found Erich sitting outside on a nearby bench. He was not wearing his uniform. As soon as he saw Andrea he raced to her side. Not paying attention, he nearly walked into a blind man standing alone by the building. Andrea's expression was somber. "Erich," she said softly, "*Vater* has forbidden me to see you anymore."

Suddenly something caught his eye. Ignoring her news, he grew serious and said, "Don't look, but we're being watched. Let's walk." After walking nearly one block, Erich asked, "Did you see that blind man?"

"The one you nearly knocked over?"

Erich smiled and nodded. "He wasn't really blind."

"How do you know?"

"Why would a blind man be wearing a watch when he can't see the time? Let's go somewhere where we can talk."

Andrea hesitated, then threw him a wicked smile. "How about your home?"

Together they walked quickly to the nearest train station and eventually made their way to his apartment. It was Andrea's first time there. The apartment was small, with only one bedroom, a living room that was no bigger than Andrea's bedroom, and a run-down kitchen with dirty dishes stacked in the sink. Seeing Andrea cringe slightly, Erich stepped up to her and said softly, "Maybe we should not have come here. I haven't had a chance to clean up."

"It looks like you need a woman around here," she responded.

"Are you volunteering?" When Andrea did not answer, Erich straightened up. "So what is it that you wanted to talk about?"

Ignoring his question Andrea unexpectedly wrapped her arms around him and buried her face into his neck. "Let's play first."

"Play?" he repeated the word, letting it linger on his lips.

"Sure. Why not? There are no blind men here to watch us."

"Ahh… Andi, what are you proposing?"

"You know, Erich." She began tugging at his jacket, slipping it off his shoulders.

"Maybe you can clarify…" he suggested.

She began unbuttoning his shirt. "Andi, are you sure you are ready for this?" he asked.

"I've never been with a man, you know," she said. Her voice turned hoarse. "Teach me everything so that I don't make a fool of myself."

Erich began to laugh. "You could never be made a fool!" he said. When he saw that she was not slowing down he straightened up and added, "First, you need to slow down… and let's get out of this kitchen."

She grabbed him by the arm and dragged him into the bedroom, where she continued to work on his buttons. "Damn these buttons!" she exclaimed. Finally, unable to undo all the buttons, she grabbed both sides of his shirt and yanked sharply downward, tearing the last few.

He smiled at her and said, "Well, there then. It looks like you've succeeded." She liked his smell… manly with a hint of cologne. He wrapped his arms around her waist and pulled her body close to his. "Are you sure, Andi?" he asked again. Andrea nodded her head, unable to speak or catch her breath fully. "Let me do the rest." He picked her up and carried her to the bed.

When she felt unexpected pain, Andrea dug her nails into his back and held on tightly. It was not what she expected, but she was not willing to stop. Her thoughts shifted to her last conversation with Walter – forbidding her to see Erich again. She smiled to herself, feeling deeply satisfied that she had won the battle. There was nothing Walter could do to keep her away from Erich. He was no longer in control. She was.

They both lay there for a long while, neither one wanting the moment to end. He kissed her several more times. "I love you, Andi," he whispered.

"I love you too," she responded. "Now about that plan to leave the Republic…" She smiled up at him.

"Soon," is all he said.

They began planning their escape the following week, and not a moment too soon. Walter was so angry at Andrea's defiance that he threw her out of the house the night she returned from Erich's apartment. Had it not been for Hanna's insistence to allow her to return home, Andrea would have had no choice other than to move in immediately with Erich. While she liked the idea, she knew that it would only complicate their plans. Erich was under constant surveillance since his brother's capture. They decided to keep their relationship discrete and spend as little time as possible together in public, knowing that soon, they would never have to hide again. They stopped going out for schnitzel or to the park. On the few occasions that Erich met up with Andrea after rehearsals he would hide and wait in the shadows around the corner of a nearby building. After meeting up, they would then take the back alleys to her apartment, where he would discretely kiss her goodnight, out of sight from the suspecting eyes of Walter and Hanna.

One week remained before the premiere of *Romeo and Juliet*. The program was scheduled to run for three days a week over the course of one month. Andrea was eager to begin for two reasons. First, after months of grueling rehearsals that resulted in blistered toes and often fatigue so severe that Andrea could have laid down in a corner of the studio and fallen asleep, she would finally be able to enjoy the fruits of her efforts. She was always happiest on stage. Second, she would soon be heading to a different life somewhere new. Meanwhile, while she concentrated on her dance, Erich was in contact with friends in the American sector. While Andrea danced, Erich worked to coordinate their escape.

After the premiere of Romeo and Juliette, Andrea's reputation as a dancer soared. The following morning she woke up to rave reviews, one of which referred to her as "The Republic's greatest treasure." Another referred to her as "a prima ballerina." After that, every performance sold out.

Two weeks before the closing of the production Andrea approached Mitzi. "Do you have a moment?" she asked.

"I always have a moment for you, Andi. First, though, I want to tell you just how proud I am of you! You are there, Andi. You are finally there, and you are still so young, with many years of great dancing ahead of you."

Andrea lowered her head slightly. "Thank you," she said.

"So, what is it that you wanted to talk about?"

"Mitzi, I have a friend who would like to see the closing production. Do you think we can get a ticket for him? I mean, everything is sold out at this point."

"Is this someone I know?"

"Not really. Well, sort of. His name is Erich. He's…"
Mitzi interrupted, "The border guard?"

"Yes," she responded. Her cheeks reddened.

"You really like this Erich, don't you?" Mitzi smiled again.

Andrea nodded. "Please don't talk to Walter or Hanna about it, though."

"I won't, but I'd like to get to know him a little better myself." Andrea gave her an inquisitive look. "Andi, I hope you don't mind me saying this, but I feel somewhat responsible for you. I mean, someone has to keep an eye on you for your mother. I don't want to see you make any mistakes that could ruin your life. You have so much going for yourself and it would be a pity to see you throw it all away."

"I can introduce you to him when he comes to the show, if we can get tickets."

"I have a better idea. Why don't you both come to our house for dinner on Thursday? I'm sure Hans would love to meet Erich as well. Let's face it. Hans knew you as a small child too, so he feels responsible."

Andrea felt her face growing flush again as she nodded her agreement. "Yes. But, again, please don't tell my parents that he'll be there."

"I have no reason to."

It was nearly ten o'clock by the time Mitzi, Hans, Erich and Andrea finished dinner. "As always, that was a delicious meal!" Andrea marveled as she stretched her arms above her head.

"You seem to be in a good mood this evening," Hans commented as Mitzi began clearing the table.

Andrea hopped out of her seat. "May I help you with the dishes, Mitzi?" she asked eagerly.

"When have you known me to refuse help when it's offered?" replied Mitzi playfully.

"I'll finish clearing the table for you," said Andrea. Once in the kitchen, Andrea asked, "So, what do you think of Erich now that you've spent more time with him?"

"He seems very nice, Andi. You can tell he really likes you too."

Andrea glanced over at her. "Yes, and I really like him."

Mitzi grew serious. "Andi, be very careful. It's obvious that he cares about you. His eyes never left you for more than a few seconds tonight. He's completely smitten. The thing is, I don't want to see you throw your life away."

"What do you mean?"

"Don't do anything stupid, Andi."

Andrea felt the heat come up into her face again. "I'm very careful. I won't do anything stupid like...." She thought for a moment. "I won't do anything stupid like get married before I turn 22. How's that?"

Mitzi pursed her lips. "Just be careful and take things slowly. Your career is very important. You're at the top of the world right now. Don't throw it all away." She washed two more plates, placing them on the towel for Andrea to dry. "So, how old is Erich anyhow?"

Andrea hesitated before answering, "My age," she blurted. When she saw Mitzi's expression she corrected herself. "He's a few years older than I am, but we have so much in common. I mean..."

"Andi," interrupted Mitzi, "you don't need to make excuses. You're no longer a little girl, you know. It was just a simple question and not an interrogation."

"Thank you." Andrea's voice drifted off. As they cleaned the kitchen, she muttered to herself, "I'm really going to miss this."

Mitzi immediately stopped working and stared at Andrea, who continued drying dishes as if she had said nothing. She reached around Mitzi, avoiding eye contact, and arranged a stack of clean plates in the cupboard to the right of Mitzi. "What are you talking about?" Mitzi finally asked.

Andrea suddenly felt awkward, not knowing how to break the news to her. She knew that Mitzi would object, seeing how many people had already been killed attempting to flee the Republic.

Andrea took a deep breath and avoided Mitzi's eyes. "I'm not staying," she finally confessed.

"You're not staying where?"

"I want to see the rest of the world."

"And where are you planning to go?"

"America," Andrea replied in one quick breath.

Suddenly Mitzi broke into laughter making Andrea even more uncomfortable. "America?" she asked between her laughter. "How?"

"We're escaping."

Mitzi grew serious. "Don't be insane, Andi. Do you know how dangerous that is?"

"It'll work. There are a lot of people who have succeeded."

"There are also a lot of people who have died trying to do it," she countered.

"Our plan will work," Andrea pressed stubbornly.

"Our?" Mitzi raised her eyebrows.

"Erich and me."

"Do Hanna and Walter know?"

"Of course not, and *please* don't tell them!"

"Andi, how can you expect me to sit back and watch you kill yourself?" she retorted.

"I'm not! We're not!" Andrea's voice went up an octave with her last words and Mitzi stepped back slightly. Then she quickly composed herself. "I'm sorry, Mitzi. You'll just have to trust me. I know what I'm doing. I mean... my mother, my real mother would understand."

Mitzi took a breath and shook her head. She stared at Andrea a moment then said, "What about your dance career? You're set up for a good life here, especially since your role as Juliet. You will also have many lead roles in upcoming productions. I can guarantee you success. On the other side you have no guarantees."

"You're not making this any easier," sulked Andrea.

"I'm not trying to."

"That's... Mitzi, you're so kind, but I've already made up my mind."

Mitzi finally backed off and said nothing more as she reached into the sink and pulled out the black stopper. Both women stood there silently and watched the murky water swirl down the drain, gurgling loudly as the last bit disappeared.

Before Andrea left the house with Erich, Mitzi took an envelope out of a drawer and handed it to Erich. "What's this?" he asked.

"Two front row tickets to our final production," she answered. "There are two in case you have someone you'd like to invite."

On their way back to Andrea's apartment Erich remarked, "That was very kind to give me these tickets." He hesitated, and then asked, "Did you give away our plan?"

"No! Of course not!" They walked the rest of the way in silence, each lost in his and her own thoughts.

CHAPTER TWENTY-SIX

JULY 1968

Andrea had become part of a privileged and elite crowd, which meant more spending power. She could have easily moved out into her own apartment, but opted to stay with Walter and Hanna, despite Walter's paranoia and watchful eye. There was no sense in moving out so soon before her planned escape.

There was only one week remaining before the final curtain call for *Romeo and Juliet*. Keeping a watchful eye out for Andrea, Hanna was staring out the living room window when she spotted a light yellow Trabant-601 pulling up to the curb. When the door to the driver's side opened and Andrea stepped out, Hanna did a double take. "Walter!" she called out. "Come see this."

"I'm busy right now. What is it?" he growled.

"Agh. 'I'm busy! I'm busy!' He's always busy," she muttered in a voice that mimicked Walter's. She then called out, "It's Andrea. I think she just drove up in a new car – a Trabant."

A few seconds later Walter stood by Hanna's side, peering out the window. "Where? Where is she? Where is the car?"

Hanna pointed to the vehicle downstairs just as the front door opened. They both whirled around to see Andrea standing in the doorway, a wide grin on her face.

"I'm right here, so don't panic. It's still daylight outside," smirked Andrea.

"You're late again," Walter barked back.

"Walter. Don't be so harsh all the time," Hanna urged. "After all, she's almost 20 now."

Andrea was not fazed by his reaction. Soon she would be gone and there was nothing Walter could do about it. "*Mutter*, come with me. I have something I want to show you."

"What is it?" Hanna asked with a wide grin on her face. Andrea took her by the hand and led her outside to the vehicle. Walter trailed closely behind, unwilling to miss anything.

Andrea placed her hand on the hood of the Trabant. "I just bought this today," she beamed. "What do you think?"

"It's very pretty," Hanna answered. "It must have been expensive, but this is wonderful. You can now drive us places."

Andrea raised her brow and grew serious. "Sorry, *Mutter*, but I have no intention of driving you any place."

"Oh… Oh… well," Hanna stammered, taken aback by Andrea's reaction. "Andi, I hope you are not upset with us. Walter doesn't mean to be so harsh. He cares about you. He just worries, and…"

"I have no intention of driving you anywhere because you are going to drive yourselves, *Mutter*."

"I don't understand."

"I bought the car for you," Andrea said softly, "and you, *Vater*." She glanced over at him, then stepped up to Hanna and pulled her gently toward the passenger side of the vehicle. She opened the door and instructed her to get in.

"Oh, Andi. This is too much. I simply can't..." Hanna broke into tears.

Andrea took her into her arms and explained, "*Mutter*, I know things have not been easy these past weeks. I know I haven't been the perfect daughter. I know that my choices aren't always what you would want for me. However, I want you to know that I recognize everything that you've done for me since the day you first took me in. I lost everything, and you gave me a new family... and a new chance at life. Through you I have been able to fulfill all my dreams. I could never repay you for calling me daughter."

Walter walked around the front of the car and approached Andrea and Hanna. "I'm sorry I've been so hard on you, Andi. I just don't want to see you get hurt. When we took you into our home, like you said, you became our daughter." He wrapped his arms around both women. "Thank you for bringing so much joy into our lives." He fought back a tear.

Andrea straightened up suddenly and began laughing. "Once we are finished watering the street, let's go for a drive!" She handed the key to Hanna. "You first."

⊁————⊁————⊁

Three days remained before the final production. Andrea lingered for a long while backstage of the *Staatsoper*, savoring the moment. She wondered if she would be able to jump-start her dance career once she started her new life. Lost in thought, she did not hear footsteps behind her. It was Christa. "What are you doing, Andi?" her friend asked as she reached her side. Seeing Christa also reminded her that she did have friends – friends and family who would likely miss her once she was gone. She suddenly felt a sense of guilt – even betrayal. The air grew still. Most of the other dancers had already departed for the evening.

To her own surprise, Andrea blurted her plans out to Christa. "I'm leaving."

"What?" Christa gave her a puzzled look.

"I'm leaving."

"I'll leave too," responded Christa. "It's getting late. Come on."

Andrea giggled. One of Christa's charms was her naiveté. "I really hate it here, Christa," she finally admitted.

"You? You of all people? *You* hate it here." Christa rolled her eyes. "That's ridiculous."

"Why is that so hard to understand?" Andrea became defensive.

"Andi, you are the star of the show. Is it dance that you suddenly loathe or the company? I just don't understand why you'd leave. The director obviously loves you. You've got it made. There are no other companies for you to join, and…"

"I really don't think you understand what I am trying to tell you," Andrea interrupted. She turned and faced Christa, looking her squarely in the eyes. "I am leaving, Christa, and not just the company."

"Are you moving out of the city then?"

"No… I mean, yes." She hesitated. "I'm…we're leaving. That's all."

The blood drained from Christa's face. "Andi," she choked out her name. "Are you saying what I think you're saying? Don't do this."

"Shhh. Someone will hear. I shouldn't have brought this up. We can talk later."

"Andi, people love you. No, you're right. I don't understand it. If I had your talent, I'd be the happiest person in the world, and I wouldn't commit suicide!"

Andrea grew frustrated. This was not the type of

response she wanted. One of her biggest struggles, after all, was leaving a successful career. "Forget it, Christa. I obviously can't talk to you about this." Andrea stormed off.

"Wait!" Christa shouted after her. "When?"

Andrea whipped around and stared at her. "When what?"

"When are you planning to leave?"

"Shhhhhh!" Andrea's face turned beet red.

"Well?"

"Don't worry. I'll be here for at least another week or more. I can't tell you when exactly though." She rushed away.

Christa shook her head, bent down, and picked up her gym bag. Just as she stepped around the corner, she came face to face with Gretchen. "So, it sounds as if your friend is planning a big escape," she sneered.

"What's it to you?" growled Christa.

"She's going to die, you know, like the rest of the cowards who leave the Republic. And if she doesn't die escaping, she'll probably become a beggar in the streets."

"Mind your own business!" Christa snapped. She turned and stomped off.

Gretchen smiled triumphantly to herself as she left the area.

Two days later, on the eve of their final curtain call, Andrea walked to the front door of the apartment, and called out, "*Mutter... Vater*, do either of you mind if I take the car?"

Hanna stuck her head from around the corner of the kitchen and answered, "Go ahead, Andi."

Andrea flashed a toothy grin before dashing out the door. She looked around carefully at her surroundings before climbing into the vehicle. Good. No one seemed to be paying attention to her. She drove away, keeping a vigilant watch in the rearview mirror for anything suspicious. No one seemed to be trailing her. She drove for about half an hour, constantly looking into her rearview mirror. Once she arrived at a worn-down repair shop, she pulled a crumpled piece of paper out of her pocket and read the address. This was it. As she maneuvered the car up close to an open garage door, a repair technician ran toward her. Andrea rolled down the window.

"Hello," the technician greeted her. "Do you have an appointment?"

"Rolf is supposed to do some repairs on my car. Is he here?" she asked.

Seconds later Rolf walked up behind the technician. "Thank you, Albert. I'll take this from here." The young technician sprinted away. Rolf turned to Andrea and instructed her to maneuver the vehicle into the garage. He then closed the garage door behind them and the room grew dark. A light snapped on and three more men appeared from behind a door apparently leading into another section of the building. Among them was Erich. Andrea got out of the car and leaped into his arms. It had been nearly two weeks since their last meeting. She planted kisses all over his face, ignoring the other men, who stood by smiling and nodding to one another.

"Erich. I would risk my life for a beauty like her any day. Congratulations, Comrade!" said one of the men.

"So, this is the famous ballerina," said Rolf. "You are even more beautiful in person, Fräulein. No wonder my cousin wants to take you with him."

Erich glanced over at Rolf then back at Andrea. He smiled and kissed her eagerly on the lips. "I've missed you, Andi. I couldn't stand not seeing you."

Andrea turned and faced Rolf. "It's good to see you again," she said.

"Again?" Rolf was taken aback.

"Yes. I'm certain we met before. It was about nine years ago in the West," Andrea explained.

Rolf scratched his head. "Wow! You must have an amazing memory because I don't remember you."

"I'm sure that was you."

"Perhaps you can refresh my memory."

"I visited the West with my friend, Christa. We were young. We snuck into the *Deutsche Oper* during its construction."

"That was you?!" Rolf grew wide-eyed. "Yes, I do remember you."

"I even delivered the note you gave me to… eh…What was his name?"

"Wolfgang," said one of the other two men, stepping forward toward Andrea.

"I remember you too!" Andrea beamed. "You practically chased me out of your office."

"You were quite the arrogant little thing, weren't you?" teased Wolfgang, who had since gained weight and become grizzled.

"Well, I hate to break up this reunion, but we need to address some concerns," said Rolf. He turned to the last man. "Would you like to tell her?" he asked.

"We can't not tell her," the third man answered.

"Tell me what?" asked Andrea, suddenly growing serious.

Erich stepped forward. "First, how about an introduction. Andi, this is Lutz. He and I have patrolled the wall together on many occasions. He happens to be a Stasi informant." Andrea's eyes grew wide. "No, don't worry," Erich assured her, waving his hand toward her. "He's a spy for the Stasi, but he's actually on our side. He's a double agent. He tells the Stasi what they want to hear, but keeps his eyes and ears open for anything that might impact our operations."

"It's nice to meet you, Lutz," Andrea said with a hint of concern in her voice.

"The pleasure is all mine, Fräulein. I'm not going to waste any more of your time, though. Your name came up at headquarters yesterday. Word has it that you are planning to flee the Republic."

Andrea's jaw dropped. "I don't understand. How could that be?" she asked, her voice climbing nearly an octave with the last two words.

"Did you tell anyone about your plans?" asked Lutz.

Andrea shook her head. "No… Well, kind of."

"Who knows about this?"

"Christa. She's my best friend. I told her the day before yesterday."

"How much did you tell her?"

"Not much, actually. She didn't give me a chance." Andrea was visibly shaken. She let out a breath. "You know, Christa was not happy with me, but she would never turn me in. We've been friends forever."

"Well, maybe it was not her, or maybe it was. These days you can't be too careful. There are informants all around us. Teachers turn in students. Children turn in their parents. Parents turn in their children. I saw a grandmother turn in her grandchildren just last week for tuning into illegal radio stations."

There was a short pause. "So, what do we do next?" asked Andrea.

"We're moving the operation up one week," said Rolf as he stepped forward.

"One week?" gasped Andrea meekly. "But that's tomorrow!"

"I'm sorry, but if you want to do this, then your best chance at success is on a day like tomorrow," explained Lutz.

"Why?" asked Andrea.

"The Stasi will be watching you closely, but we have a plan to outsmart them. Not only that, once they think you're back in your apartment, they'll lower their guard. Also, we believe that they won't likely suspect you to flee on the closing night of your greatest performance. You'll first want to celebrate your success, right? After all, who would want to leave all of that glory? Later, however, they'll be watching you more closely. Does that make sense?"

"I supposed," grumbled Andrea. "I just don't like it."

"Andi," Erich began as he gently took her hand. "You know I really care about you, right?" She nodded her head. "I don't want to do anything that could hurt you in any way. If you don't want to do this tomorrow, let me know. We can figure something else out or I can go alone."

Andrea began to voice her objections.

"Erich, you really can't postpone this yourself," Lutz interrupted.

The room grew silent once again and all eyes turned to Andrea. She stood there for a long moment, contemplating what to do. She looked at Erich and shook her head slowly from side to side. "I can't do it," she finally said.

Erich felt his heart sink. "Andi?" he muttered. His voice cracked.

Andrea shook her head again. "I can't possibly let you leave without me." She glanced up and, one by one, her eyes met each of the four men standing in a semi-circle in front of her. "Let's do it tomorrow."

Cheers erupted, but were quickly squelched. "Shhhh! Let's not bring any undue attention to ourselves. The battle has not even begun yet, and victory is still just over a day away," Wolfgang pointed out. He then walked to the side of the garage and picked up what appeared to be a mannequin that had been sitting on a nearby chair and brought it to Andrea. "Andi, I would like to introduce you to Andi."

Andrea frowned. "This is becoming strange."

Wolfgang looked at the mannequin as he spoke. "She's a great decoy." He patted the mannequin on the back.

Rolf stepped forward, his expression serious. "Let's go over our plans," he said. "We have only one shot at this. One wrong move could cost us the operation, and worse, our lives." He spent the next hour going through every detail, grilling each participant, until he felt satisfied they all knew their roles.

***

Andrea could hardly sleep that night. Rolf's instructions never stopped echoing through her mind. She tossed and turned, fearing that something might have been omitted from the plan – some important detail that could cost her life, or Erich's. The hardest part was leaving behind her loved ones. *"You can bring one small bag, large enough for only the most essential items. Other than that, you'll only have the clothes on your back,"* Rolf had explained. *"Choose wisely because there'll be no coming back for any of your possessions. Once you're gone, you can never look back."*

Feeling frustrated, Andrea stared out into the darkness, wondering how and if she would be able to restart her dance career once they settled down into their new life. To make things worse, the tick tock of the clock on her bedside table served as a reminder that life as she knew it was going to change in only a short time, hopefully for the better, but what if…?

The following morning, sunlight streamed through a crack in the curtains of Andrea's bedroom, prompting her to wake up. Despite a sleepless night, she felt wide awake and ready to greet the day. She stepped over to her desk, pulled out a sheet of paper and a pen, and began to write.

Mutter und Vater:

By the time you find this note, I will be gone. Please know that my escape is in no way a reflection on either of you. I love you very much. I always have and always will. However, I cannot stay here. I will never be completely happy living a restrained life. I believe that the world is a beautiful place, despite what we hear. Please forgive me for what I have done and don't ever forget that you will always be in my heart.

Your daughter always,
Andi

Andrea folded the letter carefully and placed it in an envelope. She opened her top drawer and put the letter beneath a shirt. *"Remember, leave nothing behind that gives any indication of your plans,"* Rolf had instructed. *Well, they are not going to look through my drawer until after I'm gone,* she figured. *What harm is there in leaving behind a note if it's hidden?*

Andrea removed a plastic bag that she had placed in the pocket of her overcoat. She walked to her closet and pulled out the two albums from beneath a stack of books. Knowing that the albums would not fit into the bag, she paged through them and pulled out many of the photographs. She wrapped them carefully in her leotard and tights and placed them into the bag. The last thing she needed would be her ballet slippers, which she placed on top of the bundled photographs in the bag.

Later on, during lunch, Andrea was lost in thought as she sat at the dining room table with Hanna and Walter. Hanna stood up to get a pot of tomato based soup made from a powder mix.

"You look lost in thought," Hanna commented as she poured some soup into each bowl. "You must be thinking about this being your last production," she guessed.

Andrea sat straight up. "What makes you say that, *Mutter*?!"

Walter's eyes grew wide. "Why do you seem so jumpy, Andi?" he asked. "The comment is harmless."

"Yes," added Hanna. "It's not as if your career is ending. There will be other productions. We've been through this before. You have your whole life ahead of you."

"Sorry," murmured Andrea. "I have a lot on my mind."

"Is something bothering you?" asked Walter before taking a sip of his tea. Andrea shook her head no.

"What time do you have to leave today, Andi?" ask Hanna.

"I need to leave by 1400," she answered.

"1400? Why so early? If you would like, one of us can drive you so that you don't have to leave so early," she offered.

"No, *Mutter*. I'm meeting up with Christa."

"Very well, then. Let me know if you change your mind."

Two hours later, bag in hand and dressed in a long black overcoat, Andrea announced she was leaving to meet Christa. As Hanna reached for her to kiss her on the cheek, Andrea wrapped her arms around her, and held her tightly.

"Whoa, Andi," Hanna said, laughing hardily. "You act as if you are going on a long trip and won't see us again for a long time."

If you only knew. Andrea let go of her and smiled. "Sorry, *Mutter*. I'll miss… Well, it's just that I'll miss being Juliet."

"There will be plenty of other roles you'll be playing. Don't let a farewell to this one ruin your day." Seeing Andrea's expression, she asked, "Andi, you seem dismayed. Is there something else going on that is bothering you?"

Dismissing her question, Andrea asked, "Did I tell you that I've seen people in the audience cry at the end when Romeo and I die?"

"It doesn't surprise me."

"Romeo thinks that Juliet is dead, but really she is only asleep," Andrea rambled. "He's so upset that he poisons himself. But then, when Romeo dies, Juliet wakes up and finds him lying on the ground. Of course, then she is so upset that..."

"She stabs herself," interrupted Hanna. "I know. We saw it already. Remember? You did a tremendous job and we are both so very proud of you. Now, don't you have to leave?"

"Yes... sorry." Andrea stood for a long moment, then, "I need to go say goodbye to *Vater* first." Andrea sauntered into the living room where Walter was sitting on the sofa, reading a newspaper. She plopped down beside him and wrapped her arms around his neck, giving him a squeeze that lasted a long moment. "Goodbye, *Vater*," she said as she gave him a kiss on the cheek. "I love you both very much." She then rose from the sofa and left the apartment.

Hanna and Walter stared at one another. "I think our little Andi must be under a good deal of stress right now," Hanna finally said, trying to explain away Andrea's sudden peculiar behavior.

"Indeed," Walter responded, barely looking up from his newspaper.

Instead of going to the theater, Andrea made her way to her favorite restaurant. The moment she walked inside, she was greeted by the familiar smell of schnitzel. Someone stepped up behind her and tapped her on the shoulder. She snapped around to see Erich standing there. It was a perfect moment to wrap her arms around him and give him a drawn out hug.

"Remember, don't worry about being too discrete at this point," Rolf had instructed the day before. *"We want people to notice you."*

"I've missed you, Erich. How good to see you here," she said blithely. He placed his hands on her shoulders and squeezed them, staring deeply into her eyes. Andrea felt her cheeks grow warm. A dark gray, woolen flat cap shaded his eyes.

"Come on," he urged. "Let's eat some lunch so that you have energy tonight for your last and most memorable performance." He winked.

"Are you still coming?" she sought reconfirmation.

"This is one performance I wouldn't dream of missing." He kissed her. "After we eat, I'll even personally drive you wherever you need to go."

"Anywhere?" she asked with a spark in her eyes.

"Anywhere."

Two hours later, per Rolf's instructions, Erich left to retrieve the vehicle while Andrea waited at the entrance to the restaurant. He pulled up five minutes later in a blue Trabant. "Hey! That looks like the car I just bought for my parents, except a different color!" Andrea beamed.

Once they drove off, Andrea glanced briefly at the back seats. They were empty. "Where's Andi?" she asked mockingly.

Erich kept glancing into the rearview mirror as he drove ahead slowly. A smile suddenly appeared on his face. "They've taken the bait. Don't look now, but it looks like they're following us, Ludwig."

"Make a couple of turns and see if they follow you, to be certain," came a man's voice from beneath a blanket on the floor behind Andrea.

"Oh!" Andrea called out startled. "Who's that?" she exclaimed.

"It's my decoy," answered Erich. "We thought it would be smarter to bring him along rather than trying to sneak him into the car later tonight. It's just a minor change. Don't be alarmed."

An open hand popped up from behind Andrea and reached around her. "How do you do? I'm Ludwig," said the voice. She reached around, took hold of the hand and shook it. "Oh, and the mannequin is squashed beside me beneath this blanket. It's like snuggling with a stiff, bony woman." Andrea heard him reposition himself with a frustrated grunt. "These floors aren't meant for humans. It would've been much more pleasant if I had a real woman with me to distract the hound dogs."

Twenty minutes later they pulled into a parking lot that was nearly empty. Erich parked his blue Trabant between a red and white van and a green sedan. He discretely looked around and saw the two black vehicles that had followed them from the restaurant. They both pulled up to the curb across the street.

"Andi, when we walk to the theater, make sure you ignore those cars as we walk past them." Andrea got out of the car. Her small bag dangled from her hand. "Whatever you do, smile and pretend to be talking to me about something… anything. You just don't want them to think we are nervous or on to them."

"But I *am* nervous," admitted Andrea. She forced a laugh then slipped her hand into Erich's. A moment later they walked past the two black vehicles and entered the theater through a back door. Once inside she led Erich through the hallways to her dressing room, where she closed the door behind them. "I guess we just wait now and it's business as usual," she sighed. Two hours remained before the performance began, which gave her ample time to prepare herself.

One hour later they heard a knock at the door. Andrea opened it to find Mitzi standing on the other side. "Hi, Andi. Someone told me that you arrived early today. Are you ready for your last curtain call?" she asked pleasantly.

"I am."

Mitzi caught a glimpse of Erich. "Hello, Erich. I'm glad you could make it this evening." She turned her attention back to Andrea. "We're having a little party backstage afterwards. It's just a little celebration of the huge success of *Romeo and Juliet*. I'll be looking forward to seeing you there."

Erich stood up and said, "I should probably go into the lobby now." Mitzi offered to accompany him to prevent him from being harassed by security and they both left.

Andrea sat quietly in front of the mirror, contemplating how to get out of the after-show gathering. Rolf had been clear in his instructions. *"Do not linger after the show. The more people and cars there are, the more challenging it will be for them to track your precise movements and so you must move while the crowd is at its peak."*

At last it was time to go on stage. Andrea struggled to maintain her character throughout the production. She found it difficult to concentrate, especially as the end neared. Her mind was abuzz with Rolf's words. *"Within 15 minutes after the curtain call, Erich will meet you at the back door as described."* Andrea pictured it in her mind. *"You should have already changed into your normal clothing and put a hat on so that you are not recognized and stopped by anyone. The only people who should recognize you are the ones tracking you."* Andrea felt herself suddenly jerked into the present when Romeo threw himself upon her character in grief, thinking Juliet was dead. She allowed her seemingly lifeless body to be picked up and tossed around, almost like a rag doll. Andrea could not help but to think, *what if this scene is a premonition?*

It was now time for her character to wake up and find Romeo dead. *Another premonition?* The scene ended without any incidents, but then the unexpected happened. After a long drawn-out curtain call, Mitzi walked onto the stage and stood by Andrea. As the audience continued to cheer, Andrea stood poised to leave the stage. However, before she could, a stout man approached her, carrying a bouquet of Red Sweet Williams, a favorite flower in the East. She gave him a half curtsey and brought the bouquet near her face to take in their fragrance. The man then waved his hand in a gesture to quiet the audience. Once the applause finally died down, he called for a microphone. As he cleared his throat, and began speaking, the audience grew completely still. "Andrea Spangenberg, it gives me great pleasure to present to you two awards. First, on behalf of the Socialist Unity Party of Germany..." He reached into his pocket and removed a small medal. Holding it in the palm of his hand, he looked out over the audience members, all of whom continued to stand, waiting for his next words. "Andrea," he continued, focusing his attention back on her. "For your continued exemplary performance and for being so instrumental in expanding the Republic's cultural greatness, you are most deserving of this Activist Honor Award. You should be proud." The audience erupted into another round of applause as he leaned over and pinned it on Andrea, who stood dumbfounded by what was happening. He put his hand up again to quiet the audience. "I have one more announcement."

He glanced over at Mitzi and nodded. "I have an even more special announcement." Looking back at Andrea he continued, "Andrea, on behalf of the Ministry of Culture, for your superb talent and undying dedication to the art of dance, it is my greatest honor to award you the official title of prima ballerina!" He shouted out the last two words, practically knocking the wind out of Andrea. She was visibly shaken, and barely able to smile.

As the audience roared, the man grinned, leaned in toward her and asked in an icy tone, "Why so serious?" Just then, the orchestra began playing the National Anthem, whereby everyone in the theater began singing:

From the ruins risen newly,
to the future turned, we stand.
Let us serve your goodwill truly,
Germany, our fatherland.
Triumph over bygone sorrow,
can in unity be won.
For we shall attain a morrow
when over our Germany,
there is a radiant sun,
there is a radiant sun.

Andrea peered down at the audience and spotted Erich standing in front. He struggled to maintain his composure, visibly concerned at how Andrea might be impacted by these two awards. Not wanting to bring any attention to himself, however, he sang along with the rest of the audience.

The time to leave was drawing near and the short stout man leaned one more time toward Andrea. As he continued smiling, his lips brushed her ear and Andrea heard him say, "Don't do anything stupid. We're watching you. Don't throw away your life." He then stood straight, winked at her, smiling broadly and continued singing.

When it was all over, Andrea felt completely numb. She headed toward her dressing room, not paying attention to her surroundings, when someone bumped her shoulder. She looked up to see Gretchen glaring at her. "When are you ever going to stop being so hateful, Gretchen?" she snapped.

"Probably next week," Gretchen sneered. She laughed as she walked away, turning back around just long enough to call out, "Oh, and by the way, Andrea, speaking of next week… Good luck. You'll need it!" Gretchen laughed again and hurried off.

Andrea felt the blood rush out of her face as she raced over to her dressing room. It was now obvious who the informant had been. *How could she have possibly found out?!* She felt confused, yet angry, with the events of the evening tearing her insides apart. She found it increasingly difficult to catch her breath. The show was over and it was now time to make her move… if she still had the nerve.

As she stepped out of her dressing room, Mitzi intercepted her. "There you are, Andi. Come and join us. We're all waiting in the back to celebrate," she said cheerfully.

"I…" Andrea hesitated. "I'm not feeling too well all of a sudden."

Mitzi stepped up to her and felt her forehead. "You look pale, but you don't feel hot. Are you going to be all right? Is this just too much good happening to you at once?" She chuckled softly.

"You could say that." Andrea took a deep, but strained breath. "Mitzi, would you be terribly upset if I head out. I just don't feel well."

"If you think you're going to be sick, by all means, go home. We can celebrate later."

"Erich will take me home," Andrea replied, holding back her urge to shout out the truth.

"I'll walk out with you…" said Mitzi.

A few minutes later they stepped out the side door and met up with Erich, who was waiting patiently in the dark. "We're running late, Andi," he said the moment she emerged from inside the theater.

Mitzi came up behind Andrea. "Late for what?" she asked. "Andrea has only one place to go, and that's home. She's not feeling well."

"Yes, well, we were going to meet up with some friends," began Erich. "I'll take her directly home instead then."

Before departing, Andrea stepped in front of Mitzi, flung her arms around her, and held her tightly. "I'll always be grateful to you for everything you've done in my life. How can I ever repay you?" Andrea gushed, unable to hold back any longer.

Mitzi returned the embrace. "Let me know how you're feeling tomorrow if you can. Take some time off too."

Andrea hugged her one last time, stopping only when she felt Erich tugging at her shoulder. They rushed through the parked cars to his Trabant. The van concealed their car from anyone who might be watching from the street. Erich walked to the driver's side of the Trabant, but rather than getting into the car, he merely tossed his flat cap onto the driver's seat, then crouched down and crept into the back seat of the green sedan. Once inside he crouched all the way down on the floor and waited. Meanwhile, Andrea got into Erich's car, and crawled through to the driver's side where she exited. She slipped into the sedan, and crouched down with Erich. They both stayed as low as they could, remaining out of view.

Meanwhile, inside the blue Trabant Ludwig had already propped the mannequin up in the passenger seat. He donned Erich's flat cap, started the ignition, and pulled away slowly, whistling to the tune of *Das Lied der Deutschen* – The Song of the Germans. He intentionally drove slowly, waiting for someone to follow him.

With so many vehicles leaving the area at once, it was difficult to discern one from the other. However, within five or six blocks Ludwig caught a glimpse of at least two black vehicles trailing him. It was too dark to make out how many men were inside the vehicles. Ludwig weaved his way through the city, careful to not lose his pursuers.

About ten minutes after Ludwig had driven away, Rolf arrived on foot and climbed into the driver's seat of the green sedan. "Are you both in here?" he asked, without looking back.

"Present and accounted for," Erich spoke out from the floor of the back seat.

Rolf waited for a moment then asked, "Andrea, how do you feel?"

Andrea let out a grunt. "I feel like I'm going to be sick. Thanks for asking."

"Wait a minute, Rolf," Erich said. "Andrea, are you having second thoughts?" Andrea pressed her lips together as her eyes narrowed. She took a deep breath. "Andi?" he asked again. His voice cracked as he said her name.

"I…" she began, then stopped. "What if I lose everything I've worked for over the past years?" She averted her eyes from him temporarily.

"I'm now a prima ballerina here. What if they don't see that on the other side?"

"After what I saw tonight, I don't think that's possible," he said sincerely.

"Come on you two. Figure this out. We really have to make our move before they realize what we've done," said Rolf impatiently from the front seat.

"Just give us another two minutes," Erich urged. "Andi, think about it this way. If you remain in the *DDR* you'll only ever dance in the *DDR*. Don't limit yourself to one small place!"

Andrea sensed the urgency mounting in his voice. "What will happen to you if I stay behind?" she asked meekly.

"Andi, I love you more than anything, but I have to go

no matter what."

"There's only one problem," she admitted.

"What's that?"

"I'll miss you." After a few more seconds she took a deep breath and said firmly, "Let's go." They kissed passionately as the car drove off. Meanwhile, Andrea felt as if her insides were being ripped apart in turmoil.

As Ludwig was about to pull up to the curb, close to Erich's apartment complex, he slowed the vehicle, watching to see what the pursuing black vehicles would do. Once he parked in front of the apartment building, he saw them roll by slowly. Ludwig pulled the cap down further over his eyes. Once the two pursuing vehicles passed by, he carefully exited the car, walked around to the passenger side, and opened the door. He reached in and picked up the mannequin, which was dressed in a black overcoat, and carried it like a sleeping child. He stretched his neck to the side and kissed the mannequin on the lips, feeling a bit foolish, yet amused by his charade. Then he entered the apartment building.

Meanwhile, in the green sedan, Rolf drew closer to the border checkpoint. "It's time," he said.

"I'll go first," Eric volunteered as he rolled underneath the seat and pressed himself against the back edge to allow enough room for Andrea. "You're next, Andi. Come on."

She inched her way back against him. "I'm not sure how long I will be able to stand this," she admitted. "It's terribly tight in here." She found it difficult to breath. Erich told

Andrea to reach over and tug on a piece of fabric dangling from the bottom edge of the back seat to close them in. "It's awfully dark in here," Andrea remarked.

Back at Erich's apartment, one of the vehicles that had been trailing Ludwig stopped up the street. The driver turned off the ignition. "It's going to be another long night," he said to his passenger. He took out a cigarette and lit it, his eyes staying on the target building, waiting for any further sign of either Erich or Andrea, but expecting none.

"We're here," Rolf said. "Be completely still and quiet." The car continued to roll for a few more seconds as Rolf carefully maneuvered through two barriers extending outward into the street.

Andrea heard Rolf roll down the window. "Identification," demanded a voice. Andrea could barely make out the sound of paper crinkling, then a cough. The guard carefully scrutinized the pages of Rolf's passport, searching for an entry stamp. He pursed his lips together. "Hmmm. You are German. What was your business here in the *DDR*?"

"I was given a special permit to visit my grandmother here. She has taken ill."

"What's wrong with her?" It was a different voice this time. Andrea's head lay on Erich's upper arm while his other arm closed in around her waist. She closed her eyes and took a slow, deep breath.

"Tuberculosis," she heard Rolf say. There was another moment of silence. Rolf leaned out the window and asked,

"Is there a problem?"

From under the back seat, they could barely make out a few words as the two guards standing outside the window conferred. "Why do you ask if there is a problem?" one guard asked Rolf. His frown was deep and penetrating.

"You just seem to be taking a long time...longer than usual," answered Rolf. He then spotted a third guard through his rearview mirror. The guard was walking in his direction, carrying a rifle in a ready position. As he reached the car, he tapped the trunk with the barrel of his rifle, kicked his heels together sharply, then walked up to the driver's side of the car.

"Open the trunk," he ordered, leaning toward the window.

"Herr..." began Rolf, searching for excuses. "I'm in rather a big hurry and..."

"Open the trunk," the guard ordered once more.

Rolf slowly pushed the door open and exited the car. He hesitated, took two steps then stopped. "I'll need the keys," he told the guard. He reached into the vehicle through the open window and removed the keys from the ignition.

"Hurry up!" stormed the guard. "We don't have all day."

Andrea could feel the heat of Erich's breath as he held her closely against his chest, cradling her in his protecting arms. At this point all Andrea could hear outside were the muffled sounds of men talking. She listened intently as two sets of footsteps came up behind the trunk. She shifted carefully. Her left hand had grown numb from having her arm pressed beneath her body.

"This is the last time I'm going to tell you to hurry and open the trunk!" bellowed the guard.

This time Andrea was certain of what she heard and her heart froze at the guard's words.

There was a moment of silence as the footsteps seemed

to increase.

"What seems to be the problem?!"

"Forgive me... But the key doesn't seem to be working," Andrea recognized Rolf's voice say.

"What? It's not the same as the ignition key?" asked a different voice.

"No."

"Then we'll just have to pry it open with a crowbar, now won't we?"

Andrea squirmed slightly. "Sh sh sh..." she heard Erich whisper into her ear as he pressed her closer to him. "Even if they open the trunk, they won't see us." He whispered so softly that she could barely hear the words. Two sets of footsteps grew fainter and fainter. *They must be walking away*, Andrea thought.

Suddenly there was a loud scuffling noise outside, followed by a car door slamming. The vehicle roared back into life as Rolf slammed his foot into the gas pedal. Whistles began blowing and, within seconds Andrea heard a series of blasts. They seemed to grow weaker and weaker as the car sped away from the scene, swerving around. After what felt like an eternity, the blasts seemed to be nothing more than a series of fire crackers.

The car spun out of control. The loud crunch of metal was deafening and for a brief second, Andrea felt as if she was going to fly straight through the side of the vehicle. The shrill sound of shattering glass took over and everything came to an abrupt halt. Andrea blacked out.

⸺✶⸺✶⸺✶⸺

Outside of Erich's apartment, just as the driver began drifting off to sleep, the radio sprang to life. "We have a break. A vehicle has slammed through the border crossing."

The driver and his passenger both sat up and glanced at each other momentarily.

The passenger craned his neck and looked up at the building they were observing. "Did you ever see the light turn on in the apartment?" he asked the driver.

"Come to think of it, no. They should have been in there by now."

They sat up straighter, glanced over at one another, then each jumped out of the vehicle. They headed directly for the building entrance and tore up the stairs. Upon reaching the entrance to Erich's apartment, they banged on the door. After knocking a second time and hearing no response, the men broke down the door. Inside, they were greeted by the lifeless mannequin, who sat on the sofa facing the door. On top of her head sat Erich's flat cap. On her face someone had painted a large red smile. The overcoat she wore was completely unbuttoned, revealing pink flesh colored plastic beneath, and on her bare chest, clearly displayed, was Andrea's Activist medal, the pin pressed through the plastic of the mannequin.

Upon regaining consciousness Andrea heard a series of muffled footsteps grow nearer and nearer. "Erich?" Her whisper bounced back at her from the inner walls of the seat. There was no answer. "Erich?" Still no answer. She shifted slightly forward. Her back felt damp – unusually damp. Erich's grip around her had loosened considerably from before. Panic suddenly seized Andrea as the dampness increased. She carefully reached behind her. Her hand slipped throughout the warm, wet substance. Finally she let out a shriek, realizing it was Erich's blood. She held her mouth tightly so that no other sound would escape.

"Is he dead?" she heard a man's voice say in broken German.

A policeman poked his head through the driver's window and carefully analyzed Rolf, whose lifeless body was hunched over the brown leather steering wheel. His right hand lay in his lap while the left one still clutched the steering wheel. His face was covered in blood. Tiny slivers of glass from the shattered windshield were lodged in his forehead. His eyes were frozen open, a look of fear and knowing. The policeman reached for his neck and tried to find a pulse. With no success he announced to the other men that the driver was dead.

"Call a tow unit. Let's get rid of this mess," he instructed the others, his tone weary. As he passed the side of the vehicle, he peered inside and thought he saw a blood stain on the floor of the back seat. It was clearly originating from beneath the back seat. He forced the door open. "Come quickly!" he called out. "It looks like there might be others somewhere inside."

Andrea then heard a series of thuds on the seat as one of the men hit it with the palm of his hand. "Is anyone in here? Speak! You're safe in West."

Andrea struggled to pull herself free. "We're in here… under the seat," came her muffled voice. "I can't move." A young man arrived moments later carrying a large, red, iron crowbar. "Help my friend," Andrea pleaded. "I think he's been hurt." She struggled again to free herself from his top arm, which now hung limply over her waist.

After taking everything apart, one of the men reached down and helped her out. "You hurt?" he asked in broken German. He was an American.

Andrea simply shook her head, then turned her attention back to Erich. Another man climbed into the back and reached in under the seat. "There's no pulse," he said.

He pulled Erich's lifeless body out onto the floor of the vehicle, then stood up and shook his head.

Hearing their words, Andrea began throwing herself back into the car, clamoring to reach for him. "Erich! Erich!" she began repeating his name over and over, but he did not respond. She stared down at his body. "No!!" she shrieked as she reached over and took him into her arms, cradling his head and stroking his face, which seemed to be the only area free of blood. She sobbed uncontrollably. His eyes were still open. She reached across and stroked them, closing them forever.

"You bleed," said the first man. "Hurt. We help you."

After a while, Andrea finally allowed herself to be placed on a gurney. As they carried her to an awaiting vehicle, she sat up long enough to see the Eastern guards off in the distance, watching. Behind them, nearly a dozen official vehicles were racing toward the border, where they came to a screeching halt. As the drivers and passengers quickly jumped out of the vehicles and began lining up, the Western guards immediately pointed their weapons toward them.

"Come on," said the American in English. "Let's get her out of here right away before we have a war on our hands." They pushed the gurney into an awaiting ambulance and raced away to safety.

CHAPTER TWENTY-SEVEN

COUNTY JAIL - NEW YORK CITY
DECEMBER 17, 1989

Stanley Nolen turned to the next page in his notebook. Andrea stopped talking momentarily. He allowed her time to collect her thoughts, then said, "You've had some rough times, haven't you?" Andrea nodded. "I never realized," he added.

Andrea smiled wearily. "I was pregnant, you know."

"What happened to the baby?"

Andrea frowned. "Miscarriage."

"I'm so sorry to hear that, Andi." He waited a moment, then sat up in his chair. "Please continue," he pressed on.

Andrea ran her fingers through her blond hair and sighed, "I'm tired." Her expression changed into a faraway stare. She took a deep breath and let it out slowly. "They won't understand," she finally said.

"Understand what?" he asked.

"Why the murder was justified."

"Justified? Let's get to that point then. Let's talk about the murder. Explain it to me. Let me be the judge this time around. Don't throw away the key just yet, Andi."

Andrea began taking several deep breaths and closed her eyes.

"Andi? Are you all right?" Stanley could see that his friend was growing weary. "Listen. Maybe you've had enough for one day. Let's just pick this up tomorrow. Okay?" Andrea nodded her head slowly. They said goodbye and Stanley called for a guard to come let him out while Andrea returned to the pod.

Later that evening, back at his office, Stanley laid out his notes and began to diagram what he had heard so far of the story, placing question marks where needed throughout his notes. He had learned a good deal about Andrea. As far as he knew, she was not the type who would murder someone in cold blood, though. He continued poring over his notes until nearly nine o'clock. Finally, he closed his notebook then rushed out the door. The following morning, anxious to hear the rest of her story, he drove directly to the county jail.

"Hello again, Andi"

She smiled back at him. "You look a little more alert today." They both sat, as before, across from one another.

"I'm relieved that you're on the case," she responded.

"Good, then. Let's begin." Looking for a starting point, he noted, "Andi, I don't think you ever told me how you ended up in the United States."

"I thought everybody knew that story," she answered curtly.

"You never talked to me about it."

"I was a defector – a high profile defector. Everyone knew exactly who I was within days after I fled the East, which really surprised me. I was a national treasure to the Socialist Unity Party of Germany. When they realized I was gone, they demanded I be returned. Fortunately, the Americans refused to hand me over. Instead they sent me to the United States. I changed my name back to Brandt as soon as I could and I immediately received a visa.

Eventually I became a naturalized citizen. I've been here ever since." She stopped and took a deep breath, holding it in as she closed her eyes. Her mind drifted away.

"Are you okay?" Stanley's voice snapped her back into the present.

Andrea nodded slowly. "After Erich died I vowed to commit myself to nothing but my dance. I didn't want to be close to anyone ever again. It seems that everyone dear to me had somehow been ripped away from me. I never want to feel that kind of pain again."

"I see. Your mother, your father, and then Erich."

Andrea's nod was barely visible. "And Erich's baby." She paused. "And in a sense, even Steve Landers. I know it's probably hard to believe, but I was actually beginning to fall for him at one point."

"Tell me about this Steve Landers. You haven't said anything about him."

"Haven't I?" Andrea smiled.

"When did you two first meet?"

Andrea thought for a long moment, reluctant to relive the last few weeks. "Steve." His name glided off her tongue while she rolled her eyes. She shook her head and said, "Steve. How could I ever have been so blind?"

CHAPTER TWENTY-EIGHT

NEW YORK CITY, NEW YORK
NOVEMBER 10, 1989

Bright lights and applause - Andrea savored these up until the last moment. She had just turned 41 years old and her time on stage was coming to a close. A new chapter in her life was about to begin when she opened the Brandt Academy of Ballet in the heart of Soho. The academy was located downstairs from the loft into which she had moved a few years earlier.

The night of her retirement from dancing turned out to be a media extravaganza, with nearly 1000 people attending the gala. Celebrities came out of the woodwork. There were politicians hoping to be seen, members of the press, and other dancers. The event was by invitation only, a fundraiser to raise money for the Brandt Foundation of the Performing Arts, which Andrea had set up to provide scholarships to future dancers. The atmosphere was buzzing with excitement as guests gathered in the lobby of the theater, eager to see what Andrea would perform for her grand finale.

Andrea sat backstage in her dressing room while Teddy, the very eccentric make-up artist, fixed her hair. She was mesmerized by the news being broadcast on a small television set to the right side of her mirror. Footage of East Germans driving in small cars through the border flashed across the screen. They were being cheered on by crowds of West Germans. Other Easterners walked across. West Germans danced atop the Wall into the night. It had to be the biggest news story since World War Two came to an end. Twenty years earlier Andrea had fled, vowing to never look back, but now all the memories flooded back to her.

Someone knocked at the door. Teddy answered it. It was Jim Veston, a director and producer of documentaries for PBS. "Ms. Brandt, we would love to do a documentary about your life," he said. He turned his attention to the television, where a scene of people lining the Wall still played. "Especially in light of what's happening right now."

Andrea smiled and agreed to participate. There was another knock at the door. A tiny, red-haired woman poked her head into the room to inform Andrea, "The guests are taking their seats in the theater and they're about ready for you on stage."

"Thank you, Jenny."

Jim Veston politely excused himself.

Ten minutes later, Andrea found her spot on the darkened stage. The audience grew quiet as an announcement came over the loudspeaker. "Ladies and gentlemen, it is my great honor, although a bittersweet moment, to introduce to you one of the greatest ballerinas of all time. Some of you may have had the privilege to see her as Odile the Swan or Camilla. This evening she bids farewell to the stage by performing one of the most beloved masterpieces, *The Dying Swan*, by Camille Saint-Saens. Please welcome New York's very own – prima ballerina, Andrea Brandt!" The audience applauded as the music began and the curtains opened. They quickly grew silent as a single spotlight shone on Andrea, who stood on point. Her arms fluttered as she stood with her back to the audience before slowly turning. The performance took just over three minutes. Her standing ovation lasted even longer, as the director of the theater brought her a bouquet of two dozen roses.

Andrea stepped up to a microphone. "Thank you," she began once the applause died down. "Thank you for being here tonight and for all your support." She spent the next 15 minutes talking about her dance career, her plans for the future, and the Brandt Foundation for the Performing Arts. Wrapping up her speech she said, "Many of you have asked me how I feel about the news coming out of Germany." She paused for a moment, carefully choosing her words. "The Wall has come down. At the same time, my world is about to change completely. My country is now non-existent, which means that everything I learned growing up is now non-existent." Andrea smiled. "So this seems to be the perfect point to start a new life, in a new country, and in a new world. When I fled to the West I was told that I could never look back. Now, however, with the stones of the Wall, we can build a bridge to unite East and West Germany to become one country again, and for the first time, I can finally look back." The crowd erupted into wild cheers as Andrea stepped down from the stage.

"That was an excellent speech," she heard a man say. He had a thick German accent. Andrea turned around to find a distinguished man in his early fifties standing before her.

Andrea blinked several times. "Do I know you?" she asked.

"I don't think so," he replied.

A string quartet suddenly sprang to life. Andrea turned to glance at the musicians as they played a sweet rendition of Mozart's String Quartet Number 17.

"I'm Steve. Steve Landers," he said. Andrea extended

her hand, which he grasped gently, brought it to his lips, and kissed. His hand was warm and his lips soft.

"Darf ich Sie auf ein Glas Wein einladen?" he asked, switching over to German. His eyes pierced right through her.

Andrea raised her brow. *"Steve Landers is an interesting name for a German man,"* she said, also switching to German.

"Wine?" he said, ignoring her comment.

"Please," Andrea replied.

He left and returned a few minutes later with two glasses and handed one to Andrea. *"So, you are from the DDR?"*

"I am. What part of Germany are you from?" Andrea asked.

"I'm actually from Switzerland," Steve replied. He watched Andrea carefully as she sipped her wine.

"Excuse me," another gentleman interrupted. "My name is Gustav. I would like to congratulate you on a beautiful performance and a splendid speech."

"Thank you," said Andrea, switching back to English as she turned to the stranger.

"How do you feel?" came another voice. This time it was Beatrice Flint, famed author and commentator for the *New York Times*.

Andrea turned to her. "I feel fine. A bit sad though."

Before long Andrea found herself surrounded by a crowd of spectators and curious onlookers. She felt the wine going to her head, then turned to Steve and shrugged. He smiled confidently before backing away.

"Perhaps another time?" he suggested. *"Let's have dinner sometime soon."* Andrea quickly pulled out a newly printed business card and pen, jotted down her home phone number on the back, and handed it to him.

After Steve left, Lisa Jennings, a dancer, choreographer, and Andrea's personal friend, came up beside her. "What's with the old German dude?" she asked discretely. Her eyes followed Steve until he disappeared into the crowd.

"You mean Steve?" asked Andrea.

"Is that his name?"

"Steve Landers," Andrea said with a nod.

"He doesn't look like a Steve. In any event, you should probably know that he's been majorly scoping you out."

"What does this mean?" asked Andrea.

"I mean he hasn't taken his eyes off of you all evening."

Andrea smiled. "He's not all together bad looking, you know."

"He's too old for you and a little weird. He told me that you reminded him of a long lost ballerina he once knew. When I asked him who, he told me it didn't matter because she killed herself."

"Oh. That's sad."

"Creepy is more like it. It was the way he said it. Then, he just walked off. Didn't even say a word. Just like that. Poof! He's gone. I'd watch that guy if I were you," Lisa warned with a mocking expression. Later on, people began dispersing for the night.

Hours later, sitting in her darkened living room, Andrea watched the news on CNN. She sat back in her recliner, sipping a steaming cup of chamomile tea. A brief segment highlighting her retirement gala flashed across the screen. She smiled. The camera honed in on her face. Behind her, she caught a glimpse of Steve Landers, who appeared to be fixated on her.

⸻✶⸻✶⸻✶⸻

Nearly one week later, after Andrea had dismissed her last class for the day, the telephone rang. She picked up the receiver. "Hello," she said, her voice cracking slightly from fatigue.

"*Guten Tag,*" a man's voice said in German. "*How is the academy progressing?*"

"*Who is this?*" Andrea asked in German.

"*Steve Landers. We met briefly at the gala last week.*" He paused momentarily. "*Maybe you don't remember me. There were so many people competing for your attention.*"

"*No, I do remember you,*" she finally said. "*How are you?*"

"*I'm doing well. Thank you for asking,*" he replied. He paused for a moment. "*Listen, I have two tickets to go see* Cabaret *tomorrow at the Imperial Theatre. Would you like to join me?*"

Andrea hesitated. She had heard about the musical. It takes place in a seedy club in 1931 when the Nazis are rising to power. The music was supposed to be excellent. *Why not,* she thought. *It could be fun.*

"*Andrea?*" she heard Steve say.

"*Yes,*" she caught herself answering, "*I would love to see it.*"

The musical was even better than Andrea had imagined. After the show, they walked to a nearby restaurant and sat at the bar. They each ordered a beer. While Steve asked numerous questions about Andrea's dance career, he volunteered very little information about himself.

"*You don't like to talk about yourself, do you?*" remarked Andrea finally after spending nearly an hour doing most of the talking.

"*Your life is far more interesting than mine,*" he countered.

"*I am sure you must have something interesting to say,*" Andrea laughed.

"*No. Really, I don't.*"

"*What about that scar on your face?*" Struggling to create a two-way conversation, Andrea pointed to a one-inch scar prominently displayed on his right cheek. "*Where did that come from?"*

"*This scar?*" He pointed to his right cheek. "*I was in a fight.*"

"*And?*"

"*That's all. I was in a fight.*"

"*Did you win at least?*"

"*Why are you so interested in my silly scar?*" he asked, smiling.

"*Because I feel as if you know everything about me, but I don't know a thing about you. I don't even know what you do for a living.*"

"*I'm in international trade.*" On that note, he paid for the drinks and they headed out.

Steve drove Andrea home and walked her to the entrance of her loft. Leaning toward her, he gave her a quick peck on the lips, then invited her to have dinner with him the following day. Andrea accepted his invitation before ducking away into her home and closing the door behind her. She then rushed over to the window and watched him as he found his way back to his car, got in, and drove away. She closed her eyes dreamily and drew in a deep breath, smiling to herself.

Over the next two weeks, Andrea spent more and more time with Steve. She found him to be mysterious, but intriguing.

"*Have you ever been married?*" he asked her on Saturday afternoon during lunch at a pizza shop. Andrea shook her head. "*We should have met ten years ago,*" he said as he took her hand into his. She simply smiled. "*Can you imagine what beautiful children we could have had together?*"

Andrea's eyebrows raised a notch. "*I'm not that old, you know,*" she said.

"*But I am,*" he pointed out.

"*I like men who are more mature,*" she countered.

"*I want to make love to you,*" he said, his voice deepening.

Andrea dropped her fork onto her empty plate, making a loud noise. *"You what?"* she gasped. She quickly recomposed herself, looked him in the eyes and whispered in a husky voice, *"Prove it."*

They went to his apartment where they made love throughout the rest of the day. After dinner, they made love again and fell asleep. The following morning she awoke with sunlight streaming through the window and onto her pillow. She opened her eyes. "Steve!" she called out. There was no answer. She rolled over and felt a piece of paper crumple beneath her shoulder. The note simply read: *Andi, I had to take care of some business. There are croissants and coffee in the kitchen. Make yourself at home. I will see you this evening. Steve.*

Andrea slipped out of bed. The cool air chilled her body. She stepped into the bathroom and slipped into the large, gray terrycloth robe hanging on a hook behind the door. She felt her stomach growl and went into the kitchen. There, she found another note for the coffee machine. Even after having been away from the German Democratic Republic for so long, she still cherished the flavor of authentic, American coffee. On the table she saw a pastry box with two croissants. She pulled one out and began consuming it with her coffee.

The telephone rang. Ignoring it, she made her way into the bathroom. As she combed her hair, the answering machine picked up. She smiled at the sound of Steve's greeting message. Then she heard a man's voice say, "Hey Max. This is Daniel. I got another job for you, Buddy. Give me a call as soon as you get this. Okay?"

Max? Who is Max? she thought. *He must have the wrong phone number.*

Just as Andrea finished combing her hair, something caught her eye. On the far edge of the bathroom sink was a torn piece of paper. On it was scribbled the name Daniel, followed by a telephone number. The note sent a cold chill through her body. She reached over, picked up the piece of paper, and analyzed it. *It's got to be a coincidence,* she thought. *Why would Steve lie about his name? Who is he?*

Hoping to quell the doubt building inside her, Andrea began searching through Steve's house for clues. She found several envelopes on a table in the entrance to his apartment. They were addressed to Steve Landers. Finally, beginning to feel guilty about rummaging through his personal belongings, she stopped and got dressed. On her way out of the apartment, as she reached for the doorknob, Andrea looked over at the desk and decided to take one last look. She began with the top drawer. Pens were strewn around haphazardly. Then, as she tried to close the drawer, something jammed it, keeping it from closing completely. She tried to open it fully again, but it would not open either. She bent down to peer into the back of the drawer. A pen had managed to get caught on top of a tiny white box. She reached in and pulled out the box to allow the pen to lie back down. Then, as she placed the box back into the drawer and pushed it toward the back, the lid fell off. She picked it up one more time and noticed a gold chain inside. It was a fine and feminine chain, not something a man would normally wear. She reached her fingers into the box and grabbed the chain. As it became unraveled, it revealed some kind of gold pendant. Looking at it more closely, her eyes narrowed, and then she froze. Andrea could not tear her eyes from the tiny ballerina surrounded by a golden wreath of carnations and roses. She returned the box, tossing it into the back of the drawer, shoved the pendant into her pocket, and raced out the door.

Andrea's stomach was churning and her pulse racing as she headed home. Finally, half an hour later, she burst through the door of her loft and hurried over to a bookshelf in the living room, where she kept the photos from the albums that Mitzi had given her years before in Berlin. She quickly thumbed through the images, then froze when she came across Ingrid's portrait. Clearly displayed around her neck was a gold locket with a ballerina in the center. The ballerina was surrounded by a wreath of carnations and roses. Andrea held the pendant up to the portrait. She found it hard to catch her breath. *This is impossible,* she thought. How can there possibly be a pendant that resembles her mother's locket? It was a unique design and they appeared to be identical. Johann had it designed especially for Ingrid. Then Andrea spotted a tiny lever carefully concealed at the bottom. It would be easy to mistake the lever as part of the design. Andrea gently pushed it to the side and the locket sprang open. Hidden inside, unchanged, were the two tiny photos of her parents. To be certain, she held the open locket up beside the two large images of her parents. There was no mistaking it. They were identical as well. *"Nein! Nein! Nein!"* she exclaimed out loud, shaking her head. Her eyes grew wild and the blood drained from her face. She found herself grasping a chair for support.

Suddenly it became clear to her: the message from Daniel on the answering machine, Steve's mysterious nature, the scar on his face. The vivid image of her mother ripping into Max's face so many years earlier, blood seeping from his wound, all flashed through Andrea's mind. Steve was Max.

In a panic Andrea ran to her front door to ensure every bolt was securely locked. She ran around closing all the curtains. She shut off the lights. Her heart pounded fiercely as she leaned up against the wall, trying to catch her breath. Just then, the telephone rang. She froze, staring at it, not daring to pick it up.

The answering machine picked up. "Hey Andi. It's Lisa.

I need to talk to you about some of the choreography on *Swan Lake*. Hey, Lady, did I tell you we were going to do that? Call me when…"

Andrea leaped toward the telephone and grabbed up the receiver. "Lisa!" she gasped. "Don't hang up."

"Are you okay? What's wrong?" Lisa asked.

"I… something horrible…" Andrea began to cry.

"Listen, I'm coming over. Just sit tight." Lisa hung up.

Once she arrived, Lisa listened carefully as Andrea told her about Max, what he had done to her family, and how she came to realize who he was. "I knew there was something I didn't like about that creep," said Lisa, nodding her head knowingly. "Seriously, you really need to go to the police."

The following morning Lisa accompanied Andrea to the police station. Overhearing part of their conversation with the clerk in record keeping, a detective stepped in to assist. "What seems to be the problem, ladies?" he asked.

"They want to report a murder, Sergeant Meade," answered a black lady officer who stood behind the desk.

"Send 'em to the General Assignment Squad," he suggested.

"Well, it seems that the murder happened more than 40 years ago," explained the woman.

"Send 'em to Cold Cases then," he barked back.

"In East Germany," she smirked.

Sergeant Meade turned to Andrea and Lisa and shook his head. "Not much the NYPD is going to do about a murder in East Germany."

Lisa began explaining Andrea's predicament with the man known as Steve Landers. "Steve Landers?" the detective raised his eyebrows. "Come over to my desk. We can talk about it more there." He led them to his department, where they made their way to his desk and all sat down. "So, tell me what's going on."

Andrea began telling him about her encounter with Steve and how she had reason to believe he had murdered her parents years earlier in Berlin.

"So you're telling me that this Max fellow, who lived in Berlin some 40 years ago and murdered your parents when you were a kid, just showed up here in New York?" asked the detective with a smirk.

"I strongly believe that," answered Andrea.

The sergeant threw his head back and rolled his eyes. "Listen, lady," he said. "There are over five billion people on this planet. Mr. Landers happens to be well respected in the community and I'm here to tell you that he has a squeaky clean background, not to mention that he also has money... a lot of money! He's one of the most generous guys I know. Gives to all the best local charities. I seriously doubt he would steal a locket from a dead woman. Do you know how crazy that sounds?"

"Yes, but..."

"Mr. Landers grew up in Switzerland. I guess next you're going to tell me that he's a Soviet spy or something!" He threw back his head and laughed.

"Sergeant Meade, I don't appreciate the way you are talking to me," Andrea snapped.

"Listen, lady..."

"No! You listen, Sergeant," Lisa jumped in. "Do you know who you're talking to? This is Andrea Brandt. She's a world renowned prima ballerina. She's the owner and director of the Brandt Academy of Dance, and..."

"She could be the pope for all I care. I don't have time for this crap. I have six new homicides, seven robberies, and a city full of thugs, the real deal, that I need to get off the streets. Just get out."

"If something bad happens, Sergeant, you'll be the one to blame," growled Lisa as they turned and began heading out.

Andrea waved her hand discretely toward her friend and said, "It's no use reasoning with fools, Lisa. I'll handle this my own way."

The sergeant closed his door behind them and picked up his telephone. "Hey Max," he began. "This is Daniel. We might have a little problem. You know that dancer, Andrea Brandt? Well, it sounds like she knows who you are." He paused, listening to the other end. "Calm down. I'm not sure... She said something about a locket... I don't know. She was talking a mile a minute. Listen, buddy, you really need to be a little more careful about your acquaintances. Getting sloppy will only land you in prison.... No, don't do anything stupid. She's only acting on a hunch at this point... Yes, she was really upset. Just stay away from her, okay? If you don't, it'll ruin everything."

The sergeant hung up the phone feeling slightly irritated, but then leaned back in his chair and chuckled. Shaking his head he recalled the day he first met Max. It was years earlier at the Port Authority of New York, where he first worked as part of the police force. He had been doing a routine inspection at the New York port and came across Max, who was hidden away in a cargo container with two naked women. Max spoke in very broken English, but he showed the young officer that he knew how to communicate when he slipped him a one hundred dollar bill to go away.

Over time, they became fast friends and eventually collaborators in one of the most elaborate international cocaine rings. Max directed operations, receiving shipments from Colombia and directing them to various European countries. At one point several of Daniel's co-workers grew paranoid about some of his relationships, and he was forced to step out of his job. Unable to prove any wrong doing, however, they transferred him to the NYPD.

—⊁————⊁————⊁—

"Are you sure you'll be all right?" asked Lisa as the two women left the police station.

"I'll be fine," answered Andrea. "You've done so much for me already."

Just then a casually dressed man, carrying a sack filled with newspapers, approached them. "Excuse me!" he said. "Would you ladies like to buy a paper?" He held one out to Andrea.

"No, thank you," she answered curtly, waving him away.

"Ms. Brandt," he said, lowering his voice. "Take the newspaper. Inside of it you will find my business card. I'll call you tomorrow and set up a meeting place."

"What's this about?" asked Andrea. "Who are you?"

"I can't talk to you here," he insisted, "but your life could be in danger. Just go home and then look at my card. It'll explain everything. I'll be in touch soon." The man immediately left the area.

"That was really weird," remarked Lisa. "I wonder who he is and what he wants."

"I guess I'll find out soon."

"Hey, Andi." Lisa stepped toward Andrea. "Maybe you shouldn't go home alone. I mean, with everything going on, maybe I should come with you, at least to make sure you get home okay."

"I'll be fine," insisted Andrea.

"Okay, but at least give me a call or something so that I know you got home safely," Lisa insisted before they hugged and parted ways.

As she made her way home, Andrea kept thinking about the locket and Max. Or was he really Steve? Sergeant Meade had managed to plant a seed of doubt in her mind. She kept mulling over and over the possibilities. Maybe Steve – Max – knew who she was all along and now he wanted to finish the job. Then there was this mysterious stranger who showed up. What could he want? Andrea rushed back to her loft. Once inside, she opened the newspaper and found a business card with the name Lloyd Trevers. Beneath the name she read the words *Central Intelligence Agency*.

The following morning the telephone rang. "Hello, Ms. Brandt," came a man's voice. "Did you have a chance to read the newspaper from yesterday?"

"News…?" She hesitated, before catching on. "Yes, I did read it."

"Can you meet me in one hour in front of the post office at the corner of Canal and Church? I'll explain everything in person."

"I have to get ready for my classes," she began to protest.

"This is more important. Just meet me." The phone went dead.

One hour later Andrea arrived at the post office, where she waited for Agent Trevers to show up. Within five minutes someone tapped her on the shoulder. She turned around. "Ms. Brandt, it's good to see you again," he said. "Come on. Act natural. I'll explain as we walk." They strolled down Canal Street toward Chinatown. It was early afternoon and the sidewalk was bustling with pedestrians. "I'm Special Agent Trevers. We've been tracking Steve Landers for some time now. After I received a tip that you were at the police station talking about him, I rushed over there." He lowered his voice to prevent from being overheard. "Listen. We could use your cooperation."

Andrea stopped walking suddenly and asked, "Do you have a badge or something?"

Agent Trevers faced her and answered, "I don't carry a badge."

"I thought policemen always carried a badge."

"Keep walking please," he instructed. They continued their walk. "I'm not a cop. I'm CIA. We're working closely with the FBI on this case. For two years now we've been trying to uncover a powerful drug ring, which seems to have one of its headquarters here in New York and another one in Switzerland. We believe Landers is one of the ringleaders. If we can learn more about him we might be able to expose the whole thing. The problem is that Landers has absolutely no criminal record, not even a speeding ticket. He's never been married, has no children, and his parents are both deceased. I was able to uncover one possible lead, though. About ten years ago three guys rented a boat for a day-long trip on Lake Meade, outside of Las Vegas. One of them, James Bogdanos, ended up dead. They found his body nearly a month later, washed up on shore with a bullet wound to his heart. The other two guys vanished into thin air. One, we know, was named Steve Landers because the boat was registered to him. The other one, we only have a first name… Max…"

"Max," Andrea repeated the name.

Agent Trevers continued, "The only evidence we were able to gather was a few drops of blood found inside the boat. The blood was type O negative. Landers' medical records have him as O negative. Of course, it's all circumstantial evidence, but less than ten percent of the population has O negative blood type."

"Did they test the murdered man's blood?"

"Absolutely. His blood type came back as A positive. So, they have a body – Bogdanos, they have this rare blood type possibly belonging to Landers, and there is no trace of the third man – no fingerprints, no blood, nothing, but several eye witnesses put three men on the boat."

Andrea stopped walking. "It was a man named Max

who killed my parents years ago."

"That might make sense then," he said.

"I don't understand."

"Well, for some reason this guy was targeting you. In fact, we even had you as a suspect briefly at first. Right now, I'm still acting on a hunch, but everything seems to tie together. I believe that this Max murdered both men, hid Landers' body so well that they never found it, then somehow got ahold of his identification in case he ever needed it. Thanks to your visit to the police department yesterday, we might have an important missing link to the puzzle. In the meantime, we can't really do anything until we get more on him. I don't know exactly why he would be targeting you unless it has something to do with your past. For now, though, we have reason to believe he'll be leaving you alone for a while. Just lie low and continue about with business as usual."

"I'll do what I can," Andrea said somewhat cynically. "Well, at least now I know I'm not crazy."

Agent Trevers smiled. "No, Ms. Brandt, you are definitely not crazy. We've been monitoring this 'Landers' or Max or whoever he is closely ever since we thought there might be a connection. We knew you started seeing him recently and, as I'm sure you can understand, we couldn't just come in and give ourselves away. We couldn't risk tipping him off. After your trip to the police station yesterday, I felt it was time to reach out to you."

"I'm afraid I can't help you much, though. I don't know that much, but I do know someone…two people actually, who might be able to give you some information. Their names are Mitzi and Hans Kaisendorf." Agent Trevers wrote the names down in a small notebook and thanked Andrea. "Tell me something, Agent Trevers. Yesterday I went to the police where I was ridiculed and practically thrown out. Maybe you should talk to them too."

Agent Trevers shook his head. "We in the CIA don't like to talk to the police force," he said firmly. "In fact, in this case, you ought to steer clear of the police right now yourself, especially Sergeant Meade. It turns out he's a mole."

"A what?"

"He keeps his eyes and ears open for Landers. He's on the wrong side of the tracks. Needless to say, going there again will only put you in danger. For now, just go about your business normally. Avoid the police and avoid Landers." He reached into his pocket and removed a business card. "If you should run into any trouble, contact this guy. Larry will keep you safe. In the meantime, we'll continue to monitor this Landers character and will be in touch if necessary."

The following day, Agent Trevers was on a plane to Berlin.

CHAPTER TWENTY-NINE

COUNTY JAIL - NEW YORK CITY
DECEMBER 18, 1989

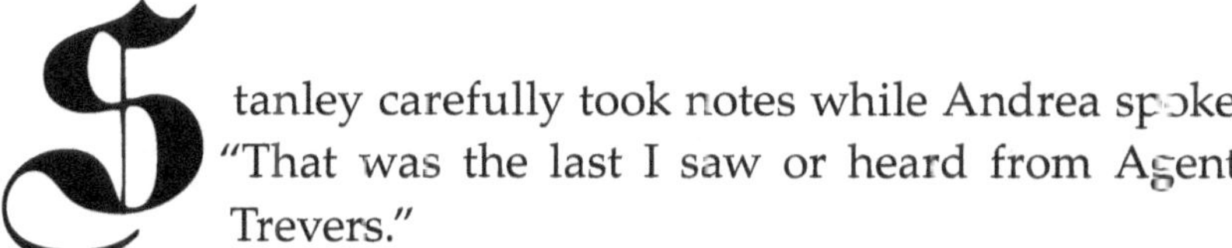

tanley carefully took notes while Andrea spoke. "That was the last I saw or heard from Agent Trevers."

"How long ago was that?" asked Stanley.

"Two weeks ago. I settled back into my routine, teaching classes and started working on choreographing Swan Lake. I saw few people outside of the academy, except for Lisa, who was helping me. I hadn't heard from Max either until…"

"Steve," Stanley interjected. "The world still knows him as Steve, and unless we can prove otherwise, there's not much we can do."

Andrea nodded, "I didn't hear from Steve until last week, when I returned from a late dinner meeting…" She stopped talking.

After an awkward moment of silence, Stanley leaned forward slightly. "And then?"

"That night is such a blur to me," she said, burying her eyes in her hands. "When I came home I went to put down my notes and noticed that I had accidentally grabbed some of Lisa's notes. I was about to call her to let her know I had them, but then someone knocked at the door. I didn't even think. I just opened the door, thinking it was Lisa coming for her notes. That's when he forced his way into my loft and knocked me down."

"Steve."

"Yes, Steve. When I tried to get up, he grabbed me and jerked me to my feet, then threw me against the wall. At some point I remember seeing him pull out a gun. I just threw myself at him. I don't really remember anything after that. The next morning Lisa came to my home and found me on the floor. I guess Steve had left the door open. Lisa took me to the hospital.

"I had been shot, but it ended up being a superficial wound. He beat me pretty badly though." Andrea stared down at the floor, unwilling to make eye contact with Stanley. "A police investigator came to talk to me. He asked so many questions. I felt like I was on trial already. After the investigator left, the hospital told me they had to keep me there for more observation. They wouldn't tell me for how long. So, I telephoned Lisa and asked her to go to my home and bring me some of my things. Lisa told me that when she arrived at my loft, the police were just leaving. They had done a complete search of my home and my studio. Lisa told me that everything was a mess. Two days later, before I even checked out of the hospital, they arrested me. I've been here since." Andrea suddenly leaned toward Stanley and looked him squarely in the eyes. "Stan, you have to get me out of here. I don't remember much, but I can't possibly be a murderer."

"I understand, Andi. I'm going as fast as I can on this, but you'll have to be patient. These things can take time."

"I heard that all the newspapers are saying that I killed Steve Landers. It's crazy. How can I kill someone who died years ago? Right?" Andrea smiled slightly, shaking her head.

"Don't worry. The truth will come out," said Stanley.

CHAPTER THIRTY

DECEMBER 19, 1989

Mike Stevens, the prosecuting attorney, sat alone at his desk going over and over evidence released by the crime lab. This was his highest-profile case ever, and an opportunity for recognition. He removed a notepad from his desk and began writing. All the rounds were 9mm rounds, but they were still awaiting more evidence. Investigators found a 9mm-short Walther PP semi-automatic pistol at the scene. It was tucked away in the holster, possibly placed there by the killer. Andrea's finger prints were found on the pistol. The voice recording found on the victim's answering machine might be linked to Andrea. According to the police, Andrea had made a menacing comment that suggested she might go after Landers.

Just then, the telephone rang. The conversation was brief. Immediately after hanging up, Stevens gathered his belongings and hurried out the door.

A short while later he was on the 23rd floor of the Jacob K. Javits Federal Office Building in lower Manhattan, sitting in an office with FBI Agent Tim Noble. "You have got to be kidding me. You're telling me to drop the charges?"

he asked.

"That's exactly what I'm telling you," answered Agent Noble. "If you don't, our entire cover could be blown and we'll never crack this case."

The prosecutor narrowed his eyes and leaned toward Agent Noble. "That's your problem. Not mine. I have a case to prosecute and that's what I'm going to do."

Just then he heard another voice behind him. "She's not guilty." The prosecutor turned around to see Agent Trevers, who had entered the room. "I can tell you unequivocally that Andrea Brandt did not murder Steve Landers. In fact, Steve Landers was murdered years ago, so that would be impossible." Agent Trevers smiled.

"What are you talking about?" snapped the prosecutor.

Agent Trevers handed him a manila envelope. "If you look through this, you'll see that the real Steve Landers was murdered around ten years ago. The guy who murdered him was the guy who got popped this time."

"Who is he?"

"That doesn't concern you right now. For now, all you need to know is that you're prosecuting the wrong person."

"So, who's the killer then?" asked the prosecutor.

"That's irrelevant as well."

"Listen, gentlemen," the prosecutor said. "You can't just bring me here and tell me to simply drop the charges. I need more than that. All the evidence handed over by the police force back up these charges."

"Well, for now I wouldn't put too much value on what the police have, at least not until we've cleaned them up a bit. You have been fed a lot of false evidence." Trevers reached across and placed a box in front of the prosecutor.

"What's that?" asked the prosecutor.

"The bullet found in the victim's shoulder came from his own gun, a 9mm-short Walther PP semi-automatic pistol. You've already seen that Ms. Brandt's prints were on it. This weapon here is an old 9mm Luger, dating from WWII. That's the weapon that killed him. Send it to the crime lab and they will tell you that the fingerprints on this one are not Ms. Brandt's. Furthermore, ballistics will prove that this is the gun that killed the victim, not the Walther PP."

The prosecutor carefully opened the box and peered inside. "What about the recording on the victim's answering machine?" he asked.

"FBI is doing an analysis of it as we speak," interjected Agent Noble. "That'll prove to be a dead end as well."

"What about Sergeant Meade's statement that Andrea Brandt made a threatening remark regarding Landers, or whoever he is?"

"That's hearsay, of course," said Agent Trevers, rolling his eyes. He glanced over at Agent Noble, who was discretely shaking his head. "Just drop the case. Don't spin your wheels on something that isn't there. Ms. Brandt did not do it, but as soon as we find someone you can prosecute, we'll let you know."

The prosecutor shook his head as he stood up. He picked up the box and left the office without saying anything more.

The following day Andrea found herself face to face with Stanley, staring at him in disbelief. "They're dismissing the charges?" she asked, wiping away a tear. Stanley smiled broadly. "What… what happened?"

"It seems that the prosecution came across certain evidence that made them realize they were going after the wrong person. They really didn't give an explanation." He shrugged. "But who cares? You're free now."

Andrea fell into his arms, overcome with relief. "How can I ever thank you, Stanley?" she cried softly.

"Well, I wish I could take the credit." He paused briefly.

"But I had nothing to do with it. I think you must have a guardian angel or something." He chuckled.

Later that day Andrea walked out of jail a free woman.

EPILOGUE

Ample natural lighting flowed through the studio windows where Andrea sat alone, mulling over her past; contemplating her future. She stared intently at her reflection in the mirror. The academy had closed temporarily after her arrest, and now she looked forward to it re-opening the following week. She was not a murderer. Everything felt surreal now that the ordeal was over. It was time to put it all behind her and jump back into her life.

Andrea stood up and walked over to the stereo to put a CD of Tchaikovsky's *Swan Lake* into her CD player. The music began with the sweet sound of the oboe. She looked forward to choreographing the production for the New York City Ballet. Just as the music reached a crescendo, she heard a knock at the door. She turned down the music, and opened the door to find an aging woman standing there. The woman, dressed in a black overcoat, wore a dark blue scarf over her head.

The woman smiled faintly and cleared her throat. "Andi," she said. Her shaky voice sounded strained. "Andi." She repeated the name several times.

Andrea wrinkled her nose and forced a smile. *"I'm sorry, but do I know you?"*

"Bitte sprechen sie auf deutsch, mein Englisch ist nicht so gut," said the woman. Her voice cracked.

"Have we met before? Do I know you?" Andrea repeated in German.

"Ahhh… Swan Lake. I love this ballet," the woman muttered, ignoring her questions. She starred at Andrea as she leaned toward the door to better hear the music coming from the room. *"Have you ever danced* Swan Lake?*"* she asked.

"I have," Andrea responded politely. The woman stood there in awkward silence. *"I'm sorry. I don't want to be rude, but I'm rather busy. Is there something I can do for you?"*

"I danced in Swan Lake *once,"* the old woman said slowly.

Andrea perked up and smiled. *"Really? How wonderful. Where?"*

"Germany." The woman's voice trailed off. *"This was many years ago."* She continued to stare intently at Andrea's face, making her feel ill at ease. As she reached up to adjust her scarf, Andrea could see that she was trembling. The woman took in a deep breath, closed her eyes momentarily, then said, *"I'm so sorry, Andi, for all the pain I put you through."* Her voice cracked. *"I wanted to turn myself in, but he wouldn't let me,"* she continued.

"I'm sorry? What are you talking about? Who?"

"Lloyd Trevers."

"Agent Trevers? I don't understand," said Andrea. *"Who are you?"*

The old woman stared into Andrea's eyes. She took a deep breath. *"My name is Ingrid. Ingrid Brandt. I'm your mother."* The tears began flowing freely down Ingrid's cheeks.

Andrea felt as if the wind had been knocked out of her. *"Impossible. My… my mother was murdered."*

Andrea covered her mouth with her hands in disbelief

as Ingrid began to explain, carefully selecting her words and speaking slowly. *"No. After they took you away from me, this monster, Max, beat me. I don't remember anything except that I woke up in a hospital in the Soviet Union. I didn't know where I was. I didn't even know who I was. I couldn't understand what anybody was saying. I finally figured out that I was in some kind of psychiatric hospital. They held me there for many years. I…"* Her voice cracked again and she shook her head slowly. *"It was a horrible place, Andi…"*

Andrea was speechless, staring wide-eyed at her mother. She tried to catch her breath, shaking her head slowly. *"Mami?"* she said, her voice cracking.

Ingrid's lower lip trembled as she nodded slowly. *"Can you ever forgive me for not being there for you all these years?"*

"Mein Gott," Andrea said as she reached for her mother. They fell into one another's arms, neither one able to hold back her tears. As they pulled away from one another, each staring at the other, there was no doubt they were mother and daughter. Andrea invited Ingrid into the studio where they sat hand-in-hand with Ingrid recounting her story.

"They sent me to the Soviet Union. They told the hospital staff members that they had found me wandering the countryside without memory or good sense," she explained. *"Nobody ever questioned it. I remained in that place for many years. I had no clue of time. They said I had retrograde amnesia and acute schizophrenia."* Ingrid closed her eyes and shook her head as she recalled the hospital. *"The conditions there were deplorable and staff members were so cruel to the patients. They especially hated me, the 'German.'"*

"Why would they diagnose you with schizophrenia?" asked Andrea.

Ingrid shook her head and shrugged. *"At first I was heavily medicated. I didn't even know what was happening most of the time."*

"*But, why?*"

"*I eventually found out that Max was quite powerful in the underworld. An important Soviet general, a man named Ivanov, was his protector. He…*"

"General Ivanov?" Andrea interrupted. She sat straight up in her chair. "*This name sounds familiar. I think I met him… Yes. It was at my school. He came to talk to us.*" Andrea scowled. "*I think he was wearing Papi's ring. Do you remember it? It had a cross on it.*"

"*Oh, Andi. Those weren't unique rings. They were distributed to many people.*"

Andrea shook her head. "*I'm sure it was Papi's. It had a little green notch in the front. A defect. I don't remember a lot but I do remember that notch.*"

Ingrid blinked several times then replied, "*I suppose. Perhaps.*"

"*But that's in the past. How did you finally ever get out of the hospital?*"

"*It took a long time. My only ally there was a young psychiatrist named Doctor Dmitri Alexandrov. He was kind and compassionate. He spoke German and spent a lot of time with me throughout the time I suffered from amnesia. Over many years the past came back to me. From then on the painful memories of you and your father became unbearable. With everything back in place… my memory… I thought they would let me return home to Germany, but they didn't. They didn't want to release me, on the pretext of acute schizophrenia. Doctor Alexandrov did not agree with the diagnosis and tried many times to convince them of my sanity. In return they threatened to take away his medical license. Eventually he stopped trying and I gave up all hope.*

"Before Gorbachev took office as General Secretary of the Communist party, many perfectly healthy people had been conveniently diagnosed with mental illness and remained locked up for various reasons."

"*I thought people were locked up because they spoke out against the Soviet government,*" Andrea chimed in.

"*Oh Andi, in my case I was locked up out of convenience to Max and the general. Max was an informant to the general, giving him many names of black market and other criminals. Not only did he help the general's career, but he also provided him with many luxuries. When General Ivanov died about 18 years ago, Max lost his protector and simply vanished, but I remained in this horrible psychiatric hospital.*"

"*How long were you there?*" asked Andrea.

"*Dr. Alexandrov was finally able to secure my release after Gorbachev took office. He had me sent back to Berlin three years ago.*"

Andrea gasped. "*You were in the hospital for over 30 years?!*"

Ingrid nodded her head slowly.

"*When I returned to Berlin, Mitzi and Hans took me in immediately. They still live in the old house, you know.*" Ingrid smiled. "*Mitzi told me all about you and how you had fled to the West. Unfortunately, we had no way of finding you or of reaching out to you. We were able to find out that you were doing well, however, because once in a while someone would somehow bring Mitzi news about you from a Western newspaper. I was going to try to find you once the Wall came down, but Agent Trevers got to us first when he came asking Mitzi and Hans questions about Max Schmidt. He showed us the photos and I immediately recognized him - Max von Euken, who apparently became Max Schmidt. It was hard to look at his picture, but the hardest thing for me was when Agent Trevers showed me a news clip of your retirement gala and there was von Euken, standing so close to you, staring at you. I was horrified, afraid he was going to hurt you.*

"*Agent Trevers devised a plan to try to trap Max and he asked for my help. So he brought me back with him to New York. He said he also wanted to reunite me with you when it was all over. As I was packing my suitcase, Mitzi came into the room and gave me your father's old pistol. They had found it tucked in the very back of one of his dresser drawers after he was killed. I decided to bring it. Three days after Agent Trevers first showed up we were on an airplane. When we arrived in New York on the tenth, Agent Trevers suggested that I hold off on meeting you. He was afraid that if we moved too quickly, it would ruin his plans."*

"What were his plans?" asked Andrea.

Ingrid shook her head. *"I really don't know. He never gave me any details. Then, shortly after we arrived in New York, he was unexpectedly called away on an emergency. He told me that he would not be gone for longer than three days and he drove me to a hotel. While he went to register me there, I waited in the car. On his seat he left a folder with the names Steve Landers and Max Schmidt written on it. I became curious and peeked inside. I found von Euken's telephone number and address and wrote them down."* Ingrid stopped and stared at Andrea for a moment.

"Before he left me, Agent Trevers made it clear that I should not reveal myself to you until the time was right. So now here I was in a strange country, with nothing to do." Ingrid closed her eyes and shook her head. *"It was very difficult because I couldn't speak much English. The front desk clerk gave me a map of the city and I decided to explore. I even came by your studio and watched you from across the street."* She smiled.

Andrea cupped her hand over her mouth. *"You... you came to the studio?"* she stammered.

"At least a dozen times. I couldn't bear to be in the same city and not see you, but the first time I saw you, it triggered a terrible rage and fear in me. Later that night, I called him."

"Max?"

Ingrid nodded. *"Yes. I threatened him and told him to meet me in a quiet alley up the street from my hotel. I gave him two days, but my anger and fear only grew each time I stopped by the studio to watch through the window. Then two days later I carried through my plans. I did it partly to protect you and partly out of revenge. I couldn't help myself. He took my life and everything I held dear away from me. I never got to see you grow up.*

"The next day, as I prepared to come see you at the studio, Agent Trevers showed up at my hotel room. He came in to tell me that Max had been murdered. That's when he saw your father's pistol. I had forgotten to close my suitcase, and there it was. He was pretty upset with me. He even accused me of ruining his case, but he decided to wait a few days to see what would happen.

"I never once imagined they would accuse you of murdering Max." Ingrid's tears welled up again. "When I found out they had arrested you, I was ready to turn myself in, but Agent Trevers insisted I give him at least three days to figure things out first. A few days later he made me put the pistol into a box. I didn't want to give it to him. It was your father's pistol, Andi. Agent Trevers explained to me that I would have to choose. I could either lose my freedom again or my daughter might lose hers. The choice was easy. After I handed over the pistol, I told him that I would give him one week, and if you were not free by then, I would turn myself in."

Just then Ingrid glanced over at the window to see Lloyd Trevers approaching the studio. *"Andi, I have to leave soon. He's coming for me."*

"Can't you stay a little longer?" Andrea raised her brow. Ingrid shook her head sadly.

Andrea then stood up, walked slowly to the door, and opened it. "Agent Trevers, it's nice to see you again. Please come in," she said calmly.

"We need to be leaving soon," he announced as Andrea approached her mother.

Andrea felt the lump in her throat growing. She swallowed carefully. "Agent Trevers, I... I... I just want to thank you for bringing my mother back to me."

He smiled at her then turned to help Ingrid to her feet. *"We need to go now,"* he said in perfect German.

Their meeting was short and bittersweet. As Agent Trevers and Ingrid headed out the door, Andrea called out in a strained voice, *"Mami!"* Ingrid turned back around. *"I love you, Mami! I always have."* She pulled the gold locket out from her shirt and hurried toward her mother. *"Please take this. Papi gave it to you!"* she insisted.

Ingrid gasped at the sight of the locket. *"Where did you find this?!"*

"It doesn't matter now," answered Andrea as she held it out to her mother.

Ingrid pushed her daughter's hand back gently and shook her head. *"But no. This belongs to you now."*

"Mami… Mami…" Andrea repeated the name. *"I will dedicate* Swan Lake *to you, Mami."*

Ingrid reached out and hugged her daughter tightly, not wanting to let go. *"Thank you, Andi. I'm so proud of you."* She pulled away and took Andrea's face gently between her hands. Their eyes locked, reluctant to turn away from one another.

"Where are you taking her?" Andrea asked Agent Trevers.

"To the airport," he answered. "She's better off returning to Germany. She'll be safe there. I need to get back to my case and pick up the pieces." He smiled and shook his head.

Andrea turned her attention back to Ingrid. *"Will I see you again?"* she asked.

"There are no longer any walls that separate us, my child. You can come home whenever you want to now."

Andrea simply smiled and nodded.

"We have to go now," Agent Trevers said in German.

Andrea stood on the sidewalk, watching as the car

began rolling away slowly. She watched until she could no longer see them. As she turned and walked back into her studio, she realized her eyes were filled with tears. Tears of sorrow from all the painful memories the recent events had brought back. Tears of joy for a new better today. Tears of hope for an even brighter tomorrow.